The Keeper of the Door

Ethel M. Dell

Contents

THE KEEPER OF THE DOOR

BY

Ethel M. Dell

I DEDICATE THIS BOOK
TO THE DEAR MEMORY OF ONE
WHO WAITS BEYOND THE DOOR
FOR THOSE HE LOVES

"And the keepers before the door kept the prison."

Acts xii. 6.

"A deep below the deep
And a height beyond the height!
Our hearing is not hearing,
And our seeing is not sight."
The Voice and the Peak.
ALFRED TENNYSON.

PART I

CHAPTER I
THE LESSON

"Then he's such a prig!" said Olga.

"You should never use a word you can't define," observed Nick, from the depths of the hammock in which his meagre person reposed at length.

She made a face at him, and gave the hammock a vicious twitch which caused him to rock with some violence for several seconds. As he was wont pathetically to remark, everyone bullied him because he was small and possessed only one arm, having shed the other by inadvertence somewhere on the borders of the Indian Empire.

Certainly Olga--his half-brother's eldest child--treated him with scant respect, though she never allowed anyone else to be other than polite to him in her hearing. But then she and Nick had been pals from the beginning of things, and this surely entitled her to a certain licence in her dealings with him. Nick, too, was such a darling; he never minded anything.

Having duly punished him for snubbing her, she returned with serenity to the work upon her lap.

"You see," she remarked thoughtfully, "the worst of it is he really is a bit of a genius. And one can't sit on genius--with comfort. It sort of flames out where you least expect it."

"Highly unpleasant, I should think," agreed Nick.

"Yes; and he has such a disgusting fashion of behaving as if--as if one were miles beneath his notice," proceeded Olga. "And I'm not a chicken, you know, Nick, I'm twenty."

"A vast age!" said Nick.

For which remark she gave him another jerk which set him swinging like a pendulum.

"Well, I've got a little sense anyhow," she remarked.

"But not much," said Nick. "Or you would know that that sort of treatment after muffins for tea is calculated to produce indigestion in a very acute form, peculiarly distressing to the beholder."

"Oh, I'm sorry! I forgot the muffins." Olga laid a restraining hand upon the hammock. "But do you like him, Nick? Honestly now!"

"My dear child, I never like anyone till I've seen him at his worst. Drawing-room manners never attract me."

"But this man hasn't got any manners at all," objected Olga. "And he's so horribly satirical. It's like having a stinging-nettle in the house. I believe--just because he's clever in his own line--that he's been spoilt. As if everybody couldn't do something!"

"Ah! That's the point," said Nick sententiously. "Everybody can, but it isn't everybody who does. Now this young man apparently knows how to make the most of his opportunities. He plays a rattling hand at bridge, by the way."

"I wonder if he cheats," said Olga. "I'm sure he's quite unscrupulous."

Nick turned his head, and surveyed her from under his restless eyelids. "I begin to think you must be falling in love with the young man," he observed.

"Don't be absurd, Nick!" Olga did not even trouble to look up. She was stitching with neat rapidity.

"I'm not. That's just how my wife fell in love with me. I assure you it often begins that way." Nick shook his head wisely. "I should take steps to be nice to him if I were you, before the mischief spreads."

Olga tossed her head. She was slightly flushed. "I shall never make a fool of myself over any man, Nick," she said. "I'm quite determined on that point."

"Dear, dear!" said Nick. "How old did you say you were?"

"I am woman enough to know my own mind," said Olga.

"Heaven forbid!" said Nick. "You wouldn't be a woman at all if you did that."

"I don't think you are a good judge on that subject, Nick," remarked his niece judiciously. "In fact, even Dr. Wyndham knows better than that. I assure you the antipathy is quite mutual. He regards everyone who isn't desperately ill as superfluous and uninteresting. He was absolutely disappointed the other day because, when I slipped on the stairs, I didn't break any bones."

"What a fiend!" said Nick.

"And yet Dad likes him," said Olga. "I can't understand it. The poor people like him too in a way. Isn't it odd? They seem to have such faith in him."

"I believe Jim has faith in him," remarked Nick. "He wouldn't turn him loose on his patients if he hadn't."

"Of course, Sir Kersley Whitton recommended him," conceded Olga. "And he is an absolutely wonderful man, Dad says. He calls him the greatest medicine-man in England. He took up Max Wyndham years ago, when he was only a medical student. And he has been like a father to him ever since. In fact, I don't believe Dr. Wyndham would ever have come here if Sir Kersley hadn't made him. He was overworked and wouldn't take a rest, so Sir Kersley literally forced him to come and be Dad's assistant for a while. He told Dad that he was too brilliant a man to stay long in the country, and Dad gathered that he contemplated making him his own partner in the course of time. The sooner the better, I should say. He obviously thinks himself quite thrown away on the likes of us."

"Altogether he seems to be a very interesting young man," said Nick. "I must really cultivate his acquaintance. Is he going to be present to-night?"

"Oh, I suppose so. It's a great drawback having him living in the house. You see, being his hostess, I have to be more or less civil to him. It's very horrid," said Olga, upon whom, in consequence of her mother's death three years before, the duties of housekeeper had devolved. "And Dad is so fearfully strict too. He won't let me be the least little bit rude, though he is often quite rude himself. You know Dad."

"I know him," said Nick. "He's licked me many a time, bless his heart, and richly I deserved it. Help me to get out of this like a good kid! I see James the Second and the twins awaiting me on the tennis-court. I promised them a sett after tea."

He rolled on to his feet with careless agility, his one arm encircling his young niece's shoulders.

"I shouldn't worry if I were you," protested Olga. "It's much too hot. Don't waste your energies amusing the children! They can quite well play about by themselves."

"And get up to mischief," said Nick. "No, I'm on the job, overlooking the whole crowd of you, and I'll do it thoroughly. When old Jim comes home he'll find a model household awaiting him. By the way, I had a letter from him this afternoon. The kiddie is stronger already, and Muriel as happy as a queen. I shall hear from her to-morrow."

"Don't you wish you were with them?" questioned Olga. "It would be much more fun than staying here to chaperone me."

Nick looked quizzical. "Oh, there's plenty of fun to be had out of that too," he assured her. "I take a lively interest in you, my child; always have."

"You're a darling," said Olga, raising her face impulsively. "I shall write and tell Dad what care you are taking of us all."

She kissed him warmly and let him go, smiling at the tuneless humming that accompanied his departure. Who at a casual glance would have taken Nick Ratcliffe for one of the keenest politicians of his party, a man whom friend and foe alike regarded as too brilliant to be ignored? He had even been jestingly described as "that doughty champion of the British Empire"--an epithet that Olga cherished jealously because it had not been bestowed wholly in jest.

His general appearance was certainly the reverse of imposing, and in this particular, to her intense gratification, Olga resembled him. She had the same quick, pale eyes, with the shrewdness of observation that never needed to look twice, the same colourless brows and lashes and insignificant features; but she possessed one redeeming point which Nick lacked. What with him was an impish grin of sheer exuberance, with her was a smile of rare enchantment, very fleeting, with a fascination quite indescribable but none the less capable of imparting to her pale young face a charm that only the greatest artists have ever been able to depict. People were apt to say of Olga Ratcliffe that she had a face that lighted up well. Her ready intelligence was ardent enough to illuminate her. No one was ever dull in her society. Certainly in her temperament at least there was nothing colorless. Where she loved she loved intensely, and she hated in the same way, quite thoroughly and without dissimulation.

Maxwell Wyndham, for instance, the subject of her recent conversation with Nick, she had disliked wholeheartedly from the commencement of their acquaintance, and he was perfectly aware of the fact. He could not well have been otherwise, but he was by no means disconcerted thereby. It even seemed as if he took a malicious pleasure in developing her dislike upon every opportunity that presented itself, and since he was living in the house as her father's assistant, opportunities were by no means infrequent.

But there was no open hostility between them. Under Dr. Ratcliffe's eye, his daughter was always frigidly polite to the unwelcome outsider, and the outsider accepted her courtesy with a sarcastic smile, knowing exactly how much it was worth.

Perhaps he was a little curious to know how she meant to treat him during her father's absence, or it may have been sheer chance that actuated him on that sultry evening in August, but Nick and his three playfellows had only just settled down to a serious sett when the doctor's assistant emerged from the house with his hands deep in his pockets and a peculiarly evil-smelling cigarette between his firm lips, and strolled across to the shady corner under the walnut-trees where the doctor's daughter was sitting. She was stitching so busily that she did not observe his approach until escape was out of the question; but she would not have retreated in any case. It was characteristic of her to display a bold front to the people she disliked.

She threw him one of her quick glances as he reached her, and noted with distaste the extreme fieriness of his red hair in the light of the sinking sun. His hair had always been an offence to her. It was so obtrusive. But she could have borne with that alone. It was the green eyes that mocked at everything from under shaggy red brows that had originally given rise to her very decided antipathy, and these Olga found it impossible to condone. People had no right to mock, whatever the colour of their eyes.

He joined her as though wholly unaware of her glance of disparagement.

"I fear I am spoiling a charming picture," he observed as he did so. "But since there was none but myself to admire it, I felt at liberty to do so."

Again momentarily Olga's eyes flashed upwards, comprehending the whole of his thick-set figure in a single sweep of the eyelids. He was exceedingly British in build, possessing in breadth what he lacked in height. There was a bull-dog strength about his neck and shoulders that imparted something of a fighting look to his general demeanour. He bore himself with astounding self-assurance.

"Have you had any tea?" Olga inquired somewhat curtly. She was inwardly wondering what he had come for. He usually had a very definite reason for all he did.

"Many thanks," he replied, balancing himself on the edge of the hammock. "I am deeply touched by your solicitude for my welfare. I partook of tea at the Campions' half an hour ago."

"At the Campions'!" There was quick surprise in Olga's voice.

It elicited no explanation however. He sat and swayed in the hammock as though he had not noticed it.

After a moment she turned and looked at him fully. The green eyes were instantly upon her, alert and critical, holding that gleam of satirical humour that she invariably found so exasperating.

"Well?" said Olga at last.

"Well, fair lady?" he responded, with bland serenity.

She frowned. He was the only person in her world who ever made her take the trouble to explain herself, and he did it upon every possible occasion, with unvarying regularity. She hated him for it very thoroughly, but she always had to yield.

"Why did you go to the Campions'?" she asked, barely restraining her irritation.

"That, fair lady," he coolly responded, "is a question which with regret I must decline to answer."

Olga flushed. "How absurd!" she said quickly. "Dad would tell me like a shot."

"I am not Dad," said the doctor's assistant, with unruffled urbanity. "Moreover, fair lady--"

"I prefer to be called by my name if you have no objection, Dr. Wyndham," cut in Olga, with rising wrath.

He smiled at something over her head. "Thank you, Olga. It saves trouble certainly. Would you like to call me by mine? Max is what I generally answer to."

Olga turned a vivid scarlet. "I am Miss Ratcliffe to you," she said.

He accepted the rebuff with unimpaired equanimity. "I thought it must be too good to be true. Pardon my presumption! When you are as old as I am you will realize how little it really matters. You are genuinely angry, I suppose? Not pretending?"

Olga bit her lip in silence and returned to her work, conscious of unsteady fingers, conscious also of a scrutiny that marked and derided the fact.

"Yes," he said, after a moment, "I should think your pulse must be about a hundred. Leave off working for a minute and let it steady down!"

Olga stitched on in spite of growing discomfiture. The shakiness was increasing very perceptibly. She could feel herself becoming hotter every moment. It was maddening to feel those ironical eyes noting and ridiculing her agitation. From exasperation she had passed to something very nearly resembling fury.

"Leave off!" he said again; and then, because she would not, he laid a detaining hand upon her work.

Instantly and fiercely her needle stabbed downwards. It was done in a moment, almost before she realized the nature of the impulse that possessed her. Straight into the back of his hand the weapon drove, and there from the sheer force of the impact broke off short.

Olga exclaimed in horror, but Max Wyndham made no sound of any sort. The cigarette remained between his lips, and not a muscle of his face moved. His hand with the broken needle in it was not withdrawn. It clenched slowly, that was all.

The blood welled up under Olga's dismayed eyes, and began to trickle over the brown fist. She threw a frightened glance into his grim face. Her anger had wholly evaporated and she was keenly remorseful. But it was no matter for an apology. The thing was beyond words.

"And now," said Max Wyndham, coolly removing the ash from his cigarette, "perhaps you will come to the surgery with me and get it out."

"I?" stammered Olga, turning very white.

"Even so, fair lady. It will be a little lesson for you--in surgery. I hope the sight of blood doesn't make you feel green," said Max, with a one-sided twitch of the lips that was scarcely a smile.

He removed his hand to her relief, and stood up. Olga stood up too, but she was trembling all over.

"Oh, I can't! Indeed, I can't! Dr. Wyndham, please!" She glanced round desperately. "There's Nick! Couldn't you ask him?"

"Unfortunately this is a job that requires two hands," said Max. "Besides, you did the mischief, remember."

Olga gasped and said no more. Meekly she laid her work on the chair by the hammock and accompanied him to the house. It was the most painful predicament she had ever been in. She knew that there was no escape for her, knew, moreover, that she richly deserved her punishment; yet, as he held open the surgery-door for her, she made one more appeal.

"I'm sure I can't do it. I shall do more harm than good, and hurt you horribly."

"Oh, but you'll enjoy that," he said.

"Indeed, I shan't!" Olga was almost in tears by this time. "Couldn't you do it yourself with--with a forceps?"

"Afraid not," said Max.

He went to a cupboard and took out a bottle containing something which he measured into a glass and filled up with water.

"Fortify yourself with this," he said, handing it to her, "while I select the instruments of torture."

Olga shuddered visibly. "I don't want it. I only want to go."

"Well, you can't go," he returned, "until you have extracted that bit of needle of yours. So drink that, and be sensible!"

He pulled out a drawer with the words, and she watched him, fascinated, as he made his selection. He glanced up after a moment.

"Olga, if you don't swallow that stuff soon, I shall be--annoyed with you."

She raised it at once to her lips, feeling as if she had no choice, and drank with shuddering distaste.

"I always have hated sal volatile," she said, as she finished the draught.

"You can't have everything you like in this world," returned Max sententiously. "Come over here by the window! Now you are to do exactly what I tell you. Understand? Put your own judgment in abeyance. Yes, I know it's bleeding; but you needn't shudder like that. Give me your hand!" She gave it, trembling. He held it firmly, looking straight into her quivering face. "We won't proceed," he said, "until you have quite recovered your self-control, or you may go and slit a large vein, which would be awkward for us both. Just stand still and pull yourself together."

She found herself obliged to obey. The shrewd green eyes watched her mercilessly, and under their unswerving regard her agitation gradually died down.

"That's better," he said at length, and released her hand. "Now see what you can do."

It seemed to Olga later that he took so keen an interest in the operation as to be quite insensible of the pain it involved. She obeyed his instructions herself with a set face and a quaking heart, suppressing a sick shudder from time to time, finally achieving the desired end with a face so ghastly that the victim of her efforts laughed outright.

"Whom are you most sorry for, yourself or me?" he wanted to know. "I say, please don't faint till you have bandaged me up! I can't attend to you properly if you do, and I shall probably spill blood over you and make a beastly mess."

Again his insistence carried the day. Olga bandaged the torn hand without a murmur.

"And now," said Dr. Max Wyndham, "tell me what you did it for!"

She looked at him then with quick defiance. She had endured much in silence, mainly because she had known that she had deserved it; but there was a limit. She was not going to be brought to book as though she had been a naughty child.

"You had yourself alone to thank for it," she declared with indignation. "If--if you hadn't interfered and behaved intolerably, it wouldn't have happened."

"What a naive way of expressing it!" said Max. "Shall I tell you how I regard the 'happening'?"

"You can do as you like," she flung back. She was longing to go, but stood her ground lest departure should look like flight.

Max took out and lighted another cigarette before he spoke again. Then: "I regard it," he said very deliberately, "as a piece of spiteful mischief for which you deserve a sound whipping--which it would give me immense pleasure to administer."

Olga's pale face flamed scarlet. Her eyes flashed up to his in fiery disdain.

"You!" she said, with withering scorn. "You!"

"Well, what about me?"

Carelessly, his hands in his pockets, Max put the question. Quite obviously he did not care in the smallest degree what answer she made. And so Olga, being stung to rage by his unbearable superiority, cast scruples to the wind.

"I'd do the same to you again--and worse," she declared vindictively, "if I got the chance!"

Max smiled at that superciliously, one corner of his mouth slightly higher than the other. "Oh, no, you wouldn't," he said. "For one thing, you wouldn't care to run the risk of having to sew me up again. And for another, you wouldn't dare!"

"Not dare! Do you think I am afraid of you?"

Olga stood in a streak of sunlight that slanted through the wire blind of the doctor's surgery and fell in chequers upon her white dress. Her pale eyes fairly blazed. No one who had ever seen her thus would have described her as colourless. She was as vivid in that moment as the flare of the sunset; and into the eyes of the man who leaned against the table coolly appraising her there came an odd little gleam of satisfaction--the gleam that comes into the eyes of the treasure-hunter at the first glint of gold.

Olga came a step towards him. She saw the gleam and took it for ridicule. The situation was intolerable. She would be mocked no longer.

"Dr. Wyndham," she said, her voice pitched rather low, "do you call yourself a gentleman?"

"I really don't know," he answered. "It's a question I've never asked myself."

"Because," she said, speaking rather quickly, "I think you a cad."

"Not really!" said Max, smiling openly. "Now I wonder why! Sit down, won't you, and tell me?"

The colour was fading from her face again. She had made a mistake in thus assailing him, and already she knew it. He only laughed at her puny efforts to hurt him, laughed and goaded her afresh.

"Why am I not a gentleman?" he asked, and drew in a mouthful of smoke which he puffed at the ceiling. "Because I said I should like to give you a whipping? But you would like to tar and feather me, I gather. Isn't that even more barbarous?" He watched the smoke ascend, with eyes screwed up, then, as she did not speak, looked down at her again. She no longer stood in the sunlight, and the passing of the splendour seemed to have left her cold. She looked rather small and pinched-- there was even a hint of forlornness about her. But she had learned her lesson.

As he looked at her, she clenched her hands, drew a deep breath, and spoke. "Dr. Wyndham, I beg your pardon for hurting you, and for being rude to you. I can't help my thoughts, of course, but I was wrong to put them into words. Please forget--all I've said!"

"Oh, I say!" said Max, opening his eyes, "that's the cruellest thing you've done yet. You've taken all the wind out of my sails, and left me stranded. What is one expected to say to an apology of that sort? It's outside my experience entirely."

Olga had turned to the door, but at his words she paused, looking back. A glimmer of resentment still shone in her eyes.

"If I were in your place," she said, "I should apologize too."

"Oh, no, you wouldn't," said Max. "Not if you wished to achieve the desired effect. You see, I've nothing to apologize for."

"How like a man!" exclaimed Olga.

"Yes, isn't it? Thanks for the compliment! Strange to say, I am much more like a man than anything else under the sun. I say, are you really going? Well, I forgive you for being naughty, if that's what you want. And I'm sorry I can't grovel to you, but I don't feel justified in so doing, and it would be very bad for you in any case. By the way--er--Miss Ratcliffe, I think you will be interested to learn that my visit to the Campions was of a social and not of a professional character. That was all you wanted to know, I think?"

Olga, holding the door open, looked across at him with surprise that turned almost instantly to half-scornful enlightenment.

"Oh, that's it, is it?" she said.

"That's it," said Max. "Quite sure you don't want to know anything else?"

Again he puffed the smoke upwards and watched it ascend.

"Why on earth couldn't you have said so before?" said Olga.

He turned at that and surveyed her quite seriously. "Oh, that was entirely for your sake," he said.

"For my sake!" said Olga. Sheer curiosity impelled her to remain and probe this mystery.

"Yes," said Max, with a sudden twinkle in his green eyes. "You know, it isn't good for little girls to know too much."

As the door banged upon her retreat, he leaned back, holding to the edge of the table, and laughed with his chin in the air.

Life in the country, notwithstanding its many drawbacks, was turning out to be more diverting than he had anticipated.

CHAPTER II
THE ALLY

A h, my dear, there you are! I was just wondering if I would come over and see you."

Violet Campion reined in her horse with a suddenness that made him chafe indignantly, and leaned from the saddle to greet Olga, who had just turned in at the Priory gates.

Olga was bicycling. She sprang from her machine, and reached up an impetuous hand, as regardless of the trampling animal as its rider.

"Pluto is in a tiresome mood to-day," remarked his mistress. "I know he won't be satisfied till he has had a good beating. Perhaps you will go on up to the house while I give him a lesson."

"Oh, don't beat him!" Olga pleaded. "He's only fresh."

"No, he isn't. He's vicious. He snapped at me before I mounted. It's no good postponing it. He'll have to have it." Violet spoke as if she were discussing the mechanism of a machine. "You go on up the drive, my dear, while I take him across the turf."

But Olga lingered. "Violet, really--I know he will throw you or bolt with you. I wish you wouldn't."

Violet's laugh had a ring of scorn. "My dear child, if I were afraid of that, I had better give up riding him altogether."

"I wish you would," said Olga. "He is much too strong for a woman to manage."

Violet laughed again, this time with sheer amusement, and then, with dark eyes that flashed in the sunlight, she slashed the animal's flank with her riding-whip. He uttered a snort that was like an exclamation of rage, and leaped clean off the ground. Striking it again, he reared, but received a stinging cut over the ears that brought him down. Then furiously he kicked and plunged, catching the whip all over his glossy body, till with a furious squeal he flung himself forward and galloped headlong away.

Olga stood on the drive and watched with lips slightly compressed. She knew that as an exhibition of skilled horsemanship the spectacle she had just witnessed was faultless; but it gave her no pleasure, and there was no admiration in the eyes that followed the distant galloping figure with the merciless whip that continued active as long as she could see it.

As horse and rider passed from sight beyond a clump of trees, she remounted her bicycle, and rode slowly towards the house.

Old and grey and weather-stained, the walls of Brethaven Priory shone in the hot sunlight. It had been built in Norman days a full mile and a half inland; but more than the mile had disappeared in the course of the crumbling centuries, and only a stretch of gleaming hillside now intervened between it and the sea. The wash and roar of the Channel and the crying of gulls swept over the grass-clad space as though already claim had been laid to the old grey building that had weathered so many gales. Undoubtedly the place was doomed. There was something eerily tragic about it even on that shining August afternoon, a shadow indefinable of which Olga had been conscious even in her childish days.

She looked over her shoulder several times as she rode in the direction in which her friend had disappeared, but she saw no sign of her. Finally, reaching the house, she went round to a shed at the back, in which she was accustomed to lodge her bicycle.

Here she was joined by an immense Irish wolf-hound, who came from the region of the stables to greet her.

She stopped to fondle him. She and Cork were old friends. As she finally returned to the carriage-drive in front of the house, he accompanied her.

The front door stood open, and she went in through its Gothic archway, glad to escape from the glare outside. The great hall she thus entered had been the chapel in the days of the monks, and it had the clammy atmosphere of a vault. Passing in from the brilliant sunshine, Olga felt actually cold.

It was dark also, the only light, besides that from the open door, proceeding from a stained-glass window at the farther end--a gruesome window representing in vivid colours the death of St. John the Baptist.

A carved oak chest, long and low, stood just within, and upon this the girl seated herself, with the great dog close beside her. Her ten-mile bicycle ride in the heat had tired her.

There was no sound in the house save the ticking of an invisible clock. It might have been a place bewitched, so intense and so uncanny was the silence, broken only by that grim ticking that sounded somehow as if it had gone on exactly the same for untold ages.

"What a ghostly old place it is, Cork!" Olga remarked to her companion. "And you actually spend the night here! I can't think how you dare."

In response to which Cork smiled with a touch of superiority and gave her to understand that he was too sensible to be afraid of shadows.

They were still sitting there conversing, with their faces to the sunlit garden, when there came the sound of a careless footfall and Violet Campion, her riding-whip dangling from her wrist, strolled round the corner of the house, and in at the open door.

She was laughing as she came, evidently at some joke that clung to her memory.

"Look at me!" she said. "I'm all foam. But I've conquered his majesty King Devil for once. He's come back positively abject. My dear, do get up! You're sitting on my coffin!"

Olga got up quickly. "Violet, what extraordinary things you think of!"

The other girl laughed again, and stooping raised the oaken lid. "It's not in the least extraordinary. Look inside, and picture to yourself how comfy I shall be! You can come and see me if you like, and spread flowers--red ones, mind. I like plenty of colour."

She dropped the lid again carelessly, and took a gold cigarette-case from her pocket. The sunlight shone generously upon her at that moment, and Olga Ratcliffe told herself for the hundredth time that this friend of hers was the loveliest girl she had ever seen. Certainly her beauty was superb, of the Spanish-Irish type that is world-famous,--black hair that clustered in soft ringlets about the forehead, black brows very straight and delicate, skin of olive and rose, features so exquisite as to make one marvel, long-lashed eyes that were neither black nor grey, but truest, deepest violet.

"Don't look at me like that!" she said, with gay imperiousness. "You pale-eyed folk have a horrible knack of making one feel as if one is under a microscope. Your worthy uncle is just the same. If I weren't so deeply in love with him, I might resent it. But Nick is a privileged person, isn't he, wherever he goes? Didn't someone once say of him that he rushes in where angels fear to tread? It's rather an apt description. How is he, by the way? And why didn't you bring him too?"

She stood on the step, with the sunlight pouring over her, and daintily smoked her cigarette. Olga came and stood beside her. They formed a wonderful contrast--a contrast that might have seemed cruel but for the keen intelligence that gave such vitality to the face of the doctor's daughter.

"Oh, Nick is playing cricket with the boys," she said. "He is wonderfully good, you know, and takes immense care of us all."

"A positive paragon, my dear! Don't I know it? A pity he saw fit to throw himself away upon that very lethargic young woman! I should have made him a much more suitable wife--if he had only had the sense to wait a few years instead of snatching the first dark-eyed damsel who came his way!"

"Oh, really, Violet! And fancy calling Muriel lethargic! She is one of the deepest people I know, and absolutely devoted to Nick--and he to her."

"Doubtless! doubtless!" Violet flicked the ash delicately from her cigarette. "I am sure he is the soul of virtue. But how comes it that the devoted Muriel can tear herself from his side to go a-larking on the Continent with the grim and masterful Dr. Jim?"

"Oh, I thought you knew that. It is for the child's benefit. Poor little Reggie has a delicate chest, and Redlands doesn't altogether suit him. Dad positively ordered him abroad, and when Muriel demurred about taking him out of Dad's reach (she has such faith in him, you know), he arranged to go too if Nick would leave Redlands and come and help me keep house. You see, Dad couldn't very well leave me to look after Dr. Wyndham singlehanded."

"My dear, of course not!" Up went the violet eyes in horror at the bare suggestion. "You scandalize me. An innocent child like you! Not to be thought of for a moment! Rather than that, I would have come and shared the burden with you myself!"

"That's exactly what I have come to ask you to do," said Olga eagerly. "Do say you can! You can't think how welcome you will be!"

"My dear, you're so impetuous!" Violet was just a year her junior, but this fact was never recognized. "Pray give me time to deliberate. You forget that I also have a family to consider. What will Bruce say if I desert him at a moment's notice?"

"I'm sure Bruce won't mind. Can't we go and ask him?"

"Presently, my child. He is not at home just at present. Neither is Mrs. Bruce." The daintiest grimace in the world testified to the opinion entertained by the speaker for the latter. "Moreover, Bruce and I had a difference of opinion this morning and are not upon speaking terms. So unfortunate that he is so difficile. By the way, he is hand and glove with the new assistant. Were you aware of that?"

"I knew that he came to tea here yesterday," said Olga.

"Oh! And how did you find that out?"

"He told me."

"You mean you asked him!"

"Indeed, I didn't!" Olga refuted the charge with indignation. "I don't take the smallest interest in his doings."

"Not really?" Her friend looked at her with a comprehending smile. "Don't you like the young man?" she enquired.

"I detest him!" Olga declared with vehemence.

Again the slender little finger flicked the ash from the cigarette. "But what a mistake, dear!" murmured the owner thereof. "Young men don't grow on every gooseberry bush. Besides, one can never tell! The object of one's detestation might turn out to be the one and only, and it's so humiliating to have to change one's mind."

"I shall never change mine with regard to Dr. Wyndham," Olga said with great determination. "I should hate him quite as badly even if he were the only man in the world."

But at that the cigarette was suddenly whisked from the soft lips and pointed full at her. "Allegro,"--it was Violet Campion's special name for her, and she uttered it weightily,--"mark my words and ponder them well! You have met your fate!"

"Violet! How dare you say such a thing?" Olga turned crimson with indignant protest. "I haven't! I wouldn't! It's horrid of you to talk like that!"

"Quite indecent, dear, I admit. But have you never noticed how indecent the truth can be? What a pity to waste such a lovely blush on me! I presume he hasn't begun to make love to you yet?"

"Of course he hasn't! No man would be such a fool with you within reach!" thrust back Olga, goaded to self-defence.

"But I am not within reach," said Violet, with a twirl of the cigarette.

"Far more so than I," returned Olga with spirit. "Anyhow, he never went out of his way to have tea with me."

A peal of laughter from her companion put a swift end to her indignation. Violet was absolutely irresistible when she laughed. It was utterly impossible to be indignant with her.

"Then you think if I am there perhaps he will be persuaded to stay at home to tea?" she chuckled mischievously. "Well, my dear, I'll come, and we will play at battledore and shuttlecock to your heart's content. But if the young man turns and rends us for our pains--and I have a shrewd notion that that's the sort of young man he is--you mustn't blame me."

She tossed away her cigarette with the words, and turned inwards, sweeping Olga with her with characteristic energy. She was never still for long in this mood.

They passed through the great hall to a Gothic archway in the south wall, close to the wonderful stained window. Olga glanced up at it with a slight shiver as she passed below.

"Isn't it horribly realistic?" she said.

The girl beside her laughed lightly. "I rather like it myself; but then I have an appetite for the horrors. And they've made the poor man so revoltingly sanctimonious that one really can't feel sorry for him. I'd cut off the head of anybody with a face like that. It's a species that still exists, but ought to have been exterminated long ago."

With her hand upon Olga's arm, she led her through the Gothic archway to a second smaller hall, and on up a wide oak staircase with a carved balustrade that was lighted half-way up by another great window of monastic design but clear glass.

Olga always liked to pause by this window, for the view from it was magnificent. Straight out to the open sea it looked, and the width of the outlook was superb.

"Oh, it's better than Redlands," she said.

"I don't think so," returned Violet. "Redlands is civilized. This isn't. Picture to yourself the cruelty of bottling up a herd of monks here in full view of their re-nounced liberty. Imagine being condemned to pass this window a dozen times in the day, on the way to that dreary chapel of theirs. A refinement of torture with which the window downstairs simply can't compete. How they must have hated the smell of the sea, poor dears! But I daresay they didn't open their windows very often. It wasn't the fashion in those days."

She drew Olga on to the corridor above, and so to her own room, a cheerful apartment that faced the Priory grounds.

"If I am really coming to stay with you, I suppose I must pack some clothes. Does the young man dress for dinner, by the way?"

"Oh, yes. It's very ridiculous. We all do it now. It's such a waste of time," said the practical Olga. "And I never have anything to wear."

"Poor child! That is a drawback certainly. I wonder if you could wear any of my things. I shouldn't like to eclipse you."

"I'm sure I couldn't, thank you all the same." Olga's reply was very prompt. "As to eclipsing me, you'll do that in any case, whatever you wear."

Violet looked at her with dancing eyes. "I believe you actually want to be eclipsed! What on earth has the young man been doing? He seems to have scared you very effectually."

"Oh, I'm not afraid of him!" Olga spoke with her chin in the air. "But I detest him with all my heart, and he detests me."

"In fact, you are at daggers drawn," commented Violet. "And you want me to come and divert the enemy's attention while you strengthen your defences. Well, my dear, as I said before, I'll come. But--from what I have seen of Dr. Maxwell Wyndham--I don't think I shall make much impression. If he means to gobble you up, he certainly will do so, whether I interfere or not. I've a notion you might do worse, green eyes and red hair notwithstanding. He will probably whip you sound-ly now and then and put you in the corner till you are good. But you will get to like that in time. And I daresay he will be kind enough to let you lace up his boots for a treat in between whiles."

Olga's pale eyes flashed. "You are positively mad this afternoon, Violet!"

"Oh, no, I'm not. I haven't had a mad spell for a long time. I am only extraordinarily shrewd and far-seeing. Well, dear, what shall I bring to wear? Do you think I shall be appreciated in my red silk? Or will that offend the eye of the virtuous Nick?"

"No, you are not to wear that red thing. Wear white. I like you best in white."

"And black?"

"Yes, black too. But not colours. You are too beautiful for colours."

"Ridiculous child! That red thing, as you call it, suits me to perfection."

"I know it does. But I don't like it. You make me think of Lady Macbeth in that. Besides, it's much too splendid for ordinary occasions. Yes, that pale mauve is exquisite. You will look lovely in that. And this maize suits you too. But you look positively dangerous in red."

"I must leave the business of selection to you, it seems," laughed Violet. "Well, I am to be your guest, so you shall make your own choice. By the way, how shall I get to Weir? Mrs. Bruce has the car, and will probably not return till late. And Bruce is using the dog-cart. That only leaves the luggage-cart for me."

"I'll fly round to Redlands for the motor. Nick won't mind. You get your things packed while I'm gone."

Olga deposited an armful of her friend's belongings upon the bed, and turned to go.

Nick's property of Redlands was less than a mile away, and all that Nick possessed was at her disposal. In fact, she had almost come to look upon Redlands as a second home. It would not take her long to run across to the garage and fetch the little motor which Nick himself had taught her years ago to drive. Lightly she ran down the oak stairs and through the echoing hall once more. The vault-like chill of the place struck her afresh as she passed to the open door. And again involuntarily she shivered, quickening her steps, eager to leave the clammy atmosphere behind.

Passing into the hot sunshine beyond the great nail-studded door was like entering another world. She turned her face up to the brightness and rejoiced.

CHAPTER III
THE OBSTACLE

Redlands had always been a bower of delight to Olga's vivid fancy. The house, long, low, and rambling, stood well back from the cliffs in the midst of a garden which to her childhood's mind had always been the earthly presentment of Paradise. Not the owner of it himself loved it as did Olga. Many were the hours she had spent there, and not one of them but held a treasured place in her memory.

As she turned in at the iron gate, the music of the stream that ran through the glen rose refreshingly through the August stillness. She wished Nick were with her to enjoy it too.

The temptation to run down to the edge of the water was irresistible. It babbled with such delicious coolness between its ferns. The mossy pathway gleamed emerald green. Surely there was no need for haste! She could afford to give herself five minutes in her paradise. Violet certainly would not be ready yet.

She sat down therefore on the edge of the stream, and gave herself up to the full enjoyment of her surroundings. An immense green dragon-fly whirred past her and shot away into the shadows. She watched its flight with fascinated eyes, so sudden was it, so swift, and so unerringly direct. It reminded her of something, she could not remember what. She wrestled with her memory vainly, and finally dismissed the matter with slight annoyance, turning her attention to a wonderful coloured moth that here flitted across her line of vision. It was an exquisite thing, small, but red as coral. Only in this fairyland of Nick's had she ever seen its like. Lightly it fluttered through the chequered light and shade above the water, shining like a jewel above the shallows, the loveliest thing in sight. And then, even under her watching eyes came tragedy. Swift as an arrow, the green dragon-fly darted back again, and in an instant flashed away. In that instant the coral butterfly vanished also.

Olga exclaimed in incredulous horror. The happening had been too quick for her eyes to follow, but her comprehension leaped to the truth. And in that moment she realized what it was of which the dragon-fly reminded her. It was of Max Wyndham sitting on the surgery-table watching her with that mocking gleam in his green eyes, as though he knew her to be at his mercy whether she stayed or fled.

It was unreasonable of course, but that fairy tragedy in the glen increased her dislike of the man a hundredfold. She felt as if he had darted into her life, armed in some fashion with the power to destroy. And she longed almost passionately to turn him out; for no disturbing force had ever entered there before. But she knew that she could not.

She went on up to the house in sober mood. It had been left to the care of the servants since Nick's departure. She found a French window standing open, and entered. It was the drawing-room, all swathed in brown holland. Its dim coolness was very different from the stony chill of the Priory. She looked around her with a restful feeling of being at home, despite the brown coverings. Many were the happy hours she had spent here both before and after Nick's marriage. It had always been her palace of delight.

As she paused in the room, she remembered that there was a book Nick had said he wanted out of the library. This room was a somewhat recent addition to the house and shut away from the rest of the building by a long passage. She passed from the drawing-room, and made her way thither.

It surprised her a little to find the door standing open, but it was only a passing wonder. The light that came in through green sun-blinds made her liken it in her own mind to a chamber under the sea. She went to a book-shelf in a dark corner, and commenced her hunt.

"If you are looking for Farrow's Treatise on Party Government," remarked a casual voice behind her, "I've got it here."

Olga started violently. Any voice would have given her a surprise at that moment, but the voice of Max Wyndham was an absolute shock that set every nerve on edge.

He laughed at her from the sofa, on which he sprawled at length. "My good child, your nerves are like fiddle-strings after a frost. Remind me to make you up a tonic when we get back! Did you bicycle over?"

Olga ignored the question. She was for the moment too angry to speak.

"Sit down," he said. "You ought to know better than to scorch on a day like this. You deserve a sunstroke."

"I didn't scorch," declared Olga, stung by this injustice. "I'm not such an idiot. You seem to think I haven't any sense at all!"

"My thoughts are my own," said Max. "Why didn't you say you were coming? You could have motored over with me."

"I didn't so much as know you would be in this direction. How could I?" said Olga. "And even if I had known--" she, paused.

"You would have preferred sunstroke?" he suggested.

"That I can quite believe. Well, here is the book!" He swung his legs off the sofa. "I dropped in to fetch it myself, as your good uncle seemed to want it, and then became so absorbed in its pages that I couldn't put it down. We seem to have a rotten Constitution altogether. Wonder whose fault it is."

Olga took the book with a slight, contemptuous glance. That he had been interested in the subject for a single moment she did not believe. She wondered that he deemed it worth his while to feign interest.

"Are you taking a holiday to-day?" she enquired bluntly.

He smiled at that. "I cut off an old man's toe at the cottage hospital this morning, vaccinated four babies, pulled out a tooth, and dressed a scald. What more would you have? I suppose you don't want to be vaccinated by any chance?"

Olga passed the flippant question over. "It's a half-holiday then, is it?" she said.

"Well, as it happens, fair lady, it is, all thanks to Dame Stubbs of 'The Ship Inn' who summoned me hither with great urgency and then was ungrateful enough to die before I reached her."

"Oh!" exclaimed Olga. "Is old Mrs. Stubbs dead?"

"She is," said Max.

She turned upon him. "And you've just come--from her death-bed?"

He arose and stretched himself. "Even so, fair lady."

Olga stared at him incredulously. "You actually--don't care?" she asked slowly.

"Not much good caring," said Max.

"What did she die of?" questioned Olga.

He hesitated for a second. Then, "cancer," he said briefly.

"Did she suffer much?" She asked the question nervously as if she feared the answer.

"It doesn't matter, does it?" said Max, thrusting his hands into his pockets.

"I don't see why you shouldn't tell me that." Olga spoke with a flash of indignation. "It does matter in my opinion."

"Nothing that's past matters," said Max.

"I don't agree with you!" Hotly she made answer, inexplicably hurt by his callous tone. "It matters a lot to me. She was a friend of mine. If I had known she was seriously ill, I'd have gone to see her. You--I think you might have told me."

She turned with the words as if to go, but Max coolly stepped to the door before her. He stretched a hand as if to open it, but paused, holding it closed.

"I was not aware that the old woman was a friend of yours," he said. "But it wouldn't have done much good to anyone if you had seen her. She probably wouldn't have known you."

"I might have taken her things at least," said Olga.

"Which she wouldn't have touched," he rejoined.

She clenched her hands unconsciously. Why was he so maddeningly cold-blooded?

"Do you mind opening the door?" she said.

But he remained motionless, his hand upon it. "Do you mind telling me where you are going?" he said.

Her eyes blazed. "Really, Dr. Wyndham, what is that to you?"

He stood up squarely and faced her, his back against the door. "I will answer your question when you have answered mine."

She restrained herself with an effort. How she hated the man! Conflict with him made her feel physically sick; and yet she had no choice.

"I am going down to 'The Ship' at once," she said, "to see her daughter."

"Pardon me!" said Max. "I thought that was your intention. I am sorry to have to frustrate it, but I must. I assure you Mrs. Briggs will have plenty of other visitors to keep her amused."

"I am going nevertheless," said Olga.

She saw his jaw coming into sudden prominence, and her heart gave a hard quick throb of misgiving. They stood face to face in the dimness, neither uttering a word.

Several seconds passed. The green eyes were staring at the bookshelves beyond Olga, but it was a stony, pitiless stare. Had he any idea as to how formidable he looked, she wondered? Surely--surely he did not mean to keep her against her will! He could not!

She collected herself and spoke. "Dr. Wyndham, will you let me go?"

Instantly his eyes met hers. "Certainly," he said, "if you will promise me first not to go to 'The Ship' till after the funeral."

She felt her face gradually whitening. "But I mean to go. Why shouldn't I?"

"Simply because it wouldn't be good for you," he made calm reply.

"How ridiculous!" They were the only words that occurred to her. She spoke them with vehemence.

He received them in silence, and she saw that a greater effort would be necessary if she hoped to assert her independence with any success.

It was essential that she should do so, and she braced herself for a more determined attempt. "Dr. Wyndham," she said, throwing as much command into her voice as she could muster, "open that door--at once!"

She saw again that glint in his eyes that seemed to mock her weakness. He stood his ground. "Fair lady," he said, "with regret I refuse."

She made a sharp movement forward, nerved for the fray by sheer all-possessing anger. She gripped the handle of the door above his hand and gave it a sharp wrench. He would not--surely he would not--struggle with her! Surely she must discomfit him--rout him utterly--by this means!

Yes, she had won! The sheer unexpectedness of her action had gained the day! Her heart gave a great leap of triumph as he took his hand away. But the next instant it stood still. For in the twinkling of an eye he had taken her by the shoulders holding her fast.

"That is the most foolish thing you ever did in your life," he said, and his words came curt and clipped as though he spoke them through his teeth.

Something about him restrained her from offering any resistance. She stood in silence, her heart jerking on again with wild palpitations. The grip of his hands was horribly close; she almost thought he was going to shake her. But his eyes under their bristling brows held her even more securely. Under their look she was suddenly hotly ashamed.

"You are going to make me that promise," he said.

But she stood silent, trying to muster strength to defy him.

"What do you want to go for?" he demanded.

"I want to know--I want to know--" She stammered over her answer; it was uttered against her will.

"Well? What?" Still holding her, he put the question. "I can tell you anything you want to know."

"But you won't!" Olga plucked up her spirit at this. "It's no good asking you anything. You never answer."

"I will answer you," he said.

"And besides--" said Olga.

"Yes?" said Max.

"You're so horrid," she burst out, "so cold-blooded, so--so--so unsympathetic!"

To her own amazement and dismay, she found herself in tears. In the same instant she was free and the door left unguarded; but she did not use her freedom to escape. Somehow she did not think of that. She only leaned against the wall with her hands over her face and wept.

Max, with his hands deep in his pockets, strolled about the room, whistling below his breath. The gleam had died out of his eyes, but the brows met fiercely above them. His face was the face of a man working out a difficult problem.

Suddenly he walked up to her, and stood still.

"Look here," he said; "can't you manage to be sensible for a minute? If you go on in this way you will soon get hysterical, and I don't think my treatment for hysterics would appeal to you. Olga, are you listening?"

Yes, she was listening--listening tensely, because she could not help herself.

"I'm sorry you think me a brute," he proceeded. "I don't think anyone else does, but that's a detail. I am also sorry that you're upset about old Mrs. Stubbs, though

I don't see much sense in crying for her now her troubles are over. I think myself that it was just as well I didn't reach her in time. I should only have prolonged her misery. That's one of the grand obstacles in the medical career. I've kicked against it a good many times." He paused.

"She did suffer then?" whispered Olga, commanding herself with an effort.

"When she wasn't under the influence of morphia--yes. That was the only peace she knew. But of course it affected her brain. It always does, if you keep on with it."

Olga's hands fell. She straightened herself. "Then--you think she is better dead?" she said.

He squared his great shoulders, and she felt infinitely small. "If I could have followed my own inclination with that old woman," he said, "I should have given her a free pass long ago. But--I am not authorized to distribute free passes. On the contrary, it's my business to hang on to people to the bitter end, and not to let them through till they've paid for their liberty to the uttermost farthing."

She glanced at him quickly. Cynical as were his words, she was aware of a touch of genuine feeling somewhere. She made swift response to it, almost before she realized what she was doing.

"Oh, but surely the help you give far outweighs that!" she said. "I often think I will be a nurse when I am old enough, if Dad can spare me."

"Good heavens, child!" he said. "Do you want to be a gaoler too?"

"No," she answered quickly. "I'll be a deliverer."

He smiled his one-sided smile. "And I wonder how long you will call yourself that," he said.

She had no answer ready, for he seemed to utter his speculation out of knowledge and not ignorance. It made her feel a little cold, and after a moment she turned from the subject.

"I am going back to the Priory," she said. "Shall I take that book, or will you?"

It was capitulation, but he gave no sign that he so much as remembered that there had been a battle. Obviously then her defeat had been a foregone conclusion from the outset.

"You needn't bicycle back," he said. "I've got the car here. And I'm going to the Priory myself."

Olga's eyes opened wide at the announcement. "In--deed!" she said, with somewhat daring significance.

"In--deed!" he responded imperturbably. "Is it a joke?"

She felt herself colouring, and considered it safer to leave the question unanswered. "I can't go back in our car," she said. "Violet Campion will be with me, so I have come to fetch Nick's."

"Oh--ho!" said Max keenly. "Coming to stay?"

Very curiously she resented his keenness. "I suppose you have no objection," she said coldly.

"I am enchanted," he declared. "But why not come with me in the car? If you take the one from here, you will only have to bring it back, for you can't house it at Weir."

"But I should have to come back in any case to fetch my bicycle," Olga pointed out.

"No, you needn't! Mitchel can ride that home, and you can drive the motor. You can drive, I'm told?"

"Of course, I can. I often drive Dad." Olga spoke with pride.

"Do you really? Why did you never tell me that before? Afraid I should want you instead of Mitchel?" He looked at her quizzically.

"It wouldn't make much difference if you did," said Olga. It was really quite useless to attempt to be polite to him if he would come so persistently within snubbing distance. Besides, she really did not owe him any courtesy, after the way he had dared to treat her.

But he only laughed at her, and turned to the door. "I shouldn't be so cocksure of that if I were you," he said, opening it with a flourish. "I have a wonderful knack of getting what I want."

She flung him the gauntlet of her contemptuous defiance as she passed him. "Really?" she said.

He took it up instantly, with disconcerting assurance. "Yes, really," he said.

And to Olga all unbidden there came a sudden little tremor of shuddering remembrance as there flashed across her inner vision the spectacle of a green dragonfly swooping upon a poor little fluttering scarlet moth.

CHAPTER IV
THE SETTING OF THE WATCH

To return to the Priory with her bete-noir seated in triumph beside her was a trick of fortune that Olga had been very far from anticipating. There was no help for it, however, for he was determined to go thither, notwithstanding her assurance that the master of the house was from home. He leaned back at his ease and watched her drive with frank criticism.

"I had no idea you were so accomplished," he remarked, as they skimmed up the long Priory drive. "I should have thought you were much too nervous to drive a car."

Olga was never nervous except in his presence, but she would have rather died than have had him know it.

"Nick taught me," she said, "years ago, when he first lost his arm. It's about the only thing he can't do himself."

"I've noticed that he's fairly agile," commented Max. "What did he have his arm cut off for? Couldn't he make himself conspicuous enough in any other way?"

Olga's cheeks flamed. "He was wounded in action," she said shortly.

Max cocked one corner of his mouth. "And so entered Parliament in a blaze of glory," he said. "Vote for the Brave! Vote for the Veteran! Vote for the One-Armed Hero! Never mind his politics! That empty sleeve must have been absolutely invaluable to him in his electioneering days."

But joking on this subject was more than Olga could bear. The sight of the empty sleeve was enough to bring tears to her eyes at times even now. To hear it thus lightly spoken of was intolerable.

"How dare you say such a thing!" she exclaimed. "As if Nick--Nick!--would ever stoop to take advantage of a thing like that. Nick, who might have won the

V.C., only--" She broke off with vehement self-repression. "I'm an idiot to argue with you!" she said.

"Don't be too hard on yourself!" said Max kindly. "Your imbecility takes quite an attractive form, I assure you. So our gallant hero occupies the shrine of your young affections, does he? It must be rather cramping for him. Is he never allowed to come out and stretch himself?"

Olga said no word in answer. Her lips were firmly closed.

"Poor chap!" said Max. "He must find it a tight squeeze, notwithstanding his size. If you don't slow up pretty soon, fair lady, you will knock the Priory into a heap of ruins."

"I know what I'm about," breathed Olga.

He caught the remark and threw it back with his customary readiness. "Do you really? I humbly beg to question that statement. If you did know, you would proceed with caution."

Olga applied her brake and brought the car adroitly to a standstill in front of the house before replying. Then she flung him a challenging glance.

"Yes," he said with deliberation. "I don't question your cleverness, fair lady;-- only your wisdom. You are too prone to let your feelings run away with you, and that is the most infectious disorder that I know."

She laughed, avoiding his eyes, and hotly aware of a certain embarrassment that made reply impossible. "Perhaps, when you have quite finished your lecture, you will get out," she said, "and let me do the same. It's hot sitting here."

"Evidently," said Max.

He turned and descended, held up a hand to her, then, as she ignored it, stooped to guard her dress from the wheel. She whisked it swiftly from his touch, and ran in through the open door, encountering the master of the house just coming out with a suddenness that involved a collision.

He held her up with a sharp, "Hullo, hullo! Why don't you look where you are going?"

And Olga, crimson and breathless, extricated herself with more of speed than dignity. "I'm so sorry, Colonel Campion. The sun is so blazing, I didn't see you. I've come to fetch Violet. She has promised to spend a few days with me while Dad is away."

Colonel Campion's thin, bronzed face was grim, but he raised no objection to the projected visit. He turned at once to Max.

"Hullo, Wyndham! You, is it? Come in and have a drink."

And Olga, feeling herself dismissed, hastened away to find her friend. She stood somewhat in awe of Colonel Campion, despite the fact that his young half-sister defied him continually with impunity. There was something fateful and forbidding about him. He made her think of a man labouring perpetually under a burden which he resented, but was compelled to bear. She wondered what he and Max Wyndham could have in common as she paused at the sea-window on the stairs to cool her cheeks. He had certainly been pleased in his gloomy fashion to see Max, though he had not troubled to give her a welcome.

She found that Violet had not proceeded much further with her packing than when she had left her more than an hour before. She was in fact lying at careless ease half-dressed upon the bed, deeply immersed in a book with a lurid paper cover. She scarcely raised her eyes at Olga's entrance.

"Back already. My dear, you are like quicksilver. Well have I named you Allegro! It suits you to perfection. Sit down--anywhere! I really can't attend to you for a few minutes. This is the beastliest thing I've ever read. You shall have it when I've finished. It's all about the Turkish massacres in Armenia--revolting--absolutely revolting--" Her voice trailed off into a semi-conscious murmur and ceased. The beautiful eyes, dilated with horror, devoured the open page.

Olga contemplated her for a moment, then went to the bedside. "Violet, do put down that hateful book! How can you read such disgusting things? Violet!" as her remonstrance elicited no response, "do get up and let us pack your things! Dr. Wyndham is downstairs."

"What?" Violet looked at her this time, but with a mazed expression as of one half-asleep. "Who? The great Objectionable himself? How did you inveigle him here? By nothing short of witchcraft, I will swear. Those pale eyes of yours are rather witch-like, do you know? Did you fly over on a broomstick to fetch him? And why?"

Olga possessed herself of the book, and shut it with decision. "I came upon him at Redlands, and as he has got the car with him, we may as well go back in it. He said he was coming here in any case."

"Really, dear? I wonder why." Violet made a futile effort to recapture her book. "You might let me have it. I must know what became of those unlucky girls when the convent was taken. They mutilated most of the nuns with their scimitars. But the pupils--Allegro, let me have it, dear! I shan't sleep a wink to-night till I know the worst."

"You won't sleep if you do," said Olga magisterially.

"You shan't read any more. It's a disgusting, filthy book and you shan't have it. Get up and dress, and don't be horrid!"

"Horrid!" Violet broke into a gay laugh and the strained look passed in a moment from her eyes. "I was all that was beautiful a little while ago. You're quite right though. It is a foul book, and the man who wrote it is a downright beast. Take it away, and never let me see it again!"

She sprang from the bed, and began to do up her hair rapidly before the glass. Olga laid down the book, and busied herself with folding the various articles of raiment that littered the room.

"I think we ought to be quick," she said.

"To be sure! We mustn't keep his Objectionable Majesty waiting. Why didn't you bring him up with you? It would have kept him amused."

"Violet! As if I could!"

"Oh, couldn't you? I thought doctors were allowed anywhere. And I am sure this young man of yours is not lightly shocked. What was he doing at Redlands?"

Olga hesitated momentarily. "He had been sent for to 'The Ship,' to attend old Mrs. Stubbs," she said then. "But he didn't get there in time."

"Oh! Is she dead? I should think he is pretty savage with her, isn't he?"

"Why should you think so?" Olga glanced round in surprise.

"He's the sort of person to resent anyone dying without his express permission, I should imagine. I know I should never dare to die with him looking on;" Lightly the gay voice made answer. The speaker turned from the glass, her vivid face aglow with merriment. "Really, Olga, if you're quite determined to do my packing, I think I will run down and entertain him."

"You needn't trouble to do that. He is with your brother." Olga proceeded deftly with her task as she spoke. "We found him in the hall as we came in."

"Bruce back already! How tiresome of him! I meant to have just left a message, and now we shall have a wordy argument instead."

"Is Colonel Campion ever wordy?" asked Olga, trying to imagine this phenomenon.

"No, I supply the words and he the argument generally. You might just hook me down the back, dear; do you mind? What do you think his latest craze is? Mrs. Bruce is run down, so nothing will serve but we must all go for a yachting cruise in the Atlantic. I have told him flatly that I will not be one of the party. I detest being on the sea, and as to being boxed up in a yacht with those two--my dear, it would be unspeakable! I should simply leap overboard, I know I should, and I told him so. He has sulked ever since."

"Ah well, you are coming to us," said Olga consolingly. "So he can go without you now with a clear conscience."

"So he can. Mrs. Bruce will be enchanted. She hates me, though she pretends not to and thinks I don't know. Isn't it funny of her? Allegro, you're a darling!" Impulsively she whizzed round and kissed her friend. "You are the one person in the world who loves me, and the only one I love!"

"Violet dearest, how can you say so?"

"The truth, dear, I assure you. I fell in love last winter when we were at Nice with a boy with the most romantic, heavenly eyes you ever saw--an Italian. And then he went and spoilt everything by falling in love with me. I hated him then. He became cheap and very nasty. He only liked my outer covering too, and was not in the least interested in the creature that lived inside."

"You apparently only cared for his eyes," observed Olga.

"Yes, exactly, dear. How clever you are! I should like to have brought them away with me as trophies. But he didn't love me enough for that, and nothing else would have satisfied me. Have you put that hateful, revolting book quite out of reach? I think you had better. If I get it again, you won't take it away so easily a second time."

"I can't think what makes you like such beastly things," said Olga, sitting down upon it firmly.

"Nor I, dear. It's just the way I'm made. I don't like them either. I hate them. That's where the fascination comes in. There! Let me put on my hat, and I am ready. I suppose I must veil myself? We mustn't dazzle the impressionable Max, must we?

He must accustom his sight to me gradually. Never mind the rest of those things, Allegro! Francoise can finish, and send them on by the luggage-cart in the evening. Come along, let us face the dragon and get it over."

She linked her arm in Olga's once more, and drew her to the door. Olga carried the book with her for safety, determined that her friend should feast no more on horrors.

"What a little tyrant you are!" laughed Violet. "I am coming to protect you from the dragon, but I shall probably end by protecting the dragon from you. Do you keep a censorious eye upon the literature he reads also?"

"I leave him quite alone," said Olga, "unless he interferes with me."

"Ah! And then, I suppose, you scratch him heartily Poor young man! But I should imagine he is quite capable of clipping your claws if they get in his way. My dear, your fate will be no easy one. I should begin to treat him kindly if I were you."

"I shall never do that," said Olga with conviction.

She was somewhat dismayed as they passed through the archway into the hall to find Max and his host still there; but as they were at the further end and apparently deeply engrossed in conversation, she decided that Violet's gay remarks were scarcely likely to have made any impression, even if they had penetrated so far.

Both men looked up at their entrance, and Max at once moved to meet them.

"I've turned up again at risk of boring you, Miss Campion," he observed. "I chanced to find myself in this direction, so had to yield to the temptation of coming here."

"Oh, don't apologize!" laughed Violet, giving him two fingers. "Of course, I know that it's Bruce you come to see. I wish you would prescribe him a temper tonic. He needs one badly, don't you, Bruce? So Granny Stubbs has given you the slip, has she? How impertinent of her! Aren't you very angry?"

Max shrugged his shoulders with a glance at Olga's tight lips. "I never expend my emotions in vain," he said. "It's a waste of time as well as energy, and I have other purposes for both."

"Then you are never angry?" enquired Violet.

"Never, unless I can punish the offender," smiled Max.

"How frightfully practical! Dear me! I shall have to be exceedingly careful not to offend you. I wonder what form your punishments usually take. Are they made to fit the crime?"

"Usually," said Max, and again he glanced at Olga.

Her eyelids flickered as though she were aware of his look, but she did not raise them.

"You make me quite nervous," declared Violet. "Do you know I have actually promised to come and help keep house for you and the redoubtable Captain Ratcliffe? I'm beginning to think I've been rather rash."

"On the contrary," said Max. "It was quite a wise move on your part, and it shall be mine to see that you do not regret it."

Her gay laugh rang through the old hall. "Bruce is looking quite scandalized, and I don't wonder. Will you and Adelaide be able to support life without me, Bruce? It's a purely formal question, so you needn't answer it if you don't wish. Oh, do let us have some tea! I'm so thirsty. Please ring the bell, Dr. Wyndham! It's close to you. Look at Olga cuddling that naughty book of mine! Don't you think you ought to take it away from her? It's not fit for an innocent maiden to handle even with gloves on."

"What book is it?" It was Colonel Campion who spoke in the harsh tone of one issuing a command.

Olga coloured fierily. "I was taking it away with me to burn on the garden bonfire," she said.

"Give it to me!" he said.

"No, don't, Allegro! It isn't yours to give. You may give it to Dr. Wyndham if you like, but not to Bruce."

"I am not going to give it to anyone," Olga said rather shortly.

"Pardon!" said Max, holding out his hand. "I should like to sample Miss Campion's taste in literature."

She drew back, but his hand remained outstretched. After a moment, reluctantly, she surrendered the book. He took it, and began to turn the pages.

"Nothing ever shocks a medical man," observed Violet. "He is inured to the worst. Come along, dear! This place is like a vault. Let us get into the sunshine and leave him to wallow till tea appears."

They went out together to Olga's immense relief, and spent the next ten minutes in playing with the motor, in the driving of which Violet had lately developed a keen interest.

When they returned, the book had disappeared and the incident was apparently forgotten. They had tea to the accompaniment of much light-hearted chatter on the parts of Violet and Max Wyndham. Colonel Campion sat in heavy silence, and Olga instinctively held aloof. There was something in Max's attitude that puzzled her, but it was something so intangible that she could not even vaguely define it to herself. All his careless banter notwithstanding, she was fully convinced in her own mind that he was not in the smallest degree dazzled or so much as attracted by the brilliant beauty that so dominated her own imagination. Though he laughed and joked in his customary cynical strain, she had a feeling that his mental energies were actually employed elsewhere. He was like a man watching behind a mask. Watching--for what?

Suddenly she remembered again the tragedy she had witnessed in the glen that afternoon, and her heart recoiled.

Was it the atmosphere of the place that made her morbid? Or was there indeed some evil influence at work in her friend's life which she by her headlong action had somehow rendered active?

Before they left the Priory, she had begun to repent almost passionately the impulse that had taken her thither. But wherefore she thus repented she could not have explained.

CHAPTER V
THE CHAPERON

I t's very kind of Olga to provide us with distractions," said Nick, as he dropped into an arm-chair, with a cigar, "but I almost think we are better off without them. If I see much of that girl, it will upset my internal economy. Is she real by any chance?"

"Haven't you ever seen her before?" asked Max.

"Several times, but never for long together. Jove! What a face she has!" He turned his head sharply, and looked up at Max who stood on the hearth-rug. "You're not wildly enthusiastic over her anyhow," he observed. "Are you really indifferent or only pretending?"

"I?" The corners of Max's mouth went down. He stuffed his pipe into one of them and said no more.

Nick continued to regard him with interest for some seconds. Suddenly he laughed. "Do you know, Wyndham," he said, "I should awfully like to give you a word of advice?"

"What on?" Max did not sound particularly encouraging. He proceeded to light his pipe with exceeding deliberation. He despised cigars.

Nick closed his eyes. "In my capacity of chaperon," he said. "It's a beastly difficult position by the way. I'm weighed down by responsibility."

"So I've noticed," remarked Max drily.

"Well, you haven't done much to lighten the burden," said Nick. "I suppose you haven't realized yet that I am one of the gods that control your destiny."

"Well, no; I hadn't." Max leaned against the mantelpiece and smoked, with his face to the ceiling. "I knew you were a species of deity of course. I've been told that several times. And I humbly beg to offer you my sympathy."

"Thanks!" Nick's eyes flashed open as if at the pulling of a string. "If it isn't an empty phrase, I value it."

"I don't deal in empty phrases as a rule," said Max.

"Quite so. Only with a definite end in view? I hold that no one should ever do or say anything without a purpose."

"So do I," said Max.

Nick's eyes flickered over him and closed again. "Then, my dear chap," he said, "why in Heaven's name make yourself so damned unpleasant?"

"So what?" said Max.

"What I said." Coolly Nick made answer. "It's not an empty phrase," he added. "You will find a meaning attached if you deign to give it the benefit of your august consideration."

Max uttered a grim, unwilling laugh. "I suppose you are privileged to say what you like," he said.

"I observe certain limits," said Nick.

"And you never make mistakes?"

"Oh, yes, occasionally. Not often. You see, I'm too well-meaning to go far astray," said Nick, with becoming modesty. "You must remember that I'm well-meaning, Wyndham. It accounts for a good many little eccentricities. I think you were quite right to make her extract that needle. I should have done it myself. But you are not so wise in resenting her refusal to kiss the place and make it well. I speak from the point of view of the chaperon, remember."

"Who told you anything about a needle?" demanded Max, suddenly turning brick-red..

"That's my affair," said Nick.

"And mine!"

"No, pardon me, not yours!" Again his eyes took a leaping glance at his companion.

Doggedly Max faced it. "Did she tell you?"

"Who?" said Nick.

"Olga." He flung the name with half-suppressed resentment. His attitude in that moment was aggressively British. He looked as he had looked to Olga that afternoon, undeniably formidable.

But Nick remained unimpressed. "I shan't answer that question," he said.

"You needn't," said Max grimly.

"That's why," said Nick.

"Oh! I see." Max's eyes searched him narrowly for a moment, then returned to the ceiling. "Does she think I'm in love with her?" he asked rather curtly.

"Well, scarcely. I shouldn't let her think that at present if I were you. In my opinion any extremes are inadvisable at this stage."

"I suppose you know I am going to marry her?" said Max.

"Yes, I've divined that."

"And you approve?"

"I submit to the inevitable," said Nick with a sigh.

Max smiled, the smile of a man who faces considerable odds with complete confidence. "She doesn't--at present."

Nick's grin of appreciation flashed across his yellow face and was gone. "No, my friend. And you'll find her very elusive to deal with. You will never make her like you. I suppose you know that."

"I don't want her to," said Max.

"You make that very obvious," laughed Nick. "It's a mistake. If you keep bringing her to bay, you'll never catch her. She's always on her guard with you now. She never breathes freely with you in the room, poor kid."

"What is she afraid of?" growled Max.

"You know best." Nick glanced up again with sudden keenness. "Don't harry the child, Wyndham!" he said, a half-whimsical note of pleading in his voice. "If you know you're going to win through, you can afford to let her have the honours of war. There's nothing softens a woman more."

"I don't mean to harry her." Max turned squarely round upon him. "But neither have I the smallest intention of fetching and carrying for her till she either kicks me or pats me on the head. I shouldn't appreciate either, and it's a method I don't believe in."

"There I am with you," said Nick. "But for Heaven's sake, man, be patient! It's no joke, I assure you, if the one woman takes it into her head that you are nothing short of a devouring monster. She will fly to the ends of the earth to escape you sooner than stay to hear reason."

Max smiled in his one-sided fashion. "Has that been your experience?"

Nick nodded. There was a reminiscent glitter in his eyes. "My courtship represented two years' hard labour. It nearly killed me. However, we've made up for it since."

"I don't propose to spend two years over mine," said Max.

Nick's eyes flashed upwards, meeting those of the younger man with something of the effect of a collision. His body however remained quite passive, and his voice even sounded as if it had a laugh in it as he made response.

"I think you're a decent chap," he said, "and I think you might make her happy; but I'm damned if she shall marry any man--good, bad, or indifferent--before she's ready."

"You also think you could prevent such a catastrophe?" suggested Max cynically.

Nick grinned with baffling amiability. "No, I don't think. I know. Quite a small spoke is enough to stop a wheel--even a mighty big wheel--if it's going too fast."

And again, more than half against his will, Max laughed. "You make a very efficient chaperon," he said.

"It's my speciality just now," said Nick.

He closed his eyes again peaceably, and gave himself up to his cigar.

Max, his rough red brows drawn together, leaned back against the mantelpiece and smoked his pipe, staring at the opposite wall. There was no strain in the silence between them. Both were preoccupied.

Suddenly through the open window there rippled in the fairy notes of a mandolin, and almost at once a voice of most alluring sweetness began to sing:

"O, wert thou in the cauld blast,   On yonder lea, on yonder lea,   My plaidie to the angry airt,   I'd shelter thee, I'd shelter thee.   Or did misfortune's bitter storms   Around thee blaw, around thee blaw,   Thy bield should be my bosom, To share it a', to share it a'."

"Or were I in the wildest waste,   Sae black and bare, sae black and bare, The desert were a paradise,   If thou wert there, if thou wert there.   Or were I monarch o' the globe,   Wi' thee to reign, wi' thee to reign,   The brightest jewel in my crown   Wad be my queen, wad be my queen."

As the song died out into the August night, Nick rose. "That girl's a siren," he said. "Come along! We're wasting our time in here."

Max stooped laconically to knock the ashes from his pipe. His face as he stood up again was quite expressionless. "You lead the way," he said. "Are you going to leave your cigar behind? I suppose cigarettes are allowed?"

"I should think so, as the lady smokes them herself." Nick opened the door with the words, but paused a moment looking back at his companion quizzically. "Good luck to you, old chap!" he said.

Max's hand came out of his pocket with a jerk. He still had it bandaged, but he managed to grip hard with it nevertheless. But he did not utter a word.

They passed into the drawing-room with the lazy, tolerant air of men expecting to be amused; and Olga, with all her keenness, was very far from suspecting aught of what had just passed between them.

She and Violet were both near the open window, the latter with her instrument lying on her knee, its crimson ribbons streaming to the floor. She herself was very simply attired in white. The vivid beauty of her outlined against the darkness of the open French window was such as to be almost startling. She smiled a sparkling welcome.

"Dr. Wyndham, I've decided to call you Max; not because I like it,--I think it's hideous,--but because it's less trouble. I thought it as well to explain at the outset, so that there should be no misunderstanding."

"That is very gracious of you," said Max.

"You may regard it exactly as you please," she said majestically, "so long as you come when you're called. Allegretto, why do you move? I like you sitting there."

"I promised to go and say good-night to the boys," said Olga, who had sprung up somewhat precipitately at Max's approach. "Sit on the sofa, Nick, and keep a corner for me! I'm coming back."

She was gone with the words, a vanishing grey vision, the quick closing of the door shutting her from sight.

Violet leaned back in her chair, and dared the full scrutiny of Max's eyes.

"What a disturber of the peace you are!" she said. "What did you want to come here for before you had finished your smoke?"

"That was your doing," said Nick. "You literally dragged us hither. I'm inclined to think it was you who disturbed the peace."

"I?" She turned upon him. "Captain Ratcliffe--"

"Pray call me Nick!" he interposed. "It will save such a vast amount of trouble as well as keep you in the fashion."

She laughed. "You're much funnier than Max because you don't try to be. What do you mean by saying that I dragged you here? Was it that silly old song?"

"In part," said Nick cautiously.

"And the other part?"

"I won't put that into words. It would sound fulsome."

"Oh, please don't!" she said lightly. "And you, Max, what did you come for?"

He seated himself in the chair which Olga had vacated. "I thought it was time someone came to look after you," he said.

"How inane! You don't pretend to be musical, I hope?"

He leaned back, directly facing her. "No," he said. "I don't pretend."

"Never?" she said.

He smiled in his own enigmatical fashion. "That is the sort of question I never answer."

She nodded gaily. "I knew you wouldn't. Why do you look at me like that? I feel as if I were being dissected. I don't wonder that Olga runs away when she sees you coming. I shall myself in a minute."

He laughed. "Surely you are accustomed to being looked at!"

"With reverence," she supplemented, "not criticism! You have the eye of a calculating apothecary. I believe you regard everybody you meet in the light of a possible patient."

"Naturally," said Max. "I suppose even you are mortal."

"Oh, yes, I shall die some day like the rest of you," she answered flippantly. "But I shan't have you by my death-bed. I shouldn't think you had ever seen anybody die, have you?"

"Why not?" said Max.

"Nobody could with you standing by. You're too vital, too electric. I picture you with your back against the door and your arms spread out, hounding the poor wretch back into the prison-house."

Max got up abruptly and moved to the window. "You have a vivid imagination," he said.

She laughed, drawing her fingers idly across the strings of her mandolin.

"Quite nightmarishly so sometimes. It's rather a drawback for some things. How are you enjoying that book of mine? Do you appreciate the Arabian Nights' flavour in modern literature?"

"It's a bit rank, isn't it?" said Max.

She laughed up at him. "I should have thought you would have been virile enough to like rank things. To judge by the tobacco you smoke, you do."

"Poisonous, isn't it?" said Nick. "I suppose it soothes his nerves, but it sets everyone else's on edge."

Violet stretched out her hand to a box of cigarettes that stood on a table within reach. "You would probably feel insulted if I offered you one of these," she said, "but I practically live on them."

"Very bad for you," said Max.

She snapped her fingers at him. "Then I shall certainly continue the pernicious habit. Do you know Major Hunt-Goring? It was he who gave them to me. He thinks he is going to marry me,--but he isn't!"

"Great Lucifer!" said Nick.

She turned towards him. "What an appropriate name! I wish I'd thought of it. Do you know him?"

"Know him!" Nick's grimace was expressive. "Yes, I know him."

"Well?"

"Rather better than he thinks."

She laughed again, lightly, inconsequently, irresistibly. "He's a fascinating creature. It is his proud boast that he has kissed every girl in the neighbourhood except me."

"What an infernal liar!" said Nick.

"How do you know?" Gaily she challenged him. "It's quite probably true. He is exceedingly popular with the feminine portion of the community. I notice that friend Max maintains a shocked silence."

"Not at all," said Max. "I was only wondering why he had made an exception of you."

She tossed her head. "Can't you guess?"

"No, I can't," he returned daringly. "I should have thought you would have been the first on the list."

"How charming of you to say so!" said Violet. "Perhaps you are not aware of the fact that the sweetest fruit is generally out of reach."

"You might have let me say that," said Nick. "But the man is a liar in any case, and I hope he will give me the opportunity to tell him so."

Violet regarded him with interest. "I had no idea you were so pugnacious. Do you always tell people exactly what you think of them? Is it safe?"

"Quite safe for him," said Max.

"Why?" Violet turned back to him, her fingers carelessly plucking at the instrument on her knee.

Max made prompt and unflattering reply. "Because he's so obviously gimcrack that no one dares do anything to him for fear he should tumble to pieces."

"Many thanks!" said Nick.

Violet's peal of laughter mingled with the weird notes of her mandolin, and Olga, returning, desired to be told the joke.

Nick pulled her down beside him on the sofa. "Come and take care of me, Olga mia! I'm being disgracefully maligned. Can't you persuade Miss Campion to sing to us, by way of changing the subject?"

"Who has been maligning you?" demanded Olga, looking at Max with very bright eyes.

He looked straight back at her with that gleam in his eyes which with any other man would have denoted admiration but which with him she well knew to be only mockery.

"I admit it, fair lady," he said. "I threw a clod of mud at your hero. I thought it would be good for him. However, you will be relieved to hear that it went wide of the mark. He still sits secure in his tight little shrine and smiles magnanimously at my futility."

Olga's hand slipped into Nick's. "He's the biggest man you've ever seen!" she declared, with warmth.

"Please don't fight over my body!" remonstrated Nick. "I never professed to be more than a minnow among Tritons, and quite a lean minnow at that."

"You're not, Nick!" declared his champion impetuously. "You're a giant!"

"In miniature," suggested Max. "He is actually proposing to go and kick Major

Hunt-Goring because--" He broke off short.

Into Olga's face of flushed remonstrance there had flashed a very strange look, almost a petrified look, as if she had suddenly come upon a snake in her path.

"Why?" she said quickly.

"Oh, never mind why," said Max, passing rapidly on. "That wasn't the point. We were trying to picture Hunt-Goring's amusement. He stands about seven feet high, doesn't he? And your redoubtable uncle--What exactly is your height, Ratcliffe?"

"Nick, why do you want to kick Major Hunt-Goring?" Very distinctly Olga put the question. She was evidently too proud to accept help from this quarter.

"It's a chronic craving with me," said Nick. "But Miss Campion has kindly undertaken the job for me. I am sure she is infinitely better equipped for the task than I am, and she will probably do it much more effectually."

"But not yet!" laughed Violet. "I like his cigarettes too well. Why do you look like that, Allegro? Doesn't he send you any?"

"If he did," said Olga, with concentrated passion, "I'd pick them up with the tongs and put them in the fire!"

Max laughed in a fashion that made her wince, but Nick's fingers squeezed hers protectingly.

"You don't like him any better than I do apparently," he said lightly. "But I suppose we must tolerate the man for Jim's sake. He wouldn't thank us for eliminating all his unpleasant patients during his absence. Now, Miss Campion, a song, please! The most sentimental in your repertoire!"

She flashed him her gay smile and flung the streaming ribbons over her arm. There was a gleam of mischief in her eyes as, without preliminary, she began to sing. Her voice was rich and low and wonderfully pure.

> In vain all the knights of the Underworld woo'd her,
> Though brightest of maidens, the proudest was she;
> Brave chieftains they sought, and young minstrels they sued her,
> But worthy were none of the high-born Ladye.

> "Whomsoever I wed," said this maid, "so excelling,

That Knight must the conqu'ror of conquerors be;
He must place me in halls fit for monarchs to dwell in;--
None else shall be Lord of the high-born Ladye!"

Thus spoke the proud damsel, with scorn looking round her
On Knights and on Nobles of highest degree;
Who humbly and hopelessly left as they found her,
And worshipp'd at distance the high-born Ladye.

At length came a Knight from a far land to woo her,
With plumes on his helm like the foam of the sea;
His vizor was down--but, with voice that thrill'd through her,
He whisper'd his vows to the high-born Ladye.

"Proud maiden, I come with high spousals to grace thee,
In me the great conqu'ror of conquerors see;
Enthron'd in a hall fit for monarchs I'll place thee,
And mine thou'rt for ever, thou high-born Ladye!"

The maiden she smil'd and in jewels array'd her,
Of thrones and tiaras already dreamt she;
And proud was the step, as her bridegroom convey'd
her In pomp to his home, of that high-born Ladye.

"But whither," she, starting, exclaims, "have you led me?
Here's nought but a tomb and a dark cypress tree;
Is _this_ the bright palace in which thou wouldst wed me?"
With scorn in her glance, said the high-born Ladye.

"Tis the home," he replied, "of earth's loftiest creatures."
Then he lifted his helm for the fair one to see;
But she sunk on the ground--'twas a skeleton's features,
And Death was the Lord of the high-born Ladye!

The beautiful voice throbbed away into silence, and the mandolin jarred and thrummed upon the floor. Violet Campion sat staring straight before her with eyes that were wide and fixed.

Olga jumped up impulsively. "Violet, why did you sing that gruesome thing? Do you want to give us all the horrors?"

She picked up the mandolin with a swish of its red ribbons, and laid it upon the piano, where it quivered and thrummed again like a living thing, awaking weird echoes from the instrument on which it rested.

Then she turned back to her friend. "Violet, wake up! What are you looking at?"

But Violet remained immovable as one in a trance.

Olga bent over her, touched her. "Violet!"

With a quick start, as though suspended animation had suddenly been restored, Violet relaxed in her chair, leaning back with careless grace, her white arms outstretched.

"What's the matter, Allegretto? You look as if you had had a glimpse of the conqueror of conquerors yourself. I shall have to come and sleep with you to frighten away the spooks."

"I don't think I shall ever dare to go to bed at all after that," said Nick.

She laughed at him lazily. "Get Max to sit up with you and hold your hand! The very sight of him would scare away all bogies."

"The sign of a wholesome mind," said Max.

She turned towards him. "Not at all! Scepticism only indicates gross materialism and lack of imagination. There is nothing at all to be proud of in the possession of a low grade of intelligence."

Max's mouth went down, and Violet's face flashed into her most bewitching smile.

"I don't often get the opportunity to jeer at a genius," she said. "You know that I am one of your most ardent admirers, don't you?"

"Is that the preliminary to asking a favour?" said Max.

She broke into a light laugh. "No, I never ask favours. I always take what I want. It's much the quickest way."

"Saves trouble, too," he suggested.

"It does," she agreed. "I am sure you follow the same plan yourself."

"Invariably," said Max.

"It's a plan that doesn't always answer," observed Nick, in a grandfatherly tone. "I shouldn't recommend it to everybody."

"And it's horribly selfish," put in Olga.

"My dear child, don't be so frightfully moral!" protested Violet. "I can't rise to it. Nick, why doesn't it always answer to take what one wants?"

"Because one doesn't always succeed in keeping it," said Nick.

"He means," said Max, a spark of humour in his eyes, "that a champion,--no, a chaperon--sometimes comes along to the rescue of the stolen article. But--from what I've seen of life--I scarcely think the odds would be on the side of the chaperon. What is your opinion, Miss Campion?"

"If the chaperon were Nick, I should certainly put my money on him," she answered lightly.

"And lose it!" said Max.

"And win it!" said Olga.

"Order! Order!" commanded Nick. "Once more I refuse to be the bone of contention between you. You will tear me to shreds among you, and even the great Dr. Wyndham might find some difficulty in putting me together again. Olga, give us some music!"

"I can't, dear," said Olga.

He frowned at her. "Why not?"

She hesitated. "I'm not in the mood for it. At least--"

"Am I the obstacle?" asked Max.

She could not control her colour, though she strove resolutely to appear as if she had not heard.

He turned to Violet, faintly smiling. "Shall we take a stroll in the garden?"

She rose, flinging a gay glance at Olga. "Just two turns!" she said.

He held aside the curtain for her, and followed her out, with a careless jest. The two who were left heard them laughing as they sauntered away. Olga rose with a shiver.

"What's the matter?" said Nick.

To which she answered, "Nothing," knowing that he would not believe her, knowing also that he would understand enough to ask no more.

She went to the piano, put aside the mandolin, and began to play. Not even to Nick, her hero and her close confidant, would she explain the absolute repugnance that the association of Max Wyndham with her friend had inspired in her.

But though she played with apparent absorption, her ears were strained to catch the sound of their voices in the garden behind her, the girl's light chatter, her companion's brief, cynical laugh. For she knew by the sure intuition which is a woman's inner and unerring vision, that jest or trifle as he might his keen brain was actively employed in some subtle investigation too obscure for her to fathom, and that behind his badinage and behind his cynicism there sat a man who watched.

CHAPTER VI
THE PAIN-KILLER

I am going over to Brethaven to see Mrs. Briggs to-day," Olga announced nearly a week later, waylaying Max after breakfast on his way to the surgery with the air of one prepared to resist opposition. "Are you wanting the car this morning, Dr. Wyndham?"

She knew that he would be engaged at the cottage-hospital that morning, but it was one of Dr. Ratcliffe's strict rules that the car should never be used unprofessionally without express permission from himself or his assistant. Naturally Olga resented having to observe this rule in her father's absence and her manner betrayed as much, but she was too conscientious to neglect its observance.

"You don't propose to go alone, I suppose?" said Max, pausing.

This was another of her father's rules and one which Olga had often vainly attempted to persuade him to rescind. Under these circumstances, Max's question seemed little short of an insult.

"I don't see what that has to do with it," she said.

Max looked at his watch, then turned squarely and faced her. "With me, you mean. Very likely not. But there is a remote connection or I shouldn't ask. Are you going to take Nick with you?"

"He is going part of the way," said Olga, striving for dignity.

"Only part?"

"As far as the station," she returned, almost in spite of herself.

"Going up to town, is he?" said Max. "Well, that doesn't help much. Take one of the boys!"

"I don't want one of the boys," Olga spoke with sudden irritation. "Violet is going with me," she said.

His face changed very slightly, almost imperceptibly. "In that case you must take Mitchel," he said.

"How absurd!" exclaimed Olga.

"No, it isn't absurd. It's quite reasonable from my point of view. If you can't take Mitchel with you, I can't spare the car."

He smiled a little as he pronounced this decision, but quite plainly his mind was made up.

Olga bit her lip in exasperation. "Do you think I am not to be trusted to take care of her?" she asked him scornfully. "I shall ask Nick if I need do anything so ridiculous!"

"Here he is," said Nick, coming lightly up behind her with the words. "What's the trouble now? If you are requiring my valuable advice, it is quite at your service."

Olga turned to him at once. "Nick, it's really too silly for words. Dr. Wyndham makes mountains out of molehills."

"That's very ingenious of him," commented Nick. "I shouldn't harass the man if I were you, Olga. He's been out all night."

Olga pounced upon this fact. "I expect Mitchel has too, then, so he just won't be able to go."

"No," said Max. "I didn't take the car or Mitchel. It chanced to be a case in the village, and I bicycled."

"Who was it?" asked Olga eagerly; and then restrained herself with annoyance. "But of course you won't tell me. You're much too professional."

"Keep to the point!" ordered Nick.

Olga slipped a coaxing arm round his neck. "Nick, don't you think it absurd that Violet and I shouldn't motor over to Brethaven without a man to take care of us? I am quite certain Dad wouldn't object."

"There you are wrong," said Max. "If your father were here, he would forbid it--as I do."

He spoke with emphasis, and glanced again at his watch as he did so.

"He doesn't object to my going alone with one of the boys," said Olga. "It's only Violet who is too precious to go motoring without a full-grown escort. As if I weren't quite capable of taking care of her!"

"It's not that at all," said Max curtly. "I can't stop to argue, so please make up your mind what you are going to do. I'm sorry you've been dragged into the discussion, Ratcliffe. I daresay it seems a senseless one to you, but I have my reasons."

Nick looked at him for a moment, a quick gleam of comprehension behind his flickering eyelids. "It won't hurt you to take Mitchel, Olga mia," he said.

"Oh, Nick!" There was deep reproach in Olga's voice, and at sound of it Max smiled with dry humour.

Nick laughed outright, openly heartless. "My beloved chicken, who is making mountains out of molehills now? I would escort you myself if I hadn't got to attend this committee meeting in town,--a million plagues upon it! Come along and open my letters for me! We are wasting time."

"I do think you needn't take his part," said Olga, as Max disappeared into the surgery. "He's quite bullying and tyrannical enough without that."

"I'm inclined to sympathize with the young man myself," said Nick. "He wouldn't bully you if you weren't so nasty."

"Nick, I'm not nasty!"

"I should detest you if I were Max," said Nick, squeezing her affectionately with his one wiry arm.

"It isn't my fault we are antipathetic," protested Olga. "For goodness' sake, Nick, don't start liking him! But I'm sure you don't in your heart of hearts. You simply couldn't."

"Why not?" said Nick.

"Oh, Nick, you don't! You know you don't! He's so cold-blooded and cynical."

"Do you want to know what he was up to last night?" said Nick.

"Yes, tell me!" said Olga.

"He was sent for last thing by some people who live in that filthy alley--near the green pond. A child was choking. They thought it had swallowed a pin. When he got there, he found it was diphtheria at its most advanced stage. The child was at death's door. He had to perform an operation at a moment's notice, hadn't got the proper paraphernalia with him, and sucked the poison out himself."

"Good heavens, Nick!" said Olga, turning very white. "And the child?"

"The child is better. It is to be taken to the hospital to-day."

"Will it--won't it--have an effect on him?" gasped Olga.

"Heavens knows," said Nick.

"And that's why he didn't come down to breakfast," she said. "How did you find out about it? He didn't tell you?"

"He couldn't help it," said Nick. "He stole my bath this morning, and when I arrived he was lying in it face downwards boiling himself in some filthy disinfectant that made the bathroom temporarily uninhabitable. Naturally I lodged a complaint, and finally got at the whole story. By the way, he said I wasn' to tell you; but I told him I probably should. That's only a detail, but I mention it in case you should be tempted to broach the subject to him. I shouldn't advise you to do so, as I think you will probably find him rather touchy about it."

"But, Nick!" Olga's eyes had begun to shine. "It was very--fine of him," she said. "I wish I'd known before I was so cross to him. I--I should have made allowances if I had known."

"Quite so," said Nick. "Well, you can begin now if you feel so inclined, though I suppose the young man did no more than his duty after all."

"Oh, Nick, a man isn't obliged to go so far as that!" she exclaimed reproachfully. "There are plenty who wouldn't."

"Doubtless," agreed Nick, looking faintly quizzical. "It was the action of a fool--but a brave fool. We'll grant him that much, shall we?"

She laughed a little, her cheek against his shoulder. "Don't poke fun at me! It isn't fair. You know he isn't a fool perfectly well."

"By Jove! You are getting magnanimous!" laughed Nick.

"No, I'm not. I'm only trying to be fair. One must be that," said Olga, whose honest soul abhorred injustice of any description.

"Oh, of course," said Nick. "You'll have to spoil him now to make up for having been so--'horrid,' I think, is the proper term, isn't it? It's the most comprehensive word in the woman's vocabulary, comprising everything from slightly disagreeable to damned offensive."

"Really, Nick!"

Nick grinned. "Pardon my unparliamentary language!"

"But Nick, I've never been--that!" protested Olga.

"A matter of opinion!" laughed Nick.

But Olga did not laugh, she only flushed a little and changed the subject.

About an hour later, Max, taking his hat from a peg in the hall, preparatory to departing for the cottage-hospital, discovered the lining thereof to be pulled away in order to accommodate a twisted scrap of paper which had been pinned to it in evident haste.

He carried the hat to the consulting-room and there detached and examined its contents. He smoothed out the crumpled morsel with his customary deliberation, drawing his shaggy red brows together over a few lines of minute writing which became visible as he did so.

"Dear Max," he read, "I'm sorry I've been a beast to   you lately. Please don't take any notice of this but let us   just be friends for the future. Yours,

"Olga."

There was no mockery in the green eyes as they deciphered the impulsive note, nor did the somewhat hard lips smile. Max stood for some seconds after reading it, staring fixedly at the paper, and when at length he looked up his face wore a guarded expression with which many of his patients were familiar. He took a pocket-book from an inner pocket and laid the crumpled scrap within it. Then, without more ado, he put on his hat and departed.

Olga was by that time spinning merrily along the road to Brethaven, having parted with Nick at the railway-station. Violet was seated beside her, and the old servant Mitchel sat sourly behind them. He had a rooted objection to the back-seat, and held the opinion that a woman at the wheel was out of place.

Olga, however, was not prepared to yield on this point at least. She had brought him against her will, and she meant to forget him if possible. But it was not long before Violet had extracted from her an account of the discussion that had resulted in Mitchel's unwilling presence. She was not very anxious to supply the information, but Violet was insistent and soon possessed herself of the full details of the argument which she seemed to find highly amusing.

"Oh, my dear, he's in love with me of course!" she said "I discovered that the first night I was with you. Hence his solicitude."

"I'm not so sure of that," said Olga.

"What! You haven't noticed it? My dear child, where are your eyes? Haven't you seen the way he watches me?"

Yes, Olga had seen it; but somehow she did not think it meant that. She said so rather hesitatingly.

"What else could it mean?" laughed Violet. "But you needn't be afraid, dear. I'm not going to have him. He's much too anatomical for me, too business-like and professional altogether. I'd sooner die than have him attend me."

"Would you?" said Olga. "But why? He's very clever."

"That's just it. He's too clever to have any imagination. He would be quite un-scrupulous, quite merciless, and utterly without sympathy. Can't you picture him making you endure any amount of torture just to enable him to say he had cured you? Oh yes, he's diabolically clever, but he is cruel too. He would take the short-est cut, whatever it meant. He wouldn't care what agony he inflicted so long as he gained his end and made you live."

"I don't think he is quite so callous as that," Olga said, but even as she said it she wondered.

"You will if he ever has to doctor you," rejoined Violet. "I wonder what Mrs. Briggs thought of him. We'll find out to-day."

Mrs. Briggs was the daughter of the old woman who had died the preceding week at "The Ship Inn," whither they were bound that morning. She had nursed Violet in her infancy, and was a privileged acquaintance of both girls.

They found her busy pastry-making, for the business of the establishment had not been suspended during her recent troubles. She greeted them both hospitably, though not without a hint of reproach, which found expression in words when she had come to the end of a detailed account of the funeral.

"I thought you'd 'a' been round long ago," she said. "Your flowers was lovely, Miss Olga. You ought to 'a' seen 'em a-layin' on pore mother. I made sure as you'd want to. And you too, Miss Violet. I kept the coffin open till the very last minute, thinkin' as you'd come."

"That was very sweet of you, Mrs. Briggs," said Violet. "It was all Dr. Wynd-ham's fault that we didn't. I'm staying there, you know, and whatever he says is law. I'm sure I don't know why, but there it is."

"Well, there!" said Mrs. Briggs. "I might 'a' known. Pore mother was frit to death o' he. 'There's black magic in 'im' she says to me. It was the day as she was took, too. 'Black magic,' she says. 'I've a-begged 'im to let me die easy, but Lor' bless yer, 'e don't take no more notice than if 'e were the Spink,'" Mrs. Briggs glanced over her shoulder. "But there's one thing as you'll both be glad to know," she said, lowering her voice confidentially, "she died easy, pore soul, in spite of 'im. 'E don't know 'ow that was."

"What?" gasped both girls in a breath.

Mrs. Briggs went to the door, peered out, softly closed it. Her eyes shone craftily as she returned. She took up her rolling-pin, holding it impressively between her floury hands.

"Two days afore pore mother went," she began, with an air of gruesome mystery, "Dr. Wyndham, 'e came and examined 'er, and 'urt 'er cruel, 'e did. I thought 'e'd 'ave killed 'er afore 'e'd finished. Well, just afore 'e left, 'e come to me with a dark blue bottle, and 'e says: 'Look 'ere, Mrs. Briggs, she won't last out the week. She's quiet now,' 'e says, 'for I've given 'er a dose as'll last for some hours. But when that's exhausted,' 'e says, 'the pain'll come back. And so I'm goin' to give you this.' 'E 'olds it up to the light, and looks at it. 'It's good stuff,' 'e says. 'It's warranted to kill pain. But it ain't a thing to play with. You give 'er a teaspoon of it,' 'e says, 'but only if she's took with bad pain. But she mustn't 'ave more than one in twenty-four hours,' 'e says. 'You mind that. And if you 'ave to give it to 'er, you send at once for me. If you don't send,' 'e says, 'I won't be 'eld responsible for the consequences.' With that 'e goes, and pore mother she seemed to take a turn, and all that day and the next she seemed to drowse like and not take much notice o' things. The neighbours come in and look at 'er, but she didn't seem to know. We 'ad two quiet nights with 'er, and then all of a sudden in the middle of the afternoon she started screamin' and writhin.' Oh, lor, Miss Olga, you never see the like. It was just as if she were bein' tortured over a slow fire. Well, Briggs, 'e was fair unmanned by it. 'For 'eaven's sake,' 'e says, 'give 'er the medicine as the doctor left, and I'll go and tell 'im as you've done it.' And off 'e goes, though it was gettin' latish and no one to attend to the bar. Well, I fetched the medicine, and I took it to 'er, and I says, ''Ere you are, mother,' I says, 'you 'ave a dose o' this. It'll kill the pain.' I gave it 'er in a teaspoon like 'e said, and she took it. But there, it didn't make no more difference to 'er than if it 'ad been water.'" Mrs. Briggs heaved a sob, and picked up a corner of her apron to wipe her eyes. "I told 'er as I dursn't give 'er any more because of what the doctor 'ad said, and I said as 'ow Briggs 'ad gone for him, and 'e'd know 'ow to quiet 'er when 'e came. But the very thought of 'im seemed to drive 'er crazy.

And then she said that about the black magic, and 'ow 'e'd never be persuaded to let 'er die easy. And then she says to me. 'But you didn't shake the bottle,' she says. 'I expect the stuff that kills the pain is all at the bottom.' And I thought there might be somethin' in it, so I fetched the bottle again and shook it up. And I thought I'd give 'er just 'alf a dose more in case she 'adn't 'ad enough. But just as I was a-goin' to pour it out there was such a rappin' down in the bar, that I 'ad to just give it 'er and run. I was back in under a minute, and there was pore mother a-sittin' up in bed and a-smilin' at me as if all 'er troubles was past, and says she, 'Annie,' she says, 'I've 'ad enough and I don't want no more,' she says; 'it's killed the pain.' And then she laid down in bed still smilin', and says she, 'You tell the doctor when 'e comes as I'm sorry to 'a' fetched 'im for nothin', but I couldn't wait--.' And--if you'll believe me, Miss Olga,--those was the last words she spoke." Again vigorously Mrs. Briggs dried her eyes. "She just dropped off to sleep as easy as easy, and I left 'er and went back to the bar. There was a stick by the bedside, and I knew I should 'ear 'er knock if she wanted me. But she didn't knock, and she didn't knock, and I kept thinkin' to myself what a nice sleep she was 'avin', and I wouldn't disturb 'er till the doctor came. And then all of a sudden, it came into my mind to wonder about that there medicine. And I just run up to see. And there I found 'er a-laying' dead, and the stuff in the bottle were 'alf-gone!"

Mrs. Briggs's information was imparted in a whisper and punctuated by sniffs. Her two listeners exchanged awe-stricken glances.

"How did you know she was dead?" asked Violet. "What did she look like?"

"My dear," said Mrs. Briggs, with solemn pride, "anyone as 'as seen death as often as I 'ave don't need to look twice."

Mrs. Briggs occupied the exalted position of layer-out in chief in Brethaven village, and right proud was she of her calling. It had been handed down from mother to daughter in her family for the past four generations. She literally swelled with importance as she resumed her narrative and her pastry-rolling at the same moment.

"Well, there she lay, pore dear, and I saw as the Lord 'ad took 'er right enough, and 'er troubles was well over. But there was this 'ere medicine-bottle, and I 'ad to think pretty quick about that; for just as I picked it up I 'eard the doctor's motor come round the corner. It came to me all in a minute, it did, and I upped with the water-jug and filled it to all but a spoonful of the top. For I knew what 'is first thought would be," said Mrs. Briggs grimly. "And I wasn't minded to let myself in for any questions. Yer see, my dear, 'e'd told me 'isself as the pore creature couldn't last the week. Well, I stuck the bottle on the shelf, and went to meet 'im. 'She's gone, sir,' I says. He come right past me without a word and stoops over the bed. And then, sure enough, quite sharp and sudden says 'e, 'You give 'er the pain-killer?' 'Just as you told me, sir,' I says, and with that I showed 'im the bottle. 'E took it into 'is 'and, and 'e give me a very straight look, and says 'e, frowning, 'Well, she'll never want any more of that.' And 'e just took it straight downstairs and emptied the bottle into the sink."

"He knew!" exclaimed Olga involuntarily.

"Lor' bless yer, no!" Mrs. Briggs's tone held unquestioning conviction. "'E was frownin' to 'isself all the time, and I could see as 'e was pretty mad that 'e'd come too late. I weren't sorry myself," she asserted boldly. "For I'd 'oped against 'ope after 'is last visit that 'e'd never see pore mother again alive. I couldn't 'a' stood it! There, I just couldn't."

Quite unexpectedly Mrs. Briggs suddenly broke down and dropped into a chair. Violet sprang to comfort, while Olga took possession of the rolling-pin and continued the pastry-making with deft hands.

After an interval poor Mrs. Briggs managed to recover somewhat of the hard demeanour that usually characterized her. "I've no call to fret," she said. "And don't you go rubbin' my dirty face with your clean 'andkerchief, Miss Violet. I ain't fit for you to touch, my dear."

"I'm only trying to get off the flour," explained Violet. "But I'm afraid you'll have to wash it after all. It's all gone into paste."

"And there's Miss Olga a-makin' my tarts for me like a ministerin' angel," said Mrs. Briggs, with a watery smile. "It's a pity you couldn't 'a' seen 'er in 'er coffin; for it was a beautiful coffin. Briggs said it was as fine a one as 'e'd seen. Well, well! She's gone, pore soul. And now you young ladies must try some of my rhubarb wine."

She rose briskly, and went to a cupboard. "We drank some of it at the funeral," she said. "And everyone liked it--even Briggs. But I thought I'd save the rest for when you came. Miss Olga always likes my rhubarb wine."

The rhubarb wine proved at least a welcome distraction, and under its genial influence Mrs. Briggs's spirits rose. She was quite cheery by the time her two visitors took their leave. They left her waving farewell from her doorstep, the patches of paste still upon her ruddy countenance, but with no other traces of her recent distress visible.

"Rum old thing!" said Violet. "I want to go round to the Priory and see Cork and Pluto next. I like to drop in unexpectedly when Bruce is away, and make sure that they are treated properly."

"We haven't much time," observed Olga.

"Oh, nonsense! Make time! We're not slaves," said Violet imperiously.

And Olga turned in the direction of the Priory without further words. It always took less time to yield to her friend's behests than to argue against them.

CHAPTER VII
THE PUZZLE

The visit to the Priory occupied some time, as Olga had foreseen. There were some things that Violet wanted to fetch from her own room and this entailed a search, for her possessions were always in the wildest disorder. Olga waited for her in the hall, chafing at the delay, since she knew that the car would be required by Max early in the afternoon to take him on his rounds.

Mitchel remained outside in the hot sunshine, severe disapproval in every line of him. Olga felt decidedly out of patience with him. As if it were her fault!

She sat on the old oak chest that Violet gaily called her coffin, and stared at the gruesome east window, while her thoughts dwelt upon the story she had just heard from Mrs. Briggs's lips. Had Max really intended to place freedom within the old woman's reach? For some reason wholly inexplicable she longed to know. She recalled the words he had uttered that day in the library of Redlands, his half-cynical talk of "a free pass," his reference to himself as "gaoler." Was it possible that she had formed a wrong impression of him? And if in this matter, perhaps in others also. Perhaps after all she had mistaken his attitude towards Violet. Perhaps after all he was human enough to feel the strong attraction of the girl's beauty. Perhaps after all he was beginning to care. And if so, what then? She felt her face burn in the coolness. Somehow she did not want him to be hurt, to suffer as she knew that other men had been made to suffer by the gay inconsequence of her friend. Only a week ago she had desired his ignominious downfall. To-day she wanted to save him from it. She had a desperate longing to warn him that Violet's favour was a thing of nought, that her treatment of him had all been planned between them beforehand, that it was all a game.

She could not picture him at any woman's feet. Yet undoubtedly Violet was hard to resist; their intimacy had grown apace during the past few days. And Violet knew so well how to wield her power, when to scorn and when subtly to flatter. She had never yet received a check in her triumphant career, and she boasted openly of her conquests.

No, Olga was fain to admit it. All her own private aversion notwithstanding, she did not want this man added to the list of victims. Cynical and even overbearing though he might be, she no longer desired to see him humiliated. And her face glowed more and more hotly as she remembered that it was she who had set the trap.

She fully realized, however, that an appeal to Violet at this stage would be worse than futile. Violet was too set on her mischievous course to do other than laugh and pursue it with renewed zest for her capture. Of course there remained Nick, chosen adviser and confidant; but for some reason Olga shrank from discussing Max with him. She had an uneasy dread lest Nick's intelligence should leap ahead of her and disclose to her with disconcerting suddenness facts and possibilities with which she was quite unprepared to reckon. She visualized his grin of amused comprehension over the means she had devised for her own deliverance and the unpleasant quandary in which it had placed her. Nick's sense of humour was at times almost too keen. She smiled faintly to herself over this reflection. She could not deny that there were points in the situation which appealed even to her own.

Yet she was more ashamed than amused. The discovery that Max was human had somehow altered everything, and made her own conduct appear dastardly. She had acted maliciously albeit, in self-defence; but now that it seemed that her point might pierce his armour, she wanted to withdraw it. She shrank unspeakably from seeing him vanquished. It would have hurt her to find him at her own feet, but the bare thought of him at Violet's--Violet who had no mercy upon old or young, who would trample him underfoot without a pang and pass gaily on--that thought was unbearable.

Of course she might be wrong. It was still possible that her original conception of him might be the correct one. He had a passion for his profession, she knew. It was quite possible that this had inspired his taking that awful risk the night before, quite possible also that a hopeless case did not appeal to him and that he had not therefore greatly cared how soon or in what manner Mrs. Stubbs had passed out through the prison-door which it was his work to guard. She realized vaguely that this form of callousness was not so hideous as she had at first deemed it. She also began to realize that for a man who had seen suffering and death in many forms and who found himself finally powerless to alleviate the one or avert the other, the inevitable end could not possess the tragic significance which it possessed for others.

Either point of view of his character was possible. She did not know him well enough to decide to her own satisfaction which was actually the true one. But the fact remained that she had delivered him to Violet to be tormented, and that before he had given any sign of suffering she had repented the rash act. He might be capable of suffering or he might not; but she had a passionate desire to know him safe before the fire had begun to kindle.

Violet's return at length broke up her reflections. She awoke from her reverie with a start to exclaim upon the lateness of the hour. It was already close upon luncheon-time.

"We shall have to scorch," laughed Violet.

And scorch they did at a rate that made the sober Mitchel swear inarticulately almost throughout the journey. They met with no mishap, however, and finally reached Weir flushed, dishevelled, but exultant.

Max came from the direction of the surgery as they entered.

"Can I speak to you a moment?" he said to Olga and drew her into her father's little smoking-room at the side of the hall almost before the words were uttered.

Olga faced him with a racing heart, burningly reminiscent of the note she had left in his hat, the note she had asked him to ignore.

He must have seen her embarrassment, for his green eyes studied her without mercy; but when he spoke it was not upon the subject of her overture.

"Look here!" he said. "Hunt-Goring is here. Do you mind if I ask him to luncheon?"

The news was unexpected. Olga gave a sharp, involuntary start. "Major Hunt-Goring!" she stammered. "Why--what is he doing here?"

"He walked over with a broken thumb for me to mend," said Max, still grimly watching her. "It's some way back to The Warren, and he's a bit used up. I fancy your father would make him lunch here under the circumstances, but you must do as you think best. It's not my house."

The colour sank rapidly from Olga's face under his look. "Oh, Dr. Wyndham," she said breathlessly, "do you think we need?"

He frowned at her agitation. "Of course, we needn't," he said. "If you don't want him, he can go to 'The Swan.' He is in the surgery at the present moment. I must go back and see how he is getting on."

"Wait a moment!" Olga broke in rapidly. "I--I'm afraid you're right. Dad would certainly keep him. Oh, why isn't Nick here? He needn't have chosen to-day to break this thumb."

"Kismet!" said Max, with a cynical lift of the shoulders. "I gather you don't like the man?"

She shrank at the question: it was almost a shudder. "No!"

He turned to the door. "Well, pull yourself together. I daresay he won't eat you. And you'll have Miss Campion to protect you. She would be proof against a dozen monsters."

He cast her a glance with the words that made her aware of a certain not very abstruse meaning behind them. Olga's cheeks burned again. Did he know, then? Had he guessed why Violet was in the house? Was that the reason of his curious vigilance, his guarded acceptance of her favours? She was possessed by an almost overwhelming desire to know, and yet no words could she find in which to ask.

"Well?" said Max, pausing in the act of opening the door. "You were going to say--"

She raised her eyes with a conscious effort, and nerved herself to speak.

"Max," she said desperately, "please don't mind my asking! It isn't from idle curiosity. Do you like her?" She saw the rough red brows go up, and swiftly repented her temerity. "I only asked," she faltered, "because--"

"Well?" Max said again. "It would be interesting to know why you asked."

She compelled herself to answer him, or perhaps it was he who compelled. In any case, with her head bent, her answer came.

"I had been thinking that perhaps you were getting fond of her, and--and--I should be sorry if that happened, because I know she isn't in earnest. I know she is only playing with you."

The words ran cut in a whisper. She dared not look at him. She could only watch with fascinated eyes the brown fingers that gripped the door-knob.

"She has told you that?" asked Max.

She quivered at the question. It was horribly difficult to answer. "I know it is so," she murmured.

She was thankful that he did not press her to be more explicit. He stood for a moment in silence; then: "Isn't it possible," he said in a very level tone, "for a woman to set out to catch a man and to end by being caught herself?"

"Not for Violet," said Olga.

"I wonder," said Max.

She looked up at him quickly, caught by something in his tone. His eyes, alert and green, looked straight into hers.

"Did you really think I was falling in love with her?" he said.

Olga hesitated.

"She thinks so?" he questioned.

"Yes." Against her will she answered. It was as if he wrung the word from her.

He smiled a grim smile. "Many thanks for your warning!" he said. "I take a deep interest in Miss Campion, as you seem to have divined. But the danger of my falling a victim to her charms is very remote. You need harbour no further anxieties on my account."

He opened the door as he spoke, and Olga passed out, uncertain whether to be glad or sorry that she had brought herself to speak.

She went upstairs to Violet and acquainted her with the fact of Major Hunt-Goring's presence and its cause.

"I do wish Nick had been here," she said in conclusion.

"He may elect to stay for ever so long. I don't know what we shall do with him."

Violet, however, was by no means dismayed by the prospect. "Oh, I enjoy Major Hunt-Goring," she said. "You leave him to me. I'll entertain him."

"Hateful man!" said Olga.

Whereat Violet laughed and pinched her cheek. "You know you like him!"

"I detest him!" said Olga quickly.

It was certainly with no excess of cordiality that a few minutes later she greeted her guest. He was standing in the hall with one arm in a sling when she and Violet descended the stairs, an immense man of about five-and-forty with a very decided military bearing and dark eyes of covert insolence.

Max was with him, and Olga experienced a very novel feeling of relief to see him there. She advanced and shook hands with extreme frigidity.

"I am sorry you have had an accident," she said.

"Very good of you," said Major Hunt-Goring, his eyes boldly passing her to rest upon Violet. "Managed to crack my thumb tinkering at my old motor. Dr. Wyndham tells me that you have been kind enough to ask me to lunch. How do you do, Miss Campion? Charmed to meet you! Someone told me you were yachting in the Atlantic."

"Heaven forbid!" said Violet. "Yachting is simply another word for imprisonment to me. I told Bruce I should certainly drown myself if I went with them."

"I should like to introduce you to a form of yachting that is not imprisonment," said Hunt-Goring.

Violet laughed. "Oh, I should have to be mistress of the yacht for that."

"Even so," he rejoined significantly.

"And I shouldn't have any men on board with the exception of the sailors," she went on.

"And the captain," said Hunt-Goring.

"Oh, dear me, no! I would be my own captain."

"You'd be horribly bored before the first week was out," observed the major, as he followed her into the dining-room.

She laughed gaily. "There isn't a single man of my acquaintance in whose company I shouldn't be bored to extinction long before that."

"Oh, come!" he protested. "You don't speak from experience. You condemn us untried."

"I know you all too well," laughed Violet.

"You know me not at all," declared Hunt-Goring. "I appeal to Miss Ratcliffe. Am I the sort of man to bore a woman?"

"I am no judge," said Olga somewhat hastily. "I never have time to be bored with anyone. Will you sit here, please? I am sorry to say my uncle is in town to-day."

"Where are the three boys?" asked Max.

Olga turned to him with relief. "They have gone for an all-day paper-chase with the Rectory crowd and taken lunch with them."

"Why didn't you go too?" he asked. "Too lazy?"

"Too busy," she returned briefly.

"That's only an excuse," said Max.

She glanced at him. "It's a sound one anyhow."

"What are you going to do this afternoon?" he asked.

"Mend."

"Mend what?"

"Stockings," said Olga.

"Great Scot!" said Max. "Do you mend the stockings of the entire family?"

"Including yours," said Olga.

"Oh, I say!" he protested. "That wasn't in the contract, was it? Pitch 'em into my room. I'll mend them myself or do without."

"One pair more or less doesn't make much difference," said Olga. "As to doing without,--well, of course, you're a man or you wouldn't make such a suggestion."

"You've thrown that in my teeth before," he observed. "I think you might re-member that I am hardly responsible for my sex. It's my misfortune, not my fault."

She smiled, her sudden brief smile, but made no rejoinder.

Major Hunt-Goring and Violet, who had undertaken to cut up his meal for him, were engrossed in a frothy conversation which it was obvious that neither desired to have interrupted.

Max glanced towards them before he abruptly started another subject with Olga.

"How is Mrs. Briggs?"

Olga coloured hotly. "Oh, she seemed all right."

Max surveyed her rather pointedly. "Well? What had she got to say about me?"

"About you?" said Olga.

He laughed and looked away. "Even so, fair lady. I conclude it was something you would rather not repeat. I had already fathomed the fact that I was not beloved by Mrs. Briggs."

"It's your own fault," said Olga, speaking on the impulse to escape from a difficult subject. "You have such a knack of making all your patients afraid of you."

"Really?" said Max.

"Oh, don't be supercilious!" she said quickly. "You know it's true."

"It must be if you say so," he rejoined, "though there again it is more my misfortune than my fault. If my patients elect to make me the butt of their neurotic imagination, surely I am more to be pitied than blamed."

"No, I don't pity you at all," Olga said. "It's want of sympathy, you know. You go and do a splendid thing like--like--" She stopped suddenly.

"Please go on!" said Max. "Let's hear my good points, by all means!"

But Olga was in obvious confusion. "I didn't mean to mention it," she said. "It just slipped out. I was really thinking of--what happened last night."

He frowned instantly. "Who told you anything about it?"

"Nick."

"I should like to wring his skinny little neck," said Max.

"How dare you?" said Olga indignantly.

"You don't think I'm afraid of you, do you?" he said, with a smile.

"No," she admitted rather grudgingly. "I don't think you are afraid of anyone or anything. But it is a pity you spoil things by being so--unfriendly."

"Are you speaking on Mrs. Briggs's behalf or your own?" asked Max.

She met his eyes with a feeling of reluctance. "Well, I do hate quarrelling," she said.

"I never quarrel," said Max placidly.

"Oh, but you do!" she exclaimed. "How can you say such a thing?"

"No, I don't!" said Max. "I go my own way, that's all. If anyone tries to stop me, well, they get knocked down and trampled on. I don't call that quarrelling. It simply happens in the natural course of things."

"No wonder people don't like you!" said Olga.

"Don't you like me?" said Max.

He put the question with obvious indifference, yet his green eyes still studied her critically. Olga poured out some water with a hand so shaky that it splashed over. He reached forward and dabbed it up with his table-napkin.

"Well?" he said.

"I don't know," she murmured somewhat incoherently.

"Don't know! But you knew this morning!" The green eyes suddenly laughed at her. "I say, don't try to drink that yet!" he said. "You'll choke if you do. Go on! Tell me some more about Mrs. Briggs! Did she give you any of that filthy concoction she calls rhubarb wine?"

"It isn't filthy! It's delicious," declared Olga. "You can't have tasted it."

"Oh, yes, I had some the day the old woman died. In fact, I was trying to sleep off the effects that afternoon, when you caught me in Uncle Nick's library. It's horribly strong stuff. I suppose that is what made you so late for luncheon?"

"Indeed, it wasn't! We went to the Priory before coming home."

"Oh! What for?"

"Some things Violet wanted."

"What things?" said Max.

She looked at him in surprise. "I'm sure I don't know. I'm not so inquisitive as you are. You had better ask Violet."

"Ask me what?" said Violet, detaching her attention from Major Hunt-Goring for a moment.

"Nothing," said Max. "I was only wondering how many glasses of rhubarb wine you had at 'The Ship.'"

Carelessly he rallied her on the subject, carelessly let it pass. And Olga was left with a newly-awakened doubt at her heart. What was the reason for the keen interest he took in her friend? Had he really told her the truth when repudiating the possibility of his falling in love with her? She fancied he had; and if so, why was he so anxious to inform himself of her most trivial doings? It was a puzzle to Olga--a puzzle that for some reason gave her considerable uneasiness. Against her will and very deep down within her, she was aware of a lurking distrust that made her afraid of Max Wyndham. She felt as if he were watching to catch her off her guard, ready at a moment's notice to turn to his own purposes any rash confidence into which she might be betrayed. And she told herself with passionate self-reproach that she had already been guilty of disloyalty to her friend.

During the rest of luncheon she exerted herself to keep the conversation general, Max seconding her efforts as though unconscious of her desire to avoid him. In fact, he seemed wholly unaware of any change in her demeanour, and Olga noted the fact with relief, the while she determined to exclude him rigidly for the future from anything even remotely approaching to intimacy. Watch as they might, the shrewd green eyes should never again catch her off her guard.

CHAPTER VIII
THE ELASTIC BOND

Major Hunt-Goring was quite obviously in his element. To Olga's dismay he showed no disposition to depart when they rose from the luncheon-table. Violet suggested a move to the garden, and he fell in with the proposal with a readiness that plainly showed that he had every intention of inflicting his company upon them for some time longer.

"It's confoundedly lonely up at The Warren," he remarked pathetically, as he lounged after her into the sunshine.

Violet laughed over her shoulder, an unlighted cigarette between her teeth. "You're hardly ever there."

"No. Well, it's a fact. I can't stand it. I'm a sociable sort of chap, you know. I like society."

"Why don't you marry?" laughed Violet.

"That's a question to which I can find no answer," he declared. "Why--why, indeed!"

"Hateful man!" murmured Olga, looking after them. "How I wish he would go!"

"Leave them alone for a spell," advised Max. "Go and mend your stockings in peace! Miss Campion is quite equal to entertaining him unassisted."

But Olga hesitated to pursue this course, and finally collected her work and followed her two guests into the garden.

Max departed upon his rounds, and a very unpleasant sense of responsibility descended upon her.

She took up a central position under the lime-trees that bordered the tennis-court, but Major Hunt-Goring and Violet did not join her. They sauntered about the garden-paths just out of earshot, and several times it seemed to Olga that they were talking confidentially together. She wondered impatiently how Violet could endure the man at such close quarters. But then there were many things that Violet liked that she found quite unbearable.

Slowly the afternoon wore away. The young hostess still sat under the limes, severely darning, but Violet and her companion had disappeared unobtrusively into a more secluded part of the garden. For nearly half an hour she had heard no sound of voices. She wondered if she ought to go in search of them, but her pile of work was still somewhat formidable and she was both to leave it. She continued to darn therefore with unflagging energy, till suddenly a hand touched her shoulder and a man's voice spoke softly in her ear.

"Hullo, little one! All alone? What has become of the fiery-headed assistant?"

She flung his hand away with a violent gesture. So engrossed had she been with getting through her work that she had not heard his step upon the grass.

"Are you just off?" she asked him frigidly. "Will you have anything before you go?"

Hunt-Goring laughed--a soft, unpleasant laugh. "Many thanks!" he said. "I was just asking myself that question. Generous of you to suggest it though. Perhaps you--like myself--are feeling bored."

He lowered himself on to the grassy bank beside her chair, smiling up at her with easy insolence. Olga did not look at him. Handsome though he undoubtedly was, he was the one man of her acquaintance whose eyes she shrank from meeting. His very proximity sent a shiver of disgust through her. She made a covert movement to edge her chair away.

"Where is Miss Campion?" she said.

He laughed again, that hateful confidential laugh of his. "She has gone indoors to rest. The heat made her sleepy. I suggested the hammock, but she wouldn't run the risk of being caught napping. I see that there is small danger of that with you."

Olga stiffened. She was putting together her work with evident determination. "I will see you off," she said.

"You seem in a mighty hurry to get rid of me," he said, without moving.

She laid her mending upon the grass and rose. "I am busy--as you see," she returned.

He looked at her for a moment, then very deliberately followed her example. He stood looking down at her from his great height, a speculative smile on his face.

"You've soon had enough of me, what?" he suggested.

Olga's pale eyes gleamed for an instant like steel suddenly bared to the sun. She said nothing whatever, merely stood before him very stiff and straight, plainly waiting for him to go.

"It's a pity to outstay one's welcome," he said. "I wouldn't do that for the world. But what about that kiss you offered me just now?"

"I?" said Olga, quivering disdain in the word.

"You, my little spitfire!" he said genially. "And it won't be the first time, what? Come now! You're always running away, but you should reflect that you're bound to be caught sooner or later. You didn't think I was going to let you off, did you?"

She stood before him speechless, with clenched hands.

He drew a little nearer. "You pay your debts, don't you? And what more suitable opportunity than the present? You are so elusive nowadays. Why, I haven't seen you except from afar since last Christmas. You were always such a nice, sociable little girl till then."

"Sociable!" whispered Olga.

"Well, you were!" He laughed again in his easy fashion. "Don't you remember what fun we had at the Rectory on Christmas Eve, and how you came to tea with me on the sly a few days after, and how we kissed under the mistletoe, and how you promised--"

"I promised nothing!" burst out Olga, with flashing eyes.

"Oh, pardon me! You promised to kiss me again some day. Have you forgotten? I hardly think your memory is as short as that."

He drew nearer still, and slipped a cajoling arm about her. "Why are we in such a towering rage, I wonder? Surely you don't want to repudiate your liabilities! You promised, you know."

She flung up a desperate face to his. "Very well, Major Hunt-Goring," she said breathlessly. "Take it--and go!"

He bent to her. "But you must give," he said.

"Very well," she said again. "It--it will be the last!"

"Will it?" he questioned, pausing. "In that case, I feel almost inclined to postpone the pleasure, particularly as--"

"Don't torture me!" she said in a whisper half--choked.

Her eyes were tightly shut; but Hunt-Goring's were looking over her head, and a sudden gleam of malicious humour shone in them. He turned them upon the white, shrinking face of the girl who stood rigid but unresisting within the circle of his arm. And then very suddenly he bent and kissed her on the lips.

She shivered through and through and broke from him with her hands over her face.

"But you didn't pay your debt, you know," said Hunt-Goring amiably. "I won't trouble you now, however, as we are no longer alone. Another day--in a more secluded spot--"

No longer alone! Olga looked up with a gasp. Her face was no longer pale, but flaming red. She seemed to be burning from head to foot.

And there, not a dozen paces from her, was Maxwell Wyndham, carelessly approaching, his hands in his pockets, his hat thrust to the back of his head, a faint, supercilious smile cocking one corner of his mouth, his whole bearing one of elaborate unconsciousness.

This much Olga saw; but she did not wait for more. The situation was beyond her. An involuntary exclamation of dismay escaped her, an inarticulate sound that seemed physically wrung from her; and then, without a second glance, ignominiously she turned and fled.

The sound of Hunt-Goring's oily laugh followed her as she went, and added speed to her flying feet.

It was several minutes later that Max entered the surgery, carrying an armful of stockings, and found her scrubbing her face vigorously over the basin that was kept there. She had turned on the hot water, and a cloud of steam arose above her head.

"Don't scald yourself!" said Max. "Try the pumice!"

"Oh, go away!" gasped Olga, with a furious stamp.

"Not going," said Max.

He fetched out a clean towel, and placed it within her reach. Then he sat down on the table and waited, whistling below his breath.

Olga grabbed the towel at last and buried her face in it. "Do you want to make me--hate you?" She flung at him through its folds.

"Don't be silly!" said Max.

"I'm not!" she cried stormily. "I'm not! It's you who--who make bad worse--always!"

He stood up abruptly. "No, I don't. I help--when I can. Sit down, and stop crying!"

"I'm not crying!" she sobbed.

"Then take that towel off your face, and behave sensibly. I'll make you drink some sal volatile if you don't."

"I'm sure you won't. I--I--I'm not a bit afraid of you!" came in muffled tones of distress from the crumpled towel.

"All right. Who said you were?" said Max. "Sit down now! Here's a chair. Now--let me have the towel! Yes, really, Olga!" He loosened her hold upon it, and drew it away from her with steady insistence. "There, that's better. You look as if you'd got scarlet fever. What did you want to boil yourself like that for? Now, don't cry! It's futile and quite unnecessary. Just sit quiet till you feel better! There's no one about but me, and I don't count."

He turned to the pile of stockings he had brought in with him, and began to sort them into pairs.

"By Jove! You're in the middle of one of mine," he said. "I'll finish this."

He thrust his hand into it and prepared to darn.

"Oh, don't!" said Olga. "You--you will only make a mess of it."

He waved his hand with airy assurance.

"I never make a mess of anything, and I'm a lot cleverer than you think. What train is Nick coming home by?"

"I don't know. The five-twenty probably."

He glanced at the clock. "Half an hour from now. And where is the fair Violet?"

"I don't know. He said she had gone in. I suppose I ought to go and see."

"Sit still!" said Max, frowning over his darning. "She is probably reading some obscene novel, and won't be wanting you."

"Max!"

"I apologize," said Max.

Olga smiled faintly. "It's horrid of you to talk like that."

"It's me," said Max.

She dried the last of her tears. "What--what did you do with him?"

"Packed him into the motor and told Mitchel to drive him home."

"I wish Mitchel would run into something and kill him!" said Olga, with sudden vehemence.

Max's brows went up. "Afraid I didn't give Mitchel instructions to that effect."

He spoke without raising his eyes, being quite obviously intent upon his darning. Olga watched him for a few seconds in silence. Finally she gave herself a slight shake and rose.

"You're doing that on the right side," she said.

"It's the best way to approach this kind of hole," said Max.

She came and stood by his side, still closely watching him.

"Dr. Wyndham!" she said at last, her voice very low.

"Please don't make me nervous!" said Max.

"Don't, please!" she said. "I want to speak to you seriously."

He drew out his needle with a reflective air. "Are you going to ask me to prescribe for you?"

"No."

"Then don't call me 'Dr. Wyndham'!" he said severely. "I don't answer to it, except in business hours."

She smiled faintly. "Max, then! Will you do me a favour?"

Max's eyes found hers with disconcerting suddenness. "On one condition," he said.

"What is it?"

The corner of his mouth went up. "I will name my condition when you have named your favour."

She hesitated momentarily. "Oh, it isn't very much," she said. "I only want you not to tell--Nick, or anyone--about--about what happened this afternoon."

"Why isn't Nick to know?" asked Max.

"He would be so angry," she said, "and he couldn't do any good. He would only go and get himself hurt."

"Would you care to know what Hunt-Goring said to me after you had effected a retreat?" asked Max.

The hot colour began to fade out of her cheeks. "Yes," she said, under her breath.

"He said--you know his breezy style: 'Don't be astonished! Miss Ratcliffe and I understand one another. In fact, we've been more or less engaged for a long time, though it isn't generally known.'"

"Max!" Olga started back as if from a blow. "He never said--that!"

"Yes, he did. I guessed it was a lie," said Max, "in spite of appearances."

She winced. "It is a lie!" she said with vehemence. "You--you told him so?"

"I was not in a position to do that," said Max. "But if you authorize me to do so--"

"Yes--yes?" she said feverishly.

"I can only do it if you accept my condition," he said.

"That means you want me to tell you everything," she said.

"No, it doesn't. I know quite as much as I need to know, and I shan't believe anything he may be pleased to say on the subject. It's up to you to tell me as much or as little as you like. No, the condition is this, and there is nothing in it that you need jib at. If you really want me to give him the lie, you must furnish me with full authority. You must put me in a position to do it effectually."

He was looking straight into her face of agitation. There was a certain remorse-lessness about him that made him in a fashion imposing. Olga quivered a little under the insistence of his eyes, but she flinched no more.

"Yes?" she said. "Well, I do authorize you. It's got to be stopped somehow. I never dreamed of his saying that."

"Quite so," said Max. "But that isn't enough. You will have to go a step further. Give me a free hand! It's the only way if you don't want Nick rushing in. Give me the right to protect you! I promise to use it with discretion."

He smiled very slightly with the words; but Olga only gazed at him uncompre-hendingly.

"How? I don't know what you mean."

He held out his hand to her abruptly. "Don't faint!" he said. "Let me tell him--

as a dead secret--that you are engaged to me!"

Olga gasped.

Max got up. "Only as a temporary expedient," he said. "I'll let you go again-- when you wish it."

His hand remained outstretched, and after a very considerable pause she laid hers within it.

"But really," she said, with an effort, "I don't think we need do anything so desperate as that."

"A desperate case requires a desperate remedy sometimes," said Max, with a humorous twinkle in his eyes "It doesn't mean anything, but we must floor this rascal somehow. Is it a bargain?"

She hesitated. "You won't tell anyone else?"

"Not a soul," said Max.

She still hesitated. "But--he won't believe you."

"He will if I refer him to you," said Max.

Olga pondered the matter. "Are you sure it's the only way?"

"If you don't want Nick to know," he said.

"And what if he--spreads it abroad?" she hazarded.

"We can always treat it as idle gossip, you know," said Max. "Imminent but not actual--the sort of thing over which we blush demurely and say nothing."

She smiled in spite of herself. "It's very good of you," she said with feeling.

"Not a bit," said Max. "I shall enjoy it. I think it ought to put an effectual stop to all unwelcome amenities on his part. We'll try it anyhow."

He released her hand, and resumed his darning, still looking quizzical.

Olga lingered, dubiously reminding herself that only a few hours before she had distrusted this man whom circumstance now made her champion.

"Scissors, please!" said Max.

She gave them to him absently. He held out the unsevered wool, his eyes laughing at her over it.

"You can do the cutting," he said.

She complied, and in the same instant she met his look. "Max," she said rather breathlessly, "I--don't quite like it."

"All right," he said imperturbably. "Don't do it!"

She paused, looking at him almost imploringly. "You're sure it won't mean anything?"

"It can mean as much or as little as you like," said Max.

"I didn't mean--quite that," faltered Olga. "But--it won't be--it never could be--like a real engagement; could it?"

"Like, yet unlike," said Max. "It will be a sort of elastic and invisible bond, made to stretch to the utmost limit, never breaking of itself, though capable of being severed by either party at a moment's notice."

Olga drew a breath of relief. "If that is really all--"

"What more could the most exacting require?" said Max.

What indeed! Yet the phrase struck Olga somehow as being not wholly satisfactory. Perhaps even then, vaguely she began to realize that the species of bond he described might prove the most inviolable of all. But she raised no further argument, doubts notwithstanding; for, in face of his assurance, there seemed nothing left to say.

CHAPTER IX
THE PROJECT

The sound of Nick's cheery, untuneful humming seemed to invest all things with a more normal and wholesome aspect. Olga went to meet him with unfeigned delight.

He put his arm around her, flashing a swift look over her as he did it. "Well, Olga mia. I trust there has been no more bickering in my absence."

"No, I've made friends with Max," she said. "Come and have tea!"

He went through the house with her to the garden where tea awaited him. Max was seated alone beside the little table under the trees.

"You're not a very large party," commented Nick.

"Best we can do under the circumstances," said Max. "The kids are still paper-chasing, and Miss Campion, overcome by the heat, has retired to bed. I propose to follow her example if the company will excuse me. I only put in two hours last night, and may have to attend another case to-night. Here, Ratcliffe, you can have my chair."

"Are you coming down to dinner?" asked Olga.

"I am," he said.

"Because you needn't. I can send it up."

"Thanks! I'll come down," said Max.

He turned away towards the house, but stopped abruptly as Violet suddenly sauntered forth. She was yawning as she came.

"Good people, pray excuse me! I'm always sleepy after a motor-run. What has become of the dear major, Allegro? You haven't banished him already!"

"Did you think he was going to live here?" said Olga, with a very unwonted touch of asperity.

"I expect he will, dear, now he knows I'm here." Violet subsided into the vacant chair with a languid smile at Nick who offered it to her. Her eyes were wonderfully bright, but the lids were heavy. "I'm horribly sleepy still," she said. "Give me some tea, quick, to wake me up! Max, I haven't the energy to amuse you, so you may consider yourself excused."

"Many thanks!" said Max. "I am going to give myself the pleasure of waiting upon you."

"Nick can do that," said Olga. "Do go and get a rest!"

"My dear, if you show yourself so anxious to be rid of him, he'll stay," protested Violet. "Haven't you discovered that yet? You should display an elegant indifference, a pray-stay-if-you've-a-mind-to-but-don't- imagine-that-I-want-you kind of attitude. There are not many men who can face that for long." She broke off to yawn. "No, thanks. Nothing to eat. I'm too sleepy. Well, Nick, have you settled the affairs of the nation satisfactorily?"

"On the contrary. The nation is trying to settle mine," said Nick.

"Oh, really! What more could anyone want you to do?"

"I'm specially qualified for many things, it seems," said Nick modestly. "What has Hunt-Goring been here for?"

"Managed to break his thumb," said Max.

"Yes, and stayed philandering all the afternoon," chimed in Violet. "How did you manage to get rid of him, Allegro? He wouldn't go for me."

"Dr. Wyndham came back early and sent him home in the car," said Olga, with a slight effort.

"I was bored to death with him," declared Violet. "I simply deserted him at last because I couldn't keep my eyes open. Give me my tea strong, please, or I shall fall asleep again under your eyes."

"Do you mind if I smoke?" said Max.

"Not in the least; quite delighted."

He offered her his cigarette-case. "P'raps you'll join me."

"No, thanks. I've been smoking all the afternoon." She stretched up her arms behind her head; they were bare to the elbow, soft and white and rounded. Her eyelids began to droop a little more. She snuggled down into the chair, plainly on the verge of slumber.

And in that moment Olga looked at Max. He was intently watching the girl, so intently that he was oblivious of everything else; and into her mind, all-unbidden, there flashed again the memory of the green dragon-fly--the monster of the stream--darting upon the little scarlet moth. It sent a curious revulsion of feeling through her. For the moment she felt physically sick.

Then impetuously, desperately, she intervened, "Violet, dear, wake up and have your tea! It's this horrid thundery weather that is affecting you. I've felt it myself. Max, you won't get much of a rest if you don't go soon."

Instantly his eyes were turned upon her, and she was conscious of the sudden quickening of her heart; for she saw at a glance that he resented her interference.

"Go on, Max!" grinned Nick. "Why can't you take a graceful hint, man? There may be another luckless little brat wanting you to-night."

"One thing at a time," said Max curtly.

He took out a cigarette and lighted it, a frown between his shaggy brows. He looked neither at Violet nor Olga but his attitude was one of stubborn determination.

"Are you waiting to see me drink my tea?" asked Violet, rousing herself in response to Olga's hand on her arm.

"I am," he said.

"Oh, well, that's soon done," she said, and raised the cup to her lips.

Max smoked on, taciturn and frowning. Violet finished her tea, and asked for more. He finished his cigarette and turned to her.

"I wonder if you would let me try one of yours."

"Not now, I'm afraid," she made answer. "I left my case upstairs."

He lighted another of his own and rose.

"Good-night!" said Nick.

"I shall be down to dinner," Max responded gruffly, and sauntered away.

"Ill-tempered cuss!" said Nick. "What's the matter with him?"

"He's jealous," said Violet.

"Of whom?" Nick was frankly curious.

"Of Major Hunt-Goring. He's been dangling after me half the afternoon. How would you like me to marry him, Allegro?"

"Who?" said Olga, turning crimson.

"Oh, not Max, you may be sure!" Her friend laughed mischievously. "Max is only an interlude."

"And Hunt-Goring the main theme?" suggested Nick.

She laughed again indifferently. "Perhaps, I can't say I'm enamoured of him, though. He's rather a brute at heart, underneath the oil-silk. Well, I'm going to lie in the hammock and sleep."

She got up, stretched luxuriously, and strolled away over the grass.

Nick watched her go with flickering, observant eyes; but he made no comment upon her. Only as she passed from sight, he made an odd little grimace as if dismissing a slightly distasteful subject from his mind. Then he turned to his niece.

"Well, my chicken, you've had a busy afternoon."

"A beastly afternoon, Nick!" she responded warmly. "And I'm very glad it's over, and I don't want to talk about it. Tell me about your doings instead! What were you wanted for?"

"Prepare for a shock!" said Nick. "I haven't got over it myself yet. They want to pack me off to India again. I told 'em I couldn't go, but they seem to take it for granted that I shall. Don't know what Muriel will say to it, I'm sure. They say it would be only a six months' job, but I have my doubts of that."

"Nick! India!"

"India, my child--naked and unadulterated India! The Imperial Commissioners have quite decided that I'm the man for the job. I kept on saying 'Can't!' and 'Won't!' But that didn't make the least difference. Old Reggie Bassett's doing, I'll lay a wager. He will have it that my genius is thrown away in England. And they inform me rather brutally that my seat in Parliament would be far more easily filled than this Sharapura post. Also the young Rajah has done me the honour to ask for me. We went pig-sticking together once--years ago, and I chanced to head off Piggie at a critical moment for young Akbar. On the strength of that, he wants me to go and be his political adviser for a few months. It seems the State is in rather a muddle. His father was a shocking old shuffler, and there are plenty of budmashes about, if report says true. But this young Rajah is anxious to get things straightened out, and the Commissioner wants a report made and so on. Altogether," Nick paused with a smile on his yellow face, "they were very persuasive," he said.

"Nick! You're going!" Olga exclaimed.

He laughed. "If you want my impartial opinion as to that," he said, "I believe I am."

She drew a deep breath. Her eyes were shining. "Oh, how I wish I were a man! I'd come with you."

"Ladies are admitted," said Nick.

"Ah! I wonder what Muriel will say," she said. "Does she like India?"

"India is a large place," he pointed out. "She doesn't like Ghawalkhand, and she isn't keen on Simla--which is sheer prejudice on her part. Sharapura she has never seen. It's a small State in the very middle of the Empire. There are rivers and jungles and tigers and snakes--quite a lot of snakes; a decent little capital and a hill-station, healthy enough though not very high. The natives are exactly like monkeys. I learnt to speak their lingo one winter from a villainous bearer I had when some of us were stationed there. There is a small native garrison in cantonments at the capital. There is also a fort and a race-course. I won the Great Mogul's Cup there--a memorable occasion. My mount was a wall-eyed lanky brute of a Waler, with the action of a camel. But he had the spirit of an Olympian, and we won at a canter."

Nick stopped. His eyes also had begun to shine. Olga was listening enraptured.

"How I wish I was Muriel!" she said. "Of course she'll want to go, Nick. It sounds perfectly enchanting."

"Especially the tigers and snakes," laughed Nick. "Poor Muriel! It's rather a shame to ask her. She had an overdose of the East at the outset, and she has never got over it."

"Oh, but that's aeons ago!" protested Olga.

"I know; but it went deep." Nick leaned back abruptly, with closed eyes. "I wonder if I can bring myself to refuse finally and conclusively--without telling her," he said ruminatively.

"Never, Nick!" Olga sprang from her chair. "You shan't think of such a thing! Nick! A heaven-sent chance like that! Oh, it wouldn't be fair. I'm sure she would say so. You must--you must tell her!"

Nick's hand clenched upon the arm of his chair. He kept his eyes shut. "You see, dear," he said, "there's the kiddie too. I'm an unnatural beast. I'd actually forgotten him for the moment. One-eyed of me, wasn't it?"

"Nick--darling!" Suddenly Olga was kneeling beside his chair; she put her arms about his neck. "You shan't call yourself anything so horrid!" she said. "Dad and I will take care of little Reggie. You know you can trust him to me, Nick. I'll watch over him day and night."

"Bless your heart!" said Nick. He lodged his head against her shoulder after the fashion she most loved. "You're a sweet little pal," he said. "But I doubt if Muriel would consent to go so far away from him, and I'm a selfish hound myself to contemplate such a thing. No; don't contradict me! It's rude. I'm that, and several other things besides. I'd no idea I was so much in the grip of the East. It's a curious thing. One feels it in the blood. It's six years--more--since I climbed on to the shelf, and I've been quite smug and self-satisfied most of the time. There's been a twinge of regret every now and then, but nothing I couldn't whistle away. But now--" his words quickened; he spoke them whimsically, yet passionately, in her ear--"between you and me, I'd give an eye, an ear, or a leg--anything I possess in duplicate--to come off the shelf, and have one more fling. I'm stiff! I'm stiff! And, ye gods, I'm only four-and-thirty! I always thought I'd go till sixty at least. I entered Parliament just to keep going; but that's only a steady progress downhill--a sort of frog's march in which you kick and are kicked, but don't do much besides. I'm a fighter, kiddie. I wasn't made to ornament the shelf. I'm not a hero; only an ordinary, restless, discontented mortal. They told me this afternoon that it was time I did something, that I was dropping out, that I should ossify if I sat still much longer. (A good term that; worthy of our friend Max!) And, by Heaven, they're right! But how can I help it? I know in my heart of hearts that it would be sheer brutality to spring this on Muriel now."

He ceased to speak, and there fell a silence. Olga's arms clasped him very tightly. Her cheek pressed his forehead. It was not often that Nick opened his heart to her thus. Only twice before had it ever happened, and on each occasion he had been in trouble--once when the woman he loved had sent back his engagement ring through her, and once again nearly two years later when that same woman--Muriel, his wife--had lain at death's door all through one dreadful night while they two, close pals, had waited huddled together in the passage outside her room. Those two occasions were sacred to Olga, never spoken of to any, shrined deep in the most inner, most secret recesses of her heart. Nick's confidence had ever been her most cherished possession. It thrilled her now with something more than pride; and through her silence her sympathy came out to him in a flood of understanding which needed no verbal expression.

She spoke at last very softly, almost in a whisper. "Nick, you know, don't you, that you are dearer to me than anyone else in the world?"

He put up his hand and patted her cheek. "What! Still?" he said.

"Still, Nick? What do you mean?"

"Nothing at all," said Nick promptly. "Go on!"

She took his hand and held it. "Nick darling, do you remember how I came and kept house for you--years ago, at Redlands, when I was a child?"

"Rather!" said Nick. "Bully, wasn't it?"

She hesitated a little. "Nick, I'm going to make a perfectly awful suggestion."

"Don't mind me!" said Nick.

She laughed faintly. "I don't, dear,--formidable as you can be. It only flashed into my mind that if Muriel feels she really can't leave Reggie, and if she can possibly bear to part with you and you with her, could you possibly put up with me as a substitute for those few months and take me instead, if Dad could spare me?"

"By Jove!" said Nick, sitting up.

"I know it's great cheek of me to suggest it," Olga hastened to say. "For of course I know I'd be a very poor substitute; but at least I could keep a motherly eye on you, and see that you were properly clothed and fed. And Muriel herself couldn't possibly love you more."

"By Jove!" Nick said again. Olga's face flushed and eager was close to his. He bent suddenly forward and kissed it. "And what about you, my chicken?" he said.

"I, Nick? I should love it!" she said, with candid eyes raised to his. "You can't imagine how much I should love it."

"You'd be homesick," said Nick.

"Nick! With you!"

He was looking at her with shrewd, flickering eyes. "Do you mean to say," he said, "that there is no one here that you would mind leaving for so long?"

"There's Dad of course," she said. "But--don't you think perhaps Muriel wouldn't mind taking care of him for me if I took care of you for her?"

Nick broke into a laugh. "Excellent, my child! Most ingenious! Jim and Muriel are fast allies. But--Jim is not the only person you would leave behind. You ought to consider that before you get too obsessed by this enchanting idea. It's pretty beastly, you know, to feel that half the world stretches between you and--someone you might at any moment develop a pressing desire to see."

Olga frowned at him. "What are you driving at, Nick?"

"I'm only indicating the obvious," said Nick.

"No, you're not, dear. You're hinting things."

"In that case," said Nick, "you are at liberty to treat me with the contempt I deserve. Look here! We won't talk about this any more to-day. The subject is too indigestible. We'll sleep on it, and see what we think of it to-morrow."

"You're not going to write to Muriel to-night?" asked Olga.

"Not to-night. They've given me a week to make up my mind."

"And when would you have to go?"

"Some time towards the end of next month, or possibly the beginning of October. But as we're not going," said Nick, "I move that the discussion be postponed."

He smiled into her eyes, a baffling, humorous smile, and rose.

"But it was a ripping idea of yours," he said. "I'm quite grateful to you for mentioning it. There are some chocolates in the hall for you. Don't give them all to Violet, charm she never so wisely."

"Oh, Nick, you darling! Fancy your remembering me! Do let's have some at once!"

They went indoors together with something of the air of conspirators, and in the close companionship of her hero Olga managed to forget that she had so recently been driven to another man for protection. In fact, the interview in the surgery, with the episode that had preceded it, was completely crowded out of her mind by this new and dazzling idea that had flashed so suddenly into her brain, and which seemed already to have altered the course of her life.

Many and startling were the visions that filled her sleeping hours that night but each one of them served but to impress upon her the same thing. When she arose in the morning she told herself with a little shiver of sheer excitement that the gates of the world were opening to her, and that soon she would actually behold those wonders of which till then she had only dreamed.

CHAPTER X
THE DOOR

When remembrance of the previous day's happenings came to Olga, she was already so deeply engrossed in household duties that she was able to dismiss the matter without much difficulty. It was one of the busiest mornings of the week, and no sooner had she finished indoors than she donned a sun-bonnet and big apron and betook herself to the raspberry-bed to gather fruit for jam.

The day was hot, and Violet had established herself in the hammock under the lime-trees with a book and a box of cigarettes. The three boys had gone with Nick on a fishing expedition, and all was supremely quiet.

The sun blazed mercilessly down upon Olga as she toiled, but she would not be discouraged. The raspberries were many and ready to drop with ripeness, and the jam-making could not be deferred. So intent was she that she really almost forgot the physical discomfort in her anxiety to accomplish her task. She had meant to do it in the cool of the previous evening, but her talk with Nick had driven the matter absolutely from her mind.

So she laboured in the full heat of a burning August day, till her head began to throb and her muscles to ache so unbearably that it was no longer possible to ignore them. It was at the commencement of the last row but one (they were very long rows) that she became aware that her energies were seriously flagging. The rest of the garden seemed to be swimming in a haze around her, but she stubbornly ignored that, and bent again to her work, fixing her attention once more with all her resolution upon the great rose-red berries that were waiting to be gathered. She must finish now. She had promised herself to clear the bed by luncheon-time. But it was certainly very hard labour, harder than she had ever found it before. She began to feel as if her limbs were weighted, and the fruit itself danced giddily before her aching eyes.

Suddenly she heard a step on the ash-path near her. She looked up, half-turning as she did so. The next instant it was as if a knife had suddenly pierced her temples. She cried out sharply with the pain of it, staggered, clutched wildly at emptiness, and fell. The contents of her basket scattered around her in spite of her desperate efforts to save them, and this disaster was to Olga the climax of all. She went into a brief darkness in bitterness of spirit.

Not wholly did she lose consciousness, however, for she knew whose arms lifted her, and even very feebly tried to push them away. In the end she found herself sitting on an old wooden bench in the shade of the garden-wall, with her head against Max's shoulder, and his hand, very vital and full of purpose, grasping her wrist.

"Oh, Max," she said, with a painful gasp, "my raspberries!"

"Damn the raspberries!" growled Max. His hand travelled up to her head and removed the sun-bonnet while he was speaking. "Don't move till you feel better!" he said. "There's nothing to bother about."

He pressed her temples with a sure, cool touch. She closed her eyes under it.

"But I must get on," she said uneasily. "I want to make the jam this after-noon."

"Do you?" said Max grimly.

She was silent for a little. He kept his hand upon her head, and she was glad of its support though she wished it had not been his.

"It must be nearly luncheon-time," she said at last, with an effort.

"It is," said Max. "We will go indoors."

"Oh, but I must pick up my raspberries first, and--there's a whole row--more--to gather yet."

"You will have to leave that job for someone else," he said. "You are not fit for it. Are you quite mad, I wonder?"

"It had to be done," said Olga. "I must finish now--really I must finish." She took his hand from her head and slowly raised it. Instantly that agonizing pain shot through her temples again. She barely suppressed a cry.

"What is it?" he said.

"My head!" she gasped. "And oh, Max, I do feel so sick."

He stood up. "Come along!" he said. "I'm going to carry you in."

She raised a feeble protest to which he paid no more attention than if it had been the buzzing of a fly. Very steadily and strongly he lifted her.

"Put your head on my shoulder!" he said, and she obeyed him like a child.

They encountered no one on the way back to the house. Straight in and straight upstairs went Max, finally depositing her upon her bed. He seemed to know exactly how she felt, for he propped her head high with a skill that she found infinitely comforting, and drew the window-curtains to shade her eyes. Then very quietly he proceeded to remove her shoes.

"Thank you very much," murmured Olga. "Don't bother!"

He came and stood beside her and again felt her pulse. "Look here," he said. "As soon as you feel a little better, you undress and slip into bed. I'll come up again in half an hour and give you something for your head. Understand?"

"Oh, no!" Olga said. "No! I can't go to bed, really. I'll lie here for a little while, but I shall be quite all right presently."

Max continued to feel her pulse. He was frowning a good deal. "You will do as I say," he said deliberately. "You are to go to bed at once, and you won't come down again for the rest of the day."

There was so much of finality in his speech that Olga became aware of the futility of argument. She felt moreover totally unfit for it. She only hazarded one more protest.

"But what about Violet?"

"She can take care of herself," he said. "I will tell her."

There was no help for it. Olga gave in without further protest. But she did venture to say as he released her hand, "Please don't bother about bringing me anything! I couldn't possibly take it."

"Leave that to me!" said Max brusquely.

He left her then, to her unutterable relief. There was no doubt about it; she was feeling very ill, so ill that the business of undressing was almost more than she could accomplish. But she did manage it at last, and crept thankfully into bed, laying her throbbing head upon the pillow with the vague wonder if she would ever have the strength to lift it again.

From that she drifted into a maze of pain that blurred all thought, and from which she only roused herself to find Max once more by her side. He was watching her closely.

"Is your head very bad?" he asked.

"Yes," she whispered.

"I've got some stuff here that will soothe it," he said.

"Just drink it down, and then see if you can get a sleep."

His tone was so gentle that had her pain been less severe Olga might have found room for amazement. As it was, she began very weakly to cry.

"Now don't be silly!" said Max. "You needn't move. I'll do it all."

He slipped his arm under the pillow, and lifted her. She commanded herself and drank from the medicine-glass he held to her lips.

"What queer stuff!" she said. "Is it--is it 'the pain-killer'?"

"What do you know about 'the pain-killer'?" he said.

She shrank a little at the question, and he did not pursue it. He laid her down again, settled the pillows, and left her.

Olga lay very still. She felt as if a strange glow were dawning in her brain, a kind of mental radiance, inexpressibly wonderful, absorbing her pain as mist is absorbed by the sun. Gradually it grew and spread till the pain was all gone, swamped, forgotten, in this curious flood of warmth and ecstasy. It was the most marvellous sensation she had ever experienced. Her whole being thrilled responsive to the glow. It was as though a door had been opened somewhere above her and she were being drawn upwards by some invisible means, upwards and upwards, light as gossamer and strangely transcendentally happy, towards the warmth and brightness and wonder that lay beyond.

Up and still up her spirit seemed to soar. Of her body she was supremely, most blissfully, unconscious. She felt as one at the entrance of a dream-world, a world of unknown unimagined splendours, a world of golden atmosphere, of ineffable rapture, and she was floating up through the ether, eager-spirited, wrapt in delight.

And then quite suddenly she knew that Max had returned to her side. His hand was laid upon her arm, his fingers sensitive and ruthless closed upon her pulse.

In that instant Olga also knew that her dream-world was fading from her, her paradise was lost. Softly, inexorably, the door that had begun to open to her closed.

The hand that grasped her drew her firmly back to earth and held her there.

In her disappointment she could have wept, so vital, so entrancing, had been the vision. Piteously she tried to plead with him, but it was as though an obscuring veil had been dropped upon her. She could only utter unintelligible murmurings. She sought for words and found them not.

And then she heard his voice quite close to her, very tender and reassuring.

"Don't vex yourself, sweetheart! It's all right--all right."

His hand smoothed her brow; she almost fancied that he kissed her hair, but she was not certain and it did not seem to matter. Surely nothing could ever matter again since the closing of that door!

A brief confusion was hers, a brief wandering in dark places, and then a slow deepening of the dark, the spreading of a great silence....

The last thing she heard was the steady ticking of a watch that someone held close to her. The last thing her brain registered was the close, unvarying grip of a hand upon her wrist....

It was many hours--it might have been years to Olga--before she awoke. Very slowly her clogged spirit climbed out of the deep, deep waters of oblivion in which it had been steeped. For a long time she lay with closed eyes, semi-conscious, not troubling to summon her faculties. At last very wearily she opened them, and found Nick seated beside her, alertly watching.

"Hullo!" she murmured languidly.

"Hullo, darling!" he made soft response. "Had a nice sleep?"

She stared at him vaguely. "What are you sitting there for?"

"Taking care of you," said Nick.

She frowned, collecting her wits with difficulty. "It's night, isn't it?"

"Half-past one," said Nick.

"My dear!" She opened her eyes a little wider. "But what are you waiting for? Why don't you go to bed?"

"I like sitting up sometimes," said Nick. "Keeps me in form."

She turned her head on the pillow. "Is Max here?"

"No," said Nick.

"But--he has been?" she persisted.

"Yes. He's been in now and then."

"Ah!" Olga frowned still more. "Am I ill, Nick?" she asked, with a touch of nervousness.

His lean hand sought and held hers. "You've had a touch of sun, dear," he said, "but you've slept it off. Max is quite satisfied about you. You'll feel a bit rotten for a day or two, but that's all."

"How horrid!" said Olga.

"Don't worry!" said Nick. "I'm here. I shall stick like a leech for the future. You will never be out of my sight again in your waking hours."

She squeezed his hand. "Poor old Nick! I'm dreadfully sorry. But I had to get those raspberries. Oh, what's that?"

She started violently at the soft opening of the door. Nick got up, but she clung to him so fast that he could not leave her side. He bent down over her.

"It's all right, darling. It's only Max with some refreshments. We'll leave you in peace as soon as you have broken your fast."

"I don't want Max," she whispered. "Please send him away!"

"I'll go like a bird," Max said, "if you will let me take your pulse first. It isn't much to ask, is it?"

He set down a tray he was carrying, and came and stood beside Nick. Outlined against the dim light shed by a shaded night-lamp, he looked gigantically square and strong.

"I won't hurt you, Olga," he said. "Won't you trust me?"

Again his voice was softened to a great gentleness; yet it compelled. In another second Nick had withdrawn himself, and Max stood alone beside her bed. He stooped low over her, put back the hair from her forehead, looked intently into her eyes.

"Are you in pain?" he asked.

"No," she whispered back.

"You are sure? It doesn't hurt you to move your eyes?"

"No," she said again.

He passed his hand again over her forehead, felt her face, her temples, finally turned his attention to her pulse. As he took out his watch, she remembered again the two things that had outlasted all other impressions before she had sunk into her long sleep. And with this memory came another. She raised her eyes to his grave face.

"Max!"

"In a moment!" said Max.

But it was many moments before he laid her hand down.

"You will be all right when you have eaten something," he said then, "and had another sleep. Is there something you want to say to me?"

His tone was kind, but his manner repressive. She wished the light had not been so dim upon his face.

"Max," she said, with an effort, "why--why did you close the door?"

She fancied he smiled, grimly humorous, at the question. She was sure his eyes gleamed mockery. He was silent for a space, and then: "Ask me some other time!" he said. She breathed a sigh of disappointment. She knew she would never have the courage. He waited a few seconds more, then as she remained silent he laid his hand again on hers and pressed it lightly.

"Good-night!" he said.

She scarcely responded, nor did he wait for her to respond. In another moment he had turned from her, and was talking in a low voice to Nick.

A minute later he went softly out, and she saw no more of him that night.

Nick remained for some little time longer, waiting on her with the tenderness of a woman. It was wonderful to note how little his infirmity hampered him. There were very few things that Nick could not accomplish with one hand as quickly as the rest of the world with two.

But Olga, having recovered the full possession of her faculties, would not permit him to sacrifice any more of his night's rest to her.

"I shall be perfectly all right," she declared. "If I'm not, you are only in the next room, and I can rap on the wall."

"Yes, but will you?" said Nick.

"Of course I will."

"Is it a promise?"

She caught his hand and kissed it. "Yes, dear Nick, a promise."

"All right," said Nick. "I'll go."

But he was obviously loth to leave her, and she detained him to assure him how greatly she loved to be in his care.

"Max tells me I am not in the least fitted to look after you," he said rather rue-fully, "and I believe he's right."

The humility of this speech was so extraordinary that it nearly took Olga's breath away.

"My dear Nick," she said, "what nonsense! Surely you don't--seriously--care what Max says?"

"Don't you?" said Nick.

She began to answer in the negative, but tripped up unexpectedly. "I--I can't quite say. I haven't really thought about it. But--anyhow--it's no business of his, is it?"

"He thinks it is," said Nick.

"Why?" She suddenly put out her hand to him with a little shiver. "Nick, you haven't told him about--that scheme of ours?"

"Yes, I have," said Nick.

"Oh, why?" There was unmistakable distress in the question.

Nick knelt down beside her. "Olga, I had to. He's a clever chap, cleverer than Jim even. I wanted to know if I'd better go on with it, if he thought--in view of to-day's misfortune--it might upset your health, supposing you were allowed to go. I couldn't run the risk of that."

"What did he say?" said Olga.

Nick chuckled a little. "He said that your normal health appeared to be up to the average young woman's, but he hadn't sounded you in any way, and--"

"And he shan't!" interjected Olga, with vehemence.

"And so couldn't say for certain," ended Nick. "But--I'll tell you this--he doesn't like our precious scheme--at all."

"Why not?" said Olga. "What has it got to do with him?"

"I don't know," said Nick.

"Why didn't you ask him?"

"My dear, you can do that in the morning--before I write to Muriel."

"I will," said Olga firmly. "It's my belief that you're afraid of him," she added, a moment later.

"No, I'm not," said Nick simply.

"Then why are you so careful of his feelings?"

"I shouldn't like to see him writhing in hell," said Nick. "I've done it myself, and I know exactly what it feels like."

"Really, Nick!"

"Yes, really, little sweetheart. You know or p'raps you don't know--what fools men can be."

"I know they can be quite unreasonable and very horrid sometimes," said Olga. "Nick dear, you'll promise me, won't you, that if Muriel agrees and Dad agrees you won't let an outsider like Max stand in our way?"

"Is he an outsider?" asked Nick humorously.

"He is so far as I am concerned," said Olga. "I can't imagine why you take any notice of him."

"Are you sure you don't yourself?" asked Nick.

"Oh, in some things perhaps. But not in a matter of this sort. I think he is very interfering," said Olga resentfully.

Nick smiled and rose. "I shouldn't be too hard on him, kiddie. Doubtless he has his reasons."

"I should like to know what they are," said Olga.

He stooped for a final kiss. "I daresay--if you were to ask him prettily--he would tell you."

"Oh, no, he wouldn't," she said. "He never tells me anything, even if I beg him." She slipped her arms round his neck and held him closely for a moment. "Nick darling, you will work that lovely scheme of ours if you possibly can--promise me!--in spite of anything Max may say or do!"

"You don't mind hurting his feelings?" asked Nick.

"Oh, well,"--she hesitated--"he couldn't care all that. It's only his love of interference."

"Or his love of you? I wonder which!" whispered Nick.

"Nick! Nick!" Wonder, dismay, incredulity, mingled in the cry.

But Nick had already slipped free from the clinging of her arms, and he did not pause in answer.

"Good-night, Olga mia!" he called back to her softly from the door. "Don't forget to knock on the wall if you feel squeamish!"

And with that he was gone. The latch clicked behind him, and she was alone.

CHAPTER XI
THE IMPOSSIBLE

Could it be true? Sleeping and waking, sleeping and waking, all through the night Olga asked herself the question; and when morning came she was still unconvinced. Nothing in Max's manner had ever given her cause to imagine for an instant that he cared for her. Never for an instant had she seriously imagined that he could care. Till quite recently she had believed that a very decided antipathy had existed between them. True, it had not thriven greatly since the writing of her note; but that had been an event of only two days before. She was sure he had not cared for her before that. He could not have begun to care since! And if he had, how in wonder could Nick have come to know?

Certainly he knew most things. His uncanny shrewdness had moved her many a time before to amazement and admiration. This quickness of intellect was hers also, but in a far smaller degree. She could leap to conclusions herself and often find them correct. But Nick--Nick literally swooped upon the truth with unerring precision. She had never known him to miss his mark. But this time--could he be right this time? It was such a monstrous notion. Its very contemplation bewildered her, carried her off her feet, made her giddy. She began to be a little frightened, to cast back her thoughts over all her intercourse with Max to ascertain if she had ever given him the smallest reason for loving her. Most emphatically she had never felt drawn towards him. In fact, she had often been repelled. In all their skirmishes she had invariably had the worst of it. He had simply despised her resistance, treating it as a thing of nought. And yet--there was no denying it--their intimacy had grown. Who but an intimate friend could have made that suggestion for encompassing her deliverance from the persecutions of that hateful man? Her face burned afresh over the memory of this. It had certainly been a desperate remedy--one to which she would never have given her consent could she for a single instant have suspected that it had been dictated by anything more than a friendly desire for her welfare.

Surely, argued her practical mind, he could never have been so foolish as to let himself care deeply for one who so obviously had only the most casual regard for him! She knew women did these silly things, but surely not men--and hard-headed men like Max!

Besides, what could he possibly see in her? Was it not Violet upon whom his attention was constantly focussed? And small wonder, his own repudiation of sentiment notwithstanding! Did not all men look at her with dazzled eyes? Even Nick paid her that much homage, though Olga was privately a little doubtful as to whether he altogether liked her brilliant friend.

No, she had never for an instant seriously contemplated this possibility which Nick had whispered into her ear. She wondered what had made him do it? Had he meant to put her on her guard. Or--staggering thought!--had he thought to wake her heart to some response? Was he taking Max's part? Did he want her to be kind to him?

She pictured Max's wrath, sardonically expressed, should he ever become acquainted with that move of Nick's. She fancied he did not much like Nick and that suspicion of itself was quite sufficient to present him in an unfavourable light to her half-involuntary criticism. How could she ever possibly begin to care for a man who did not admire her hero? Oh, why had she ever placed herself under an obligation to him, ever consented to the forging of that bond between them, elastic though it might be?

Of course it could be severed. He had said so. And severed it should be at once. But why had she ever suffered it? It weighed upon her intolerably now that she realized in what foundry its links had been cast. Even her enemy's impertinences would be easier to bear--now that she knew.

Again, as morning broke, she told herself that this thing was an impossibility after all, that Nick had been misled, or had spoken in jest. It seemed the only sane conclusion by the practical light of day, and, reassured, at last she slipped into untroubled slumber. Yes, she was sure Max was much too shrewd to let himself be caught by a girl who did not even want him. He would never waste his valuable time over such as she.

Yet while she slept, a curious memory came to her--a memory that was half a dream--of a hand that had stroked her head with a sure and soothing touch, of lips very near her hair that had whispered words of tenderness. It was not a disturbing dream by any means. She slept through it into a deeper peace with a smile upon her face.

She was finally aroused without ceremony by Violet, who skipped airily into the room, clad in a daring sea-green wrapper that revealed more of her charms than it concealed.

"Oh, my dear soul, are you awake?" was her greeting, as she perched herself on the foot of the bed. "I've just had the very sweetest note from Hunt-Goring accompanied by a box of the most exquisite Eastern cigarettes--'Companions of the Harem,' he says they are called. And how are you feeling now, you poor wan thing? What interesting shadows you have developed! I wish I could make my eyes look like that. The revered Max suffered agonies about you last night, and nearly slew me with a glance because I dared to touch my mandolin after dinner. Poor little Nick was rather blue too though he did at least try to be courteous. What made you go and get sunstroke, Allegretto? Rather unnecessary, wasn't it? He was quite obviously at your feet without that. Of course you realize how completely my wiles have been thrown away on him. I declare I was never so humiliated in my life. However, I daresay I shall get over it. If I don't, I shall take refuge in Hunt-Goring's harem. Good gracious! What now?"

A smart rap at the door had interrupted her plans for her future. She sprang off the end of Olga's bed, and stood poised on one foot, listening.

"Can I come in?" asked Max on the other side of the door.

Olga's face flushed scarlet. Violet shot her a glance of mock dismay.

"My dear, I wonder which would be the least improper," she said. "To go or to remain?"

"For pity's sake, put something on!" urged Olga. "There's my dressing-gown. Take that!"

But Violet had already snatched up a bath-towel which she draped about her with scarf-like effect.

"This will do quite well and is infinitely more artistic. Pray come in, Dr. Wyndham! The patient is quite ready for you."

Max came in. He scarcely looked at either girl, but halted just inside the room, holding the door wide open.

"One at a time, Miss Campion, please!" he said curtly.

"Dear, dear!" laughed Violet, with audacious mirth. "Then you had better call again later when I have concluded my visit."

He turned his eyes straight upon her; they were piercingly green in the morning light. "Your visit," he said, "is a direct violation of my orders. I must trouble you to conclude it at once."

He had never used that tone to her before. She opened her eyes very wide, meeting his look with the utmost nonchalance.

"Dear me!" she said. "How fierce we are this morning! And what if Olga prefers my company to yours?"

"That has nothing to do with it," he returned. "I am here professionally.".

"And if Olga is not requiring your professional services?" she suggested daringly.

"Oh, Violet dear, I think you had better go," interposed Olga nervously. "You can come back again when you are dressed."

Violet's beautiful eyes suddenly gleamed. She moved to the door, stepping daintily with her bare feet.

"Dr. Wyndham," she said, "I congratulate you on your conquest. It has been a ridiculously easy capture, but I warned her she had met her fate long ago. No doubt she has wisely decided that to run away any longer would be a waste of energy. En tout cas,--" she made an airy gesture of the hands,--"my blessing be upon you both!"

And with that, lightly she crossed the threshold, and was gone, flitting like a sunbeam from the room.

Quietly Max closed the door. He did not look at Olga, but walked straight to the window and stood there with his back turned and his hands in his pockets, staring outwards.

"I hope you don't object to an early visit," he said, after a moment. "I want to get my rounds done in good time to-day, and I didn't like to leave without seeing you first."

"I don't mind at all," stammered Olga in reply. "But--really, there's no reason for you to--to bother about me. I've had a good night, and--and I'm going to get up."

"Really?" he said. "You're not going raspberry picking, I hope?"

She laughed somewhat tremulously. Violet's vindictive thrust had embarrassed rather than hurt her. She looked at the great square shoulders that intervened between her eyes and the morning sunshine, and wondered why he did not turn. Was it possible that he could be feeling embarrassed too? She could scarcely imagine it; but yet the position was sufficiently intolerable for him also.

"I'm afraid the raspberries will have to go," she said regretfully, "unless the boys--"

"They would probably eat 'em as fast as they picked 'em," observed Max grimly. "I know boys."

Again, rather feebly, she laughed. "It seems a pity," she said.

"I shouldn't worry," said Max. "Besides, it's Sunday. You couldn't make jam on Sunday in any case."

"I could, though," said Olga, "if the fruit wouldn't keep till Monday."

He laughed. "What an admirably practical spirit!"

"Thank you!" said Olga. "That's the first nice thing you have ever said to me."

"Oh, no, it isn't!" said Max. "May I come and take a survey now?"

"I can't imagine what you are waiting for," she returned with renewed spirit.

She could meet him on the old fencing-ground without a tremor; at least so she fancied. But the next instant he disconcerted her in the most unexpected fashion.

"I have been waiting for your pulse to steady down," he said coolly.

"Oh!" said Olga.

He left the window and came to her side. She gave him her hand with an abrupt, childish movement.

"It's great nonsense!" she said, with burning cheeks. "You can't possibly make me out ill."

She saw one side of his mouth go up. He took out his watch, but he looked at her.

"You don't imagine that I want to keep you as a patient, do you?" he said.

"You know you always like people best when they are ill," she retorted.

"Do I?" he said.

"Well, don't you?"

"I wonder what makes you think so," he said.

She looked straight up at him with something of defiance. "You never bother to be nice to people unless they are ill."

He frowned a little. "I've been as nice as you would let me," he said.

"Yes, yes," said Olga rather hurriedly. "Of course we are friends. But, Max, there's something I want to say to you. It's very particular. Be quick with my pulse!"

He let her hand slip from his. "It's about a hundred and fifty," he observed, "but that seems to be the normal rate with you. I don't think you had better talk to me now unless it's to be a professional consultation. You can get up if you want to, and I will give Nick a list of the things you are not to do."

He would have gone with the words, but imperiously she detained him.

"You must wait a minute now. I want to speak about--about that compact we made the other day. You--you knew I was only joking, didn't you? You didn't--really--? tell Major Hunt-Goring--that?"

"Yes, I did," said Max. "And do you generally go and cry into the surgery towel when you are enjoying a joke?"

"Oh, Max! You told him?" Her face was tragic. "And what did he say?"

"He congratulated me," said Max.

"Max!"

"My dear girl, I'm telling you the truth; but really, since you have discharged yourself as cured, this has become a highly improper situation. Don't you think we had better postpone this discussion to a more suitable moment?"

Max was openly laughing into her face of distress. She suddenly felt abundantly reassured. He could not--surely--look and speak like this if he dreamed of wooing her in earnest!

"I don't want any discussion," she hastened to tell him. "Only--please, do go and tell Major Hunt-Goring that--that--there's been a mistake, and--in short--"

"In short that you've thrown me over?" said Max. "Oh, thanks, no! You can tell him that--if you wish!"

"He must be told," she said.

"I don't see why." Max smiled upon her with good-natured indulgence. "Have you suddenly taken fright at something?" he asked.

She smiled also, but a little anxiously. "I'm afraid it wasn't a very wise move after all. I want to put an end to it."

"You can't put an end to an engagement that doesn't exist," he said. "You will have to wait till I propose, and then you can go and tell everyone--including Hunt-Goring--that you have said No."

It was impossible to treat the matter seriously. She had a feeling that he was deliberately restraining her from so doing, deliberately offering her an easy means of escape from her own indiscretion. She seized upon it, eager to convince him that she had never deemed him in earnest.

"Do propose soon then!" she said. "And let us get it over!"

He turned to the door. "Given a suitable opportunity," he said, "if shall be done to-night."

"To-night!" she echoed sharply.

She caught the mocking gleam of his eyes for an instant, and her heart misgave her.

"Really, Max!" she said, in a tone of protest.

"Yes, really," said Max. "Good-bye!"

He was gone. She heard him stride away down the passage, and go downstairs. A little later she heard the banging of the surgery-door and the sound of his feet on the gravel. They passed under her window. They paused.

"Olga," he called up to her, "do you mind if a pal of mine comes to lunch?"

Her heart gave a great jolt at the sound of his voice. She swallowed twice before she found her own.

"Who is it?" she called then.

"Someone very nice," he assured her, and she caught a laugh in the words. "Someone you'll like."

"Anyone I know?" she asked.

"No."

She heard him strike a match to light a cigarette. He would not be looking up-wards then. Impulse moved her. She left her bed and went to the window.

He was standing immediately below her, a thick-set, British figure of immense strength. A brisk breeze was blowing. She watched him nursing the flame between his hands, firm, powerful hands, full of confidence. The flame flickered and went out. Instantly he threw up his head and saw her. His cigarette was alight.

She drew back sharply as he waved her an airy salute.

"Adieu, fair lady!" called the mocking voice. "I conclude the aforementioned pal may come, then?"

He did not wait for her answer. She heard him whistling cheerily as he went in the direction of the coach-house, and the ting of his bicycle-bell a moment after as he rode away. When that reached her ears, Olga sat down very suddenly on the edge of her bed with the limpness of relaxed tension, and realized that she was feeling very weak.

CHAPTER XII
THE PAL

Nick's letter to his wife was written that morning while Olga lay on the study-sofa, comfortably lazy for once, and listened to the scratching of his pen.

The boys had been sent to church, Violet was again devouring a book and smoking Major Hunt-Goring's cigarettes in the hammock, and all was very quiet.

"I suppose I had better write to Jim too," Nick said, as he looked up at length from his completed epistle.

"I was just thinking I would," said Olga.

"No. Writing is strictly prohibited by your medical adviser." Nick grinned over his shoulder. "I'll send him a line myself."

"Don't let him be worried about me," said Olga. "I really don't know why I'm being so lazy. I feel quite well."

"And look--charming," supplemented Nick.

"Don't be silly, dear! You know I'm as hideous as--"

"As I am? Oh, no, not quite, believe me. I always pride myself I am unique in that respect. Now you mustn't talk," said Nick judiciously, "or you will spoil my inspiration. Who's that going across the lawn?"

He was writing rapidly as he spoke. Olga raised herself on her elbow to look.

"How on earth did you know? I never heard anyone. Oh!"

"What's the matter?" said Nick.

"It's Major Hunt-Goring!"

Nick ceased to write and peered into the garden. "It's all right. He's only violeting. An interesting pastime!" He turned unexpectedly and gave her one of his shrewd glances. "You don't seem pleased," he observed.

"Oh, Nick, he's so hateful! And--and Violet actually likes him."

"Every woman to her taste," said Nick. "Why shouldn't she?"

Olga was silent.

Nick returned to his writing. "I'll go and kick him for you if you like," he said. "Let me just finish my letter to Jim first, though, or it may never get written."

His pen resumed its energetic progress, and Olga fell into a brown study.

Half an hour later Nick turned swiftly and looked at her. Her eyes met his instantly.

"Not asleep?" he said.

"No, Nick. Only thinking."

"What about?"

"India," said Olga.

He got up and came and sat on the edge of the sofa. "Look here, kiddie," he said, "if you've thought better of it, just mention the same before I post these letters. I shall understand."

She smiled at him, her quick, sweet smile. "Nick, you're a darling! But I haven't."

"Quite sure?" said Nick.

"Quite sure," she replied with emphasis.

He looked a little quizzical. "By the way, did you ask Max--what you wanted to know?"

She knew that she coloured, but she faced him notwithstanding. "No, I didn't. I decided it wasn't important enough."

"Oh, all right," said Nick. He got up. "Now can I trust you to lie quietly here while I go and post these letters?"

"Of course you can," she said.

"I shan't be more than five minutes," he said, turning to the door.

She watched him go, and then closed her eyes, slightly frowning. She wished with all her heart that Major Hunt-Goring had not seen fit to come again, even though it was obviously her friend and not herself that he had come to see.

She was still pondering the unpleasant subject when the housemaid suddenly presented herself at the open door.

"Cook wants to know what she's to do about the raspberries, miss."

"Raspberries!" said Olga, with a start. "Oh, I'm afraid they're done for. It's no good thinking about them. I will go round to-morrow, and see if there are any left worth having. But I expect they will all be spoilt by this hot sun."

The girl looked at her, slightly mystified. "But they've been gathered, miss. Didn't you know? Cook thought you had done them yourself before you took ill."

Olga put her hand to her head. "No, I didn't. I hadn't finished. I dropped them all too."

"Well, they're in the pantry now, miss, and cook was wondering if she hadn't better start the jam first thing in the morning."

"Who brought them in?" asked Olga quickly.

The housemaid didn't know. She departed to ask.

Olga leaned back again on her cushions. She was growing a little tired of in-activity, notwithstanding the undeniable languor that had succeeded the previous day's headache.

The sound of voices in the hall outside, however, dispelled her boredom almost before she had time to recognize it. She suddenly remembered Max's pal, and started up in haste to smooth her rumpled hair. Surely Max would not be so inconsiderate as to bring him straight in to her without a moment's preparation!

This was evidently his intention, however, for she heard their footsteps drawing nearer, and she was possessed by a momentary shyness so acute that she nearly fled through the window. It really was too bad of Max!

"Come in here!" she heard him say, and with an effort she braced herself to encounter the stranger.

He entered, paused a second, and came forward. And in that second very strangely and quite completely her embarrassment vanished. She found herself shaking hands with a large, kindly man, who looked at her with deep-set, friendly eyes and asked her in a voice of marvellous softness how she was.

Her heart warmed to him on the instant, and she forgave Max forthwith.

"I am quite well," she said. "Have you walked from the station? Please sit down!"

He was years older than Max, she saw, this man whom the latter had so airily described as his pal. There was a bald patch on the back of his head, and his brows were turning grey. His face was clean-shaven, and she thought his mouth the kindest and the saddest she had ever seen.

"Yes, I walked," he said. "Max brought me across the fields. It was very pleasant. There is a good breeze to-day."'

"I am sure you must be thirsty," Olga said, mindful of the honours of the house. "Max, please go and find something to drink and bring it here!"

"No, no, my dear fellow! I can wait," protested the newcomer. But Max had already departed upon his errand. He turned back smiling to the girl. "I know you were lying on the sofa when I came in. Please lie down again!"

"I've had more than enough of it," she assured him. "I don't think lying still suits me. I only did it to please Nick. He will be in directly."

"Nick is your brother?" he asked.

Olga's smile flashed out. "Not quite. He is three parts brother to one part uncle. That is to say, he is Dad's half-brother, but nearer my age than Dad's."

He nodded in humorous comprehension. "And your father is away, Max tells me. I hope you don't mind being taken by storm like this? I am sorry to miss him, for we are old friends. We don't often meet, as I haven't a great deal of time at my disposal. I reserved to-day, however, as I rather particularly wanted to see Max."

"You will manage to come again perhaps, when Dad is at home," said Olga.

He smiled courteously. "I shall certainly try. And you are his eldest daughter?"

"His only daughter," she said. "There are three boys as well."

"Ah! And you have been left in charge?"

"Nick and I," she said; and then moved to sudden confidence, "I expect you have heard of Nick, haven't you? Nick Ratcliffe of Wara! He is an M.P. too."

"Oh, is he that Ratcliffe?" Her listener displayed immediate interest. "Yes, of course I have heard of him, Miss Ratcliffe. He is a man of renown, isn't he? It will give me much pleasure to meet him."

"You'll like him awfully!" said Olga, with shining eyes.

It was at this point that Nick himself pushed open the door with a peremptory, "Now then, Olga, what about your promise? Hullo!" He stopped short, and stood blinking rapidly at the visitor. "I thought it was Hunt-Goring you had got here," he observed. "Introduce me, please!"

Olga hesitated in momentary confusion. "Max didn't tell me your name, you know," she said to the stranger. "This is Captain Ratcliffe of Wara."

"Monkey!" said Nick briefly. "Plain Ratcliffe of no-where in particular is my description."

The big man rose with outstretched hand. "I know you well by repute, and I am very pleased to meet you. My name is Whitton--Kersley Whitton."

"Goodness!" ejaculated Olga. "Max might have told me!"

He laughed at her quietly. "Told you what? Didn't he say I was a friend of his?"

"So you've been entertaining a celebrity unawares!" laughed Nick. "I hope you have been on your best behaviour, my child."

"But Miss Ratcliffe must be accustomed to celebrities," said Sir Kersley Whitton, "since she has to entertain you and Max Wyndham every day."

"Is Max a celebrity too, then?" asked Olga quickly.

"He is going to be one," the great doctor answered, with conviction.

"You mean he will--someday--be like you?" she said.

He smiled at that. "He will be a greater man than I am," he said.

"An interesting collection!" commented Nick. "Heroes past, present, and to come! You will pardon me for putting myself first. My little halo went out long ago."

"Nick! How absurd you are!"

"My dear, it's my role to be absurd. I am the clown in every tragedy I come across--the comic relief man--the buffoon in every side-show. Hence my Frontier laurels, because I kept on dancing when everyone else was dead. The world likes dancers--virtuous or otherwise." Nick broke off with his elastic grimace. "If I go on, you'll think I'm trying to be clever. Sir Kersley, come and have a drink!"

"I'm bringing drinks," said Max's voice from the hall. "I say, Ratcliffe,"--he entered with the words--"do go and dislodge that leech Goring. He's in the garden with Miss Campion. Tell him I don't want to see either him or his beastly thumb for a week. I'll call in next Sunday, if I've nothing better to do. Say I'm engaged if he asks for me now."

"I'll say you're dead if you like," said Nick cheerily. "Shall I say you're dead too, Olga?"

"Say she's engaged also," said Max.

Olga glanced up sharply, but he was not looking at her. He was occupied in pouring out a drink for his friend, which he brought to him almost immediately.

"That's how you like it measured to a drop. Sorry there's no ice to be had. It doesn't grow in these parts."

"I'd have got out the best glass if I'd known," murmured Olga regretfully.

Max threw up his head and laughed. "What a good thing I didn't tell her, eh, Kersley?" He leaned a careless hand on Sir Kersley's shoulder. "She doesn't know what a taste you have for the simple life."

Olga's eyes opened wide at the familiarity of speech and action. Sir Kersley faintly smiled.

"Since Miss Ratcliffe received me so kindly as a friend of yours," he said, "I hope she will continue to regard me in that light, and dispense with all unnecessary ceremony. Miss Ratcliffe, I drink to our better acquaintance!"

"How nice of you!" said Olga.

"I return thanks on Miss Ratcliffe's behalf," said Max. "How long has the Hunt-Goring monstrosity been here?"

Olga's face clouded. "Oh, ages! Do you think Nick will persuade him to go?"

"He can't stop to lunch if he isn't asked," said Max.

"An unwelcome visitor?" asked Sir Kersley.

"Yes, a neighbour of ours," explained Olga. "He lives about two miles away at a place called The Warren. He is retired from the Army. He shoots and hunts in the winter and loafs all the summer."

"A very horrid man," said Max with a twinkle. "He broke his thumb the other day and we haven't been quit of him since. You see, Miss Ratcliffe has a most beautiful friend staying with her with whom we all fall in love at first sight. Some of us fall out again and some of us don't. Hunt-Goring--presumably--belongs to the latter category."

"And you?" asked Sir Kersley.

"Oh, I am too busy for frivolities of that sort," said Max. "My mind is entirely occupied with drugs. Ask Miss Ratcliffe if it isn't!"

Olga looked a little scornful. It suddenly seemed to her that Max Wyndham required a snub. She was spared the trouble of administering one, however, by the reappearance of the housemaid.

She rose. "Do you want me, Ellen?"

"Oh, no, miss. It's all right," was Ellen's breezy reply. "I only just come to say as it was Dr. Wyndham as brought in them raspberries--early this morning."

Ellen disappeared as Max popped the cork of a soda-water bottle with unexpected violence. He clapped his hand over the top and carried it bubbling to the window.

"Awfully sorry," he said. "The beastly stuff is so up this weather."

Olga followed him with his glass. "Thank you for rescuing my raspberries," she said.

Max rubbed himself down with a handkerchief and took the glass from her. He was somewhat red in the face. He looked at her with a queer smile.

"Confound that girl!" he said.

"Have you discovered any specially beneficial properties In raspberries?" asked Sir Kersley in the tone of one seeking information.

"Not yet. I'm experimenting," said Max.

And Olga laughed, though she could scarcely have said why.

"There goes Nick, escorting the undesirable," observed Max, a moment later. "I begin to think there really must be a spark of genius in that little uncle of yours. Hunt-Goring looks as if he had been kicked, while the swagger of Five Foot Nothing defies description. Ah! And here comes Miss Campion! She looks as if--" He broke off short.

Olga bent forward sharply to catch a glimpse of her friend, and then as swiftly checked herself and remembered her guest. She moved sedately back into the room, only to discover that he also had risen, to look out of the window over Max's shoulder.

Instinctively she glanced at him. His deep-set eyes were fixed intently as if held by a vision. But his face was drawn in painful lines. She had a curious feeling of foreboding as she watched him. There was something fateful in his look. It passed in a moment. Almost before she knew it, he had turned back to her and was courteously conversing.

She gave him her attention with difficulty. Her ears were strained to catch the sound of Violet's approach. She was possessed by a ridiculous longing to rush out to her, to keep her from entering this man's presence, to warn her--to warn her--Of what? She had not the faintest idea.

By a great effort of will, she controlled herself, but the impulse yet remained--a striving, clamouring force, impotent but insistent.

There came the low, sweet notes of Violet's voice. She was singing a Spanish love-song.

Sir Kersley Whitton fell silent. He looked at the door. Max wheeled from the window. Olga waited tensely for the coming of her friend.

The door swung back and she entered. With her careless Southern grace she sauntered in upon them.

"Good Heavens!" she said, breaking off in the middle of her song. "Is it a party of mutes?"

Olga hastily and with evident constraint introduced the visitor, at sound of whose name Violet opened her beautiful eyes to their widest extent.

"How do you do? I had no idea a lion was expected. Why wasn't I told?"

"He is not one of the roaring kind," said Max.

Violet was looking with frank curiosity into Sir Kersley's face. "I'm sure I've met you somewhere," she said. "I wonder where."

He smiled slightly--a smile which to Olga's watching eyes was infinitely sad.

"I don't think you have," he said. "You may have seen my portrait."

"Ah, that's it!" She regarded him with a new interest. "I have! I believe I've got it somewhere."

"Do you collect the portraits of celebrities?" asked Max.

She shook her head. "Oh, no! It's among my mother's things. It must have been taken years ago. You were very handsome--in those days, weren't you?"

"Was I?" said Sir Kersley.

"Yes. That's why I kept you. There was a bit of your hair with it, but I burnt that." Violet's brows knitted suddenly. "My mother was handsome too," she said. "I wonder why you jilted her!"

Sir Kersley made a slight movement, so slight that it seemed almost involuntary. "That, my child," he said quietly, "is a very old story."

She laughed her gay, winning laugh. "Oh, of course! I expect you have jilted dozens since then. It's the way of the world, isn't it?"

He looked into the exquisite face, still faintly smiling. "It's not my way," he said.

There fell a sudden silence, and Olga sent an appealing glance towards Max. He came forward instantly and clapped a practical hand upon his friend's shoulder.

"Come and have a wash, Kersley!" he said, and with characteristic decision marched him away.

As they went, Violet broke once more into the low, sweet refrain of her Spanish love-song.

CHAPTER XIII
HER FATE

"How extraordinary men are!" Violet stretched her arms high above her head and let them fall. Her eyes were turned contemplatively towards the sinking sun. "This man for instance who might have been--who should have been--my father. He loved her, you know; he must have loved her, or he wouldn't have remained single all these years. And she worshipped him. Yet on the very eve of marriage--he jilted her. Extraordinary!"

"How do you know she worshipped him?" Olga spoke with slight constraint; it seemed to her that the matter was too sacred for casual discussion.

"How do I know? My dear, it is written in black and white on the back of his photograph. 'The only being I have it in me to love--sovereign lord of my heart!' Fancy writing that of any man! I couldn't, could you?"

"I don't know," said Olga soberly.

Violet laughed. "You're such a queer child! One day you come flying to me for protection, and almost the day after, you--"

"Please, Violet!" Olga broke in sharply. "You know I don't like it!"

"Oh, very well, my dear, very well! The subject is closed. We will return to the renowned Sir Kersley. He was watching me all luncheon-time. Did you notice?"

Olga had noticed. "Are you very like your mother?" she asked.

"I am better-looking than she ever was," said Violet, without vanity. "You see, my father, Judge Campion (he was nearly sixty when he married her, by the way), was considered the handsomest man in India at the time. She was a Californian, and very Southern in temperament, I believe. I often rather wish I could have seen her, though she would probably have hated me for not being the child of the man she loved. She died almost before I was born however. I daresay it's as well. I'm sure we shouldn't have got on."

"Violet! How can you say those things?"

"I always say whatever occurs to me," said Violet. "It's so much simpler. Mrs. Briggs was all the mother I ever knew or wanted. Of course as soon as Bruce settled down, I was taken to live with them. But I never liked either of them. They always resented the Judge's second marriage."

"Why didn't he take care of you himself?" asked Olga.

"My dear, he was dead. He died before she did. He was assassinated by a native before they had been married three months. I've always thought it was rather poor-spirited of her to die too; for of course she never cared for him. She must have married him only to pique Kersley. By the way, Major Hunt-Goring met them in his subaltern days. He said everyone fell in love with her. I supposed that included himself, and he smiled and said, 'Calf-love, senorita!' Allegro, I wonder if I really like that man."

"I'm sure you don't," said Olga quickly. "You couldn't."

"But I must amuse myself with someone," reasoned Violet pathetically. "Besides, he gives me such lovely cigarettes. Have one, Allegretto. Do!"

"No!" said Olga almost fiercely.

"I will, Miss Campion." Coolly Max came forward from the open window behind them. "You promised me one, you know."

"Did I?" She tossed him her cigarette-case carelessly. "They are not made for masculine palates. However, as you are so anxious--"

"Thank you," he said.

He opened the case. Violet was lying back with eyes half-closed. Olga's eyes were keenly watching. He glanced up and met them.

Abruptly he held up a warning finger. For one instant his eyes commanded her, compelled her. Then deliberately he extracted two cigarettes, slipped one into his pocket, stuck the other between his lips. She watched him in silence.

He returned the case to its owner with the slight, cynical smile she knew so well, and began to smoke.

"What time is Sir Kersley Whitton going?" asked Violet.

"Soon. His train starts at seven."

Olga rose suddenly. "Well, I am going to the evening service," she announced, with a touch of aggressiveness. "Are you coming, Violet?"

"No, dear," said Violet.

"Nor you either," said Max, blowing a cloud of smoke upwards.

She looked at him. "Why not?"

"Doctor's orders," he said imperturbably.

Violet laughed a little. Olga's face flamed.

"That is absurd! I am going!"

"Where's Nick?" said Max unexpectedly.

"Somewhere in the garden with Sir Kersley. I believe they went to see the vine."

"Then go to him," said Max; "tell him I have forbidden you to go to church to-night, and see what he says."

"I won't," said Olga.

She passed him without a second glance, and went indoors.

Violet laughed again. Max turned towards her. "Excuse me a moment!" he said, and therewith followed Olga into the house.

He overtook her at the foot of the stairs and stopped her without ceremony.

"Olga, what do you want to go to church for?"

She turned upon him in sudden, quivering anger. "Max, leave me alone! How dare you?"

His hand was on her arm. He kept it there. He looked steadily into her eyes.

"I dare because I must," he said. "You have had a tiring day, and you will end it with a racking headache if you are not careful."

"What does it matter?" she flashed back.

He did not answer her. "What are you so angry about?" he said. "Tell me!"

She was silent.

"Olga," he said, "it isn't quite fair of you to treat me like this."

"I shall treat you how I like," she said.

"No, no, you won't!" he said.

His voice was quiet, yet somehow it controlled her. Her wild rebellion began to die down. For a few seconds she stood in palpitating silence. Then, almost under her breath: "Max," she said, "why did you take that other cigarette?"

She saw him frown. "Why do you want to know?"

Her hands clenched unconsciously. "You are always watching Violet--always spying upon her. Why?"

"I can't tell you," he said briefly and sternly.

"You can," she said slowly, "if you will."

"I won't, then," said Max.

She flinched a little, but persisted. "Don't you think I have a right to know? It was I who brought her here. She is--in a sense--under my protection."

"What are you afraid of?" Max demanded curtly.

She shivered. "I don't know. I believe you are trying to get some power over her."

"You don't trust me?" he said, in the same curt tone.

"I don't know," she said again.

"You do know," he said.

She was silent. There seemed nothing left to say.

He released her arm slowly. "I am sorry I can't be quite open with you," he said. "But I will pledge you my word of honour that whatever I do is in your friend's interest. Will that make things any easier?"

Her eyes fell before his. "I--was a fool to ask you," she said.

He did not contradict the statement. "You are going to have a rest now," he said, "before the headache begins."

It had begun already, but she did not tell him so. "I would rather go to church," she said.

Max looked stubborn.

"I always do go," she protested into his silence. "It will do me good to go."

"All right," he said, with his one-sided smile. "Then I must go too, that's all."

"What for?" she asked quickly.

"To bring you home again when you begin to be ill."

"I'm not going to be ill!" she declared indignantly.

"No," he said. "And you're not going to church either. I'm sorry to thwart your pious intentions, but in your father's absence--"

"Oh, don't begin that!" she broke in irritably.

"Well, don't you be silly!" said Max good-humouredly. "You know you don't really want to go. It's only because you are cross with me."

"It isn't!" she said.

"All right. It isn't. Now go and lie down like a good child! I shall come and prescribe for you if you don't."

Was it mockery that glinted in his eyes as he thus smilingly quelled her resistance? She asked herself the question as she slowly mounted the stairs. It was a look she had come to know singularly well of late, a look that she resented instinctively because it made her feel so small and puny. It was a look that told her more decidedly than any words that he would have his way with her, resist him as she might.

She heard the church-bells ringing as she went to her room, but the impulse to obey their summons had wholly left her. She lay down wearily upon her bed. She wished there were not so many problems in life. She had an uneasy sensation as of being caught in the endless meshes of an invisible net that compassed her whichever way she turned.

She did not sleep, but the rest did her good. Undeniably it had been a tiring day. It was growing dark when a tentative scratch at the door told her of Nick's presence there.

She called him eagerly in. "Has Sir Kersley gone? I hope he didn't think me rude. Max made such a fuss about my resting. So I thought--"

"Quite right, my chicken!" Nick came softly to her side. "Max explained your absence. How's the head?"

"Oh, it's all right now. Nick, how soon will Dad and Muriel get your letters?"

"The day after to-morrow," said Nick.

She took his hand and squeezed it. "And we shall hear--when?"

"On Thursday night--with luck," said Nick.

She carried the hand impulsively to her lips. "Nick, you are a darling!"

He laughed. "Same to you! But we won't count on it too much or we may find ourselves crying for the moon, which is the silliest amusement I know. How do you like Sir Kersley Whitton?"

"Oh, very much. You heard about--about Violet's mother having been engaged to him, I suppose?"

"He told me himself," said Nick.

"What did he tell you, Nick?"

Nick hesitated momentarily. "He spoke in confidence," he said then.

"You won't tell me?" she asked quickly.

"Sorry; I can't," said Nick.

Olga sat up. A sudden idea had begun to illumine her brain. "Nick tell me this--anyhow! Did Violet's mother do--something dreadful?"

"Look here, Olga mia!" said Nick severely. "I know you can't help being a woman, but you're not to look at your neighbour's cards. It's against the rules."

She laughed a little. "Forgive me, Nick! I suppose supper is ready. I'll come down."

They went down together, to find Violet thrumming her mandolin in the twilight for the benefit of Max who was stretched at full length on the drawing-room sofa. The three boys were scudding about the garden like puppies.

As Olga and Nick entered, Violet looked up from her instrument. "I'm wondering if Sir Kersley would like to adopt me as well as Max. Do you think he would?"

"Exceedingly doubtful," said Max, rising.

"Why?"

"You would take up too much of his valuable time," he rejoined. "A man has to think of that, you know."

"Only horrid sordid men like you!" she retorted.

He uttered his dry laugh. "A professional man must think of his career."

She tossed her head. "Is that your creed--that there is no time for a woman in a professional man's life?"

Max laughed again. "She mustn't be too beautiful, anyhow."

She sprang suddenly to her feet. The mandolin jarred and jangled upon the ground. "Are you listening, Allegro?" she said, and through her deep voice there ran a sinister note that seemed to mingle, oddly vibrant, with the echoing strings of the instrument. "A professional man can admit only a plain woman into his life. The other kind is too distracting, since he must think of his career."

Nick cut in upon the words with the suddenness of a sabre-thrust. "Oh, we all say that till we meet the right woman, and then, be she lovely or hideous, the career bobs under like a float and ceases to count."

Max grunted. "Does it? Well, you ought to know."

"Let's go and have supper," said Olga, and turned from the room.

Violet stooped to pick up her mandolin. Nick lingered to summon the boys.

Max entered the dining-room in Olga's wake.

"Give me five minutes in the surgery presently," he said as he did so.

She glanced round at him sharply. "Why?"

He raised his brows. "Because I ask you to." He halted at the sideboard to cut some bread. "Going to refuse?" he asked.

"No," said Olga.

"Thanks!"

He went on with his cutting with the utmost serenity, and almost immediately they were joined by the rest of the party.

It was a somewhat rowdy meal. Violet appeared to be in one of her wildest moods. Her eyes shone like stars, and her merriment rippled forth continuously like a running stream. The boys were uproarious, and Nick was as one of them. In the midst of the fun and laughter, Olga sat rather silent. Max, drily humorous, took his customary somewhat supercilious share in the general conversation, but he made no attempt to draw her into it. She almost wished he would do so, for she felt as if he purposely held aloof from her.

Rising from the table at length, she was aware of an urgent impulse to shirk the interview for which he had made request. Valiantly she held it in check, but it did not have a very soothing effect upon her nerves.

The whole party rose together, and she slipped away to the kitchen to discuss domestic matters with the cook. She knew that Max saw her go, knew with sure intuition that he would seize the opportunity of her return to secure those few minutes alone with her that he had desired.

She was not mistaken. He was waiting for her by the baize door that led to the surgery when she emerged. With a brief, imperious gesture he invited her to pass through. The door closed behind them, and they were alone together.

"Come along into the consulting-room," said Max.

She turned thither without question. The room was in darkness. Max went forward and lighted the gas. Then, without pause, he wheeled and faced her.

"Are you angry with me still?"

Olga stood still by the table. "You haven't brought me in here to--quarrel, have you?" she said, a hint of desperation in her voice.

He smiled very slightly. "I have not. Sit down, won't you? You're looking very fagged."

He pulled forward an arm-chair, and she sat down with a nervous feeling that she was about to face a difficult situation. He relaxed into his favourite position, lounging against the table, his hands deep in his pockets.

"I want a word with you about Hunt-Goring," he said.

She looked up startled. "What about him?"

"He was here to-day, wasn't he?" proceeded Max.

"Yes. He came to see Violet."

Max grunted. "I suppose you know his little game?"

Olga's eyes widened. "No, I don't. What is it?"

He looked at her for a moment or two in silence. "Do you really imagine that you succeed in effacing yourself when you hide behind the beautiful Miss Campion?" he asked then.

The quick colour rose in her face. "What an absurd question!" she said.

"Why absurd?"

"As if anyone could possibly prefer me to Violet!"

"I know at least two who do," said Max.

"Who?" She flung the question almost angrily, as though she uttered it against her will.

Very deliberately he answered her. "Hunt-Goring and myself."

She started. Her face was burning now. Desperately she strove to cover her confusion, or at least to divert his attention from it. "I am quite sure Major Hunt-Goring doesn't! He--he wouldn't be so silly!"

"We are neither of us that," remarked Max with a twist of the lips that was hardly a smile. "I suppose you don't feel inclined to tell me exactly what the fellow's hold over you is."

"You said you didn't want to know!" she flashed back.

Max's green eyes were regarding her very intently. She resented their scrutiny hotly, but she could not bring herself to challenge it.

"Quite so, fair lady, I did," he responded imperturbably. "But as this affair has developed into something of the nature of a duel between the gallant major and myself it might be as well, for your sake as much as mine, that I should know what sort of ground I am standing on."

"A duel!" echoed Olga.

He smiled a little. "Hunt-Goring has no intention of letting you stay engaged to me if he can by any means prevent it."

"Oh, Max!" She met his look for an instant. "But--but--what can it really matter to him--one way or the other?"

"I conclude he wants you for himself," said Max.

She turned suddenly white. "He doesn't! He couldn't! Max!" She turned to him almost imploringly. "He doesn't really want me! It's not possible!"

"I should say he wants you very much indeed," said Max. "But you needn't be scared on that account. He isn't going to have you."

That reassured her somewhat. She essayed a shaky laugh. "You'll think me a shocking coward," she said. "But--do you know, I'm horribly frightened at him."

"Are you frightened at me too?" Max enquired unexpectedly.

She shook her head without looking at him.

"Quite sure?" he persisted.

She raised her eyes with a feeling that he must be convinced of this at all costs. "Of course I'm not," she said.

He leaned down towards her on one elbow, his hands still deep in his pockets. "Will you be engaged to me in earnest then?" he said. "Will you marry me?"

She stared at him. "Max!"

The humorous corner of his mouth went up. "Don't let me take your breath away! I say, what's the matter? You're as white as a ghost. Do you want some sal volatile?"

She forced a rather piteous smile. "No--no! I'm quite all right. But, Max--"

He pulled one hand free and laid it upon her clasped ones. "You can't stand me at any price, eh?"

She shook her head again. "Are you suggesting that I should--marry you, just to get away from Major Hunt-Goring?"

"I suppose you would rather marry me than him," said Max.

She laughed faintly. Her eyes were upon his hand--that hand which she had so ruthlessly stabbed not so very long before. The red scar yet remained. For the first time she felt genuinely sorry for having inflicted it.

"But there is no question of my marrying him, is there?" she said at last. "He has never even hinted at such a thing."

"That's true," said Max grimly. "You see, he has begun to realize by this time that you are not precisely fond of him."

She shivered involuntarily. "I hate him, Max!"

"He thrives on that," observed Max drily.

"Oh, not really!" she protested. "He couldn't want to marry me against my will."

"My good child," said Max, "if you had had the bad taste to flirt with him, he would have tired of you long ago. As it is--" he paused.

She looked up. "As it is?"

He uttered a curt laugh, and sat up, thrusting his hand back into his pocket. "Well--he won't be happy till he gets you."

Olga sprang to her feet. "But, Max, he couldn't marry me against my will! That sort of thing isn't done nowadays."

Max looked at her, his shrewd eyes very cynical. "Quite true!" he said.

"Then--then--" She stood hesitating, looking at him doubtfully--"what is there to be afraid of?" she asked at length.

"Oh, don't ask me!" said Max.

She felt the blood rush back to her face, and turned sharply from him.

"You--you don't help me much," she said.

He got to his feet abruptly. "You won't accept my help," he returned. "You've got yourself into a nasty hole, and you can't climb out alone, and you won't let me pull you out."

Olga was silent.

He stood a moment, then turned to the doctor's writing-table and sat down. "It's no good talking round and round," he said. "You'll have to tell Nick or your father. I can't do anything further. It's not in my power."

He opened a blotter with an air of finality, found a sheet of paper, and began to write.

Olga turned at the sound of his pen, and watched him dumbly. He had apparently dismissed her and her small affairs from his mind. His hand travelled with swift decision over the paper. He was evidently immersed in his own private concerns. He wrote rapidly and without a pause.

Very suddenly, without turning, he spoke again. "How did you like Kersley?"

The question astonished her. She had almost forgotten their visitor of a few hours before. But she managed to answer with enthusiasm.

"I liked him immensely."

"He is the greatest friend I possess," Max said, still writing. "He made me."

"I thought you seemed very intimate," observed Olga.

He laughed. "We are. I pulled him through a pretty stiff illness once. The mischief was that he wanted to die. I made him live." A note of grim triumph sounded in his voice, but he still continued to write.

"Was he grateful?" Olga asked.

"No. He fought like a mule. But I had my own way. It was tough work. I crocked up myself afterwards. And then it was his turn." Max jerked up his head. "After that," he said, "we became pals. He was only my patron before; since, we have been--something more than brothers."

He paused. Olga said nothing. She was wondering a little why he had chosen to make this confidence.

Suddenly he turned in his chair and enlightened her. "If you want to know what sort of animal I am," he said, his eyes going direct to hers, "if you want to know if I am worthy of a woman's confidence--in short, if I'm a white man or--the other thing, ask Kersley Whitton. For he is the only person in the world who knows."

The words were blunt, perhaps all the more so for the unwonted touch of fiery feeling which Olga was quick to detect in their utterance. They moved her strangely. It was almost as if he had flung open his soul to her, challenging her to enter and satisfy herself. And something very deep within her awoke and made swift response almost before she knew.

"But I don't need to ask him, Max," she said. "I know that for myself."

"Really?" said Max.

He stretched out his hand to her, without rising. His manner had changed completely. It was no longer passionate, but intensely quiet.

She came to him slowly, feeling compelled. She laid her hand in his.

His eyes were still upon hers. "I can't marry you against your will, can I?" he said. "It's not done nowadays."

She smiled a little. "I'm not afraid of that."

"Shall we go on being engaged, then," he said, "and see how we like it? We won't tell anyone yet--if you'd rather not."

She hesitated. "But--if I go to India with Nick?"

He frowned momentarily. "Well. I shouldn't ask you to marry me first."

Olga's face cleared somewhat. This was reassuring. It might very well lead to nothing after all.

"But," said Max impressively, "you wouldn't get engaged to any other fellow without letting me know."

She laughed at that. "I certainly shan't marry anyone out there."

Max looked grim. "You will give me the first refusal in any case?"

"But I needn't promise anything?" she said quickly.

"No, you needn't make any promise. Just bear me in mind, that's all; though I don't suppose for a moment that you could forget me if you tried," said Max with the utmost calmness.

"Why do you say that?" said Olga rather breathlessly.

It suddenly seemed to her that she had gone a little further than she had intended. She made an instinctive effort to get back while the way remained open.

But she was too late. She felt his hand tighten. For a moment she caught that gleam in his eyes which always disconcerted her.

And then it was gone, even as his hand released hers. He turned back to the writing-table with his supercilious smile.

"Because, fair lady," he said, "you have met your fate. If Hunt-Goring pesters you any further, of course you will let me know. Hadn't you better go now? The little god in the shrine will be jealous. And I have work to do."

And Olga went, somewhat precipitately, her heart throbbing in such a clamour of confused emotions that she hardly knew what had happened or even if she had any real cause for distress.

CHAPTER XIV
THE DARK HOUR

He had not made love to her! That was the thought uppermost in Olga's mind when the wild tumult of her spirit gradually subsided. He had not so much as touched upon his own feelings at all. Not the smallest reason had he given her for imagining that he cared for her, and very curiously this fact inclined her towards him more than anything else. Had he proposed to her in any more ardent fashion, she would have been scared away. Possibly he had fathomed this, and again possibly he had not wanted to be ardent. He was hard-headed, practical, in all he did. She was sure that his profession came first with him. He probably thought that a wife would be a useful accessory, and he was kind-hearted enough to be willing to do her a good turn at the same time that he provided for his own wants.

Violet's malicious declaration regarding a professional man's preference for a plain woman recurred to her at this point and made her feel a little cold. She did not know very much about men, and she had to admit to herself that it might quite easily be the truth. And then she thought of Hunt-Goring, reflecting with a shudder that that explanation would not account for his preference, if indeed what Max said were true and he actually did prefer her to Violet at whose feet he was so obviously worshipping.

She wondered if she ought to tell Max all about the man, and shuddered again at the bare thought. Not that there was much to tell, but even so, it was enough to set the blood racing in her veins and to make her hotly ashamed. She remembered with gratitude that he had not pressed her to be open on this point. He had left the matter almost at the first sigh of her reluctance to discuss it. She liked him for that. It furnished proof of a kindly consideration with which she had not otherwise credited him. It also furnished proof that he did not think very seriously of the matter. And for that also, lying awake in the moonlight, Olga secretly blessed her champion. Hard of head and cool of heart he might be, but he was undoubtedly a white man through and through.

From that she began to wonder if she really had met her fate, and if so, what life with him would be like, whether she would find it difficult, whether they would quarrel much, whether--whether they would ever fall in love. Of course there were plenty of people in the world who didn't, excellent people to whom romance in that form came not. Olga had always been quite sure that she was not romantic. She had always loved cricket and hockey and all outdoor sports. She had even--quite privately--been a little scornful over such shreds of romance as had come beneath her notice, dismissing them as paltry and ridiculous. Possibly also Violet's scoffing attitude towards her adorers had fostered her indifference.

No, on the whole she decided that it was verging upon foolish sentimentality to contemplate the possibility of falling in love. She was convinced Max would think so, even pictured to herself the one-sided smile that such nonsense would provoke. Doubtless he deemed her too sensible to waste time and thought over anything so absurd. He would even quite possibly be extremely annoyed if she ever ventured beyond the limits of rational friendship which he had marked out. Olga's sense of humour vibrated a little over this thought. He was always so scathing about her worship of Nick. He would certainly find no use for such feminine trash himself.

And yet--and yet--through her mind, vague as a dream, intangible yet not wholly elusive, there floated once more the memory of a voice that had reassured, a hand that had lulled her to rest. Had he really spoken that word of tenderness? Had his lips really touched her hair? Or had it all been a trick of her fancy already strung to fantastic imaginings by that magic draught?

She told herself that she would have given all she had to know if the dream were true and then found herself trembling from head to foot lest haply she might one day find that it had been so. Yes, on the whole she was relieved, thankful beyond measure, that he had not made love to her. Things were better as they were.

The church clock struck one as she arrived at this comfortable conclusion, and she turned her back to the moonlight and composed herself for slumber. Her thoughts wandered off down another track;--India as Nick had described it to her, a land of rivers and jungles, tigers and snakes, natives that were like monkeys, horses that moved like camels, pigs with tusks that had to be hunted and slain. Elephants too! He had left out the elephants, but they crowded in royal array into Olga's quick imagination. She and Nick would often go elephant-riding in the jungle. Mysterious word! It held her like a spell. Tall trees and winding undergrowth, a gloom well-nigh impenetrable, creatures that hid and spied upon them as they passed! Perhaps they would go tiger-hunting together. She thrilled at the thought, picturing herself creeping down one of those dim glades, rifle in hand, in search of the enemy. Nick would certainly have to teach her to shoot. He was a splendid shot, she knew. She believed that she could be a good shot too. It would not be easy to mark the striped body sliding through the undergrowth, but it would be a serious thing to miss. Olga's eyes closed. She began to wander down that jungle path, in search of the monster that lurked there. The lust of the hunt was upon her. She was about to secure the largest tiger that had ever been seen.

Her breath came quickly. Her blood ran hot. She forgot all lesser things in the ardour of the chase. The elephants had disappeared. She was running on foot through the jungle, eager and undismayed. Ah! What was that? Something that moved and was still. Two points that shone out suddenly ahead of her! Green eyes that gleamed triumphant mockery! Her heart stopped beating. Those eyes! Those eyes! They struck terror to her soul.

Headlong she turned and fled. Back through the jungle with the anguished speed of fear. The ground was sodden. It seemed to hold her flying feet. She tore them free, only to plunge deeper at every step, while behind her, swift and remorseless, followed her fate.

Wildly she struggled, powerless but persistent, till at last her strength was gone. She sank in utter impotence.

And then he came to her, he lifted her, he held her in his arms, pressed sickening kisses upon her lips; and suddenly she knew that she had fled from a myth to hurl herself into the power of her enemy. She had eluded her fate but to find herself at the mercy of a devil.

Gasping and half-suffocated she awoke, starting upright in a cold sweat of fear. Her heart was pumping as if it would burst. Her starting eyes searched and searched for the face of her captor. Her ears were strained for the sound of his soft, hateful laugh.

Ah! He was at the door! She heard a hand feeling along the panels, heard the handle turn! As one paralyzed she sat and waited.

Softly the door opened.

"Allegro!" whispered a hushed voice.

Olga turned swiftly with outflung arms. "Oh, come in, dear! Come in! I've had such a ghastly dream! You've come just in the nick of time."

Softly the door closed. Violet came to her, wonderful in the moonlight, a white mystery with shining eyes. She stood beside the bed, suffering herself to be clasped in her friend's arms.

"What have you been dreaming about?" she said.

"Oh, sheer nonsense of course," said Olga, hugging her in sheer relief. "All about that hateful Hunt-Goring man. Get into bed beside me and help me to forget him!"

But Violet remained where she was.

"Allegro," she said, "I've had--a bad dream--too."

"Have you, dear? How horrid!" said the sympathetic Olga. "What can we both have had for supper, I wonder?"

Violet uttered a hard little laugh. "Oh, it wasn't that! I haven't been asleep at all. I generally do sleep after Hunt-Goring's cigarettes. But to-night I couldn't. They only seemed to make things worse." She sat down abruptly on the edge of the bed. "Don't cuddle me, Allegro! I'm so hot."

Olga leaned back on her pillows, with a curious sense of something gone wrong. "Shall I light a candle?" she said.

"No. It's light enough. I hate an artificial glare, Allegro!"

"Well, dear?" said Olga gently.

Violet was sitting with her back to the moonlight, her face in deep shadow. Her black hair was loosely tied back and hung below her waist. Olga stretched out a hand and touched the silken ripples caressingly.

Violet threw back her head restlessly. "I'm going to give up Hunt-Goring," she said.

"My dear, I am glad!" said Olga fervently.

Violet laughed again. "I only encouraged him for the sake of his cigarettes. But

I'm going to give up them too. The opium habit grows on one so."

"Opium!" echoed Olga sharply.

"Opium, dear child! It's a cunning mixture and most seductive. The astute Max little knew what he was inhaling this afternoon." Violet's words had a curious tremor in them as of semi-tragic mirth.

Olga listened in horrified silence. So this was the secret of Max's peculiar behaviour! If he did not know by this time, then she did not know Max Wyndham.

"Yes," Violet went on. "Hunt-Goring is counting on those cigarettes of his to get me under his influence. I know. But I'm tired to death of the man. I'm going to pass him on to you."

"I hate him!" said Olga quickly.

"Oh, yes, dear! But he has his points. You'll find he can be quite amusing. Anyhow, take him off my hands for a spell. It isn't fair to make me do all your entertaining."

"Why don't you snub him?" said Olga, with some impatience. "It certainly isn't my fault that he comes here."

"Allegro, don't be horrid! I didn't refuse to help you when you wanted help." There was actually a pleading note in Violet's voice.

Olga responded to it instantly, with that ready warmth of hers that was the secret of her charm. "My dear, you know I would do anything in my power for you. But I can't--possibly--be nice to Major Hunt-Goring. I do detest him so."

"You detest Max Wyndham," said Violet quickly. "But you manage to be nice to him."

The words rang almost like an accusation. For the moment Olga felt quite incapable of replying. She lay in silence.

"Allegro!" Again she heard that note of pleading, vibrant this time, eager, almost passionate.

With an effort Olga brought herself to answer. "I've changed my mind about him. We are friends."

"Friends!" Violet sprang from the bed, and stood tense, quivering, with an arrow-like straightness that made her superb. Her eyes glittered as she faced the moonlight that poured through the unshaded window. "Does that mean you--care for him?" she demanded.

Olga hesitated. Violet in this mood was utterly unfamiliar to her, a strange and tragic personality before which she felt curiously small and ill at ease, even in some unaccountable fashion guilty.

"Dear, please don't ask me such startling questions!" she said. "I can't possibly answer you."

"Why not?" said Violet. Her hands were clenched. Her whole body seemed to be held in rigid control thereby.

"Because--" again Olga hesitated, considered, finally broke off lamely "I don't know."

"You do know!" There was actual ferocity in the open contradiction. Violet was directly facing her now. Her eyes shone so fiercely, so unnaturally, bright that a queer little sensation of doubt pricked Olga for the first time, setting every nerve and every muscle on the alert for she knew not what. "You do know, Allegro! And so do I!" The full voice took a deeper note, it throbbed the words. "Do you think I haven't watched you, seen what was going on? Do you think it has all been nothing to me--nothing to see you spoiling my chances day by day--nothing to feel you drawing him away from me--nothing to know--to know--" she suddenly flung her clenched hands wide open to the empty moonlight--"to know that you have set your heart on the only man I ever loved--you who wanted me to help you to get away from him--and have shouldered me aside?"

Her voice broke. She turned to the girl in the bed with eyes grown terrible in their wild anguish of pain. "Allegro!" she cried. "Allegro! Give him up! Give him up--if not for my sake--for your own! You couldn't--be happy--with him!"

With the words she seemed to crumple as though all power had suddenly left her, and sank downwards upon the floor, huddling against the bed with agonized sobbing, her black head bowed almost to the floor.

Olga was beside her in an instant, stooping over her, wrapping warm arms about her. "My darling, don't, don't!" she pleaded. "You know I would never do anything to hurt you. I never dreamed of this indeed--indeed!"

Violet made a passionate movement to thrust her away, but she would not suffer it. She held her close.

"Violet dearest, don't cry like this! There is no need for it. Really, you needn't be so distressed. There, darling, come into bed with me. You'll be ill if you cry so.

Violet! Violet!"

But Violet was utterly beyond control, and her paroxysm of weeping only grew more and more violent, till after some minutes Olga became seriously frightened. She stood up, and began to ask herself what she must do.

It was then that to her intense relief the door slid open and Nick's head was poked enquiringly in.

"Hullo!" he said softly. "Anything wrong?"

She motioned him to enter, being on the verge of tears herself.

"Nick, she's hysterical! What am I to do?"

"Better fetch Max," he said.

But the words were hardly out of his mouth before Max himself pushed the door wide open and entered!

He bore a small lamp in his hand which threw his somewhat grim features into strong relief. He made a weird figure in his night-attire, and his red hair looked as if it had been brushed straight on end.

He looked at neither Olga nor Nick, merely for a single instant at the shivering, sobbing girl on the floor, ere he set down his lamp with decision and turned to the washing-stand.

Olga stood and watched him as one fascinated. He was quite deliberate in all he did. With the utmost calmness he took up a tumbler and poured out some cold water.

Then very quietly he went to Violet, bent over her, gathered the dark hair back upon her shoulders.

She started at his touch, started and cried out in wild alarm, raising her head. And Max, with a set intention which seemed to Olga scarcely short of brutal, dashed a spray of water full into her deathly face.

She flinched away from him with another cry, gasping for breath and staring up at him as one in nightmare terror.

"You!" she uttered voicelessly. "You!"

He held what was left of the water to her lips. "Drink!" he said with insistence.

She tried feebly to resist. Her teeth chattered against the glass.

"Drink!" Max said again relentlessly.

Olga stooped swiftly forward and slipped a supporting arm around her. Violet drank a little, and turned to her, weakly sobbing.

"Allegro, send him away! Send him away!"

"Yes, dear, yes; he's going now," murmured Olga soothingly.

Max gave the glass to Nick with the absolute detachment of the professional man, and proceeded to take Violet's pulse. He watched her closely as he did so, with shaggy brows drawn down.

Violet gazed at him wide-eyed. She was no longer sobbing, but she shivered from head to foot.

"Yes," said Max at last, in the tone of one continuing an interrupted conversation. "Well, now you are going back to bed."

Violet shrank against Olga. "Let me stay with you, Allegro!" she murmured piteously.

"Of course you shall, dear," Olga made quick reply.

But in the same instant she saw Max elevate one eyebrow and knew that this suggestion did not meet with his approval.

"You will sleep better in your own room," he said. "Come along! Let me help you."

He put his arm about her and lifted her to her feet; but she clung fast to Olga still.

"I won't go without you, Allegro," she cried hysterically.

"My dear, of course not!" Olga answered. She caught up her dressing-gown and wrapped it round her friend. "You're as cold as ice," she said.

They helped her back to her own room between them, almost carrying her, for she seemed to have no strength left.

Max said nothing further of any sort till she was safely in bed, then somewhat brusquely he turned to Olga.

"Put on your dressing-gown and go down to the surgery! I want a bottle out of the cupboard there. It's a poison bottle, labelled P.K.R.; you can't mistake it. Third shelf, left-hand corner. The keys are in your father's desk. You know where. Put on your slippers too, and take a candle! Mind you don't tumble downstairs!" His eyes travelled to the doorway where Nick hovered. "Go with her, will you?" he said. "Bring back a medicine-glass too! There's one on the surgery mantelpiece."

He turned back to Violet again, stooping low over her, his hand upon her wrist.

Olga fled upon her errand with the speed of a hare, leaving Nick to follow with a candle. Even as she went she heard a cry behind her, but she sped on with a feeling that Max was compelling her.

When Nick joined her a few seconds later she had already found the keys and was fumbling in the dark for the cupboard-lock.

They found the medicine-bottle exactly where Max had said, and Olga snatched it out, seized the glass, and was gone. She was back again in Violet's bedroom barely two minutes after she had left it, but the instant she entered she was conscious of a change. Violet was lying quite straight and stiff with glassy eyes upturned. Max was bending over her, tight-lipped, motionless, intent. He spoke without turning his head.

"Just a teaspoonful--not a drop more. The rest water."

Olga poured out the dose, controlling her hands with difficulty.

"Not a drop more," he reiterated. "There's sudden death in that. Finished? Then give it to me!"

He raised Violet up in bed and took the glass from Olga. A curious perfume filled the room--a scent familiar but elusive. Olga stood breathing it, wondering what it brought to mind.

Max held the glass against the pale lips, and suddenly she remembered. It was the magic draught he had given to her two days before.

Violet seemed to be unconscious, but she drank nevertheless very slowly, with long pauses in between. Gradually the glassy look passed from her eyes, the long lashes drooped.

Max held out the empty glass to Olga. "You go back to bed now," he said. "She will sleep for some time."

"I can't leave her," Olga whispered.

He was lowering the senseless girl upon the pillow and made no reply. Having done so, he stooped and set his ear to her heart for a space of several seconds. Then he stood up and turned quietly round.

"You can't do anything more. Thanks for fetching that stuff! Why didn't you put on your slippers as I told you?"

His manner was perfectly normal. He left the bedside and took up the medicine-bottle, holding it against the lamp.

"Are you sure she will be all right?" whispered Olga.

"Quite sure," he said.

She turned her attention to the bottle also. "What is that stuff?" she asked.

He looked at her, and for an instant she saw his sardonic smile. "It's sudden death if you take enough of it," he said.

"Yes, I know," said Olga. "It's what you call 'the pain-killer,' isn't it?"

"Exactly," said Max, "Hence the legend on the label. But what do you know about the pain-killer? Who told you about it? I know I didn't."

"It was Mrs. Briggs," said Olga, and then turned hotly crimson under his eyes.

There fell a sudden silence; then, "You go back to bed," said Max. "And you are to settle down and sleep, mind. Don't lie awake and listen."

"You are sure she will sleep till morning?" said Olga, lingering by the bed.

"Yes." He put his hand on her shoulder, and wheeled her towards the door. "There's Nick waiting to tuck you up. Run along! I am going myself immediately."

She went, more to escape from his presence than for any other reason. There was undoubtedly something formidable about Max Wyndham at that moment notwithstanding his light speech, something that underlay his silence, making her curiously afraid thereof.

She did not lie and listen when she returned to bed, but a very long time passed before she slept.

CHAPTER XV
THE AWAKENING

Olga slept late on the following morning, awaking at length with a wild sense of dismay at having done so. She leaped up as the vivid memory of the night's happenings rushed upon her, and, seizing her dressing-gown, ran out into the passage and so to Violet's room.

Very softly she turned the door-handle, and peeped in. The curtains were drawn, but the morning-breeze blew them inwards, admitting the full daylight. Violet was lying awake with her face to the door.

"That you, Allegro? Come in!" she called. "I've had the oddest night."

Olga slipped in and went to her. The beautiful eyes were very wide open. They gazed up at her wonderingly. The forehead above them was slightly drawn.

"I've been dead," said Violet slowly. "I've just come to life."

"My darling!" Olga said.

"Yes. Isn't it queer? It was so strange, Allegro. I went right up to the very door of Paradise. But I suffered a lot first. I suffered--horribly. And when I got there--the door was shut in my face." Violet uttered a curious little laugh that had in it a note of pain. "That was when I died," she said.

Olga stooped to kiss her. "It was a dream," she said.

"Oh, but it wasn't," said Violet. She threw her arms unexpectedly around Olga's neck, and held her very tightly, as if she were afraid. "Allegro," she said under her breath, "I believe I left my soul behind. It's up there, waiting for the door to open. I hope it won't get lost."

The words sent a sharp chill through Olga. She held her friend closely, protectingly. "Darling, I don't think you are quite awake yet," she said very tenderly. "Stay in bed for a little while, and I'll dress and get your breakfast."

"Oh, no! Oh, no! I'm going to get up!" Quickly Violet made reply, almost feverishly. "I couldn't possibly lie still and do nothing. I've got to find the way out. It's very dark, but I daresay I shall manage. Blind people learn to, don't they? And that's what has happened to me, really. I've gone blind, Allegro, blind inside."

She put Olga from her, and prepared to rise. Her eyes were very bright, but there was a curiously furtive look about them. They seemed afraid to look.

"Wait anyhow till you have had some tea," urged Olga. "I'll run down and order it."

"No, don't go, Allegro! Don't leave me! I don't want to be alone." Impetuously Violet stretched out her hands to her. "Don't go!" she pleaded. "I'm so afraid--he--will come. And I don't want him to know anything about it. You won't tell him? Promise, Allegro!"

"Who, dear?" Olga asked the question though she knew the inevitable answer. She was becoming seriously uneasy, though she sought to reassure herself with the thought that Violet's nerves were of the high-strung order and could scarcely have failed to suffer from the strain they had undergone.

Violet answered her with obvious impatience. "Why, Max, of course! Who else? Promise you won't tell him, Allegro!"

"Tell him what, dear?" questioned Olga.

Violet started up from her bed and sprang to the open door. She closed it and stood facing Olga with arms outstretched across it. Her breath came pantingly through dilated nostrils.

"You're not to tell him--not to tell him--what I have just told you. If he knows I'm trying to get out, he'll stop me. Don't you understand? Oh, don't you understand?" A fury of impatience sounded in her voice; she quivered from head to foot. "He keeps the door," she said. "And he never sleeps. Why, even last night he was there. Didn't you see him? Those dreadful green eyes--like--like a tiger in the dark? Olga--" suddenly and passionately she began to plead "--you won't tell him, dearest! You couldn't be so cruel! Can't you see what it means to me? Don't you realize that it's my better self that's gone? And I've got to follow--I must follow. If he doesn't know, perhaps I shall manage to slip through when he isn't looking. Dear, you wouldn't have me kept a prisoner--against my will? He's so hard, Allegro--so hard and merciless. And he keeps the door so close. I should have got away last night if it hadn't been for him. So you won't tell him, will you? You'll promise me you won't!"

Olga listened to the appeal with a heart that seemed turned to stone. She knew not what to say or do.

"It's my only chance!" urged Violet, in a voice that was beginning to break. "Oh, how can you hesitate? Are you all in league against me? Allegro! Allegro!"

"There, dear, there! It's all right. Don't worry!" Swiftly Olga collected herself and spoke. "There's nothing to be afraid of. No one shall keep you against your will."

"You promise, Allegro?" Violet looked at her doubtfully, yet as if she wished to be reassured.

"Yes, of course, dear. Now really you must let me go and dress. It's eight o'clock, and I shan't be ready for breakfast."

Violet came slowly away from the door. She did not look wholly satisfied, but she said no more; and Olga hastened back to her room with deadly misgiving at her heart. She felt as if there were tragedy in the very air. It seemed to be closing in upon her, a dread mist of unfathomable possibilities.

She dressed with nervous haste, and hurried downstairs, wondering a little that Max had not bestirred himself to ascertain the effect of his treatment.

She wondered still more when she found him calmly established behind the morning paper in an arm-chair in the dining-room. He laid it aside at her entrance, and rose to greet her.

"Well?" he said, with her hand in his.

She looked up to find his eyes piercingly upon her. They shone intensely green in the morning light.

She removed her hand somewhat abruptly. There was something in his manner that she resented, without knowing why. "Well?" she said.

"How do you find yourself this morning?" asked Max.

"I'm perfectly well, thank you," said Olga briefly.

"Ready to start jam-making?" he suggested.

Olga went to the coffee-urn. "I really don't know," she said. "I've had other things to think about."

He smiled a little, the superior, one-sided smile she most detested. "You mustn't let the fruit go bad," he observed, "after all my trouble."

Olga peered into the coffee-urn, without replying. Max in an exasperating mood could be very exasperating indeed. He pulled out the chair next to her, and sat down.

"And how is the beautiful Miss Campion?" he said.

Olga looked at him. She could not help it.

"Well?" said Max.

She coloured hotly. "I wonder you haven't been to see for yourself," she said.

"Perhaps I have," said Max.

She turned from his open scrutiny, and began to pour out the coffee with a hand not wholly steady.

"I presume--if you had--you wouldn't ask me," she said.

He lodged his chin on his hand, the better to study her. "In making that presumption, fair lady," he said, "you are not wholly justified. Has it never occurred to you that I might entertain a certain veneration for your opinion on a limited number of subjects?"

Olga set down the coffee-urn and squarely turned upon him. "Have you seen her this morning?" she asked him point-blank.

"Yes, I have seen her," he said.

"Then you know as much as I do," said Olga.

"Not quite," he returned. "I soon shall however. Did she seem pleased to see you this morning?"

"Of course," said Olga.

"And why 'of course'? Do you never disagree?" He asked the question banteringly, yet his eyes were still upon her, unflaggingly intent.

"We never quarrel," said Olga.

"I see. You have differences of opinion; is that it? And what happens then? Is there never a tug of war?" Max's smile became speculative.

"No, never," said Olga.

"Never?" He raised his red brows incredulously. "Do you mean to say you give in to her at every turn? She can be fairly exacting, I should imagine."

"I would give her anything she really wanted if it lay in my power," said Olga very steadily.

"Would you?" said Max. He suddenly ceased to smile. "Even if it chanced to be something you wanted rather badly yourself?"

She nodded. "Wouldn't you do as much for someone you loved?"

"That depends," said Max cautiously.

"Oh, of course!" said Olga quickly. "You're a man!"

He laughed. "You've made that remark before. I assure you I can't help it. No, I certainly wouldn't place all my possessions at the disposal of even my best friend. There would always be--reservations."

He looked at her with a smile in his eyes, but Olga did not respond to it. An inner voice had suddenly warned her to step warily. She took up the coffee-urn again.

"I wouldn't give much for that kind of friendship," she said.

"But is it always in one's power to pass on one's possessions?" questioned Max. "I maintain that the possessions are entitled to a voice in the matter."

"I don't understand you," said Olga, in a tone that implied that she had no desire to do so.

"No?" said Max indifferently. "Well, I think unselfishness should never be carried to extremes. Some women have such a passion for self-sacrifice that they will stick at nothing to satisfy it. The result is that unwilling victims get offered up, and you will admit that that is scarcely fair."

Olga handed him his coffee. "Will you cut the ham, please?" she said.

"Do you catch my meaning yet?" asked Max, not to be thwarted.

She shook her head. "But really it doesn't matter, and it's getting late."

"Sorry to keep you," he replied imperturbably, "but when I take the trouble to expound my views, I like to guard against any misunderstanding. Just tell me this, and I shall be satisfied. If you were at a ball, and you had a partner you liked and who liked you, and you came upon your friend crying because she wanted that particular partner--would you give him up to her?"

"Of course I should," said Olga. "I don't call that a very serious self-sacrifice."

"No?" said Max. He gave her a very peculiar look, and pursed his lips for an instant as if about to whistle. "And if the unfortunate partner objected?"

Olga began vigorously to cut some bread. "He would have to put up with it," she said.

Max rose without comment and went to the ham. There followed a somewhat marked silence as he commenced to carve it. Then: "Pardon my persistence, fair lady," he said. "But just one more question--if you've no objection. Suppose you were my partner and Hunt-Goring the forlorn friend, do you think I should be justified in passing you on to him? It would be a considerable self-sacrifice on my part."

"Oh, really!" exclaimed Olga, in hot exasperation. "What absurd question will you ask next?"

He looked across at her with a complacent smile. "You see, I'm only a man," he said coolly. "But that illustrates my point. It's not always possible to pass on all one's possessions, is it? It may answer in theory but not in practice. I think you catch my meaning now?"

"Hadn't you better have your breakfast?" said Olga, with a glance at the clock.

Max's eyes followed hers. "Where's Nick? Has he overslept himself?"

"He has not," said Nick, entering at the moment. "It is not a habit of his. Well, Olga, my child, how goes the world this morning?"

She turned with relief to greet him. His genial personality was wonderfully reassuring. He kissed her lightly, and took up his correspondence.

"Let me open them!" she said.

He stood by and watched her while she did it. She was very deft in all her ways, but to-day for some reason her hands were not quite so steady as usual.

Nick threw a sudden glance across at Max while he waited. "Miss Campion all right this morning?" he asked.

"Apparently," said Max, staring deliberately at a point some inches above Nick's head.

Nick pivoted round abruptly, and found Violet standing in the doorway directly behind him. He went instantly to meet her.

"Hullo, Miss Campion! You're just in time for breakfast. Come and have some!"

His tone was brisk and kindly. He took her hand and drew her forward. She submitted listlessly. Her face was white and her eyes deeply shadowed. She scarcely raised them as she advanced.

"Hullo, Nick!" she said indifferently. "Hullo, Allegro! No, I don't want any breakfast. I'm not hungry to-day." She reached the table, and for the first time seemed to become aware of Max, seated on the opposite side of it.

Her eyes suddenly opened wide. She stood still and faced him. "I want my cigarettes," she said, with slow emphasis.

Olga glanced at him sharply, in apprehension of she knew not what. Max's face, however, expressed no anxiety. He even faintly smiled.

"What! Haven't you got any? I shall be happy to supply you with some," he said, feeling in his pocket for his own case.

She leaned her hands upon the table in a peculiar, crouching attitude that struck Olga as curiously suggestive of an angry animal.

"I don't want yours," she said, in a deep voice that sounded almost like a menace. "I want my own!"

Max looked straight at her for a few seconds without speaking. Then, "I am sorry," he said very deliberately. "But you mustn't smoke that sort any more. They are not good for you."

"And you have dared to take them away?" she said.

He shrugged his shoulders. "I had no choice."

"No choice!" She echoed the words in a voice that vibrated very strangely. "You speak as if--as if--you had a right to confiscate my property."

"I have a right to confiscate that sort," said Max.

"What right?" She flung the question like a challenge, and as she flung it she straightened herself in sudden splendid defiance. All the pallor had gone from her face. She glowed with fierce, pulsing life.

Max remained looking at her. There was a glint of mercilessness in his eyes. "What right?" he repeated slowly. "If you saw a blind man walking over a precipice, would you say you hadn't the right to stop him?"

"I am not blind!" she flung back at him. "And I refuse to be stopped by you--or anyone!"

Max raised his red brows. "You amaze me," he said. "Then you are aware of the precipice?"

She clenched her hands. "I know what I am doing--yes! And I can guide myself. I refuse to be guided by you!"

"Violet!" Nervously Olga interposed. "Never mind now, dear! Do sit down and have some breakfast! The eggs are getting cold."

"Quite so," said Nick, putting down his letters abruptly. "The coffee also. Olga, you may tear up all my correspondence. It's nothing but bills. Miss Campion, wouldn't you like to butter some toast for me? You do it better than anyone I know. And I'm deuced hungry."

She turned away half-mechanically, met his smile of cheery effrontery, and suddenly flashed him a smile in return.

"What a gross flatterer you are!" she said "Allegro, aren't you jealous? Which piece of toast do you fancy, Nick? Can I cut up some ham for you as well?"

The tension was over and Olga breathed again. Max continued his breakfast with an inscrutable countenance, finished it, and departed to the surgery.

Violet did not so much as glance up at his departure. She was wrangling with Nick over the best means of attacking a boiled egg with one hand.

There was no longer the faintest hint of tragedy in her demeanour. Yet Olga went about her own duties with a heart like lead. She was beginning to understand Max's attitude at last; and it filled her with misgiving.

CHAPTER XVI
SECRETS

The rest of that day was passed in so ordinary a fashion that Olga found herself wondering now and then if she could by any chance have dreamed the events of the night.

During the whole of the morning she was occupied with her jam-making, while Violet lazed in the garden. Nick had planned a motor-ride in the afternoon, and they went for miles, returning barely in time for dinner. Violet was in excellent spirits throughout, and seemed unconscious of fatigue, though Olga was so weary that she nearly fell asleep in the drawing-room after the meal. Max was in one of his preoccupied moods, and scarcely addressed a word to anyone. Only when he bade her good-night she had a curious feeling that his hand-grip was intended to convey something more than mere convention demanded. She withdrew her own hand very quickly. For some reason she was feeling a little afraid of Max.

Yet on the following morning, so casual was his greeting that she felt oddly vexed with him as well as with herself, and was even glad when Violet sauntered down late as usual and claimed his attention. Violet, it seemed, had decided to ignore his decidedly arbitrary treatment of her. She had also apparently given up smoking, for she made no further reference to her vanished cigarettes, a piece of docility over which Olga, who had known her intimately for some years, marvelled much.

She was obliged to leave her that afternoon to go to tea with an old patient of her father's who lived at the other end of the parish, Violet firmly refusing at the last moment to accompany her thither. Nick had promised to coach the boys at cricket practice that day, and Olga departed with a slight feeling of uneasiness and a determination to return as early as possible.

It was not, however, easy to curtail her visit. The patient was a garrulous old woman, and Olga was kept standing on the point of departure for a full half-hour. In the end she almost wrenched herself free and hurried home at a pace that brought her finally to her own door so hot and breathless that she was obliged to sit down and gasp in the hall before she could summon the strength to investigate any further.

Recovering at length, she went in search of Violet, and found her lounging under the limes in luxurious coolness with a book.

She glanced up from this at Olga's approach and smiled. There was a sparkle in her eyes that made her very alluring.

"Poor child! How hot you are! People with your complexion never ought to get hot. What have you been doing?"

She stretched a lazy hand of welcome, as Olga subsided upon the grass beside her.

"I've been hurrying back," Olga explained. "I thought you would be lonely."

"Oh dear, no! Not in the least." Violet glanced down at her book, a little ruminative smile curving the corners of her red mouth.

Olga peered at the volume. "What is it? Something respectable for once?"

"Not in the least. It is French and very highly flavoured. I daresay you wouldn't understand it, dear," said Violet. "You're such an ingenue ."

Olga made a grimace. "I'd rather not understand some things," she said bluntly.

Violet uttered a low laugh. "Dear child, you are so unsophisticated! When are you going to grow up?"

"I am grown up," said Olga. "But I don't see the use of studying the horrid side of life. I think it's a waste of time."

"There we differ," smiled Violet. "Perhaps, however, it doesn't matter so much in your case. It is only women who travel and see the world who really need to be upon their guard."

Olga smiled also at that. "Shall I tell you a secret?" she said.

"Do, dear!" Violet instantly stiffened to attention. The smile went out of her face; Olga almost fancied that she looked apprehensive.

"It's quite a selfish one," she said, seeking instinctively to reassure her. "It's only that--perhaps--when the autumn comes--I may go to India with Nick."

"Oh! Really! My dear, how thrilling!" The words came with a rush that sounded as if the speaker were wholeheartedly relieved. The smile flashed back into Violet's face. She lay back in her chair with the indolent grace that usually characterized her movements. "Really!" she said again. "Tell me all about it."

Olga told her forthwith, painting the prospect in the brilliant colours with which her vivid imagination had clothed it, while Violet listened, interested and amused.

"You'll remember it's a secret," she wound up. "We haven't heard from Dad or Muriel yet, and of course nothing can be settled till we do. If either should object, of course it won't come off."

"Oh, I won't tell a soul," Violet promised. "How exciting if you go, Allegro! I wonder if you will get married."

Olga laughed light-heartedly. "As if I should waste my precious time like that! No, no! If I go, I shall fill up every minute of the time with adventures. I shall go tiger-hunting with Nick, and pig-sticking, and riding, and--oh, scores of things. Be-sides, they're nearly all Indians at Sharapura, and one couldn't marry an Indian!"

"Couldn't one?" said Violet. "Wouldn't you like to be a ranee, Allegro? I would!" She looked at Olga with kindling eyes. "Just think of it, dear! The power, the mag-nificence, the jewels! Oh, I believe I'd do anything for riches."

"Violet! I wouldn't!"

Olga spoke with strong emphasis and Violet laughed--a short, hard laugh. "Oh, no, you wouldn't, I know! You were born to be a slave. But I wasn't. I was born to be a queen, and a queen I'll be--or die!" She suddenly glanced about her with the peculiar, furtive look that Olga had noticed the day before. "That's why I wouldn't marry Max Wyndham," she said, "for all the riches in the world! He is the One Impossible."

Olga felt her colour rising. She made response with an effort. "Don't you like him, then?"

"Like him!" Violet's eyes came down to her. They expressed a fiery chafing at restraint that made her think of a wild creature caged. "My dear, what has that to do with it? I wouldn't marry a man who didn't worship me, whatever my own feelings might be; and it isn't in him to worship any woman. No, he would only grind me under his heel, and I should probably kill him in the end and myself too." A passionate note crept into the deep voice. It seemed to quiver on the verge of tragedy; and then again quite suddenly she laughed. "But I don't feel in the least murderous," she said. "In fact, I'm at peace with all the world just now. Listen, Allegro! You've told me your secret. I'll tell you one of mine. But you must swear on your sacred honour that you will never repeat it to a soul."

Olga was in a fashion used to this form of affidavit. She had been the recipient of Violet's secrets before. She gave the required pledge with the utmost simplicity, little dreaming how soon she was to repent of it.

Violet leaned towards her and spoke in low, confidential tones. "So amusing, dear! I know you won't mind for once. It's Hunt-Goring again. He really is too ridiculous for words. He has hired a yacht, you must know--a nice little steam-yacht, Allegro. He walked over this afternoon to tell me about it. Don't look so horrified! There's much worse to come." She laughed again under her breath. "He has asked me--in fact, persuaded me--to go for a little trip in it one day next week. Of course I said No at first; and then he said you could come too to make it proper; so I consented. I'm sure you won't mind for once, and a breath of sea air will do me good."

She laid a hand of careless coaxing upon Olga's shoulder. But Olga's demeanour was very far from acquiescent.

"But, Violet!" she exclaimed, "how could you possibly accept for me? I'm not going! No; indeed, I'm not! Neither must you. It's the maddest project I ever heard of! Whatever made you imagine for one moment that I would agree to go?"

"Don't be ridiculous, Allegro!" Violet sounded quite unmoved. "Of course you'll go, unless--" she smiled a trifle maliciously--"you mean me to go alone, as I certainly shall if you are going to be tiresome about it. You wouldn't like me to do that, I suppose?"

Olga gazed at her helplessly. "Violet, what am I to say to you? How could you and I go off for a whole day with that detestable man? Why, it--it would start everyone talking!"

"My dear, no one will know," said Violet with composure. "Haven't you sworn to keep it a dead secret? He won't talk and neither shall I. So, you see, it's all perfectly safe. Not that there would be anything improper about it in any case. He is as old as you and me put together,--older I should say."

"Oh, but he's such a fiend!" burst forth Olga. "You said you were going to give him up only the other night."

"When?" said Violet sharply.

Olga hesitated. It was the first time she had made direct reference to that midnight episode.

"When did I say that?" insisted Violet.

Half-reluctantly Olga made reply, while Violet leaned forward and listened intently. "The night before last. You came to my room late, don't you remember?"

Violet's eyes had a startled look. "Yes?" she breathed. "Yes? What else?"

Olga looked straight up at her. "Dear, I don't think we need talk about it, need we? You were not yourself. I think you were half-asleep. You had been smoking those hateful cigarettes."

"Ah, but tell me!" insisted Violet. "Why did I come to you? What did I say? Was--was Max there?"

"He came in," faltered Olga. "He--guessed you weren't well. He helped you back to your own room. Don't you remember?"

"Yes--yes--I remember!" Violet's brows were drawn with the effort; there was a look of dawning horror in her eyes. "I remember, Allegro!" she said, speaking rapidly. "He--he was very brutal to me, wasn't he? He made me tell him where to find the cigarettes, and then--and then--yes, he took them away. I've hated him ever since." Again that vindictive note sounded in her voice. "I won't bear brutality from any man," she said. "Do you know, if I didn't hate him, I believe I should be afraid of him? I know you are, Allegro."

"Perhaps; a little," Olga admitted.

"Ah! I knew it. He can do anything he likes with you. But I am different." She lifted her head proudly. "I am no man's slave," she said. "He thinks that he has only to speak, and I shall obey. He was never more mistaken in his life."

"But, Violet, he was only treating you as a patient," Olga protested. "And he only took the cigarettes because--"

"I know why he took them." Quickly Violet interrupted. "And remember this, Allegro! Whatever happens to me in the future you must never, never let him attend me again. I suffered more from his treatment than I have ever suffered before, and I can never go through it again. You understand?" She looked at Olga with eyes that had in them the memory of a great pain. "It was torture," she said. "He forced his will upon mine. He crushed me down, so that I was at his mercy. It was like an overpowering weight. I thought my heart would stop. I don't know--even now--how it was I didn't die."

"He gave you the pain-killer, dear," said Olga soothingly. "That was what made you well again."

"The pain-killer!" Violet gazed at her bewildered. "What is--the pain-killer?" she said.

Olga shook her head. "I don't know what it is. He wouldn't tell me. He calls it--sudden death."

Violet gave a great start. "Good heavens, Allegro! And he gave me that?"

"Only enough to make you sleep," explained Olga. "He gave me some the other day, when the heat upset me. I liked it."

Violet's eyes were glittering very strangely. "And you--came back again after it?" she said. "Allegro, are you--sure?"

"Of course," said Olga. "I don't know what you mean, dear. Of course I came back, or I shouldn't be here now."

"No--no, of course not!" Violet lay back in her chair, gazing straight up through the limes at the flawless August sky. "So that is why I didn't die," she said. "He only let me go--half-way. If I'd only had a little more--a little more--" She broke off suddenly and threw a quick side glance at Olga. "What queer creatures doctors are!" she said. "They spend their whole lives fighting, with the certainty that they are bound to be conquered in the end."

"They are splendid!" said Olga, with shining eyes.

"Oh, do you think so? I never can. If they fought suffering only, it would be a different thing. That I could admire. But to fight death--" Violet made a curious little gesture of the hands--"it seems to me like tilting at a windmill," she said. "Everyone must die sooner or later."

"But no one wants to go before his time," observed a cool voice behind them. "Or if he does, he's a shirker and deserves to be kicked."

Both girls started as Max strolled carelessly up, hands in pockets, and propped himself against a tree close by.

His eyes travelled over Olga's face as he did so. "You've been overheated," he remarked.

She pulled her hat forward with a nervous jerk. "Who can help it this weather?"

He grunted disapproval. "You never see me in that condition. Pray continue your oration, Miss Campion! It was not my intention to interrupt."

But Violet had suddenly reopened her book and buried herself therein.

Max twisted his neck and peered over. After a brief space he grunted again and relaxed against the tree.

"Do you read French?" Olga asked, feeling the silence to be slightly oppressive.

He laughed drily. "Not that sort. I have no taste for it."

"But you know the language?" Olga persisted, still striving against silence.

"I've studied it," said Max. He paused a moment; then, "The best fellow I ever knew was a Frenchman," he said.

She looked up at him, caught by something in his tone. "A friend of yours?"

He took off his hat with a reverence which she would have deemed utterly foreign to his nature. "Yes, a friend," he said. "Bertrand de Montville."

"Oh, did you know him?" exclaimed Olga. "Why did you never tell me before? I shall never forget how miserable I was because he didn't live to be reinstated in the French Army. But it's years ago now, isn't it?"

"Six years," said Max.

"Yes, I remember. How I should like to have known him! But I was at school then. And you knew him well?"

"I was with him when he died," he said.

"Oh!" said Olga, and then with a touch of shyness, "I'm sorry, Max."

"No," he said. "You needn't be sorry. He was no shirker. His time was up."

"But wasn't it a pity?" she said.

He smiled a little. "I don't think he thought so. He was happy enough--at the last."

"But if he had only been vindicated first!" she said.

"Do you think that matters?" Max's smile became cynical.

"Surely it would have made a difference to him?" she protested. "Surely he cared!"

He snapped his fingers in the air. "He cared just that."

Violet looked up suddenly from her book. "And you--did you care--just that too?"

He seemed to Olga to contract at the question. "I?" he said. "I had other things to think about. Life is too short for grizzling in any case. And I chanced to have my sister to attend to at the same time."

"You have a sister?" said Olga, swift to intervene once more.

He nodded. "Did I never tell you? She is married to Trevor Mordaunt the writer. Ever heard of him?"

"Why, yes! Nick knows him, I believe."

"Very likely. He has an immense circle of friends. He's quite a good sort," said Max.

"And where do they live?" asked Olga, with interest.

"In Suffolk chiefly. Mordaunt bought our old home and gave it to Chris--my sister--when they married. My elder brother manages the estate for him."

"How nice!" said Olga. "And what is your sister like?"

Max smiled. "She is my twin," he said.

"Oh! Like you then?" Olga looked slightly disappointed.

Max laughed. "Not in the least. Can you imagine a woman like me? I can't. She has red hair or something very near it. And there the resemblance stops. I'll take you to see her some day--if you'll come."

"Thank you," said Olga guardedly.

"Don't mention it!" said Max. "There are two kiddies also--a boy and a girl. It's quite a domestic establishment. I often go there when I want a rest. My brother-in-law is good enough to keep special rooms for the three of us."

"Is there another of you then?" asked Olga.

"Yes, another brother--Noel. By the way, he won't be going there again at present, for he sailed for Bombay to join his regiment a year ago. That's the sum complete of us." Max straightened himself with a faintly ironical smile. "We are a fairly respectable family nowadays," he observed, "thanks to Mordaunt who has a reputation to think of. But we are boring Miss Campion to extinction. Can't we talk of something more amusing?"

Violet threw back her head with a restless movement, but she did not meet his eyes. "I am accustomed to amusing myself," she said.

He stooped to pick up a marker that had fallen from her book. "It is a useful accomplishment," he observed, as he handed it to her, "for those who have time to cultivate it."

She raised her arms with the careless, unstudied grace of a wild creature. Her eyes were veiled.

"I assure you it is far more satisfying than tilting at windmills," she said.

Max straightened himself. There seemed to Olga something pitiless about him, a deadliness of purpose that made him cruel. And in that moment she became aware of a strong antagonism between these two that almost amounted to open hostility.

"A matter of opinion," said Max. "I suppose we each of us have our patent method of killing time."

Violet uttered an indolent laugh. "Yours is a very strenuous one," she observed. "I believe you imagine yourself invincible in your own particular line, don't you?"

"Not at present," said Max, with his twisted smile.

She laughed again, mockingly. "Irresistible then, shall we say?"

He had turned to go, but he paused at the question and looked back at her, grimly ironical. Olga had a feeling that the green eyes comprehended her also.

"No," he said, with extreme deliberation. "Not even that. But--since you ask me--the odds are certainly very greatly in my favour."

And with that he turned on his heel, still smiling, and sauntered away.

As he went, Violet stooped towards Olga with a face gone suddenly white, and grasped her arm.

"Remember, Allegro!" she said. "Not a word about Hunt-Goring--to anyone! Not one single tiny suspicion of a hint!"

And Olga, looking into her eyes, read terror in her soul.

CHAPTER XVII
THE VERDICT

It's a difficult position," said Nick.

"It's a damnable position," said Max. He stared across the white table-cloth with eyes that brooded under down-drawn brows. "I don't anticipate any sudden development if I can keep her off that cursed opium. But--I'd give fifty pounds to have her people within reach."

"Do you know where they are?" said Nick.

Max shrugged his shoulders. "They are cruising about the Atlantic to give Mrs. Bruce, who is neurotic, a rest-cure. Of course, when I undertook to keep an eye on the girl, I never anticipated this. Her brother was anxious about her, I thought somewhat unnecessarily. It was that blackguard Hunt-Goring who precipitated matters. I've given him a pretty straight warning, though Heaven alone knows what effect it will have."

"What did you say to him?" questioned Nick.

"I said that I had just discovered that he had been giving her cigarettes that contained opium. I warned him that it was criminally unsafe, that her brain was peculiarly susceptible to drugs, and that he would probably cause her death if he persisted; also, that if he did I would see that he was held responsible. What more could I say?"

"That was fairly direct certainly," said Nick. "And he?"

"He asked me to dine," said Max.

Nick laughed. "And you didn't accept?"

"Would you have accepted?" Max turned on him almost savagely.

"I think I should," said Nick. "There's nothing like studying the enemy from close quarters. But go ahead! Tell me more! When do you expect her people back?"

"Possibly in a fortnight. They have been gone that time already--rather more. And they expected to make a month of it."

Nick nodded. "We ought to be able to hold the fort for that time. What did your friend Sir Kersley think?"

Max lifted one eyebrow. "What did he say to you about it?"

Nick struck a match for his cigarette with considerable dexterity. "About Violet--practically nothing. About her mother--a good deal."

"I wonder why." Max spoke somewhat curtly.

Nick lighted his cigarette with a whimsical expression. "You don't seem to have noticed what an excellent confidant I make," he said.

"Ah, I know you are safe." There was conviction in Max's tone. "But Kersley is such a reserved chap. And--that ancient affair ruined his life."

"I gathered that," said Nick. "As a matter of fact, I knew a little of the affair before we met. He had been a doctor in my old regiment. It was five years after he retired that I joined; but most of the fellows knew the story. It reached me one way or another. I was deuced sorry for him when I heard the truth. Most people out there were of the opinion that he had treated her badly--was, in fact, to a very great measure responsible for the tragedy."

"That of course was not so," said Max deliberately. "She was responsible from first to last. She knew of the taint in her veins. He did not--till he detected it."

"Rather hard on her!" remarked Nick.

"Would you have married her?" The green eyes fixed him with sudden stern intentness.

Nick blinked rapidly for a few seconds. "I daren't answer that question," he said at length. "You see, I'm not a doctor."

Max rose abruptly. "Are doctors the only beings whoever think of the next generation?" he asked bitterly.

"There is a saying," said Nick, "that 'Love conquers all things.'"

"Pshaw!" said Max. "It never conquered heredity."

"I withdraw the proposition," said Nick. "But, I say, Wyndham!" He paused.

"Well?" Max swung round aggressively with hands in his pockets.

"Suppose the woman you loved developed that disease--would you throw her over?" Nick spoke tentatively.

Max flung back his head and stared at the ceiling. "Why do you ask?"

"Because I want to know what you are made of," replied Nick with simplicity.

Max turned and slowly walked to the window. "Yes," he said, with his back turned, "I should."

Nick was silent.

After a moment Max glanced round at him. "You wouldn't, I suppose?"

"No," said Nick.

"You would marry her regardless of the consequences?"

"If I were an ordinary man--perhaps," said Nick. "If I were a doctor--" he paused--"if I were a doctor, Max," he said again with a sudden smile, "I think I should tackle the situation from another standpoint. Either way, if she loved me and I loved her, I would marry her. As to the consequences--there wouldn't be any."

Max grunted. "Of course you are the exception to every rule."

"Who told you that?" thrust in Nick.

"It's been dinned into me ever since I met you." Half-churlishly Max made reply, and turning fell to pacing the room with the measured tread of one trained to step warily.

"And you believe it?" Nick leaned back in his chair peering forth through eyes half-closed.

"I do--more or less."

"Thanks!" said Nick. "And how goes the courtship?"

Max frowned heavily, without speaking.

"Pardon my asking," said Nick, "and consider the question answered!"

Max stopped squarely in front of him. "It doesn't go," he said briefly.

Nick's glance darted over him for an instant. "What method have you been employing? Coercion? Persuasion? Indifference? Or strategy?"

Max's hands showed clenched inside his pockets. "I'm leaving her alone," he growled.

"Then change your tactics at once!" said Nick. "Try an advance!"

"That's just the mischief. In the present damnable state of affairs, I am powerless. Violet Campion is hating me pretty badly, and--she--is thinking it clever to follow suit. She is avoiding me like the plague."

"That's sometimes a good sign," said Nick thoughtfully.

"Not in this case. It only means she is afraid of me."

Nick's glance flashed up at him again. "For any special reason?"

"I have given her none."

"Violet again?" queried Nick.

"Probably."

Nick ruminated. "You don't think it advisable to tell her how things are?"

"I?" The brief word sounded almost hostile. Max resumed his pacing on the instant. "I'm not an utter brute, Ratcliffe," he said, "whatever I may appear."

Nick sent a cloud of smoke upwards. "Would you call me a brute if I told her?" he asked.

"Yes, I should." Curt and prompt came the answer. "What is more, I won't have it done."

"She is a sensible little soul," contended Nick.

"She may be. But it would increase the difficulties a hundredfold. The girl herself would probably suspect something, and that would almost inevitably precipitate matters. No, the only possible course is to leave things alone for the present. The symptoms are slight, and though it is impossible to say from moment to moment what will happen, the chances are that if we can keep Hunt-Goring from doing any further mischief, the disease may remain in a stationary condition for some time. In that case you may manage to get Olga away on this tom-fool expedition of yours to India before any serious development takes place."

"I see," said Nick. "And you are convinced that a serious development is inevitable?"

"Absolutely." Max came strolling back from the window with eyes fixed and far-seeing. "It is as plain as a pike-staff to any professional man. Kersley detected it at once--as I knew he would; and that was before the midnight episode in Olga's room. Yes, it's bound to come. It may be gradual. It may even take the form of paralysis. But with her temperament I don't think that very likely. It will probably come suddenly as a sequel to some shock or violent agitation. But come--sooner or later--it must."

He spoke slowly, with the deliberation of absolute certainty. Reaching the mantelpiece he lodged himself against it and smoked with his eyes on the ceiling.

Nick watched him with a veiled scrutiny from the depths of his chair. "So that is the verdict," he said at last.

Max nodded without speaking.

"And how long have you known?"

"About a month."

"But you knew them before then?"

Max looked down at him with a slight gesture that passed unexplained. "As long as I have known the Ratcliffes," he said.

"It must have been something of a shock to you," suggested Nick.

Max's jaw hardened. "I was infinitely more interested in her when I knew," he said.

"Really?" said Nick.

"Yes, really." Max spoke with finality. "I assure you I am not impressionable," he added a moment later with the cynical twist of the lips that Olga knew so well. "And I never play with fire. That form of amusement doesn't attract me."

A sudden humorous glitter shone between Nick's half-closed eyelids. "But even serious people burn their fingers sometimes," he observed. "I presume you haven't proposed yet?"

"Yes, I have." Max spoke with dogged assertiveness.

Nick jerked upright. "The deuce you have!"

"You needn't excite yourself," Max assured him grimly. "We are not officially engaged yet--or likely to be. You needn't stick your spoke in. She knows I shan't marry her against her will."

"Oh, that's settled, is it?" Nick's eyes flashed over him with lightning rapidity.

"It is." Max began to smile. "And the marriage will take place some time before the end of next year."

The door opened abruptly while he was speaking, but he finished his sentence with extreme deliberation in spite of the fact that it was Olga who entered,--Olga, flushed and eager, vivid, throbbing with excitement. If she heard his words she paid no heed to them, but broke at once into breathless speech.

"Oh, Nick, it's the post! It's the post! A letter from Dad and another from Muriel; both for you!"

Nick stretched out his hand to her. "Come over here, kiddie! We'll read them together."

She sprang to him, knelt beside him, and warmly hugged him. Max remained propped against the mantelpiece, looking on, ignored by both.

"Muriel's first!" commanded Nick; and, with hands that shook, Olga slit open the envelope.

He put his arm about her shoulders as she withdrew the sheet and opened it out. "Yes, you can read it too. I know what's in it, bless her heart!"

So together they read the closely-written pages. There was silence in the room as they did so, broken only by the crackling of the paper, while Max Wyndham kept a motionless watch, his shaggy brows drawn close.

Suddenly Olga lifted her face. "Oh, Nick, isn't she a darling? I--I--it makes me feel such a beast!"

Nick's hand pinched her cheek in answer. His lips twitched a little, but he did not speak or raise his eyes.

She leaned her cheek against his shoulder. "I won't read any more, Nick. It's too private. May I open Dad's?"

He took his wife's letter between his fingers and dexterously folded it. "All right, Olga mia! Let us hear the verdict of the great Dr. Jim!"

He glanced up at Max with the words and instantly looked away.

Olga had apparently forgotten his very existence. She opened her father's letter still in quivering haste, and again there was a silence of several seconds while they read.

It was broken in a fashion which not one of the three anticipated. Quite suddenly Olga's lips began to quiver. She raised her head with the agitated gesture of one straining for self-control; and then in a moment the tears were running down her cheeks, and she covered her face and sobbed.

"Kiddie! Kiddie!" remonstrated Nick.

But it was Max who stooped and swiftly lifted her, holding her against his heart, stroking the fair hair with his steady capable hand. And surely there was magic in his touch, for almost immediately her weeping ceased. She looked up with slightly startled eyes, and drew herself gently but quite definitely from him.

"Thank you," she said, with a quaint touch of dignity. "You're very kind. Nick dear, I'm sorry. I--I'm all right now. Dad's very sweet to put it like that, pretending he doesn't mind a bit. I don't know how ever I shall say good-bye to him."

"You are really going then?" said Max.

She looked at him with a fleeting smile. "Yes, really!" she said.

"I congratulate you," he said.

Nick chuckled. "He is pretending he doesn't mind, too, Olga."

Olga flushed a little. "Oh, Max never pretends," she said. "Do you, Max?"

He smiled in his grim fashion. "It is not for me to contradict you," he said. "Permit me to congratulate you instead, and to hope that the East will not take as great liberties with your complexion as it has with Nick's."

"I'd rather be like Nick than anyone else in the world," she declared, with one arm wound about her hero's neck.

"Curious, isn't it?" grinned Nick.

"Almost incredible!" said Max.

"But quite true!" asserted Olga with vehemence.

Max swung around with his hands in his pockets, and sauntered to the door. Reaching it, he glanced back for a moment at the eager, girlish face, unperturbed, inscrutable.

"Strange as it may seem," he said, "I personally would rather that you remained like yourself."

"What cheek!" said Olga, as the door shut.

"Oh, isn't he allowed to say that?" enquired Nick.

She nestled to him, albeit half in protest. "Do let's talk about important things!" she said.

And Nick at once took the hint.

CHAPTER XVIII
SOMETHING LOST

Had Olga been a little less engrossed with the all-absorbing prospect that had just opened before her, she might have regarded as somewhat unusual the fact that Violet made no further mention of the proposed trip with Major Hunt-Goring during the week that followed. But, such was her preoccupation, she had even ceased to remember his existence. Little more than six weeks lay between her and the great adventure to which she was pledged, and she had already commenced her preparations. A visit to town would of course be inevitable, but this could not take place till Muriel's return at the end of the month. Nevertheless Olga, being woman to the core, found many things to do at home, and immersed herself in sewing with a zest that provoked Nick to much mirth.

Violet watched her lazily, with occasional offers to help which were seldom meant or taken seriously.

"I believe I shall come after you, Allegro," she said once. "It will be very dull without you."

"You know you are never dull in the shooting season," was Olga's sensible reply. "You never have time to think of me then."

"Quite true, dear," Violet admitted. "I wonder what sort of crowd Bruce will collect this year, and if any of them will want to marry me. He is always furiously angry when that happens. I can't imagine why. It amuses me," said Violet, with a yawn.

"Perhaps he doesn't want you to get married," suggested Olga.

"Apparently not. And yet I am sure he would be thankful to be rid of me. We never agree." The beautiful eyes gleamed mischievously. "I suppose he will expect me to marry a husband of his selection by-and-bye. He is very mediaeval in some things."

"I don't believe you ever mean to marry at all," said Olga.

"Oh, yes, indeed I do!" Violet uttered her soft, low laugh. "But I am mediaeval too, Allegro. Have you never noticed? I am waiting for the first man who is brave enough to run away with me."

It was on the day following this conversation that she prevailed upon Olga to leave her numerous occupations for an hour or so and motor her over to Brethaven to pay another visit to her old nurse, Mrs. Briggs. Nick wished to go over to Redlands to sort some papers, and offered his company as far as his own gates.

"You can walk to 'The Ship' from there," he said to Olga. "It's only half a mile, and after that you can run about the shore and amuse yourselves till I am ready to go back."

"Don't get up to mischief!" said Max briefly.

Violet gave him a quick look from under her lashes, but said no word.

It was a hot morning with a hint of thunder in the atmosphere. With Olga at the wheel, they set off soon after breakfast, leaving Max pumping his bicycle at the surgery-door with grim energy. He was going to the cottage-hospital that morning, a fact which left the motor at liberty till the afternoon.

Mile after mile of dusty road slid by, and Olga, with her heart in the future, sang softly to herself for sheer lightness of heart. She had ceased to trouble about Max, since he, quite obviously, had no intention of obtruding himself upon her. The problem--if problem there were--was evidently one that would keep until her return from India, and Olga was child enough to feel that that event was far too remote to trouble her now.

So, with a gay spirit, she piloted her two friends on that summer morning. No presentiment of evil touched her, no cloud was in her sky. Gaily she sped along the sunny road, little dreaming that that same sun that so gladdened her was to set upon the last of her youth.

The car was in a good mood also, and they hummed merrily past the little stone church of Brethaven and up to the great iron gate of Redlands just as the clock in the tower struck ten.

"Good business!" commented Nick, as he descended to open the gate. "That gives me two hours and a half. Don't be later than twelve-thirty, Olga mia, for starting back."

Olga promised, as she dexterously turned the car and ran in up the drive. He sprang upon the step, and so she brought him to his own door.

"Good-bye, Nick!" she said then, lifting her bright face.

He bent and lightly kissed her. "Good-bye! Don't go and get drowned, either of you, for my sake! Yes, you can leave the car here. It won't rain at present."

He stood on his own step and watched them go, with a motherly smile on his wrinkled face.

"Bless their hearts!" he murmured, as he finally turned away. "I'll swear it's all a mistake. She looks like a queen this morning; and as for Olga, if she has really given her heart to that ugly doctor chap I have never yet seen a woman in love."

He entered the house with the words, and straightway dismissed them from his mind.

"We will go to the shore first," Violet decreed. "Mrs. Briggs won't be expecting us so early. I hear that some more of the Priory land has been slipping into the sea. We must go and see it."

So to the shore they went. The slip was not a serious one. They made their way to the spot over loose sand and rocks, and dropped down in a sandy hollow to rest.

"Poor old Priory!" said Violet. "It's sure to be swallowed up like the rest some day. I wonder if I shall live to see it."

"Oh, surely not!" said Olga.

Violet laughed. "Do you think I am destined to die young then?"

"I can't imagine you dying or growing old," said Olga, with simplicity.

"My dear, what gross flattery!" Violet laughed again, her eyes upon the glittering sea. "Immortal youth! How divine it sounds! Allegro, I should hate to be old." She stretched out her arms to the sky-line. "I want to keep young for ever," she said. "Do you really think I shall? I sometimes think--" she paused.

"What?" said Olga.

She turned round to her with a little gesture of confidence. "I sometimes have a feeling, Allegro, that I must be getting old or dull or plain already. Men don't make love to me so much as they did."

"My dear, what nonsense!" exclaimed Olga, with burning cheeks.

"No, listen! It's true." There was almost a sound of tears in the deep voice. "It's quite true, Allegro. I am not so attractive as I was. I feel it. I know it. Something is lost. I don't know what it is. It went from me that night--you remember!--and it hasn't returned. I thought it was my soul at first. I still sometimes wonder." She laid a hand that quivered and clung upon Olga's arm. "And the dreadful part of it is, Allegro, that Max knows. He looks at me with the most deadly knowledge in his eyes--such wicked eyes they are, all green and piercing, and so cruel--so cruel."

A great shiver went through her, and then all in a moment--before Olga could utter a word--her mood had changed. She leaped suddenly to her feet, all sparkling animation and excitement.

"See! There is a yacht just come round the headland! How close it is! Oh, Allegro, wouldn't you love to go on the water this stifling day?"

"An easy wish to gratify!" observed a voice close to them.

Olga turned with a violent start. Violet merely glanced over her shoulder and smiled. Hunt-Goring, stepping lightly in canvas shoes, came airily forward over the sand, and bowed low.

"I am the deus ex machina," he said. "The yacht is mine--and entirely at your service."

Olga's face was crimson. She got quickly to her feet and stood stiffly silent.

Hunt-Goring was looking remarkably elegant, attired in white drill with a yachting cap which he carried in his hand.

"I seem to have come at an opportune moment," he said. "Really, the fates are more than kind. The yacht is making for Brethaven jetty to take me on board. If you ladies will come with me for a couple of hours' cruise, I need scarcely say how charmed I shall be."

He was looking at Violet as he spoke, and she made instant and impulsive reply. "Of course we will! It will be too delicious--the very thing I was longing for. What lucky chance sent you our way, I wonder?"

She gave him her hand, which he took with a gallantry that sent a quiver of disgust through Olga. With a sharp effort she spoke, hurriedly, nervously, but very much to the point.

"It's very good of you, but we can't possibly come. We must be getting back. You are going to see Mrs. Briggs, you know, Violet. And we promised Nick we wouldn't be late starting home from Redlands."

Violet's quick frown appeared like a sudden cloud. "My dear child, what nonsense! As if Mrs. Briggs mattered! And as for Nick, he won't be ready for more than two hours. You heard him say so."

But Olga stood her ground. "I don't see how we can possibly go--anyhow without telling Nick first. In fact, I would rather not."

Hunt-Goring was smiling--the smile of the man who has heard it all before. "Miss Olga is evidently afflicted with a tender conscience," he observed. "But if you really have two hours to spare and really care to go on the water, I do not see how Nick can reasonably object. Of course I have no desire to persuade you. I only beg that you will follow your inclinations."

"Of course!" said Violet quickly. "And we are coming--at least I am. Allegro, you can please yourself, but it will be very horrid of you if you won't come too."

Olga's pale eyes sparkled. "That depends on one's point of view," she said, with a touch of warmth. "You know what I think about it. I told you the other day."

"My dear, that is too ridiculous," declared Violet. "I never heard such rubbish in my life. Besides, it's only for a couple of hours. Major Hunt-Goring," appealing suddenly, "do tell her how absurd she is! What possible objection could there be to our going out with you for a morning's cruise?"

"None, I should say," smiled Hunt-Goring. "But doubtless Miss Olga has made up her mind and discussion would be only a waste of time. Shall we start?"

"Yes, we will!" agreed Violet impetuously. "I am simply dying for a breath of sea air. Ah, do give me a cigarette! I finished my last this morning."

And then Olga's eyes were opened, and she knew the reason of this man's ascendancy over her friend. The certainty went through her like the stab of a sword, and hard upon it came the realization that to desert Violet at that moment would be an act of treachery. So strong was the conviction that she did not dare to question it. It was as if a voice had spoken in her soul, and blindly she obeyed.

"I will come too," she said.

Violet beamed upon her instantly. "Well done, Allegro! I thought you couldn't be so unkind as to stay behind when I wanted you."

"A woman's second thoughts are always best," observed Hunt-Goring.

She looked him straight in the eyes. "I am going for Miss Campion's sake alone," she said.

He smiled at her with covert insolence. "You are a true woman," he said.

"Is that intended for a compliment or otherwise?" asked Violet.

"Otherwise, I think," said Olga, in a very low voice.

"Acquit me at least of idle flattery!" said Hunt-Goring, with a laugh.

CHAPTER XIX
THE REVELATION

It was certainly a perfect day for a cruise. The sea lay blue and still as a lake, so clear that the rocks made purple shadows in its crystal depths. Under any other circumstances, Olga would have revelled in the beauty of it, but there was no enjoyment for her that day. She stood on the deck of the yacht as she steamed away from the jetty, and watched the uneven shore recede with a feeling of impotence that was not without an element of fear. For it seemed to her that she was a prisoner, looking her last upon the liberty of her youth.

The vessel was of no inconsiderable size and moved swiftly through the still water, cleaving her way like a bird through space. It was not long before they passed the jutting headland that hid the little fishing-village from view; but Olga still stood motionless at the rail, fighting down the cold dread at her heart.

She could hear Violet's voice on the other side of the deck, gaily chattering to Hunt-Goring. The scent of their cigarettes reached her, and she clenched her hands. She was sure now that he had been supplying Violet with them secretly. She had been too deeply engrossed with her own affairs to think of this before, and bitterly did she blame herself for this absorption.

Poor Olga! It was the prelude to a life-long self-reproach.

They were heading out to sea now, running smoothly into the glaring sunshine. It poured upon her mercilessly where she stood, but she was scarcely aware of it. She gazed backward at the shore with eyes that saw not.

Suddenly a soft voice spoke at her shoulder. "What! Still sulking? Do you know you are remarkably like a boy?"

She turned with a great start, meeting the eyes she feared. "I don't know what you mean," she said, drawing sharply back.

He laughed his smooth, easy laugh. "I mean that you are behaving like a cub in need of chastisement. Do you seriously think I am going to put up with it--from a chit like you?"

She looked him up and down with a single flashing glance of clear scorn. "How much do you think I am going to put up with?" she said.

He leaned his arms upon the rail in an attitude of supreme complacence. "I may be the villain of the piece," he observed, "but I have no desire to be melodramatic. I have come over here to talk to you quietly and sensibly about the future. Of course if you--"

"What have you to do with my future?" she thrust in fiercely. She would have given all she had to be calm at that moment, but calmness was beyond her. Though her fear had utterly departed, she was quivering with indignation from head to foot.

Hunt-Goring kept his face turned downwards towards the swirl of water that leaped by them. He was quite plainly prepared for the question.

"Since you ask me," he responded coolly, "I should say--a good deal."

"In what way?" she demanded.

She could see that he was still smiling--that maddening, perpetual smile, and she thought that her sheer abhorrence of the man would choke her. But with all her throbbing strength she held herself in check.

He did not answer her at once. She waited, compelling herself to silence.

At length quite calmly he turned and faced her. "Well now, Olga, listen to me," he said. "I am a good deal older than you are, but I am still capable of a certain amount of foolishness. What I am now going to say to you, I have wanted to say for some time, but you have been so absurdly shy with me that--as you perceive--I have been obliged to resort to strategy to obtain a hearing."

He paused, for Olga had suddenly gripped the rail as if she needed support. Her face was deathly, but out of it the pale eyes blazed in fierce questioning.

"What do you mean?" she said. "What strategy?"

He laid his hand upon hers and gripped it hard. "Don't be hysterical!" he said. "I am paying you the compliment of treating you like a woman of sense."

She shrank away from him, but he continued to grip her hand with brutal force till the pain of it reached her consciousness and sent the blood upwards to her face.

Then he let her go.

"Yes," he said coolly, "I have been laying my mine for some time now. It has not been particularly easy or particularly pleasant, but since I considered you worth a little trouble I did not grudge it. The long and the short of it is this: I fell in love with you last winter. You may remember that I caught your brothers poaching on my ground, and you came to me to beg them off. Well, I granted your request--for a consideration. You may remember the consideration also. You had been at great pains to snub me until that episode. I made you pay for the snubbing. I imposed a fine--do you remember?"

"I have loathed you ever since," she broke in.

"Oh, yes," he said. "I know that. That was what started the mischief. I am so constituted that resistance is but fuel to the flame. In that respect I believe I am not unique. It is a by no means remarkable trait of the masculine character, you will find. Well, I made you pay. It was to be two kisses, was it not? You gave me one, and then for some reason you fled. That left you in my debt."

"It is a debt I will never pay!" she declared passionately. "I will die first!"

He laughed. There was something in his eyes--something intolerable--that made her avert her own in spite of herself. In desperation she glanced around for Violet.

"She is asleep," said Hunt-Goring.

She turned on him then like a fury. "You mean you have drugged her!" she cried.

He shrugged his shoulders. "Not to that extent. You can wake her if you wish, but I think you had better hear me out first--for her sake also. It is better for all parties that we should come to a clear understanding."

With immense effort she controlled herself. "Very well. What do you wish me to understand?"

"Simply this," said Hunt-Goring. "I know very well that your engagement to Wyndham was simply a move in the game, and that you have not the faintest intention of marrying him. That is so, I think?"

She was silent, taken by surprise.

"I thought so," he continued. "You see, I am not so easy to hoodwink. And now I am going to act up to my villain's role and break that engagement of yours-

-which is no engagement. To put it quite shortly and comprehensibly--I am going to marry you myself."

She stared at him in gasping astonishment. "You!" she said. "You!"

He laughed into her eyes of horror. "You will soon get used to the idea," he said. "You see, Wyndham doesn't really want you, and I do. That is the one extenuating circumstance of my villainy. I want you so badly that I don't much care what steps I take to get you. And so long as you continue to hate me as heartily as you do now, just by so much shall I continue to want you. Is that quite plain?"

She was still staring at him in open repulsion. "And you think I would marry you?" she said breathlessly. "You think I would marry you?"

"I think you will have to," said Hunt-Goring, with his silky laugh. "I love you, you see." He added, after a moment, "I shan't be unkind to you if you behave reasonably. I am well off. I can give you practically anything you want. Of course you will have to give also; but that goes without saying. The point is, how soon can we be married?"

"Never!" she cried vehemently. "Never! Never!"

He looked at her, and again her eyes fell; but she continued, nevertheless, with less of violence but more of force.

"I don't know what you mean by suggesting such a thing. I think you must be quite mad--as I should be if I took you seriously. I am not going to marry you, Major Hunt-Goring. I have never liked you, and I never shall. You force me to speak plainly, and so I am telling you the simple truth."

"Thank you," said Hunt-Goring. "Well, now, let us see if I can persuade you to change your mind."

"You will never do that," she said quickly.

He smiled. "I wonder! Anyhow, let me try! It makes no difference to you that I love you?"

"No," she told him flatly. "None whatever. In fact, I don't believe it."

"I will prove it to you one day," he said. "But let that pass now, since it has no weight with you. I quite realize that I shall not persuade you to marry me for your own sake or for mine. But--I think you may be induced to consider the matter for the sake of--your friend."

"In what way?" Breathlessly she asked the Question. for again it was as if a warning voice spoke within her, bidding her to go warily.

He paused a moment. Then: "Has it never struck you that there is something rather--peculiar--about her?" he asked suavely.

She brought her eyes back to his in sharp apprehension. "Peculiar? No, never! What do you mean?"

"Are you quite sure of that?" he insisted.

She began to falter in spite of herself. "Never, until--until quite lately. Never till you gave her those--abominable--cigarettes."

"Believe me, there is no harm whatever in those cigarettes," he said. "I smoke them myself constantly. Try them for yourself if you don't believe me. They contain a minute quantity of opium, it is true, but only sufficient to soothe the nerves. No, those cigarettes are not responsible. That peculiarity which you have recently begun to notice is due to quite another cause. Surely you must have always known that she was different from other girls. Have you never thought her excitable, even unaccountable in some of her actions? Has she never told you of strange fancies, strange dreams? And her restlessness, her odd whims, her insatiable craving for morbid horrors, have you never taken note of these?"

He spoke with deliberate emphasis, narrowly watching the effect of his words.

Olga's hands were gripped fast together; her wide eyes searched his face.

"Oh, tell me what you mean!" she entreated, a piteous quiver in her voice. "Tell me plainly what you mean!"

"I will," he said. "Violet Campion's mother was a homicidal maniac. She killed her husband--this girl's father--in a fit of madness one night three months after their marriage. It happened in India, and was put down to native treachery in order to hush it up, but it was well known that no native was responsible for it. During the six months that followed, she was kept under restraint, hopelessly insane. It was in her blood--the worst form of insanity known. At the birth of the child she died. That will explain to you my exact meaning, and if you need corroboration you can go to Max Wyndham for it. She has begun to develop symptoms of her mother's complaint. All her peculiarities arise from incipient madness!"

"Oh, no!" Olga whispered, with fingers straining against each other. "It's not possible! It's not true!"

"It is absolutely true," he said. "And you know it is true. At the same time it is just possible that the disease may be arrested. Wyndham himself will tell you this. We discussed the matter quite recently. It may be arrested even for years if nothing happens to precipitate it. Of course her people will never let her marry, but she is not, I fancy, the sort of young woman to whom wedded bliss is essential. Naturally, all this has been kept from her. There are not many people who know of it. I am one, because I knew her mother both before and after her marriage, being a young subaltern at the time and stationed at the very place where the tragedy occurred. Wyndham is another, being the protege of Kersley Whitton to whom the girl's mother was engaged and who was the first to discover the fatal tendency. She married Campion mainly out of pique because Whitton threw her over. He was a man of sixty, and his son was grown up at the time. I have often thought that he behaved with remarkable magnanimity when he adopted the child of the woman who had murdered his father."

Olga shivered suddenly and violently. The horror of the tale had turned her cold from head to foot. She no longer questioned the truth of it. She knew beyond all doubting that it was true.

The sun still shone gloriously, and the yacht slipped on through the shining water, throwing up the sparkling foam as she went. But to Olga the whole world had become a place of darkness and of the shadow of death. Whichever way she turned, she was afraid.

"Oh, why have you told me?" she said at last. "Why--why have you told me?"

"Can't you guess?" said Hunt-Goring.

"No!" Yet her breath came sharply with the word. If she did not guess, she feared.

He looked down at her for the first time unsmiling. "I have told you," he said, "that I mean to marry you, and--in keeping with the part of villain which you have assigned to me--I don't much care what I do to get you."

She met his look with all her quivering courage. "But what has this to do with that?" she said.

She saw his face harden, become cruel. "Miss Campion is nothing to me," he said brutally. "Either you give me your most sacred promise to marry me before the end of the year, or--I shall tell her the truth here and now, as I have just told it to you."

She shrank as though he had struck her. "Oh, you couldn't!" she cried out wildly. "You couldn't! No man could be such a fiend!"

He came a step nearer to her, and suddenly his eyes glowed with a fire that scorched her to the soul. "You had better not tempt me!" he said. "Or I may do that--and more also!"

She put her hands up to shield her face from his look, but he caught them suddenly and savagely into his own, overbearing her resistance with indomitable mastery.

"Promise me!" he said. "Promise me!"

His lips were horribly near her own. She strained away from him tensely, with all her strength. "I will not!" she panted. "I will not!"

"You shall!" he declared furiously. "Do you think I will be beaten by a child like you? I tell you, you shall!"

But still desperately she struggled against him, repeating voicelessly, "I will not! I will not!"

He gripped her fast, holding her face up mercilessly to his own. "You think I won't do it?" he said.

"I know you won't!" she gasped back. "You couldn't! No man--no man could!"

"I swear to you that I will!" he said.

"No!" she breathed. "No! No! No!"

She saw the fury on his face suddenly harden and turn cold. Abruptly he set her free.

"Very well," he said. "Marry you I will. But first I will show you that I am a man of my word."

He swung round upon his heel to leave her. But in that instant the warning voice cried out again in Olga's soul, compelling her to swift action. She sprang after him, caught his arm, clinging to it with all her failing strength.

"You will not!" she gasped out in an agony of entreaty. "You could not! You shall not!"

He stopped, looking down without pity into her face of supplication. "Then give me that promise!" he said.

She shook her head. "No, not that--not that!"

"Why not?" he insisted. "Are you hoping to catch your red-haired doctor? You are not likely to secure anyone else, and he will probably prove elusive."

She flinched at the gibing words, but still she held him back. "No, no! I don't want to marry anyone. I have always said so."

"Have you said so to him?" asked Hunt-Goring.

She was silent, but the quick blood ran to her temples betraying her.

"I thought not," he said. "So that is the explanation, is it? That is why you will have none of me, eh?"

"Oh, how can you be so hateful?" she cried vehemently.

He laughed. "You won't let me be anything else, I assure you I would be ami-ability itself if you would permit. Well now, which is it to be? You say you don't want to marry anyone. That, we have seen, is only a figure of speech. But since the red-haired doctor is not wanting you and I am--"

"You are wrong!" she broke in, with sudden heat.

Some hidden fire within her had kindled into flame at his words; it burned with a fierce strength. For the first time she challenged him without any sense of fear.

He looked at her in unfeigned astonishment. "I beg your pardon?"

"You are wrong!" she said again, and it was as if some inner force inspired the words. She spoke without conscious volition of her own. "Max Wyndham has asked me to marry him--and marry him I will!"

She never knew with what triumphant finality she spoke, but the effect of her words was instant and terrible. Even as they left her lips, she saw the dark blood rise in a wave to his forehead, swelling the veins there to purple cords. His eyes became suddenly bloodshot and glittered devilishly. His hands clenched, and she almost thought he was going to strike her.

With a desperate effort she faced him without a tremor, instinctively aware that courage alone could save her.

For fully thirty seconds he said no word, and as they slipped away she saw the dreadful wave of passion gradually recede. But even then he continued to glare at her till with a quiet movement she took her hand from his arm and turned away.

Then, as she stood at the deck-rail, at last he spoke. "So that is your last word upon the subject?"

She answered him briefly, "Yes."

She kept her face turned seawards. She was suddenly and overwhelmingly conscious of bodily weakness. All her strength seemed to have gone into that one great effort, that at the moment had seemed no effort at all. She felt as if she were going to faint, and gripped herself with all her quivering resolution, praying wildly that he might not notice.

He did not notice. For a few seconds more he stood behind her, while she waited, palpitating, for his next move. Then, very suddenly he turned and left her.

And Olga, instantly relaxing from a tension too terrible to be born, covered her face with her hands and shuddered over and over again in sick disgust.

It was many minutes before she recovered, minutes during which her mind seemed to be almost too stunned for thought. Very gradually at length she began to remember the words she had last uttered, the weapon she had used; and numbly she wondered at herself.

No, she had scarcely acted on her own initiative. Her action had been prompted by some force of which till that moment she had had no knowledge, a force great enough to lift her above her own natural impulses, great enough to help her in her sore strait, and to make all other things seem of small importance.

What would Max have said to that emphatic declaration of hers? But surely it was Max, and none other, who had inspired it. Surely--surely--ah, what was this that was happening to her? What magic was at work? She suddenly lifted her face to the dazzling summer sky. A brief giddiness possessed her--and passed. She was as one over whom a mighty wave had dashed. She came up from it, breathless, trembling, yet with a throbbing ecstasy at her heart such as she had never known before. For the impossible had happened to her. She realized it now. She--Olga Ratcliffe, the ordinary, the colourless, the prosaic--was caught in the grip of the Unknown Power, that Immortal Wonder which for lack of a better name men call Romance. And she knew it, she exulted in it, she stretched out her woman's hands to grasp it, as a babe will seek to grasp the sunshine, possessing and possessed.

In that moment she acknowledged that the bitter struggle through which she had just come had been indeed worth while. It had exhausted her, terrified her; but it had shown her her heart in such a fashion as to leave no room for doubt or misunderstanding. Even yet she quivered with the rapture of the revelation. It thrilled her through and through. For she knew that Max Wyndham reigned there in complete and undisputed possession. No other man had entered before him, or would ever enter after....

Slowly, reluctantly, she came back from her Elysium. She descended to earth and faced again the difficulties of the way.

She opened her eyes upon the yacht still running seawards, and decided that they must turn. She wondered if Hunt-Goring had regained his self-control, if he were ashamed of himself, if possibly he might bring himself to apologize, and what she should say to him if he did. Her heart felt very full. She knew she could not be very severe with him if he were really repentant.

Then she remembered Violet,--her friend....

CHAPTER XX
THE SEARCH

For the third time Nick looked at his watch. It was nearly one. He jumped to his feet with a grimace.

"What on earth are those girls up to?"

Rapidly he locked drawer after drawer of his writing-table, gathered up a sheaf of papers, and turned to go.

The library at Redlands overlooked a wide lawn that led through shrubberies to the edge of the cliff, up the face of which had been cut a winding path. He paused a moment considering this. Would they return from the shore by that way? If so, he would miss them if he went in search of them by the drive.

Impatiently he turned back towards the window, and in that moment he caught sight of a flying figure crossing the lawn,--Olga, with a white, strained face, hatless, dishevelled, gasping.

Nick's one arm fought with the heavy window and flung it up. In another second he had leaped out to meet her. She ran to him, stumbled ere she reached him, fell against him, helpless, sobbing, exhausted.

He held her up. "What is it? Violet? Is she drowned?" he questioned rapidly.

"No--no!" She gasped the words as she lay against his shoulder.

"All right then! Take your time! Come and sit down!" said Nick.

He supported her to the low window-sill, and she sank down upon it, still clinging to him with agonized gasping, voiceless and utterly spent.

He stood beside her, strongly grasping her hand. "Keep quite quiet!" he said. "It's the quickest in the end."

She obeyed him, as was her custom, leaning her head against him till gradually her breath came back to her and speech became possible.

"Oh, Nick!" she whispered then. "That any man--could be--so vile!"

"What man?" said Nick sharply.

"Major Hunt-Goring."

He stooped swiftly and looked into her face. "What has he been doing?"

"I'll tell you!" she said. "I'll tell you!"

And then, arrested possibly by something in that flashing regard, she raised herself and looked straight up at him.

"I can only tell you everything," she said, "if you will promise me not to go and quarrel with him--in fact, not to go near him. Will you promise, Nick?"

"I will not," said Nick.

"You must!" she said. "You must!"

"I will not," he said again.

She held his hand imploringly. "Not if I ask you--not if I beg you--"

"Not in any case," he said. "Now tell me the truth as quickly as you can."

She shook her head. "Nick, I can't. He is quite unscrupulous. He might kill you!"

"So he might," said Nick grimly. "He's crazy enough for anything. What has he been doing?"

"Is he crazy?" she said, catching at the word.

"He's drug-ridden," said Nick, "and devil-ridden too upon occasion. Now tell me!"

She began to cry with her head against his arm. "Nick,--I'm frightened! I can't!"

"Oh, damn!" said Nick to the world at large. And then he gently released himself and knelt beside her. "Look here, Olga darling! There's nothing to frighten you. I'm not a headlong fool. There! Dry your eyes, and be sensible! What's the beast been up to? Made love to you, has he?"

His bony hand grasped hers again very vitally, very reassuringly. Almost insensibly she yielded herself to his control. Quiveringly she began to tell him of the morning's happenings.

Perhaps it was as well that she did not see Nick's face as she did so, or she might have found it difficult to continue. As it was she spoke haltingly, with many pauses, describing to him Hunt-Goring's arrival and invitation, her own dilemma, her final surrender.

"I couldn't help it, Nick," she said, still fast clinging to his hand. "I couldn't let her go alone."

"Go on," said Nick.

And then she told him of Hunt-Goring's overture, her own sick repulsion for the man, his persistence, his brutality.

At that abruptly Nick broke in. "Before you go any farther--has he ever made love to you before?"

She answered him because she had no choice. "Yes, Nick. But I always hated him."

"And you didn't tell me," he said.

There was no note of reproach in his tone, yet in some fashion it hurt her.

"Nick--darling, you--you've only got one arm," she said. "And he's such a great, strong bully."

Nick uttered a sudden fierce laugh. His hand was clenched. "You women!" he said, and for some reason Olga felt overwhelmingly foolish.

"Well, finish!" he commanded. "No half-measures, mind! Just the whole truth!"

And Olga stumbled on. She repeated with quivering lips Hunt-Goring's story of the taint in Violet's blood, of the tragedy that had preceded her birth.

"Nick," she said, turning piteous eyes upon his face, "I know it must be partly true, but do you think it is really quite as bad as that? I believed it at the time. But--but--perhaps--"

He shook his head. "It's true," he said briefly.

"True that she is going--mad? Oh, Nick--Nick!"

He slipped his arm around her. "And the devil told her, did he?"

She leaned her forehead on his shoulder in an agony of quivering recollection. "Because I wouldn't listen to him--because--because--"

"Pass on," said Nick. "He told her. What happened?"

But she could not tell him. "It was too dreadful--too dreadful!" she moaned.

"Where is she now?" he pursued. "You can tell me that anyhow."

"She has gone to Mrs. Briggs," Olga whispered. "She said she would know everything. She had been her nurse from the beginning. She--she is in a terrible state,

Nick. I only came away to tell you. I thought you would be getting anxious, or I wouldn't have left her. I ran up the cliff path. It was quickest."

"We will go back to her in the motor," Nick said.

He got to his feet, his arm still about her, raising her also.

"Come now!" he said. "Pull yourself together, kiddie! You will need all the strength you can muster. Come inside and have a drain of brandy before we start!"

He led her within. She was shivering as one with an ague, but she made desperate efforts to control herself.

Nick was exceedingly matter-of-fact. There was never anything tragic about him. He made her drink some brandy and water, and while she did so he scribbled a brief note.

"I will send off my own man in the motor with this to Max," he said. "He had better come."

Olga looked up sharply. "It's no manner of use sending for him, Nick. She vows she will never see him again."

"We will have him all the same," said Nick. "He is the man for the job."

He went off and despatched his message, and then, returning, went out with her to the motor in which they had arrived so gaily but a few hours before.

"Now go steady, my chicken!" he said, as he got in beside her. "It wouldn't serve anyone's turn to have a spill at this juncture."

His yellow face smiled cheery encouragement into hers, and Olga felt subtly comforted.

"Oh, I am glad I've got you, Nick," she said. "You're such a brick in any trouble."

"Don't tell anyone!" said Nick. "But that's my speciality."

The midday sun was veiled in a thick haze, and the heat was intense. The dust lay white upon the hedges, and eddied about their wheels as they passed. The sea stretched away indefinitely into the sky, leaden, motionless, with no sound of waves.

"I am sure there will be a storm," said Olga.

"A good thing if there is," said Nick.

"Yes, but Violet is terrified at thunder. She always has been."

"It won't break yet," he said.

Almost noiselessly the motor sped along the dusty road. All Olga's faculties became concentrated upon her task, and she spoke no more.

They reached the village. It seemed to be deserted in the slumbrous stillness. There was not so much as a dog to be seen.

Suddenly Nick spoke. "What became of Hunt-Goring?"

The colour leaped into her pale, tense face. "He landed us at the jetty, and went away again in his yacht."

"Let us hope he will go to the bottom!" said Nick.

She shook her head, a gleam of spirit answering his. "Men like that never do."

They ran unhindered through the village and came to "The Ship." The inn-door gaped upon the street. There was not a soul in sight.

Olga brought the car to a stand. "We had better go straight in, Nick."

"Certainly," said Nick.

She peeped into the bar and found it empty. Together they entered the narrow passage. The unmistakable odour of beer and stale tobacco was all-prevalent. The air was heavy with it. They reached the foot of the steep winding stairs, and Olga paused irresolutely.

"There doesn't seem to be anyone downstairs. Will you wait while I run up?"

"No," said Nick. "I'm coming too."

They ascended therefore, and commenced to search the upper regions. But the same absolute quiet reigned above as below. Only the loud ticking of a cuckoo-clock at the head of the stairs aggravated the stillness.

Olga opened one or two doors along the passage and looked into empty rooms, and finally turned round to Nick with scared eyes.

"What can have happened? Where can she be gone?"

As she uttered the words, there fell a heavy footstep in the sanded passage below, and the sound of a man's cough came up to them.

Nick wheeled. "Hi, Briggs! Is that you?"

"Briggs it is," said a thick voice.

Nick descended the stairs with Olga behind him, and encountered the owner thereof at the bottom. He was a large-limbed man with a permanent slouch and a red and sullen countenance that very faithfully bore witness to his habits. He stood and regarded Nick with a fixed and somewhat aggressive stare.

"Where's the missis?" he said.

"That's just what I want to know," said Nick.

Briggs uttered an uneasy guffaw as if he suspected the existence of a joke that had somewhat eluded him. His eyes rolled upward to Olga, and back to Nick.

"Well, she ain't 'ere seemin'ly," he remarked.

"Don't you know where she is?" demanded Nick.

Briggs grinned foolishly. "That's tellin'!" he observed facetiously.

Nick turned from him. "Come along, Olga! They are not here evidently. It's no use trying to get any sense out of this drunken beast."

"But, Nick--" said Olga in distress.

"We will go down to the shore," he said. "Here, you Briggs! Stand back, will you?"

Briggs was blocking the narrow passage with his great bull-frame, and showed no disposition to let them pass. He seemed to think he had a grievance, and he commenced to state it in a rambling, disjointed fashion, holding them prisoners on the stairs while he did so.

Nick bore with him for exactly ten seconds, and then, clean and straight, with lightning swiftness, his one hand shot forward. It was a single hard blow, delivered full on the jaw with a force that nearly carried Nick with it, and it sent the offender staggering backwards on his heels in bellowing astonishment. The opposite wall saved him from falling headlong, but the impact was considerable, and tendered him quite incapable of recovering his He subsided slowly onto the floor with a flood of language that at least testified to the fact that his injuries were not severe.

Nick's arm went round Olga in a flash. He almost lifted her over the legs of the prostrate Briggs and hurried her down the passage. As they emerged into the smoky sunlight, she heard him laugh, and marvelled that he could.

"On second thoughts," he said, with the air of one resuming an interrupted discussion, "I think we will go to the Priory. If she is not there, she is probably on the way."

"She would go by the cliffs," Olga said.

"Yes, I know. But Mrs. Briggs is with her. We had better motor," said Nick.

So they set off again along the glaring road.

It began to seem like a nightmare to Olga. She drove as one pursued by horrors unspeakable. Once or twice Nick spoke to her, and she knew that she obeyed his instructions, though what they were she could never afterwards remember. On and on they went, flying like cloud-shadows on a windy day, yet--so it seemed to Olga--drawing no nearer to their goal, until quite suddenly she found herself staring at the great Priory gate-posts with their huge stone balls while Nick wrestled with the fastenings of the gates.

They opened before her, and she drove slowly through with a curious sensation as of entering an unknown country, though she had known the Priory grounds from childhood. Nick clambered in beside her as she went, and then they were off again running swiftly up the long drive with its double line of yews to the house.

Memory awoke within her then, and she called to mind that day that seemed so long ago when she had encountered Violet, superbly confident, conquering the rebellious Pluto. The cry of a gull came to her now as then, and it sounded like a cry of pain.

They came within sight of the old grey walls. Silent and tragic, they stood up against the mist-veiled sky. The sunlight had turned to an ominous copper glow. And in that moment Olga was afraid, with that sick apprehension of evil that comes upon occasion even to the brave. She gave no sign of it, but it was coiled like a serpent about her heart from then onwards.

The front-door stood open, its Gothic archway gaping wide and mysterious. Still with that nightmare dread upon her, she descended and passed into the old chapel of the monks.

The stained window at the end cast a lurid stream of light along half its length. She caught her breath in an irrepressible shudder. She thought she had never before realized how gruesomely horrible that window was.

Nick's hand closed upon her elbow, and she breathed again. "Shall we go and investigate upstairs?" he said.

Mutely she yielded to the suggestion. They went down the long vault-like hall, and turned through the archway in the south wall close to the window. As they did so, a sudden sound rent the ghostly stillness, a sound that echoed and echoed from wall to wall, dying at last into a shrill thread of sound that seemed to merge into the cry of a sea-gull over the leaden waters. As it died, there came a noise of running feet in the corridor above, and a white-faced maid-servant rushed gasping down the wide oak stairs.

Olga sprang to intercept her. "Jane, what is the matter? Where is Miss Violet? Have you seen her?"

She caught the terrified girl by the shoulders, holding her fast while she questioned her.

Jane stopped perforce in her headlong flight. "Oh, lor, Miss Olga, do let me go! Miss Violet's upstairs--with Mrs. Briggs. She's in a dreadful taking, and don't seem to know what she's doing. Did you hear her scream? Mrs. Briggs says it's hysterics, but it don't sound like that to me. It's made my blood run cold."

Olga released as swiftly as she had captured her, and started for the stairs. Nick was close behind her. They ascended almost together, past the great window that looked upon the sea, and so on to the oak-panelled corridor that led to Violet's room.

The great wolf-hound Cork came to meet them here, wagging a wistful tail and lifting questioning eyes. He made no attempt to hinder their advance, obviously regarding them as friends in need.

Olga's hand caressed him as she passed, and he came and pressed against her as she stopped outside the closed door. Softly she turned the handle, only to discover that the door was locked. She bent her head to listen, and heard a broken sobbing that was like the crying of a child.

Her face quivered in sympathy. She stooped and put her lips to the key-hole. "Violet--Violet darling--let me in! Let me be with you!"

Instantly the sobbing ceased, but it was Mrs. Briggs's voice that made answer. "You can't come in, Miss Olga, only unless you're by yourself. Miss Violet's still very upset-like, and she ain't wanting anyone but me."

There was authority in the announcement. Mrs. Briggs was not without considerable strength of character, and she knew how to keep her head in an emergency.

Olga looked at Nick.

"I should wait if I were you," he counselled. "She is sure to want you later on."

She nodded silently, and bent over Cork. The strain of the past few hours was beginning to tell upon her. Her tears fell unrestrained upon the great dog's head.

Nick strolled away to the head of the stairs, and stood there like a sentinel, searching the blurred expanse of sea through the open window with alert, restless eyes.

Several minutes passed; then there came the sound of the key turning in the lock. Olga stood up hastily, dashing away her tears. Mrs. Briggs's head appeared in the aperture.

"Miss Olga," she said in a strenuous whisper, "Miss Violet would like to speak to you if so be as you're alone. But she won't have anyone else."

"There is only Captain Ratcliffe here," said Olga.

"Then p'raps he'll be good enough to wait outside," said Mrs. Briggs, with the air of a general issuing his orders. "You can come in, Miss Olga, and for pity's sake soothe the pore dear as much as you can. She's well-nigh wore herself out."

Olga glanced round for Nick, and found him at her side.

"Look here, Olga," he said, speaking in a rapid whisper, "you are not to lock that door. Understand? I say it!"

She hesitated. "But if------"

"I won't have it done," he said. "You must pretend to lock it. Mind, if I find that door locked, I shall have it forced, and take you away."

"But she may ask me, Nick," Olga objected.

"If she does, you must lie to her," he said inexorably.

Olga abandoned the discussion somewhat reluctantly, anticipating difficulties.

He laid his hand for an instant on her arm as she prepared to enter. "You understand I am in earnest, don't you?" he said.

She looked into his queer, yellow face with a feeling that was almost awe as she answered meekly. "Yes, Nick."

"And don't forget it," he said, as he let her go.

CHAPTER XXI
ON THE BRINK

I s that you, Allegro? There is no one with you?"

Violet raised herself from her pillows, turning a haggard face to meet her friend. She looked as if years had passed over her. Her great eyes shone out of dark circles. They looked beyond Olga in evident apprehension.

"It's only me, darling," said Olga, going swiftly to her.

Feverish hands caught and held her. "Goodness, child! How cold you are!" exclaimed Violet. "Mrs. Briggs, I can do without you now. You had better go and look after Briggs." She broke into a brief laugh. "He always gets up to mischief as soon as your back is turned."

"He can very well look after 'imself," said Mrs. Briggs austerely. "And I'm not a-goin' to leave you like this, my dearie. But I'll tell you what I will do. I'll go down to the kitchen and make them lazy hussies stir themselves and get you a meal of some sort."

In the days when Mrs. Briggs had been Violet's nurse she had reigned supreme in the Priory kitchen, and she still regarded it as an outlying portion of her dominions.

Violet leaned back upon her pillows with exhaustion written plainly on her pale face. "Oh, do as you like, Nanny! But I don't want anything. I've got my cigarettes."

Mrs. Briggs grunted, and turned to go. The patient Cork here seized the opportunity to assert himself, and gently but firmly pressed into the room.

"Drat the dog!" said Mrs. Briggs.

"Leave him alone!" Violet commanded. "He knows how to take care of me."

As Cork was fully determined to enter, no effort on Mrs. Briggs's part would have availed to stop him, and Mrs. Briggs, realizing this, sniffed and departed.

The huge animal lay down by the foot of the bed and heaved a sigh of satisfaction as he dropped his nose upon his paws.

And then Violet turned her face to Olga, sitting on the bed, and whispered, "Does he know?"

"Who?" whispered back Olga.

"Max, of course! Who else?"

Olga hesitated. Violet's hands were gripping her very tightly. "Know what, dear?" she said at last.

A quick frown drew Violet's forehead. "Oh, you know what I mean. Does he know about my going mad? Have you told him?"

"My dearest,"--keen distress rang in Olga's voice--"don't--don't talk like that! You're not mad! You're not mad!"

Violet's frown changed into a very strange smile. "Oh yes, but I am," she said. "I've been mad for some time now. It's been gradually coming on, but to-day--to-day it is moving faster--much faster." Her low voice quickened. "I haven't much sanity left, Allegro. I can feel it slipping from me inch by inch like a paid-out rope. Only enough left now to know that I am mad. When I don't know that any longer, I shall have lost it all."

"Dearest! Dearest!" moaned Olga. "Won't you try to forget it--try to think of other things for a little?"

Violet continued as if she had not heard her. "You know, it's curious that it never occurred to me before. I've had such queer sensations--all sorts of funny things going on inside me. It began like a curious thirst--a very horrible sort of craving, Allegro. That was what made me take to those cigarettes. I never felt it when I was smoking them. They made me so deliriously sleepy. It was terrible when--he--took them away. I felt as if he had pushed me over a deep abyss. I really can't do without them. They make me float when I'm going to sink."

She paused, and passed a weary hand across her brow. "Why have I been crying so, Allegro? I hardly ever cry. Was I sorry for someone? Was it my mother? Fancy her doing--that!" The heavy eyes grew suddenly wide and bright. "I wonder if she would have killed me too if she had lived. I know exactly what made her do it. I should have done it myself--yes, and revelled in it. Can't you imagine it? The night and the darkness, and oneself lying there pretending to be asleep and waiting--waiting--for the man one hated." Suddenly the wide eyes glowed red. "Think of it--think of it, Allegro!--how one would feel for the point of the knife when one heard his step, and hide it away under the pillow when at last he came in. How one's flesh would creep when he lay down! How one's ears would shout and clamour while one waited for him to sleep! And then--and then--when he began to breathe slowly and one knew that he was unconscious--how inch by inch one would draw out one's hand with the knife and raise the bedclothes, and plunge it hard and deep into his breast! Would he struggle, Allegro? Would he open his eyes to see his own life-blood spout out? Would he be frightened, or angry, or just surprised? I think he would be surprised, don't you? He wouldn't give his wife credit for hating him so much. Men don't, you know. They never realize how far hatred will drive a woman until it pushes her over the edge. I think he would hardly believe his own eyes even then, unless he saw her laughing!" A burst of wild laughter broke from Violet's lips, but she smothered it with her handkerchief.

"I mustn't laugh," she said, "though I'm sure she did. And I want to talk to you seriously, Allegro."

"Dear, do lie down and rest!" Olga urged her gently. "That hateful story has given you a shock. Do try and remember that there's nothing new about it. It all happened years ago. And you are no different now than you were this morning before you heard it."

Violet leaned her head back again upon the pillows, but her eyes roved unceasingly. "But then I was mad this morning," she said, "only I didn't know it. Do you know, I think madness is a sort of state in which people lose their souls and yet go on living. Or else the soul goes blind. I've thought of that too. But I think my soul has gone on. I shall go and find it presently. You must help me."

"Of course I will help you, darling," Olga promised soothingly.

"Yes. But it won't be easy," said Violet, frowning upwards. "I've got to go into a great space of lost souls, and I shan't find it very easily. It was his fault. He never ought to have brought me back that night. That's the worst of doctors. They are so keen about the body, but they don't study the soul at all. They behave exactly as if the soul weren't there."

"Look here, dear," said Olga, with sudden inspiration, "wouldn't you like to talk to Nick about it? He's so clever. I always ask him about puzzling things."

"Nick?" Violet's eyes came round to her. "He's a soldier, isn't he? He has killed people."

"I don't know. I suppose so," said Olga. "He is just outside. May I fetch him?"

"Oh, yes, I don't mind Nick. He's got some sense. But I won't have Max, Allegro. He is not to come near me. I've found him out, and I hate him!" The deep voice suddenly grew deeper. A flame of fierce resentment leaped up in the roving eyes. "I know now exactly why he has been so attentive all this time. I thought--I used to think--he was in love with me--like other men. But I know now that he was only making a study of me, because he knew that I was going mad. Bruce must have told him that. I've often wondered why he and Bruce were so friendly. I know now that they were in league against me. Bruce never liked me--naturally. No one ever liked me but you, Allegro."

"Shall I call Nick?" said Olga, gently bringing her back to the point.

"Oh, if you like. But no! Cork would never let any man come in here. I will come downstairs. We'll have some lunch, and then smoke." Violet sprang from the bed with sudden decision. "Heavens!" she exclaimed, as she caught a glimpse of herself in her glass. "What a hag I look! I can't go down in this. It looks like a bedgown. Find me something, Allegro! That red silk will do. I believe everything else is at Weir. You will have to send my things back, for I am going to stay here now. I've had enough of Max Wyndham's tyranny. I must have my own way or I shall rave."

With impulsive hands she tore off her tumbled muslin dress, and arrayed herself in the flaming evening robe which Olga had once condemned. Olga raised no protest now. She gave her silent assistance. The horrors of that day had so closed in upon her that she felt fantastically convinced that nothing she did or left undone could make any difference, or hinder for the fraction of an instant the fate that so remorselessly pursued them and was surely every moment drawing nearer. The fear at her heart had so wound itself into her very being that she was no longer conscious of it. It possessed her like an evil spell.

So she stood by, sometimes helping, always watching, while her friend's tragedy leaped from point to point like a spreading forest-fire breeding destruction.

"You are not afraid of me, Allegro?" Violet asked her suddenly, as she arranged her black hair with swift, feverish movements.

And Olga answered with truth. "No, dear. I should never be that."

"Not whatever happened? That's right. I'm not really dangerous--so long as you keep Max out of my way. But, mind--I must never see him again, never--never--while I live!" She turned from the glass, facing Olga with eyes in which an awful fire had begun to burn. "I know him!" she said. "I know him! He will want to shut me up--to keep me as a specimen for him--and men like him--to study. He and Bruce will do it between them if they get the chance. But they won't--they won't! Allegro--darling, you must help me to get away. I can't--can't--be imprisoned for life. You will help me? Promise me! Promise!"

"I promise, dearest!" Olga made answer very earnestly.

Something of relief softened the agony in the dark eyes. Very suddenly Violet took her friend's face between her hands and passionately kissed her on the lips.

"I love you, Allegro!" she said. "And I trust you--and you only--till death."

It was then--at first but dimly--that Olga began to realize that the burden laid upon her might be heavier than she could bear, and yet that she alone must bear it even if it crushed her to the earth.

Passing out at length into the passage, she felt Violet's hand close with a convulsive pressure upon her arm, and she knew that here was fear such as she had never before encountered or imagined,--the deadly, unfathomable fear of a mind that hovered on the brink of the abyss.

She caught the hand warmly, protectingly, into her own. And she swore then and there a solemn, inward oath that, cost what it might, the trust reposed in her should not be in vain. When her friend turned to her for help in extremity, she should not find her lacking.

For of such stuff was Olga Ratcliffe fashioned, and her loyalty was that same loyalty which moves men even unto the sacrifice of their lives.

CHAPTER XXII
OVER THE EDGE

Marshalled by Mrs. Briggs, the Priory servants brought them luncheon, laying a table at one side of the great entrance-hall, for all the lower rooms were shuttered and closed.

Violet, with the great dog Cork vigilant and silent beside her, sat before it as one wrapt in reverie. Now and then she roused herself to answer at random some remark from Nick, but for the most part she sat mutely brooding.

The meal was but a dreadful farce to Olga. She was waiting, she was listening, she was watching. It seemed ludicrous to her stretched nerves to be seated there with food before her, when every instant she expected the devastating power that lurked behind the stillness to burst forth and engulf them. It was like sitting at the very mouth of hell, feeling the blistering heat, and yet pretending that they felt it not.

Darker and darker grew the day. They sat in a close, unearthly twilight. Though the huge entrance-door was flung wide, no breath of air reached them, no song of birds or sound of moving leaf. Once Olga turned her eyes to the far glimmer of the east window, but she turned them instantly away again, and looked no more. For it was as though a hand were holding up a dim lantern on the other side to show her the dreadful scene, casting a stain of crimson across the space where once had stood the altar.

Looking back later, she realized that it was only Nick's presence that gave her strength to endure that awful suspense. She had never admired him more than she did then, his shrewdness, his cheeriness, his strength. There was not the faintest suggestion of strain in his attitude. With absolute ease he talked or he was silent. Only in the deepening gloom she caught now and then the quick glitter of his eyes, and knew that like herself he was watching.

Slowly the minutes wore away, the darkness grew darker. From far away there came a low, surging sound. The storm-wind was rising over the sea.

Nick turned his head to listen. "Now for one of our patent storms!" he said. "Brethaven always catches it pretty strong. Remember that night you developed scarlet fever, at Redlands, Olga mia, and your devoted servant went down to a certain cottage on the shore to fetch a certain lady to nurse you?"

Olga did remember. It was one of the cherished memories of her childhood. "I told Muriel a secret about you that night, Nick," she said, responding with an effort.

He nodded. "For which act of treachery you possess my undying gratitude. Did you ever hear that story, Miss Campion?"

He offered her his cigarette-case with the words, and she turned her brooding eyes upon him. "Thanks!" she said. "I will have one of my own. Yes, I know that story. Your wife must be a very brave woman."

"She had me to take care of her," pointed out Nick.

Violet laughed with a touch of scorn.

"Oh, quite so," he said. "But I bear a charmed life, you should remember. No one ever drowns in my boat."

She leaned her chin upon her hand, and surveyed him through the weird twilight. "You are a strong man," she said slowly, "and you don't think much of Death."

"Not much," said Nick, striking a match on the heel of his boot.

The flame flared yellow on his face, emphasizing its many lines. His eyelids flickered rapidly, never wholly revealing the eyes behind.

"You wouldn't be afraid to die?" she pursued, still watching him.

His cigarette glowed and he removed the match; but the flame remained, burning with absolute steadiness between his fingers.

"I certainly shan't be afraid when my turn comes," he said, with confidence.

"Tell me," she said suddenly, "your idea of Death!"

His look flashed over her and back to the match he still held. The flame had nearly reached his fingers.

"Death," he said, "is the opening--and the closing--of a Door."

She leaned eagerly forward. "You think that?"

"Just that," said Nick. He smiled and blew out the match, just in time. "But--as you perceive--I am afraid of pain--that is, when I think about it."

She scarcely seemed to hear. "And have you ever seen anyone die?"

"Plenty," said Nick.

"Ah, I forgot! You've killed men, haven't you?" There was suppressed excitement in her voice.

Nick threw up his head and smoked towards the oak-beamed roof. "When I had to," he said, with brevity.

"Ah!" The word leaped from her like a cry of triumph. "Did you ever kill anyone with a knife? What did it feel like?"

"I shan't tell you," said Nick rudely. "It isn't good for anyone to know too much."

An abrupt silence followed his refusal. The surging of the sea had risen to a continuous low roar; and from the garden came the sound of trembling leaves. The storm was at hand.

"Do you think I don't know?" said Violet, and laughed.

Quickly Olga rose, as if her nerves were on edge, and went towards the open door. As she did so, a violet glare lit the hall from end to end, quivered, and was gone. She stopped dead, and in the awful silence that succeeded she heard the wild beat of her heart rising, rising, rising, in a tumult of sudden fear.

Violet remained at the table, staring, as one transfixed. She was gazing at the open door. Nick leaned swiftly forward and took her hand. So much Olga saw in the dimness before the thunder with a fierce crash burst forth overhead.

Ere it died away there came a shriek, wild, horrible, unearthly. It pierced Olga through and through, turning her cold from head to foot. Another shriek followed it, and yet another; and then came a dreadful, sobbing utterance in which words and moans were terribly mingled.

Olga caught at her self-control, as it were, with both hands, and went swiftly back to the table. Violet was on her feet. She had wrenched herself free, and was wildly pointing.

"No! No! No!" she cried. "Take him away!" Mortal terror was in her starting eyes. Suddenly perceiving Olga, she turned and clung to her. "Allegro! You promised! You promised!"

Then it was that Olga realized that someone had entered during that awful peal of thunder, and was even then advancing quietly down the hall. It needed not a second flickering flash to reveal him. Her heart told her who it was.

With Violet pressed close in her arms, she spoke. "Max, stop!"

She never knew whether it was the note of authority or of desperation in her voice that induced him to comply; but he stopped on the instant a full twenty feet from where they stood.

"What's the matter?" he said.

Brief, matter-of-fact, almost contemptuous, came his query. Yet Olga thrilled at the sound of it, feeling strengthened, reassured, strangely unembarrassed.

"It's this horrid storm," she said. "Violet's upset. Ah, here is Mrs. Briggs! Darling, wouldn't you like to go upstairs and lie down again till it's over? Do, dearie! I'll look after Nick and Max."

But Violet's straining arms clung faster. "He'll follow me!" she whispered.

"No, indeed he won't, dear. I won't allow it," said Olga, and she spoke with absolute confidence born of this new, strange feeling of power. "You needn't be afraid of that," she said, with motherly, shielding arms about her. "Won't you go with Mrs. Briggs? I will come up presently. Really there's nothing to be afraid of. The storm won't hurt you."

"And you won't let Max come?" Violet was suffering herself to be led towards the further door. She was shivering violently and moved spasmodically, as though the impulse to escape strongly urged her.

"I promise," Olga said.

She passed under the archway with her, paused there while another furious burst of thunder rolled above them: then gently surrendered her to Mrs. Briggs, and turned back herself into the hall.

She found Max and Nick standing together in the gloom.

"I came up here on the chance," the former was saying, "and got here just in time. Hullo! Is that a wolf?"

It was Cork, who crouched bristling against the table, with bared fangs, watching him. Olga went to him and took him by the collar.

"He's all right," she said. "I think he doesn't like strangers."

She led him also across the hall, took him to the foot of the stairs, and re-turned.

She felt Max's eyes upon her as she came up. He seemed to be regarding her in a new light.

"Well?" he said. "Why this hysteria? Is it due to the storm or--some other cause?"

She hesitated, finding it somehow difficult to give an answer to his cool ques-tioning.

"I'll tell him, shall I?" said Nick.

She came and slipped her hand into his. "Yes, Nick."

He squeezed her fingers hard. "Our friend Hunt-Goring has been sticking his oar in," he said. "This--hysteria has been caused by him."

"You mean he has told her the whole story?" said Max.

"Yes," said Olga.

He considered the matter for a few seconds in silence. "And how long has this sort of thing been going on?" he asked then.

Again she hesitated.

He looked at her. "It's no good trying to keep anything from me," he observed. "I've seen it coming for a long while."

"Oh, Max!" she burst forth involuntarily. "Then it really is--"

A vivid flash of lightning and instant crashing thunder drowned her words. In-stinctively she drew nearer to Nick. On many a previous occasion they had watched a storm together with delight. But to-day her nerves were all a-quiver, and its vio-lence appalled her.

As the noise died away, Max looked about the shadowy place. "Is there any means of lighting this tomb?" he asked.

Apparently there was not. Olga believed there were some electric switches somewhere but she had forgotten where.

Max began to stroll about in search of them.

"Here comes the rain!" said Nick. "It will be lighter directly."

The rain came quite suddenly in an immense volume, that beat with deafen-ing force upon the roof, drowning all but the loudest crashes of thunder. For a few seconds the darkness was like night. Then, swift and awful, there came a flash that was brighter than the noonday sun. It streaked through the stained-glass window, showing the dreadful picture like a vision to those below it, throwing a stream of vivid crimson upon the floor; then glanced away into the dark.

There came a sound like the bursting of shell that shook the very walls to their foundation. And through it and above it, high and horrible as the laughter of storm-fiends there came a woman's laugh....

In that instant Nick's hand suddenly left Olga's. He leaped from her side with the agility of a panther, and hurled himself into the darkness of the archway that led to the inner hall.

Something dreadful was happening there, she knew not what; and her heart stood still in terror while peal after peal of that awful laughter rang through the pealing thunder.

Then came another flash of lighting, keen as the blade of a sword, and she saw. There, outlined against the darkness of the archway, red-robed and terrible, stood Violet. Her right hand was flung up above her head, and in her grasp was a knife that she must have taken from the table. She was laughing still with white teeth gleaming, but in her eyes shone the glare of madness and the red, red lust of blood.

The picture flashed away and the thunder broke forth again, but the fiendish laughter continued for seconds till suddenly it turned to a piercing scream and ceased. Only the echoes of the thunder remained and a dreadful sound of struggling on the further side of the archway, together with a choking sound near at hand as of some animal striving against restraint.

Olga stumbled blindly forward. "Nick! Nick! Where are you? What has happened?" she cried, in an agony.

Instantly his voice came to her. "Here, child! Don't be scared! I'm holding the dog."

She groped her way to him, nearly falling over Cork, who was dragging against his hand.

The great dog turned to her, whining, and, reassured by her presence, ceased to resist.

"That's better," said Nick, with relief. "Can you hold him?"

She slipped her hand inside his collar! "Nick! What has happened?" she whispered, for her voice was gone.

Dimly she discerned figures in the inner hall, but there was no longer any sound of struggling. And then quite suddenly Max came back through the archway.

"Lend me a hand, Ratcliffe!" he said. "I'm bleeding like a pig."

CHAPTER XXIII
AS GOOD AS DEAD

S o cool was his utterance, so perfectly free from agitation his demeanour, that Olga wondered if she could have heard aright. Then she saw him go to the table and prepare to remove his coat, and she knew that there could be no mistake.

The frozen horror of the past few seconds fell from her, and strength came in its place--the strength born of emergency. "I shall help you better than Nick," she said.

"If you don't faint," said Max.

She spoke a reassuring word to Cork and let him go. He moved away at once in uneasy search for his mistress, and she turned round to Max. Nick was already helping him out of his coat.

The storm had lulled somewhat, and the gloom had begun to lighten. As she drew near him she saw his right arm emerge from the coat. The shirt-sleeve was soaked with blood from shoulder to cuff.

"It's the top of the shoulder," said Max. "Only a flesh wound. Make a wet pad of one of those table-napkins and bind it up tight. I'll go back to the cottage-hospital presently and get it dressed."

With the utmost calmness he issued his directions, and Olga found herself obeying almost mechanically. Nick helped her to cut away the shirt and expose the wound. It was a deep one, and had been inflicted from the back.

"Quite a near shave," said Max, with composure. "That flash of lightning came just in time. I saw the reflection in one of those oak panels."

"Will this stop the bleeding?" asked Olga doubtfully.

"Yes, if you get the pressure on the right place. Pull it hard! That's the way!

Don't mind me!" He was speaking through clenched teeth. "I daresay Nick knows all about first aid."

Nick did; and under his supervision the injury was bandaged at length with success.

"First-rate!" said Max approvingly. "I congratulate the pair of you. Now I will have a brandy and soda, if you have no objection. Olga must have one too. I'm never anxious about Nick. He always comes out on top."

He watched Olga pour him out a drink according to instructions. The storm was passing, and every instant the gloomy place grew lighter. Glancing at him, as she placed the tumbler before him, she saw his face fully for the first time, and noted how drawn and grey it was.

He smiled at her abruptly. "All right, Olga! You must drink the first quarter."

"Oh, no!" said Olga quickly.

"Oh, yes!" he rejoined imperturbably. "Tell her to, Nick! I know your word is law."

Nick had strolled across the hall to pick up something that lay upon the floor. As he returned, Olga was hastily gulping the prescribed dose.

Max turned towards him. "Yes. Take care of that!" he said. "It's done enough damage." He took the glass that Olga held out to him, and deliberately drained it. Then he rose, and took up his coat. "I must get into this if possible," he said.

Silently, with infinite care, Olga helped him.

Nick stood with the knife in his hand. "What are you going to do now?" he said.

Max's brows went up. "My dear fellow, what do you suppose? I am going to attend to my patient."

"Where is she?" said Nick.

"Upstairs. Mrs. Briggs went to look after her. I'm going to give her a composing draught," said Max, plunging his hand into a side-pocket.

"Oh, Max!" exclaimed Olga.

He turned to her. "There will be no repetition of this," he said grimly. "Miss Campion is exhausted and probably more or less in her right mind by now."

"But she won't be if you go to her," Olga said, and in her eagerness she drew near to him and laid a light hand on his sleeve. "Max, you mustn't go to her--indeed--indeed. I have promised her that you shall not. As you have seen for yourself, the very sight of you is enough to send her demented."

"Oh, it's for her sake, is it?" said Max; but he stood still, suffering her hand on his arm.

Her eyes were raised to his, very earnestly beseeching him. "Yes, for her sake," she said. "You would do her much more harm than good. Let me take the composing draught to her! Oh, Max, really it is the only way. Please be reasonable!"

Her voice trembled a little. She knew well that where his patients were concerned he would endure no interference. Again and again he had made this clear to her. But this was an exceptional case, and she prayed that as such he might view it.

She wondered a little that Nick did not come to her aid, but he stood aloof as if unwilling to be drawn into the discussion. Max seemed to have completely forgotten his existence.

"Look here," he said finally. "The matter isn't so desperate as you seem to think, but if I give in, so must you. There are several questions I shall have to ask, and I must have a clear answer."

"I will tell you anything in my power," she said.

"Very well," he said. "Tell me first--if you can--why Miss Campion hates me so violently."

His manner was curtly professional. He looked straight into her eyes with cool determination in his own.

She answered him, but her answer did not come very easily. "I think she feels that you have had her under supervision all along, and she resents it."

"Quite true," he said. "I have. Is that why she wants to kill me?"

"Not entirely." Olga was plainly speaking against her will.

But Max was merciless. "And the other reason?"

She locked her fingers very tightly together. "It--it would be a breach of confidence to tell you that," she said.

"I see," said Max. "She was annoyed because I didn't fulfil expectations by falling in love with her. She misunderstood my attitude; was that it? You did so yourself at one time, if I remember aright."

"Yes," admitted Olga reluctantly.

"I don't know quite how you managed it," he commented. "However, we are none of us infallible. Now tell me--without reservation--exactly what passed this morning between you two girls and Hunt-Goring."

With quivering lips she began to tell him. There were certain items of that conversation with Hunt-Goring, of which, though they were branded deep upon her mind, she could not bring herself to speak. It was a difficult recital in any case, and the grim silence with which he listened did not make it any easier.

"Have you told me everything?" he asked at last.

She answered steadily. "Everything that concerns Violet!"

He looked at her very closely for a few moments, and she saw his mouth take a cynical, downward curve.

"Hunt-Goring has my sympathy," he observed enigmatically. "Well, I think you are right. I had better keep out of the way for the present. I shall know better what course to take in the morning. Her state of mind just now is quite abnormal, but she may very well have settled down a little by that time. She will probably go through a stage of lethargy and depression after this. Her brother should be back again in a week's time. We may manage to ward off another outbreak till then. But, mind, you are not to be left alone with her during any part of that week. There must always be someone within call."

"I shall be within call," said Nick.

Max glanced at him. "Yes, you will be quite useful no doubt. But I must have a nurse as well."

"A nurse!" exclaimed Olga.

He looked back at her. "You don't seriously suppose I am going to leave you and Mrs. Briggs--and Nick--in sole charge?"

"But, Max," she protested, almost incoherent in her dismay, "she will be herself again to-morrow or the next day! This isn't going to last!"

"What do you mean?" he said.

She controlled herself with a sharp effort, warned of the necessity to do so by his tone.

"I mean that--hysteria--isn't a thing that lasts long as a rule."

"It isn't hysteria," he said.

She flinched in spite of herself. "But you think she will get better?" she urged.

He was silent a moment, looking at her. "I will tell you exactly what I think, Olga," he said then, in a tone that was utterly different from any he had used to her before. "For you certainly ought to know now. The tale you heard this morning was true--every word of it. I heard it myself from Bruce Campion and also from Kersley Whitton. Kersley was engaged to marry her mother when he detected in her a tendency to madness which he afterwards discovered to be an hereditary taint in her family. It is a disease of the brain which is absolutely incurable. It is in fact a peculiarly rapid decay caused by a kind of leprous growth which nothing can arrest. In some cases it causes total paralysis of every faculty almost at the outset, in others there may be years of violent mania before the inevitable paralysis sets in. Either way it is quite incurable, and if it takes the form of madness it is only intermittent for the first few weeks. There are no lucid intervals after that."

He paused. Olga was listening with white face upturned. She spoke no word; only the agony in her eyes spoke for her.

He went on very quietly, with a gentleness to which she was wholly unaccustomed. "It has been coming on for some little time now. I hoped at first that it would be slow in developing, and so at first it appeared to be. Sometimes, at the very beginning, it is not possible to detect it with any certainty. It is only when the disease has begun to manifest itself unmistakably that it moves so rapidly. It was because I feared a sudden development that I asked Sir Kersley to come down. He was of the opinion that that was not imminent, that three months or even six might intervene. I feared he was mistaken, but I hoped for the best. Of course a sudden shock was more than sufficient to precipitate matters. But I knew that she was less likely to encounter any in your society than anywhere else. Nick wanted me to warn you, but--rightly or wrongly--I wouldn't! I thought you would know soon enough."

He paused again, as if to give her time to blame him; but still she spoke no word, still she waited with face upturned.

He went on gravely and steadily. "I knew that opium was a very dangerous drug for her to take in however minute a quantity, but I hoped I had put a stop to that. I could not foresee to-day's events. Hunt-Goring is no favourite of mine, but I never anticipated his taking such a step. I did not so much as know that he was in a position to do so. He suppressed that fact on the sole occasion on which Miss

Campion's name was mentioned between us."

Olga spoke for the first time, her stiff lips scarcely moving. "I think he is a devil," she said slowly.

Max made a gesture expressive of indifference on that point. "People who form the drug habit are seldom over-squeamish in other respects," he said. "He has certainly hastened matters, but he is not responsible for the evil itself. That has been germinating during the whole of her life."

"And--that--was why Sir Kersley jilted her mother?" Olga spoke in a low, detached voice. She seemed to be trying to grasp a situation that eluded her.

"It was." Max answered with a return to his customary brevity; his tone was not without bitterness. "Kersley was merciful enough to think of the next generation. He was a doctor, and he knew that hereditary madness is the greatest evil--save one--in the world. Therefore he sacrificed his happiness."

"What is the greatest evil?" she asked, still with the air of bringing herself painfully back as it were from a long distance.

He was watching her shrewdly as he answered. "Hereditary vice--crime."

"Is crime hereditary?"

"In nine cases out of ten--yes."

"And that is worse than--madness?"

"I should say much worse."

"I see." She passed a hand across her eyes, and very suddenly she shivered and seemed to awake. "Oh, is it quite hopeless?" she asked him piteously. "Are you sure?"

"It is quite hopeless," he said.

"She can never be herself again--not even by a miracle?"

"Such miracles don't happen," said Max, with grim decision. "It is much the same as a person going blind. There are occasional gleams for a little while, but the end is total darkness. That is all that can be expected now." He added, a hint of compassion mingling with the repression of his voice: "It is better that you should know the whole truth. It's not fair to bolster you up with false hopes. You can help now--if you have the strength. You won't be able to help later."

"But I will never leave her!" Olga said.

"My dear child," he made answer, "in a very little while she won't even know you. She will be--as good as dead."

"Surely she would be better dead!" she cried passionately.

"God knows," said Max.

He spoke with more feeling than he usually permitted himself, and at once changed the subject. "What we are at present concerned in is to make her temporarily better. Now you know this stuff?" He took a bottle from his pocket. "I am going to put it in your charge. Give her a teaspoonful now in a wine-glass of water, as you did before. I hope it will make her sleep. If it doesn't, give her a second dose in half an hour. But if she goes off without that second dose, all the better. Remember, it is rank poison. She ought to sleep for some hours then, and when she wakes I think she will probably be herself for a little. That's quite clear, is it?"

He was looking at her closely as he handed her the bottle; but she met the look with absolute steadiness. She had plainly recovered her self-control, and was ready to shoulder her burden once more.

"I quite understand," she said.

He laid his hand for a moment on her arm, and smiled at her with abrupt kindliness.

"Stick to it, Olga!" he said. "I am counting on you."

She smiled back bravely, though her lips quivered. She did not say a word.

But Nick answered for her, his arm thrust suddenly about her waist. "And so you can, my son," he said. "She is the pluckiest kid I know."

CHAPTER XXIV
THE OPENING OF THE DOOR

A llegro!"

The utterance was very faint, yet it reached Olga, sitting, as she had sat for hours, by her friend's side, watching the long, still slumber that had followed Max's draught.

She bent instantly over the girl upon the bed, and warmly clasped her hand. "I am here, darling."

The shadows were lengthening. Evening was drawing on. Very soon it would be dark.

"Allegro!" The low voice said again. It held a note of unutterable weariness, yet there was pleading in it too. The hand Olga had taken closed with a faint, answering pressure.

"Are you wanting anything?" whispered Olga, her face close to the face upon the pillow, the beautiful face she had watched, with what a passion of devotion, during the long, long afternoon.

"Have you been here all the time?" murmured Violet.

"Yes, dear."

"How sweet of you, Allegro!" The dark eyes opened wider; they seemed to be watching something very intently, something that Olga could not see. "I suppose you thought I was asleep," she said.

"Yes, dear."

"I wasn't," said Violet. "I was just--away."

Olga was silent. The clasp of her hand was very close.

"My dear," Violet said, "I've been there again."

"Where, dearest?"

"I've been right up to the Gate of Heaven," she said. "It's very lovely up there, Allegro. I wanted to stay."

"Did you, dear?"

"Yes. I didn't mean to come back again. I didn't want to come back." A sudden spasm contracted her brows. "What happened before I went, Allegro? I'm sure something happened."

Very tenderly Olga sought to reassure her. "You were ill, dear. You were upset. But you are better now. Don't let us think about it."

"Ah! I remember!" Violet raised herself abruptly. Her eyes shone wide with terror in the failing light. "Allegro!" she said. "I--killed him!"

"No, no, dear!" Olga's hand tenderly pressed her down again. "He is only--a little--hurt. You didn't know what you were doing."

But recollection was dawning in the seething brain. One memory after another pierced through the turmoil. "I had to do it!" she whispered. "He is so cruel. He keeps me back. He holds the door when I want to get away. Allegro, why won't he let me go? I'm nothing to him. He doesn't love me. He doesn't--even--hate me." A great shudder ran through her. She fell back upon the pillow as though her strength were gone. "Oh, why won't he open the door and let me go?" She moaned piteously. "Why does he keep bringing me back? I know I shall kill him. I shall be driven to it. And it's such a horrible thing to do--that dreadful soft feeling under the knife, and the blood--the blood--oh, Allegro!" She tried to raise herself again, and was caught into Olga's arms. She turned her face into her neck and shuddered.

"I'm not mad now," she whispered. "Really I'm not mad now! But I soon shall be. I can feel it coming back. My brain is like--a fiery wheel. Oh, don't let it come again, Allegro! Help me--help me to get away--before it comes again!"

Olga strained her to her heart, saying no word.

"They'll shut me up," the broken whisper continued. "I shall never find my soul again. I shan't even have you, and there's no one else I love. All the rest are strangers. Only he will come and look at me with his cruel, cold green eyes, and I shall kill him--I know I shall kill him--unless they bind me hand and foot. Allegro! Allegro!" She was shivering violently now. "Perhaps they will do that. It's happened before, hasn't it? 'Bound hand and foot and cast into outer darkness.' That's hell, isn't it? Oh, Olga, shall I be sent to hell if I kill him?"

"My darling, hush, hush!" Olga's arms held her faster still. "There is no such place," she said--"at least not in the sense you mean. You are torturing yourself, dear one, and you mustn't. Don't dwell on these dreadful things! You are quite, quite safe, here in my arms, with the love of God round us. Think of that, and don't be afraid!"

"But I am afraid," moaned Violet. "It's the outer darkness, Allegro. And you won't be there. And the door will be shut--always shut. Oh, can't you do anything to save me? You're not like Max. You're not paid to keep people back. Can't you-- can't you find a way out for me? Couldn't you open the prison-door before he comes again, and let me slip through? I've never been a prisoner before. I've always come and gone as I liked. And now--twice over--he has dragged me back from the Gate of Paradise. Oh, Allegro, I shall never get there unless you help me. Quick, dear, quick! Help me now!"

She had turned in Olga's arms. She raised an imploring face. She clung about her neck.

"Isn't there a way of escape?" she urged feverishly. "Can't you think of one?"

But Olga looked back in silence, white and still.

"Allegro, don't you love me? Don't you want me to be happy?" Incredulity, despair were in the pleading voice. "Don't you believe in paradise either, Allegro? Do you want me to be shut away in the dark--buried alive--buried alive?"

There was suddenly a note of anguish in the appeal. Violet drew herself slowly away, as though her friend's arms had ceased to be a haven to her.

But instantly, with a swiftness that was passionate, Olga caught her back.

"I would die for you, my darling! I would sell my soul for you!" she said, and fierce mother-love throbbed in her voice. "But what can I do? O God! what can I do?"

Her voice broke, and she stilled it sharply, as if taken off her guard.

"Can't you open the door for me?" Violet begged again. "Don't you know how?"

But still Olga had no answer for the cry. Only she held her fast.

There followed a long, long pause; then again Violet spoke, more collectedly than she had spoken at all.

"Do you know what that man said to me this morning? He told me I should be a homicidal maniac--like my mother. I didn't realize at the time what that meant. I was too horrified. I know now. And it was the truth. That's what I want you to save me from. Allegro, won't you save me?"

"My darling, how can I?" The words were spoken below Olga's breath. The gathering darkness was closing upon them both.

Violet freed a hand and softly stroked her cheek. "Don't be afraid, dear! No one--but I--will ever know. And I-- Allegro, I shall bless you for ever and ever. Wait!" She suddenly started, with caught breath. "Are we alone?"

"Mrs. Briggs is outside, dear," Olga told her gently.

"Oh! Dear old Nanny! She would never hold me back. She would understand. Do you remember how she told us--that afternoon--about her mother?"

Yes, well Olga remembered. She had never forgotten. Back upon her mind flashed that vivid memory, and with it the memory of Max's eyes, green and intent, searching her face on the night that he had asked, "What do you know about the pain-killer?"

Violet's voice brought her back. "Where is he, Allegro? Is he still here?"

"No." Almost unconsciously Olga also spoke in a whisper. "He has gone back to Weir," she said. "He had to go; but--"

"But he will come back?" gasped Violet.

"Yes."

"Ah! And he may be here--at any time?" The words came quick and feverish; again that painful trembling seized her.

"He won't come in here," Olga said steadfastly.

"He will! He will!" breathed Violet. "I know him. There is nothing--he will not do--for the sake of his--profession." She broke off, gripping Olga with tense strength. "And I've nothing to defend myself with!" she panted. "They have taken--the knife--away!"

Tenderly Olga soothed her panic. "It will be all right, dear. I can take care of you. I can keep him away."

Violet relaxed against her again, exhausted rather than reassured. "And where is Nick?" she murmured presently.

"Downstairs, darling; in the hall."

"On guard," said Violet quickly. "What shall I do? Oh, what shall I do?"

"My dearest, no! Only he wouldn't leave me. You know what pals we are," urged Olga. "Besides, you like Nick."

"Oh, yes; he amuses me. He is clever, isn't he? What was that he said about--about the opening--and the shutting--of a Door?"

Spasmodically the words fell. The failing brain was making desperate efforts against the gathering dark.

"He was speaking of Death," said Olga, her voice very low.

"Yes, yes! He said he wouldn't be afraid. And I'm sure he knew. He must have seen Death very often."

"I don't know, darling."

"Of course, the opening of the Door is to let us escape," ran on the feverish whisper. "And then it shuts, and we can't get back. But no one ever wants to get back, Allegro. Who ever wanted to go back into the prison-house--and the dreadful, dreadful dark?"

But Olga made no answer. With set face and quiet eyes she was waiting. And already at the heart of her she knew that when the moment came she would not flinch.

"And how lovely to be free--to be free!" Soft and eager came the whisper from her breast. "Never to be dragged back any more. To leave the dark behind for ever and ever. For it isn't dark up there, you know. It's never dark up there. You can see the light shining even through the Gates. And God couldn't be angry, Allegro. Do you think He could?"

"Not with you, my darling! Not with you!"

"So you'll let me go," said Violet, with growing earnestness. "You'll help me to go, Allegro? You will? You will?"

"My darling, I will!" Quick and passionate came the answer. The time had come.

For a few moments the arms that held her tightened to an almost fierce embrace; then slowly relaxed.

"Dear heart, I knew you would," said Violet.

She leaned back upon her pillow as Olga gently let her go, and through the deepening dusk she watched her with eyes of perfect trust.

There followed a pause, the tinkle of glass, the sound of liquid being poured out. Then Olga was with her again, very still and quiet.

Softly the door opened. "Anything I can do, Miss Olga?" murmured Mrs. Briggs.

"Nothing, thank you," said Olga.

"That young Dr. Wyndham--'e's just come back," said Mrs. Briggs.

Olga turned for a moment from the bed. The glass was in her hand.

"Go down to him, Mrs. Briggs," she said. "Ask him to wait five minutes."

"Allegro!" There was agonized appeal in the cry.

She turned back instantly. "It's all right, dearest. It's all right. Mind how you take it! There! Let me! Your hand is trembling."

She leaned over her friend, supporting her, holding the glass to her lips.

"Drink it slowly!" she whispered to the quivering girl. "You are quite safe--quite safe."

And Violet drank,--at first feverishly, then more steadily, and at last she took the glass into her own hand and slowly drained it. Olga waited beside her, took it quietly from her; set it down.

"Quite comfy, sweetheart?"

"Quite," said Violet. And then, "Come quite close, Allegro dear!"

Olga sat down upon the bed, and took her into her arms, "You don't mind the dark?" she whispered.

And Violet answered. "No. I've passed it. I'm not afraid of anything now."

There fell a silence between them. A great, all-enveloping peace had succeeded the turmoil. Violet's breathing was short but not difficult. She lay nestled in the sheltering arms like a weary child. And slowly the seconds slipped away.

There came a faint sound outside the door as of muffled movements, and Cork, from his post at the foot of the bed, raised his head and deeply growled.

Sleepily the head on Olga's shoulder stirred. "It doesn't matter now," said Violet's voice, speaking softly. "He can never bring me back again." And then, still more softly, in a kind of breathless ecstasy, "The Door is opening, Allegro--darling! Let me--go!"

The words went into a deep sigh that somehow did not seem to end. Olga waited a moment or two, listening tensely, then rose and laid her very tenderly back upon the pillow. She knew that even as she did so, her friend passed through ...

Slowly she turned from the bed, as one in a dream, unconscious of tragedy, untouched by fear or agitation or any emotion whatsoever. All feeling seemed to be unaccountably suspended.

The figure of a big man met her on the threshold. She looked at him with wide, incurious eyes, recognizing him without surprise.

"You are too late," she said.

He started, and bent to look at her closely.

From the deep shadow behind her arose Cork's ominous growl. She turned back into the room.

"May I come in?" Sir Kersley asked in his gentle voice.

With her hand upon Cork's collar, she answered him. "Yes, come in. I am afraid it is rather dark. Will you wait while Mrs. Briggs brings a candle?"

Someone else had entered behind Sir Kersley. She heard a quick, decided tread; and again more ferociously Cork growled.

"Take that dog away!" ordered Max.

Mechanically she moved to obey, Cork accompanying her reluctantly. In the passage she found a strange woman in a nurse's uniform, and Nick. He came to her instantly, and she felt his arm about her with a vague sensation of relief.

"Still sleeping?" he asked.

She answered him quite calmly; at that moment it was no effort to be calm.

"No, Nick; she has gone away."

"What?" he said sharply.

"Won't you take her downstairs?" interposed the nurse, and Olga wondered a little at the compassion in her voice. "She would be the better for a cup of tea."

"So she would," said Nick. "Come along, Olga mia!"

His arm was about her still. They went down the wide dim stairs, he and she and the great wolf-hound who submitted to Olga's hand upon him though plainly against his own judgment.

There were candles in the hall, making the vast place seem more vast and ghostly. The east window was discernible only as a vague oblong patch of grey against the surrounding darkness.

"The electric light has gone wrong," said Nick, as she looked at him in momentary surprise.

"I see," she said. "It must have been the storm." She looked down at Cork pacing beside her. "Poor fellow!" she murmured. "He doesn't understand."

"Come and sit down!" said Nick.

Tea had been spread in the place of luncheon. He led her to the table and pulled forward a chair. She sank into it with a sudden shiver.

"Cold?" he said.

"Yes, horribly cold, Nick," she answered.

She tried to smile, but her lips were too stiff. A very curious feeling was creeping over her, a species of cramp that was mental as well as physical. She leaned back in her chair, staring straight before her, seeing nothing.

Nick went round to the tea-pot. She heard him pouring out, but she could not turn her head.

"I ought to do that," she said.

"All right, dear. I'm capable," he answered.

And then in his deft fashion he came to her with the cup, and sat on the arm of her chair, holding it for her.

"Don't try to talk," he said. "Just drink this and sit still."

She leaned her head against him, feeling his vitality as one feels the throb of an electric battery.

"Do you think God is angry with me, Nick?" she said. "She wanted to go--so dreadfully."

"God is never angry with any of us," he answered softly. "We are not big enough for that. There, drink it, sweetheart! It will do you good."

She raised her two hands slowly, feeling as if they were weighted with iron fetters. With flickering eyes he watched her, in a fashion compelling though physically he could not help. She lifted the cup and drank.

The candlelight reeled and danced in her eyes. Her dazed senses began to awake. "Nick!" she exclaimed suddenly and sharply.

"Here, darling!" came his prompt reply.

She set down the empty cup, and clasped her hands tightly together. "Nick!" she said again, in a voice of rising distress.

His hand slid down and held hers. "What is it, kiddie?"

She turned to him impulsively. "Oh, Nick, I've made a great mistake--a great mistake! I ought not to have let her go alone. She will be frightened. I should have gone with her."

"My child," Nick said, "for God's sake--don't say any more! This isn't the time."

And even as she wondered at the unwonted vehemence of his speech, she knew that they were no longer alone.

Max came swiftly through the shadowy archway and moved straight towards her. A white sling dangled from his neck, but it was empty. She thought his hands were clenched.

Scarcely knowing what she did, she rose to meet him, forcing her rigid limbs into action. He came to her; he took her by the shoulders.

"Olga," he said, "how did this happen?"

She faced him, but even as she did so she was conscious of an awful coldness overwhelming her, as though at his touch her whole body had turned to ice. His eyes looked straight into hers, searching her with intolerable minuteness, probing her through and through. And from those eyes she shrank in nameless terror; for they were the eyes of her dream, green, ruthless, terrible. He looked to her like a man whose will might compel the dead.

For a long, long space he held her so, silent but merciless. She did not attempt to resist him. She felt that he had already forced his way past her defences, that he was as it were dissecting and analyzing her very soul. She had not answered his question, but she knew that he would not repeat it. She knew that he did not need an answer. And then the coldness that bound her became by slow degrees a numbness, paralyzing her faculties, extinguishing all her powers. There arose a great uproar in her brain, the swirl as of great waters engulfing her. She raised her head with a desperate gesture. She met the searching of his eyes, and goaded as it were to self-defence, with the last of her strength, she told him the simple truth.

"I have opened the Door!" she said. "I have set her free!"

She thought his face changed at her words, but she could not see very clearly. She had begun to slip down and down, faster and ever faster into a fathomless abyss of darkness from which there was no deliverance. And as she went she heard his voice above her, brief, distinct, merciless: "And you will pay the price." ... The darkness closed over her head....

CHAPTER XXV
THE PRICE

That darkness was to Olga but the beginning of a long, long night of suffering--such suffering as her short life had never before compassed--such suffering as she had never imagined the world could hold.

It went in a slow and dreadful circle, this suffering, like the turning of a monstrous wheel. Sometimes it was so acute that she screamed with the red-hot agony of it. At other times it would draw away from her for a space, so that she was vaguely conscious that the world held other things, possibly even other forms of torture. Such intervals were generally succeeded by intense cold, racking, penetrating cold that nothing could ever alleviate, cold that was as Death itself, freezing her limbs to stiffness, congealing the blood in her veins, till even her heart grew slower and slower, and at last stood still.

Then, when it seemed the end of all things had come, some unknown power would jerk it on again like a run-down watch in which the key had suddenly been inserted, and she would feel the key grinding round and round and round in a winding-up process that was even more dreadful than the running-down. Then would come agonies of heat and thirst, a sense of being strung to breaking-point, and her heart would race and race till, appalled, she clasped it with her fevered hands and held it back, feeling herself on the verge of destruction.

And through all this dreadful nightmare she never slept. She was hedged about by a fiery ring of sleeplessness that scorched her eyeballs whichever way she turned, giving her no rest. Sometimes indeed dreams came to her, but they were waking dreams of such vivid horror as almost to dwarf her reality of pain. She moved continually through a furnace that only abated when the exhausted faculties began to run down and the deathly chill took her into fresh torments.

Once, lying very near to death, she opened her sleepless eyes upon Max's face. He was stooping over her, holding her nerveless hand very tightly in his own while he pressed a needle-point into her arm. That, she knew, was the preliminary to the winding-up process. It had happened to her before--many times she fancied.

She made a feeble--a piteously feeble--effort to resist him. On the instant his eyes were upon her face. She saw the green glint of them and quivered at the sight. His face was as carved granite in the weird light that danced so fantastically to her reeling brain.

"Yes," he said grimly. "You are coming back."

Then she knew that his will, indomitable, inflexible, was holding her fast, heedless of all the longing of her heart to escape. Then she knew that he, and only he, was the unknown power that kept her back from peace, forcing her onward in that dread circle, compelling her to live in torment. And in that moment she feared him as the victim fears the torturer, not asking for mercy, partly because she lacked the strength and partly because she knew--how hopelessly!--that she would ask in vain.

He did not speak to her again. He was fully occupied, it seemed, with what he had to do. Only, when he had finished, he put his hand over her eyes, compelling them to close, and so remained for what seemed to her a long, long time. For a while she vibrated like a sensitive instrument under his touch, and then very strangely there stole upon her for the first time a sense of comfort. When he took his hand away, she was asleep....

Max turned at last from the bed, nodded briefly to the nurse, and went as silently as a shadow from the room.

Another shadow waited for him on the threshold, and in the light of the passage outside the room they stood face to face.

"She will live," said Max curtly.

"And--" said Nick. He was blinking very rapidly as one dazzled.

"Yes; her reason is coming back. She knew me just now."

"Knew you!"

Max nodded without speaking.

Nick turned his yellow face for a moment towards the open window on the stairs. His lips twitched a little. He said no word.

Max leaned against the wall, and passed his handkerchief over his forehead. Sharp as a ferret, Nick turned.

"Come downstairs, old chap! You've been working like a nigger for the past fortnight. You'll knock up if you are not careful."

Max went with him in silence.

At the foot of the stairs he spoke again. "I shall hand her over to Dr. Jim now. She will do better with him than with me as she gets more sensible."

And so a new presence came into Olga's room, and the figure of her dread appeared no more before her waking eyes. Not at first did she realize the change, for it was only fitfully that her brain could register any definite impression. But one day when strong hands lifted her, something of familiarity in the touch caught her wavering intelligence. She looked up and saw a rugged face she knew.

"Dad!" she said incredulously.

"Of course!" said Dr. Jim bluntly. "Only just found that out?"

She made a feeble attempt to cling to him, smiling a welcome through tears. "Oh, Dad, where have you been?"

"I?" said Dr. Jim. "Why, here to be sure, for the past week. Now we won't have any talking. You shut your eyes like a sensible young woman and go to sleep!"

He had always exacted obedience from her. She obeyed him now. "But you won't go away again?" she pleaded.

"Certainly not," he said, and took her hand into his own.

The last thing she knew was the steady pressure of his fingers on her pulse.

From that time her strength began very slowly to return. The suffering grew less and less intense, till at last it visited her only when she tried to think. And this she was sternly forbidden to do by Dr. Jim, whose word was law.

She was like a little child in those days, conscious only of the passing moment, although even then at the back of her mind she was aware of a monstrous shadow that was never wholly absent day or night. Her father and the nurse were the only people she saw during those early days, and she came to watch for the former's coming with a child's eager impatience.

"I dreamed about Nick last night," she told him one morning. "I wish he would come home, don't you?"

"What do you want Nick for?" he said, possessing himself of her wrist as usual.

"I don't know," she said, knitting her brows. "But it's such a long while since he went away."

He laid his hand on her forehead, and smoothed the lines away. "If you're a good girl," he said, "you shall go and stay with Nick at Redlands when you are well enough."

She looked up at him with puzzled eyes. "I thought Nick was in India, Daddy."

"He was," said Dr. Jim. "But he has come back."

"Then he is at Redlands?" she asked eagerly.

He met her look with his black brows drawn in a formidable frown. "Go slow!" he said. "Yes, he is staying at Redlands."

"Oh, may he come and see me?" she begged.

Dr. Jim considered the point. "If you will promise to keep very quiet," he said finally, "I will let you see him for five minutes only."

"Now?" she asked eagerly.

"Yes, now," said Dr. Jim.

He rose with the words and went out of the room, leaving her struggling to fulfil his condition.

She thought he would return to satisfy himself on this point, but he did not. When the door opened again it was to admit Nick alone.

She held out her arms to him, and in a second he was beside her, holding her fast.

"My poor little chicken!" he said, and though there seemed to be a laugh in his voice she fancied he was in some fashion more moved than she.

"They've cut off all my hair, Nick," she said. "That's the worst of scarlet fever, isn't it?"

"Hair will grow again, sweetheart," he said. "At least, yours will. Mine won't. I'm going as bald as a coot."

They laughed together over this calamity which was becoming undeniably obvious.

"You never did have much thatch, did you, Nick?" she said. "And I suppose India has spoilt what little you had."

"It's nice of you not to set it down to advancing years," said Nick. "Muriel does."

"Muriel? Have you seen her lately?"

"This morning," said Nick.

"Oh?" There was surprised interrogation in Olga's voice. "Where is she, then?"

"At Redlands," said Nick; then, seeing her puzzled look: "We're married, you know, sweetheart."

"Oh?" she said again. "I didn't know."

"It's some time ago now," said Nick. "We've got a little kiddie called Reggie. He's at Redlands too."

"I remember now," Olga smiled understanding. "How is Reggie?" she asked.

"Oh, going strong," said Nick. "He'll soon be as big as I am."

She stretched up a shaky hand to stroke his parchment face. "You're the biggest man I know, Nick," she said softly. "Dad says I may come and stay with you at Redlands. Will you have me?"

"Rather!" said Nick. "There's your own room waiting for you."

"Dear Nick!" she murmured. "You are good to me."

She lay still for a few seconds, holding his hand. Her eyes were wandering round the room. They reached him at last, alert and watchful by her side.

"Nick!" she said.

"What is it, kiddie?"

"There's something I can't remember," she said. "And it hurts me when I try. Nick, what is it?"

He answered her at once with great gentleness. "It's nothing you need worry your head about, dear. I know and so does Jim. You leave it to us till you are a bit stronger."

But she continued to look at him with trouble in her eyes. "I feel as if someone is calling me," she said.

"But that is not so," said Nick quickly and firmly. "Believe me, there is nothing for it but patience. Wait till you are stronger."

She submitted to the mandate, conscious of her own inability to do otherwise; but there was a touch of reproach in her voice as she said, "I thought you would help me, Nick."

"I will," he promised, "when the time comes."

That comforted her somewhat, for she trusted him implicitly; and when Dr. Jim came in he found her quite tranquil.

Thereafter Nick was permitted to see her for a little every day, and she welcomed his visits with enthusiasm.

She would have welcomed Muriel also, but Dr. Jim had decreed that one visitor in the day was enough. She would see Muriel as soon as she was well enough to go to Redlands.

"I really think I am well enough to go now," she confided to Nick one morning. "Do try and persuade Dad."

Nick undertook to do so, with the result that late that night Dr. Jim came in, wrapped her in blankets, head and all as though she had been an infant, and carried her away.

It was a masterly move and achieved with such precision on his part that she had scarcely time to be surprised or excited before she was lying, still in his arms, in a motor and travelling rapidly through the darkness. He uncovered her face then and gave her his blunt permission to come up and breathe.

She clung to him delightedly. "Oh, Dad, isn't it fun? But you're going to stay at Redlands too?"

"For the present," said Dr. Jim.

"Who is taking your patients?" she asked him unexpectedly.

"A fellow from London, a youngster," said Dr. Jim. "Now no more talking, my girl! I'll have you in bed in five minutes and you must be fast asleep in ten."

She laid her cropped head down upon his shoulder, and asked no more.

But she could not wholly repress her astonishment when she abruptly found herself at Redlands. The adventure had all the suddenness of a fairy-tale. "We must have been scorching!" she exclaimed. "Why, we seem to have flown here!"

"It's necessary sometimes," said Dr. Jim.

His words did not wholly explain matters, but they effectually closed her lips; and she asked no more as he bore her up to the room she always occupied when staying in Nick's house. And thereafter she slept more peacefully and naturally than she had slept for a very long time.

In the morning she found another wonder awaiting her; for it was not the nurse who came to her bedside, but Muriel, grave and gentle and motherly, and somehow the sight of her seemed to unveil much that till then had been a mystery to Olga.

She greeted her very lovingly. "You can't imagine what it feels like to see you again," she whispered, with her arms round Muriel's neck. "But I do hope you and Dad haven't hurried back from Switzerland because of me."

Muriel smiled at her with great tenderness. "My darling, don't you know how precious you are?"

"Then you did!" said Olga. "I feel a horrid pig. How is Reggie?"

"He is splendid," said Reggie's mother, in the deep voice that always indicated depth of feeling also. "Much too gay and giddy to come and see you yet. Even Jim is satisfied with him. I couldn't ask for more than that, could I?"

She brought her a cup of milk and sat by the bed while she drank it. There was never any perturbing element in Muriel's presence. She carried ever with her the gracious quietness of a mind at rest.

Olga drank her milk with a most unwonted feeling of serenity. "Reggie certainly mustn't come near me yet," she said. "It would be awful if he caught it."

"There is nothing to catch, dear," said Muriel, as she took back the cup.

"Not scarlet fever?" said Olga in surprise.

"You haven't had scarlet fever," Muriel told her gently. "It was brain fever, following upon sunstroke. That is why we have to keep you so quiet."

"Oh!" said Olga. "Nick never told me that!"

"I don't suppose Dr. Jim would let him. But I told him I should." Muriel's hand, cool and reassuring, held hers. "There is no object in keeping it from you," she said. "You are getting well again, and you always had plenty of sense, dear. I know you will be sensible now."

"I'll certainly try," said Olga.

She lay quiet then for some time, apparently engrossed in thought though not distressed thereby. She turned her head at last and asked a sudden question.

"Will Nick go to India without me, Muriel?"

"No, dear. He is going to wait till you can go too," Muriel answered.

"Oh, Muriel!" She carried the quiet hand impulsively to her lips.

Muriel smiled. "Are you so anxious to go?"

"I should just think I am! But I know I'm horridly selfish. How can you bear to let him go?"

"My dear," Muriel said, "I don't think I could bear to keep him when I know he wants to go. You will have to take care of him for me."

"Oh, I will!" said Olga earnestly.

Very little more passed between them on the subject then, but it filled Olga's mind throughout the day, even to the exclusion of that sinister shadow that still lurked at the back of her consciousness.

Nick did not visit her until the evening, and then she at once began to talk of the topic that so occupied her thoughts.

"Do you know, I had actually forgotten about going to Sharapura, Nick?" she said. "I'm so glad I've remembered. It's something to be quick and get well for."

"Hear, hear!" said Nick, with a whoop of delight.

She laughed at his enthusiasm, and he suddenly recollected himself and entreated her to keep calm.

"If Jim knew I had made you laugh, he'd kick me to a jelly, and give you a blue pill."

Whereat she laughed a little more. "That would be more like Max than Daddy Jim." And there suddenly she stopped short, the colour flooding her pale face. "Why," she said, frowning confusedly, "I had forgotten Max too. How is Max?"

"He's all right," said Nick lightly. "Shall I give him your love?"

"Oh, no!" she said quickly. "Don't give him anything of mine! He--wouldn't understand."

"All right, my chicken," said Nick, with cheery unconcern. "He's got a little brother in the East by the way. I wonder if we shall run across him."

She did not echo the wonder. Her forehead was drawn in the old, painful lines, and she scarcely responded to the rest of his airy conversation.

When Dr. Jim visited her later in the evening he grunted disapproval.

"What's the matter now?" he asked her, with keen eyes on her troubled face.

"I don't know," she murmured wistfully.

"Yes, you do. Come, tell me!" He sat down on the edge of the bed with the evident determination to get at the root of the matter.

She held back for a little, but finally, finding him obdurate, sat up and drew herself within the circle of his arm.

"There, my dear! What is it?" said Dr. Jim.

She hid her face on his shoulder. "Dad, it--it's something to do with Max," she whispered.

"Max? Who is Max?" demanded Dr. Jim inquisitorially, the while he cuddled her close.

"Oh, you know, dear,--Dr. Wyndham," she murmured.

"Oh! So you call him Max, do you?" said Jim drily. "That's an innovation, so far as I am concerned."

"I couldn't help it," she faltered, hiding her face a little lower. "He made me."

"Did he indeed?" said Dr. Jim. "Well? What's the trouble?"

"I--I can't remember," she whispered forlornly.

"Are you in love with him?" asked Dr. Jim abruptly.

She lifted her face with a great start. "No!" she gasped breathlessly.

He looked at her with a semi-humorous frown. "Well, that's something definite to go upon anyhow. Can't stand him at any price, eh?"

She smiled a little doubtfully. "I couldn't at one time. But now--now--"

"Yes? Now?" said Dr. Jim.

"I'm just--afraid of him," she said, a piteous quiver in her voice.

"What for?" Dr. Jim sounded stern, but his hold was very comforting.

"That's just it," said Olga. "I don't remember. I can't remember. But I know he is angry--for some reason. I think--I think I must have done--something he didn't like. Anyhow--I know he is angry."

Dr. Jim grunted again. "Does that matter?" he asked after a moment.

She clung to him very fast. "It will matter--when I see him again."

"And if you don't see him again?" said Dr. Jim.

"Oh, Dad!" she said, with a deep breath.

"Well?" he persisted. "Would that simplify matters? Would that set your mind at rest?"

"Oh, yes, it would!" she said, with immense relief.

He gave her an abrupt kiss, and laid her down. "Very well then. That's settled," he said. "You shan't see him again. Now go to sleep!"

But though she knew he would keep his promise, she was not wholly satisfied, nor did sleep come to her very readily. Her mind was vaguely disturbed. The thought of Max had set her brain in a turmoil which she literally dared not attempt to pursue to its source. She was beginning to be desperately afraid of the mystery she could not penetrate.

She was not so well in the morning, and Dr. Jim rigidly refused to allow either Nick or Muriel at her bedside.

He himself was there during the greater part of the day, watching her, waiting upon her, with a vigilance that never slackened. She suffered a good deal of pain, but his unremitting care did much to alleviate it, and in the evening she was better again, albeit considerably weakened.

After that, her progress was slow, and finding the effort of thought beyond her, she was forced wearily to give up the attempt to think. Even when at length her strength returned sufficiently for her to be carried downstairs and laid on a couch in the garden, the mystery still remained a mystery, and for some reason unintelligible even to herself she had grown content to leave it so. She avoided all thought of it with a morbid dread that was in part physical; for any attempt at concentration in those days always entailed a headache that rendered her practically blind and speechless for hours.

Meantime, they sought to keep her occupied with thoughts of her coming adventure in the East with Nick. There were many preparations to be made, and Muriel tackled them with a steady energy that could not fail to excite Olga's interest. She even roused herself to assist, though Dr. Jim would not permit her to do much, and would often rise and take the work out of her hands when her eyes began to droop.

She had her hours of great depression also, when life was nothing but a burden and she would weep without knowing why. On these occasions Nick was invaluable. He had a wonderful knack of banishing those tears, and in his cheery presence the burden was never insupportable.

It was on Nick's wiry strength that she leaned when she tottered forth for her first walk in the garden. She would probably have wept over her weakness if he had not made her laugh at it instead. It was a morning of soft misty sunshine in the early autumn, and a robin trilled his gay greeting to them as they slowly crept along.

"Jolly little beggar!" said Nick. "Robins always appeal to me. They know how to be cheerful in adversity. Care to go down to the glen, sweetheart? I'll haul you back again."

Yes, Olga would go to the glen. It was a favourite haunt with both of them. The sun glinted on the narrow pathway as they went. The twinkle of the stream was like fairy laughter, with every now and then a secret gurgle as of a laugh suppressed.

They halted on the mossy bank, Nick's arm affording active support. Olga looked down thoughtfully into the running water.

"The last time I was here," she said slowly, "was on the day I went to the Priory to--ask--Violet--to come and stay with me. That must be ages ago."

"Oh, ages!" said Nick.

She turned to him with a puzzled air. "I wonder Violet hasn't been to see me, Nick. Where is she?"

His flickering eyes were searching the stream. "She's gone away," he said.

"Oh! Where has she gone?"

"Haven't a notion," he said indifferently.

"I wonder I haven't heard," mused Olga. "I suppose she hasn't written?"

"Not to my knowledge," said Nick. His attention was obviously still fixed upon the babbling water.

"Oh, well, she hardly ever does write," commented Olga. "And you don't know where she is gone?"

"I do not," said Nick.

At this point his preoccupation seemed to strike her. "What are you looking at?" she asked.

He nodded towards a clump of ferns that fringed the bank. "I thought I saw my friend the scarlet butterfly. There is a beauty lives hereabouts. Yes; by Jove, there he is! See him, Olga?"

Even as he spoke the scarlet butterfly emerged from its hiding place and fluttered down the stream.

Olga uttered a sharp cry that brought Nick's eyes to her face. "What's the matter, kiddie? What is it?"

For a moment she was too overcome to tell him. Then: "Oh, Nick," she said, "I saw that butterfly the last time I was here. It was fluttering along just like that. And then--all of a sudden--a dreadful green dragon-fly flashed out on it, and--and--I didn't see it any more."

"Cheer up!" said Nick. "Evidently it escaped."

"Oh, I wonder!" she said, in a voice of puzzled distress. "I do wonder!"

His shrewd glance returned to the moth quivering like a flower petal in the breeze. "Well, there it is!" he said cheerily. "Let's give it the benefit of the doubt."

Her face did not wholly clear. "I wish I knew," she said. "Do you really think it can be the same, Nick?"

"I've never seen more than one," said Nick, "so it would appear to be a more artful dodger than you took it for. I don't see friend dragon-fly anywhere about."

She shuddered suddenly and convulsively. "No, and I hope he isn't here. Do you know what he made me think of? Max; so strong, so merciless, and so horribly clever."

"I'm clever too," said Nick modestly.

"Oh, but in a different way," protested Olga.

Again his quick eyes flashed over her. "I think you are rather hard on Max myself," he said unexpectedly.

"I?" said Olga.

"Yes, you, my dear. You've no right to regard him in that unwholesome light. He doesn't deserve it. He is quite a decent sort; a little too managing perhaps, but that's just his way. You might go further and fare much worse."

He paused, but Olga said no word. She only palpitated against his arm.

He continued after a moment with the quick decision characteristic of him. "I'm not going to pursue the subject, but just this once--in justice to the man--I must have my say. You asked me once if I liked him, and I was not in a position to tell you. I will tell you now. I like him thoroughly. He's a man after my own heart, straight and clean and staunch. If you ever want someone to trust--trust him! He'd stand by you to perdition."

"Oh, do you think that of him, Nick?" she said, as one incredulous.

"Yes, dear, I do," said Nick. "Well, that's all I have to say. Suppose we begin to crawl back!"

But Olga waited a moment, watching with fascinated eyes the speck of scarlet that still trembled in the sunshine. It fluttered from sight at last, and with a sigh she turned.

"I wonder if it got away!" she murmured again, as if to herself. "I do wonder!"

But to Max, in spite of Nick's spirited eulogy, she made no further reference.

Nick dined at his brother's house at Weir that evening, alone with Max Wyndham. The boys had gone back to school, and the house was almost painfully quiet. Even Nick seemed to feel a certain depression in the atmosphere, for his cheerful chatter was decidedly fitful, and when he and Max were seated opposite to one another smoking it ceased altogether.

Out of a long silence came Max's voice. "When did you say you were starting for the East?"

"Three weeks next Friday," said Nick.

Max grunted, and the silence was renewed.

It was Nick's voice, cracked and careless, that next broke the spell. He seemed to speak on the edge of a laugh. "It's just six years ago since the woman I wanted went to India. Curious, isn't it?"

"What's curious?" said Max.

Nick explained, still with a suspicion of humour in his words: "Well, the funny part of it was that she hoped and believed she was going to get away from me. However, I viewed the matter otherwise, and--I followed her."

"Did you though?" said Max. "And how did the lady take it? Was she pleased?"

"My dear chap, she didn't know." The laugh was more apparent now. Nick removed his cigar to indulge it. "I was most careful not to get in her way, you understand. I was simply there--if wanted."

"And events proved you justified, I suppose?" Max sounded interested after a cynical and quite impersonal fashion.

"They did," said Nick. His own elastic grin appeared for an instant and was gone. "Events can generally be trimmed to suit your purpose," he said, "if you are sufficiently in earnest."

"That has not been my experience," observed Max briefly.

"Perhaps you haven't tried," said Nick.

Silence descended once more, and Nick was rude enough to fall asleep.

An hour later he awoke with extreme alertness in response to a remark from

Max as to the lateness of the hour.

"Yes, by Jove," he said. "I must be getting back. By the way, Wyndham, did I mention to you that Sharapura is the name of the place we are going to? It's quite an interesting corner of the Empire, and declared by medical experts to be a top-hole neighbourhood for studying malaria."

"Is that a recommendation?" asked Max grimly.

Nick's smile was geniality itself. "It is," he answered; "a very strong recommendation." He thrust out a friendly hand. "Good-night, my son, and good luck to you!"

Max's grip was hard and sustained. He looked into the grinning, humorous face, and almost in spite of himself his own mouth took a humorous twist.

"So that's what you came to say, is it?" he said. "Well, good-night, you old rotter, and--thanks!"

Nick mounted his horse and rode back in the moonlight, singing a tuneless but very sentimental love lyric to the stars.

PART II

CHAPTER I
COURTSHIP

It must be great fun gettin' married," said the chief bridesmaid pensively to the best man. "Why don't you go and get married, Noel?"

"I'm going to," said Noel.

"Oh, are you?" with suddenly-awakened interest. "Soon?"

Noel screwed up his Irish eyes and laughed. "In twelve years or thereabouts."

"Oh!" A pair of wide blue eyes regarded him attentively. "Twelve years is a very long time," observed the chief bridesmaid gravely.

"It is, isn't it?" said Noel, with a large sigh.

"P'raps you'll be dead then," suggested the chief bridesmaid.

"What a jolly idea! P'raps I shall. In that case, the marriage will not take place."

She sat down on his knee, and slipped a kindly arm round his neck. "I hope you won't be dead, Noel," she said, in the careful tone of one not wishing to be taken too seriously.

The best man smiled all over his merry face. "I shall do my best to survive for your sake," he said.

She nodded thoughtfully. "But why aren't you goin' to get married sooner?"

He surveyed her with his head on one side. "My little sweetheart is only pocket size at present," he said. "I'm waiting for her to grow up."

"Oh! Is she little like me?" asked the chief bridesmaid, looking slightly disappointed.

"She's just like you, sweetheart," said Noel, with cheery assurance. "She has eyes of wedgewood blue, and hair of golden down, a mouth like a rose, and the jolliest little turn-up nose in the world. And she's going to be six next birthday."

This classic description was an instant revelation to the chief bridesmaid. She blushed very sweetly, with pleasure unfeigned in which shyness had no part. "Oh, Noel!" she breathed, in rapturous anticipation. "But why must we wait till we're growed up?"

"We!" said Noel, who was twenty-two and a crack shot in the Regiment.

She kissed him propitiatingly. "I mean--dear Noel--. why can't we go and get married now? I'm sure Mummy wouldn't mind."

"H'm! I wonder!" said Noel.

"I do love you so very much," said the chief bridesmaid, with eyes of shining sincerity. "And you are just the beautifullest soldier I ever saw!"

He threw back his head in a laugh that showed his white teeth, to his small adorer's huge delight. He was certainly a very gallant figure in his red and gold uniform with his sword dangling at his side; and his winning Irish ways gained him popularity wherever he went.

It was true that the chief bridesmaid's mother shook her head at him, and called him fickle, but then his fickleness was of so open and boyish an order that it could hardly be regarded as a fault, especially since no one--with the exception of the chief bridesmaid--ever took him seriously. And to her at least young Noel Wyndham was always tenderly faithful in his allegiance.

On the present occasion, though nominally he had been acting as best man to a brother officer, he had spent most of his time in the service of the muslin-frocked, bare-legged atom who now sprawled upon his knee with all the privilege of old acquaintance, assuring him of her whole-hearted devotion and admiration.

He had just been giving her tea and wedding-cake, of which latter she had eaten the sugar and he the cake, a wise division which had pleased them both.

"Will we have a cake just like this when we're married, Noel?" she asked seductively, casting an affectionate glance towards the empty plate.

"Oh, rather!" said Noel. "Several storeys high, big enough to last a whole year."

"Oh, Noel!" she murmured ecstatically.

And, "Oh, Noel!" said her mother, suddenly coming up behind them.

The chief bridesmaid laughed roguishly over Noel's shoulder. "I like weddin's," she said.

Noel set her down and rose. "My dear Mrs. Musgrave, I've been hunting for you everywhere. Have you had any tea?"

She smiled at him with amused reproof. A very sweet smile had Mrs. Musgrave, but it was never very mirthful. She had lost all her mirth with her youth. Though she could not have been much over thirty, her hair was silver white.

"I was only in the next room," she said. "Yes, thank you; the padre gave me tea. We must be going. Peggy and I. Will left some time ago, directly after the bride and bridegroom."

"Ah, Will is a paragon of industry. I believe he thinks more of that beastly old reservoir of his than of the whole population of Sharapura put together. But surely you needn't go yet? Don't!" pleaded Noel, with his most persuasive smile.

"No, don't let's, Mummy!" begged the child, clinging to her hero's hand. "Noel and me, we're goin' to be married, we are."

"So we are," said Noel. "And we're going to church on the Rajah's state elephant, and we're going to make him trumpet all the way there and all the way back. I hope we are not springing it on you too suddenly," he added, with a laugh. "It's the usual thing, isn't it, for the best man to marry the chief bridesmaid?"

"I should say it depended a little on their respective ages," smiled Mrs. Musgrave. "Are you going to find my 'rickshaw? It is later than I thought, and I am expecting visitors."

"Ah, I know," said Noel. "Captain and Mrs. Nick of Wara, isn't it?"

"Not Mrs. Nick," she corrected him. "I wish it had been. She is my greatest friend. But she can't leave England because of their child."

"There's a lady of some description coming in his train," asserted Noel. "I have it on unimpeachable authority."

"Yes, she is his niece. I knew her as a child, a giddy little thing--rather like Nick himself."

"Mrs. Musgrave! Is that how you describe one of our most celebrated heroes? Nick Ratcliffe--the one and only--the most romantic specimen of our modern British chivalry--beloved of women like yourself, respected by men like me! Did I hear aright?"

She laughed. "Oh, don't be absurd! He is the least imposing person in the world, I assure you."

"And the lady, his niece?" questioned Noel. "Is she married by the way?"

"Oh, no. She is quite a girl."

"A real live girl in this wilderness!" ejaculated Noel. "I say, may I drop in a little later and see her? Dear Mrs. Musgrave, say Yes!" He stooped and gallantly kissed her hand. "As your daughter's fiance, I think you might ask me to dine. I'll be so awfully good if you will. I say, Peggy, ask Mummy to invite me to dinner to-night, and I'll come and say good-night to you in bed."

"Oh, yes!" cried Peggy, jumping with eagerness. "He may come, mayn't he, Mummy? And I'll save up my prayers," she added to Noel, "and say them to you!"

"Hear, hear!" said Noel. "Come, Mrs. Musgrave, you haven't the heart to refuse me such an innocent pleasure as that. I'm sure you haven't, so thank you kindly, I'll come. Shall I?"

"Of course you are quite irresistible," said Mrs. Musgrave. "But I don't--really-- think it would be very kind of me to have guests on their first night. The poor child is sure to be too tired for chatter."

"But I shan't chatter," protested Noel. "I'll be as quiet as a mouse. Come, Mrs. Musgrave, don't be cruel! Remember you're dealing with your future son-in-law, who is absolutely devoted to you; and don't refuse me the only favour I've ever asked!"

He gained his end. Noel Wyndham was an adept at that, having made a study of it all his life.

Mrs. Musgrave, reflecting that the most fascinating young officer in the cantonment could scarcely be unwelcome in the eyes of a young English girl, however tired she might be, finally allowed herself to be persuaded by cajolery on his part and earnest pleading on Peggy's to include him at her dinner-table.

"If you don't mind taking the risk of being de trop," she said, "you may come."

"I'll take any risk," he declared ardently; and, having gained his point, kissed her hand again and departed to summon her 'rickshaw, with Peggy mounted on his shoulder.

CHAPTER II
THE SELF-INVITED GUEST

When Noel Wyndham entered Mrs. Musgrave's drawing-room that night, he was wearing his most alluring smile. He was evidently prepared to charm and be charmed; and his host, who privately regarded this addition to the party as a decided nuisance, could not but extend to him a cordial welcome. Will Musgrave, though grave and even by some deemed austere, was never churlish. He was a civil engineer of some repute, and had earned for himself a reputation for hard work which was certainly well deserved.

Nick Ratcliffe had been his close friend from boyhood, and the chance that had stationed him within a short distance of the native city of Sharapura in which Nick was for the next few months to take up his abode was regarded by both as a singularly happy one. It was not surprising therefore that he could not bring himself to look upon Noel's advent on that, their first evening together, with much enthusiasm.

His wife had broken the news with semi-humorous apologies. "I couldn't resist him, Will. You know what that boy is. Really I didn't ask him. He asked himself."

"Oh, all right," Will had replied, with resignation. "You'll have to look after him, and see he doesn't try to flirt too outrageously at first sight."

"I'll try," she had assented somewhat dubiously.

For Noel always flirted with every woman he met, herself included, and it was really quite impossible to stop him, or even to discourage him. He only laughed at snubs, and pursued his airy flights with keener zest.

She was not in the drawing-room when the self-invited guest arrived, and it fell to her husband to receive and entertain him. Noel, however, was extremely easy to entertain at all times. He was never bored.

"It was so awfully good of Mrs. Musgrave to let me come," he observed to his host, on shaking hands. "I had to beg jolly hard, I can tell you. She thought your other visitors might consider me one too many. But I'm sure they won't, and I'm immensely keen on meeting them. Have they arrived?"

"Two hours ago," said Will Musgrave.

"That's all right. My brother-in-law knows Ratcliffe, but I've never had the good luck to meet him. Something of a fire-eater, isn't he?"

Will laughed. "Oh, quite a giant in his own line."

Noel nodded. "Just as well. They are wanting a giant pretty badly up at the city if report says true. That young Akbar needs a firm hand. He passed us on parade yesterday, went by like the devil, kicking up a dust fit to choke the lot of us. Beastly young cad!"

"Ah! He isn't over fond of the Indian Army," said Will.

"The Indian Army would give him a damn good hiding if it got the chance," returned Noel, in righteous indignation. "I hope Ratcliffe will rub that into him well. The place is simply swarming with malcontents, and he encourages them. I believe they even flatter themselves we are afraid of 'em."

"I shouldn't say anything of that kind before Miss Ratcliffe," said Will. "She has just got over a severe illness, and may be nervous."

"Great Scotland! This isn't the place for anyone with nerves!" ejaculated Noel. "I heard this morning that there's a most ferocious man-eater in the Khantali district. I'm longing to have a shot at him, but they say he's as cunning as Beelzebub, and never shows unless he has some game on. And the jungle's so beastly thick all round there. It doesn't give anyone a chance. Why can't His Objectionable Excellency turn his hand to something useful, and clear some of it away? By the way, I tried to catch a karait khit, who is a very officious person when he isn't wrapt in contemplation of nothing in particular, interfered and killed the little beast before I had time to explain. I told him he was a silly ass, but he seemed to think he had done something praiseworthy. What's the best remedy for a karait's bite?"

"The only known remedy is to sit down and die with as good a grace as possible," said Nick, entering at the moment. "But it's just as well to be sure it is a karait before you take those measures, as there are more hopeful remedies for other species." He held out his hand to Noel with a cheery smile. "Pleased to meet you. I have already made the acquaintance of one member of your illustrious family."

"Have you though?" said Noel. "That's rather a handicap for me, isn't it?"

Nick's glance travelled swiftly over him and passed. "If you're as good a chap as your brother, you'll do," he said.

"Oh, I'm not," said Noel hastily. "If you're talking about Max, he's the only respectable Wyndham there is, and that's only because he hasn't time to be anything else. He wrote and told me you were coming here. I was at Budhpore then, but I set to work double quick and got myself transferred."

"What for?" said Nick.

Noel winked confidentially. "I wanted to see the fun," he said.

Again for the passage of a second Nick's eyes regarded him, and then over the shrewd, yellow face there flashed a sudden smile. "Are you a cricketer?" said Nick.

"You bet I am!" said Noel boyishly.

Nick nodded. "I was myself once."

"Only once, Nick?" protested Musgrave, with a smile that was scarcely humorous.

Nick turned to him with a semi-rueful grimace. "Oh, my cricketing days are over. All I'm good for now is to teach other fellows the rules of the game."

At this point a high voice made itself heard in the distance, imperiously demanding Noel's presence.

"Oh, Jupiter!" exclaimed Noel. "That's Peggy! Excuse me, you chaps! She has been saving up her prayers for my benefit, and I came early on purpose!"

He was gone with the words, with all an ardent lover's alacrity, and Will Musgrave smiled.

"He's a heady youngster, but there's real stuff in him."

"Sound, is he?" said Nick.

"I should say so; but fancy he's a bit fiery," said Will.

There was nothing to denote fieriness in Noel's attitude as he composed himself a few seconds later for the ceremony of Peggy's devotions. It was a very simple ceremony, but conducted with extreme decorum, Peggy's ayah being sternly dismissed as a preliminary.

Noel sat on the edge of the bed while its small owner knelt upon it, head bowed in hands and lodged upon his shoulder. He had made a tentative movement to encircle her with his arm, but this had been gently but quite firmly forbidden.

"You mustn't cuddle while I'm sayin' my prayers," said Peggy. "You must put your hands together and shut your eyes. That's what Mummy does."

Noel complied with these instructions, but when Peggy was fairly launched he ventured to violate the last and steal a look at the fair head that rested against his shoulder.

Peggy was saying the Lord's Prayer with evident enjoyment. Noel listened with respect. There was the swish of a woman's dress in the passage outside. He listened to that also, his dark eyes watching the half-open door. His attention began to wander.

"Noel!" said a small, hurt voice at his side.

Noel's eyes shut as if at the pulling of a string. "Sorry, Peg-top! Go ahead!"

"You mustn't call me Peg-top when I'm sayin' my prayers!" protested Peggy. "I wanted you to say Amen."

"Amen," said Noel humbly.

"It's no good now." There was a sound of tears in Peggy's voice. "You've just spoilt it all."

"Oh, I say!" pleaded Noel. "Well, try again! I'll say it next time."

"Can't," said Peggy. "It's wrong to keep on sayin' the same thing."

"I never heard that before," said Noel.

"It's in the Bible," asserted Peggy.

"Is it?" Noel sounded faintly incredulous.

"Yes, it is." There was a touch of indignation in Peggy's rejoinder. "It's what the heathen do," she said.

Noel ventured to open his eyes, and found hers fixed severely upon him. "Well, I'm awfully sorry," he said. "What had we better do?"

"You're not sorry," said Peggy accusingly. "Your eyes are all laughy."

"I'll swear they're not," declared Noel. "But I say, hadn't you better finish? Then we can have a cuddle."

"But I can't finish," said Peggy.

"Why not?"

"'Cos you interrupted, and I can't begin again." There was more than the sound of tears this time; the blue eyes were suddenly swimming in them. "And I haven't said my hymn, and you don't care a bit," she said in a voice that quivered ominously. Matters were evidently getting desperate.

"Yes, but you can say the rest," argued Noel, with the feeling that he was losing ground every instant. "What do you generally say next?"

"No, I can't. It wouldn't be sayin' them properly, and God doesn't listen if you don't say them properly."

Here was a formidable difficulty; but Noel's brain was fertile. He had a sudden inspiration. "Look here!" he said. "I'll say the first part again for you, and you can say Amen. I haven't said mine yet, you know, so it doesn't matter for me. Then you can go on and finish. Will that do?"

Peggy gave the matter her grave consideration, and decided that it would. "But you must kneel down," she said.

There was no sound in the passage now. Noel peered in that direction, but detected nothing. Patiently he slipped on to his knees, and began to recite the Lord's Prayer.

Considering the difficulties under which he laboured, he acquitted himself with considerable credit. Peggy at least was fully satisfied, a fact to which her fervent "Amen"! abundantly testified. She took up her own petitions at once quite impressively, albeit with slightly accelerated speed to make up for lost time. At the end of her hymn she paused.

"Would you like me to ask God to make me grow up quick so that we can be married soon, Noel?" she asked.

"I shouldn't." said Noel.

"Not?" The wedgewood-blue eyes opened wide.

"No. Very likely you won't want to marry me when you're grown up," Noel explained.

Peggy was amazed at the bare suggestion of such a possibility. "Why, of course I'll want to marry you," she declared, hugging him. "You're the wery nicest man that ever was."

"No, I'm not. I'm a rotter," Noel made brief and unvarnished reply. "No one knows what I am--except myself. And no one ever will," he added almost fiercely. And then, with lightning change of front, he laughed. "Never mind! We'll go on being sweethearts. That's better than nothing, isn't it?"

Peggy was looking at him very seriously. "I'd go on lovin' you even if--if--you was to kill someone," she said.

"Thanks, Peg-top! Well, I've never done that yet, though there's no knowing how soon I may begin," said Noel carelessly.

"Oh, but it's very wicked to kill people." There was shocked reproof in Peggy's tone.

"Depends," said Noel judicially. "Sometimes it's the only thing to do."

"Oh, Noel!" Peggy's disapproval was evidently struggling with her loyalty.

Something white gleamed in the doorway, and Noel's eyes suddenly sparkled. He abandoned the argument without a second thought.

"Pray come in!" he said. "Peggy is holding a reception. She always receives at this hour. Now, Peggy, stand up and tell this lady my name!"

"May I really come in for a moment?" said Olga. She stood hesitating on the threshold, a slim, girlish figure. "Don't let me disturb you! Mrs. Musgrave thinks she must have left her rings here. How do you do?"

She gave her hand to Noel who had moved to meet her He laughed audaciously into her face.

"Awfully pleased to meet you, Miss--er--Ratcliffe! Why didn't you come in before? I was in a beastly tight fix, and should have been glad of your assistance. I knew you were there."

"Did you?" she said. The smile that had grown so rare flashed over her face in response to his. "I wasn't eavesdropping really," she assured him. "I was only waiting for a suitable moment to present myself."

"Could any moment be anything else?" he asked her, bowing deeply.

She laughed at that without the faintest coquetry. "Very easily, I should say. Isn't little Peggy going to bed?"

"Of course she is," said Noel. "Hop in, infant! We've been officiating at a wedding to-day, she and I, and the excitement has turned our heads a little. That's the way, mavourneen!" as Peggy, a little shy in the presence of the newcomer, slipped into her bed. "You didn't introduce me though, did you?"

Peggy held his hand in embarrassed silence.

"Peggy scarcely knows me herself yet," said Olga. "Don't you think we might manage without?"

"I dared not have suggested it myself," said Noel, with an ease that belied him. "If we do that, we may as well pretend we're old acquaintances at once."

"Perhaps," said Olga. She was searching for her hostess's rings and spoke with a somewhat absent air.

"Especially as my name is Wyndham," he said.

She stopped short in her search and seemed to stiffen. Then slowly she turned towards him. "You are Max's--Dr. Wyndham's--brother!"

"I have that honour," said Noel drily.

She stood quite still for a moment; then: "I knew he had a brother in India," she said. "But I didn't know we were likely to meet."

"That," said Noel, "was partly his doing and partly mine. He wrote and told me that Captain Ratcliffe was coming to Sharapura, and I at once took steps to get myself transferred to the battalion here."

"Oh! Then you know Nick?"

"By repute," smiled Noel. "A good many people in India can say the same, though he may be without honour in his own country."

"Indeed he isn't!" said Olga proudly. "He is a hero wherever he goes."

"And you have come to take care of him?" asked Noel.

She faced him. "Did you know I was coming?"

"No. I thought it was Mrs. Ratcliffe. Max writes an abominable fist."

She seemed relieved. "Yes, I have come to take care of him. He never takes care of himself."

"And you know how to make him do as he is told?" asked Noel.

She smiled. "Oh, yes, I am quite capable. It isn't the first time I have taken care of him. We are very old pals."

"I envy you both," said Noel. "Is this what you are looking for?"

He had spied a ring under the edge of Peggy's biscuit-plate. He held it out to her with a graceful flourish.

But at this point Peggy, who had begun to feel neglected, overcame her shyness and shrilly intervened.

"Noel, that's not the way! You should say, 'With this ring--'"

"Peggy!" Noel interrupted, "you're going too fast. I'm much too old to travel at that pace. I will say good-night to you before you get me into trouble."

He stooped to kiss her, but Peggy was clinging like a marmoset round his neck when he stood up again. His brown face laughed through her curls.

"We're a horribly spoony couple," he said to Olga. "We've known each other just six weeks, and we got engaged to-day."

"Do you often get engaged like that?" asked Olga.

"Oh, rather!" said Noel. "It's much more fun than getting married. Cheaper too, and not so monotonous!" Again he laughed. "I assure you it's the easiest thing in the world to get engaged. Never tried it?"

It was unpardonably audacious; but that was Noel Wyndham's way, and somehow no one ever took offence.

Olga did not take offence, but she winced ever so slightly; a fact which Noel obviously failed to observe, being occupied with the difficult task of releasing himself from Peggy's ardent embraces.

When he finally obtained his freedom and stood up, Olga had passed out again into the passage. He threw a last kiss to his small sweetheart, and hurried after her.

CHAPTER III
THE NEW LIFE

I t isn't in the least what I thought it would be," said Olga.

"Nothing ever is," said Nick.

He was sprawling on a charpoy on the verandah of their new abode, smoking a cigarette with lazy enjoyment.

Though within sound of the native city, their bungalow stood well outside. It was surrounded by a compound of many tangled shrubs that gave it the appearance of being more isolated than it actually was. Not so very far away from it, down in the direction of Will Musgrave's growing reservoir, there stood a dak-bungalow; and immediately beyond this were corn-fields and the native village that clustered along the edge of the river. The cantonments were well out of sight, more than a mile away along the dusty road, further than the polo-ground and race-course.

Behind the bungalow, approached only through a dense mass of tall jungle grass, stretched the jungle, mile upon mile of untamed wilderness, home of wild pig and jackals, monkeys and flying foxes. Very quiet by day was that long dark tract of jungle, but at night strange voices awoke there that seemed to Olga like the crying of unquiet spirits. Neither by day nor night did she feel the smallest desire to explore it.

The native city of Sharapura held infinitely greater fascinations for her. Some of its buildings were beautiful, and she was keenly interested in its inhabitants. She never entered it, however, save under Nick's escort. He was very insistent upon this point, and he would never suffer her to linger in the long, narrow bazaar, with its dim booths and crafty, peering faces.

Down by the river there was a mosque about which pigeons circled and cooed perpetually, but beggars were so plentiful all round it that it was next to impossible to pause near the spot without being beset on all sides, a matter of real regret to the English girl, who longed to wander or stand and admire at will.

In His Excellency the Rajah she was frankly disappointed. He had been educated in England, and had acquired a patronizing condescension of demeanour which she found singularly unattractive. He never treated her with familiarity, but she did not like the look of his dusky eyes. They always smiled, but to her there was something unpleasant behind the smile. In her private soul she deemed him treacherous.

He invariably wore European costume, with the exception of his green turban with its flowing puggaree. He was an excellent and graceful horseman, and spoke English with extreme fluency.

Nick spent a good many hours of every day at the Palace, and they were always on the best terms; yet Olga never saw him go without a pang of anxiety or return without a thrill of relief.

Probably her recent severe illness had had a lasting effect upon her nerves, for she was never easy in his absence, though Daisy Musgrave did much to reassure her. She had taken Olga under her wing as naturally as though they had been related, and they were much together.

The old life had begun to seem very far away to Olga, her childhood as remote as a half-forgotten dream. The blank space in her memory remained as a patch of darkness through which her thread of life had run indeed but of which no record remained. She had ceased to attempt to read the riddle, half in dread and half in sheer helplessness. It did not seem to matter. Surely, as Max had once said to her, nothing mattered that was past.

She did not spare much thought for Max either just then, instinctively avoiding all mention of him. She had a vague consciousness that was more in the nature of a nightmare memory than an actual happening, that they had parted in anger. Sometimes there would rush over her soul the recollection of piercing green eyes that searched and searched and would not spare, and her heart would beat in a wild dismay and she would shrink in horror from the vision. But it was not often that this came to her now. She had learned to ward it off, to put away the past, to live in the present.

For nearly a month she had been established with Nick in the bungalow on the outskirts of the city, and the novelty of things had begun to wear off. She was not strong enough to go out very much, and beyond a few calls with Nick and a dinner or two at the cantonments she had not seen much of the social life of Sharapura.

That night, however, they were to attend a State dinner at the Palace, to which all the officers of the battalion and their wives had been bidden. Olga was relieved to know that the Musgraves were also going, for at present she was intimate with no one else, with the possible exception of Noel, who visited them in a fashion which he described as "entirely unofficial" almost every day. He seemed to entertain a vast admiration for Nick, and as Olga was wholly in sympathy with him on this great point, they did not find it difficult to agree upon smaller matters. She even bore with his bare-faced Irish compliments, mainly because she knew he did not mean them and she found it easier to be amused than offended.

The new life was undeniably one of considerable interest, and now and then, more particularly when she went for her morning ride with Nick--a function which Noel almost invariably attended when off duty, appearing with a brazen smile and not the faintest suggestion of an excuse--the old zest would awake within her, almost deluding her into the belief that her lost youth had returned.

She still had her hours of depression and strange heart-heaviness so alien to her nature, and even in her lighter moments she was far more restrained than of yore--shrewd still, quick of understanding still, but infinitely graver, more womanly, more reserved.

Nick, who watched her as tenderly as a mother, sometimes asked himself if after all he and Jim had done the right thing. Her remoteness worried him. She seemed to live in a world of her own, asking no questions, making no confidences. Not that she ever barred him out. He was well aware that she had not the vaguest desire to keep him at a distance. But her old spontaneity, her child-like demonstrativeness, seemed to have gone, and a nameless shadow haunted the eyes that once had been so clear.

They often sat together on the verandah as now, when the day's work was done, sometimes talking, sometimes silent, always in complete accord.

Olga's remark that the India to which Nick had introduced her was wholly unlike her expectations had been called forth by some comment of his upon the Rajah's exceedingly British tastes.

"I thought things would be much more primitive," she said.

And Nick laughed, and after a long draught of whisky and soda observed that possibly they were more primitive than she imagined. After which he stretched himself luxuriously, and asked her if she were aware that they were within a week of Christmas Day.

"Of course," she said. "Did you imagine I had forgotten? It seems so strange to have nothing to do."

He sat up very abruptly with his knees drawn up to his chin and blinked at her with extreme rapidity. "Olga," he said, "I believe you're homesick."

The colour that of old had been so quick to rise faintly tinged her face as she shook her head. "Oh, no, Nick! Don't be absurd! How could I be, with you?"

"I'm not absurd--on this occasion," returned Nick.

"It's the fashion for absentees to be homesick all the world over at Christmas-time. However, we are not bound to follow the fashion. How are we going to celebrate the occasion? Have you any ideas to put forward?"

"None, Nick."

He nodded. "That makes it all the easier for me. Shall we give a picnic at Khantali--you and I? It won't be much fag for you if you drive over with Daisy Musgrave. Noel can take most of the provisions in his dog-cart. He's a useful youngster. How does that strike you? There is a ruined temple or a mosque at Khantali, I believe, and you like that sort of thing."

He paused. She was listening with far-away eyes. "Yes, I shall like that," she said. "It is very nice of you to think of it."

Nick straightened his knees and got up. "Do you know what I would do if I had two hands, Olga mia?" he said.

She looked up questioningly. His face was for the moment grim.

"I would take you by the shoulders and give you a jolly good shaking," he said.

She opened her eyes in astonishment. "Really, Nick!"

"Yes, really," he said. "You didn't hear a word of what I said just now."

"Oh, but I did!" she protested, flushing in earnest this time. "I heard you and I answered you."

"Oh, yes, you answered me," he said, "as kindly and indulgently as if I had been prattling like Peggy Musgrave. I won't put up with it any longer, my chicken. Understand?"

He put his hand under her chin and turned her face upwards.

She quivered a little and the tears sprang to her eyes. "I'm sorry, Nick," she said.

He shook his head at her. "I won't have you sorry. That's just the grievance. Be hurt, be indignant, be angry! Sulk even! I know how to treat sulks. But don't cry, and don't be sorry! I shall be furious if you cry."

She smiled up at him wistfully, saying nothing.

"Fact of the matter is," proceeded Nick, "you're spoilt. It's high time I put my foot down. If you don't wake up, I'll make you take a cold bath every morning and swing dumb-bells for half an hour after it."

She began to laugh. "I love to see you playing tyrant, Nick."

He let her go. "I'm not playing, my child. I'm in sober, deadly earnest. Have you made up your mind yet what you're going to say to young Noel when he asks you to marry him?"

She started. "Oh, really, Nick!" she said again, this time with a touch of annoyance in her tone.

He smiled as he heard it. "It's coming, I assure you. You see, the station is short of girls, and our young friend is impressionable. He is the sort of amorous swain who gets engaged to a dozen before he settles down to marriage with one. The question for you to decide is, are you going to be one of the dozen?"

"No, that I certainly am not." Olga spoke with undoubted emphasis, and having spoken rose and laid her hands upon Nick's shoulders. "I don't think he would be so silly as to ask me," she said. "And if he did, I certainly should not be silly enough to say Yes."

"I'm glad to hear that anyway," said Nick briskly. "I was afraid you might accept him out of sheer boredom."

"Nick! I'm not bored!"

He looked at her quizzically, as if he did not quite believe her.

"I am not bored," she reiterated, with something like vehemence. "I am happier with you than with anyone else in the world."

"Really?" said Nick, still smiling.

"Don't you believe me?" she said.

He laughed. "Not quite, dear; but that's not your fault. What are you going to wear to-night?"

Nick could switch himself from one subject to another as easily as a monkey leaps from tree to tree, and when once he had made the leap no persuasion could ever induce him to return. Olga knew this, and abandoned the discussion, albeit slightly dissatisfied.

They separated soon after to dress for the Rajah's dinner. Olga had chosen a dress of palest mauve, and very fair and delicate she looked in it. In a crowd of girls she would doubtless have been passed over by all but the most observant, but she was not one of a crowd at Sharapura. There were not many girls in that region, or Noel Wyndham's volatile fancy had scarcely strayed in her direction.

She told herself this with a faint smile, as she took a final glance at herself when her ayah had finished. There never had been any personal vanity about Olga, and that night she told herself she looked positively ugly. What in the world did Noel see in her, she wondered? It seemed incredible that any man could find anything to admire in the colourless image that confronted her.

And yet as she went up the Palace steps with Nick into the blaze of light that awaited them, he was the first to greet her, and she saw his eyes kindle at the sight of her after a fashion that made her heart contract with a sudden pain for which at the moment she was wholly at a loss to account.

"I say, you look topping!" he said, smiling down at her with pleasing effrontery. "Do you know you are very nearly late? I've been watching out for you for the past ten minutes."

"What a waste of time!" said Olga; but she returned his smile, for she could not do otherwise.

"No! Why? I had nothing better to do," he assured her. "And my patience is well rewarded. Hope you're keen on music. I've brought my banjo for the Rajah's edification. It's better than a tomtom anyway. I wonder if the fates have put us next to each other. I'll lay you five rupees to a sixpence that they haven't."

Olga refused to take this generous offer, saying she had no sixpences to spare him, a remark which he declared to be both premature and uncalled for.

"You shouldn't kick a man before he's down," he said. "It's bad policy. If you have to sit next to me after that, it will serve you right."

But when she found that he actually was to be her neighbour she was far from quarrelling with the destiny that made him so. He was so blithe and gay of heart, so blandly impudent, the very wine seemed to shine the redder for his presence. It was not in her nature to flirt with any man, but it was utterly impossibly not to enjoy his society. Less and less did she believe that his butterfly pursuit of her had in it the smallest element of serious intention. He was altogether too young and giddy for such things. She dismissed the matter without further misgiving.

CHAPTER IV
THE PHANTOM

Without Noel she would have found that State dinner as dreary as it was pompous. The Rajah was occupied with discussing the laws of British sport with Colonel Bradlaw who regarded himself as an authority on such matters, and expressed his opinions ponderously and at extreme length.

Nick was far away down the long table, seated beside Daisy Musgrave, obviously to their mutual satisfaction. A bubbling oasis of gaiety surrounded them. Evidently the general atmosphere of state and ceremony was less oppressive in that quarter.

"Where would you be without me to take care of you?" said Noel, boldly intercepting her glance in their direction.

"I am not at all bad at taking care of myself," she told him.

"I say--forgive me--I don't believe that," said Noel, with calm effrontery. "You would simply fall a prey to the first ogre who came along."

Olga elevated her chin slightly. "That shows how much you know about me."

"I know a great deal," said Noel, with an ardent glance. "And that's what makes me want to know much more. You know, you're horribly tantalizing, if you will allow me to say so."

"In what way?" She spoke coolly; there was a hint of challenge in the grey eyes she turned upon him.

He laughed without embarrassment. "I can't quite explain. There's something so elusively attractive--or do I mean attractively elusive?--about you. I call you 'the will-o'-the-wisp girl' to my own private soul."

"I hope your own private soul is too sensible to encourage such nonsense," said

Olga severely.

He looked at her, sheer mischief dancing in his Irish eyes. "Come and see it some day and judge for yourself!" he said. "I can fix up a seance any time. It would always be at home to you. I'm sure you would get on together."

It was hard to restrain a smile; Olga permitted herself one of strictly limited proportions.

"I will show you a glimpse presently if you would care to see it," proceeded Noel.

"Oh, please don't trouble!" said Olga.

"Afraid of being bored?" he asked.

She laughed. "Perhaps."

He leaned towards her. Her laugh was reflected in his eyes, but she did not hear it in his voice as he said, "Do you mean that? Do I really bore you?"

She met his look for a moment, and her heart quickened a little. Quite suddenly she realized that this man, young though he was, possessed a wonderful power of attraction. She wondered if he himself were aware of it, and rapidly decided that he had made the discovery in his cradle. Of one thing she was certain. She did not want to fall in love with him. He drew her indeed, but it was against her will.

"Well?" he said. "Have you made up your mind yet?"

She smiled. "Oh, no, you don't bore me," she said.

"Thanks awfully! It's not generally considered a family failing of the Wyndhams. Every other rascality under the sun, but not that."

"What a fascinating family you seem to be!" said Olga.

He made a wry face. "In a sense. Did you find Max fascinating?"

He put the question carelessly; yet she suspected he had a reason for asking it. She felt the tell-tale blood rising in her face.

"You don't like him?" said Noel.

She hesitated.

"I don't mind your saying so in the least," he assured her. "He's a queer chap--a bit of a genius in his own line; but geniuses are trying folk to live with. How did he get on with your father?"

"Oh, Dad likes him," she said.

"He's not much of a ladies' man," remarked Noel. "I suppose he has chucked that job by this time, and gone back to Sir Kersley Whitton. Lucky beggar! He seems to be able to do anything he likes."

"I didn't know he was going to leave," said Olga quickly.

"No? I believe he said something about it in his letter to me. He is always rather sudden," said Noel. "Too much beastly electricity in his composition for my taste."

"Do you often hear from him?" Olga asked abruptly.

"Once in a blue moon. Why?" His dark eyes interrogated her, but she would not meet them.

"I just wondered," she said.

"No. I scarcely ever hear," said Noel. "He wrote, I suppose, to tell me of your good uncle's advent. He had probably heard from my sister that some of us were stationed here. Anyhow I lost no time in getting myself transferred for the pleasure of making his acquaintance. I was inclined to regret the move just at first. It's rather a hole, isn't it? But the moment I saw you--" Olga stiffened slightly, and he at once passed on with the agility of a practised skater on thin ice: "I say, what a ripping little sportsman your uncle is! He is actually talking of taking up polo again. Did you know?"

"Polo!" Olga stared at him. "Nick! How could he?"

"Heaven knows! I suppose he would hang on with his knees, and swipe when he got the chance. He'd need some deuced intelligent ponies though."

"He couldn't possibly do it!" Olga declared. "He mustn't try."

"Think you can prevent him?" asked Noel curiously.

"He won't if I beg him not to," she said.

"Oh, that's how you manage him, is it? Does he always come to heel that way?"

Olga's eyes flashed a loving glance down the table towards her hero. "There is no one in the world like Nick," she said softly.

"It's good to be Nick," remarked Noel, with his impudent smile. "It's quite evident that he can do no wrong."

She laughed and turned the subject. Nick was too near and dear to discuss with an outsider.

They began to talk of polo. A match had been arranged for Boxing Day. Noel was a keen player, and had plenty to say about it.

The Rajah was also a keen player, and after a little he disengaged himself from Colonel Bradlaw's endless reminiscences and joined in the conversation, which speedily became general.

A display of fireworks had been provided for the entertainment of the guests, and when the long State dinner was over they repaired to a marble balcony that overlooked some of the Palace gardens.

Will Musgrave came and joined Olga as she stepped out between the carved pillars. She greeted him with a smile of welcome. They were old friends. As a child she had known him before his marriage, though she had seen nothing of him since. There was something in the quiet strength of the man that appealed to her. He gave her confidence.

"Well, Olga," he said, "how do you like India?"

They stood together by the fretted marble balustrade, looking down upon the illuminated gardens that stretched away dim and mysterious into the night.

Olga did not directly answer the question. "I am not really acquainted with her yet," she said.

He uttered a short sigh. "She is a hard mistress. I don't advise you to get too intimate. She has a way of turning and rending her slaves, which is ungrateful, to say the least of it."

"But you are not sworn to her service for ever," said Olga.

He laughed with a touch of sadness. "Until she kicks me out. Like Kipling's Galley Slave, I'm chained to the oar. It's all very well so long as one remains in single blessedness, but it's mighty hard on the married ones. Take my advice, Olga; never marry an Indian man!"

"I'm never going to marry anyone," said Olga, with quiet decision.

"Really!" said Will Musgrave.

She turned her head towards him. "You sound surprised."

He smiled a little. "I beg your pardon. I was only surprised at the way in which you said it--as if you had been married for years, and knew the best and the worst."

There was a slight frown on Olga's face. She looked as if she were trying to remember something. "Oh, no, it wasn't like that," she said. "But somehow I don't feel as if I could ever like a man well enough to marry him. I don't want to fall in love."

"Too much trouble?" suggested Will.

She nodded, the frown still between her eyes. "It doesn't seem worth while," she said rather vaguely. "It's such a waste."

Will looked at her with very kindly eyes. "I see," he said gently.

She met the look and read his thought. Almost involuntarily she answered it. "I've never been in love myself," she told him simply. "But somehow I know just what it feels like. It's a wonderful feeling, isn't it? Like being caught up to the Gates of Paradise." She paused, and the puzzled frown deepened. "But one comes back again--nearly always," she said. "That's why I don't think it seems worth while."

"I see," Will said again. He was silent for a moment while a great green rocket rushed upwards with a hiss and burst in a shower of many-coloured stars. Then as they watched them fall he spoke very kindly and earnestly. "But it is worth while all the same--even though one may be turned back from Paradise. Remember-- always remember--that it's something to have been there! Not everyone gets so far, and those who do are everlastingly the richer for it." He paused a moment, then added slowly, "Moreover, those who have been there once may find their way there again some day."

Another rocket soared high into the night and broke in a golden rain. From a few yards away came Nick's cracked laugh and careless speech.

"Here comes the *chota-bursat*, Daisy! It's high time you went to the Hills."

Daisy Musgrave's answer was instant and very heartfelt. "Oh, not yet, thank Heaven! We have three months more together, Will and I."

"You must make him leave his beastly old reservoir to the sub when the hot weather comes," said Nick, "and go for a honeymoon with you."

"If he only could!" said Daisy.

A sombre smile crossed Will's face as he turned it towards his wife. "I'm listen- ing, Daisy," he said.

She came quickly to his side, and in the semi-darkness Olga saw her hand slip within his arm. "I'm feeling sentimental to-night," she said, in a voice that tried hard to be gay. "It's Nick's fault. Will, I want another honeymoon."

"My dear," he made answer in his deep, quiet voice, "you shall have one."

The rattle of squibs drowned all further speech, and under cover of it Olga made her way to Nick.

"They're awfully fond of each other, those two," she confided to him.

"Bless their hearts! Why shouldn't they?" said Nick tolerantly. "Are you getting tired, my chicken? Do you want to go home to roost?"

She was a little tired, but he was not to hurry on her account. "It's quite restful out here," she said.

He put his arm about her. "What did the infant Don Juan talk about all dinner-time?"

She laughed with a touch of diffidence. "He is quite a nice boy, Nick."

"What ho!" said Nick. "I thought he was making the most of his time."

She pinched his fingers admonishingly. "Don't be a pig, Nick! We--we talked of Max--part of the time."

"Oh, did we?" said Nick.

"Yes. Did you know he was thinking of leaving Dad?"

"I did," said Nick.

There was a moment's silence; then: "Dear, why didn't you tell me?" she asked, her voice very low.

"Dear, why should I?" said Nick.

She did not answer, though his flippant tone set her more or less at her ease.

"Any more questions to ask?" enquired Nick, after a pause.

With an effort she overcame her reticence. "He has actually gone then?"

"Bag and baggage," said Nick.

"Nick, why?"

"I understand he never was a fixture," said Nick.

"No. I know. But--but--I didn't think of his going so soon," she murmured.

"You don't seem pleased," said Nick.

"You see, I had got so used to him," she explained. "He was like a bit of home."

"I'm sure he would be vastly flattered to hear you say so," said Nick.

She laughed rather dubiously. "Has Dad got another assistant then?"

"I don't know. Very likely. You had better ask him when you write."

"And he has gone back to Sir Kersley Whitton?" she ventured.

"My information does not extend so far as that," said Nick.

She turned her attention to the blaze of coloured fire below them, and was silent for a space.

Suddenly and quite involuntarily she sighed. "Nick!"

"Yours to command!" said Nick.

She turned towards him resolutely. "Be serious just a moment! I want to know something. He didn't leave Dad for any special reason, did he?"

"I've no doubt he did," said Nick. "He has a reason for most of his actions. But he didn't confide it to me."

She gave another sharp sigh, and said no more.

Colonel Bradlaw came up and joined them, and after a little the Rajah also. He stationed himself beside Olga, and began to talk in his smooth way of all the wonders in the district she had yet to see.

She wished he would not take the trouble to be gracious to her, but he was always gracious to European ladies and there was no escape. The British polish over the Oriental suavity seemed to her a decidedly incongruous mixture. She infinitely preferred the purely Oriental.

"My shikari has told me of a man-eater at Khantali," he said presently. "You have not seen a tiger-hunt yet? I must arrange an expedition, and you and Captain Ratcliffe will join?"

Olga explained that she had never done any shooting.

"But you will like to look on," he said.

She hesitated. "I am afraid," she said, after a moment, "I don't like seeing things killed."

"No?" said the Rajah politely.

She wondered if the dusky eyes veiled contempt, and felt a little uncomfortable in consequence of the wonder.

"You have never killed--anything?" he asked, in a tone of courteous interest.

"Nothing bigger than a beetle," said Olga.

"Really!" said the Rajah.

This time she was sure he was feeling bored, and she began to wish that Noel would reappear and lighten the atmosphere.

As if in answer to the wish, there came the sudden tinkle of a stringed instrument in one of the marble recesses behind them, and almost immediately a man's voice, very soft and musical, began to sing:

"O, wert thou in the cauld blast,
 On yonder lea, on yonder lea,
My plaidie to the angry airt,
 I'd shelter thee, I'd shelter thee.

Or did misfortune's bitter storms
 Around thee blaw, around thee blaw,
Thy bield should be my bosom,
 To share it a', to share it a'."

The voice ceased; the banjo thrummed on. Olga's hands were fast gripped upon the marble lattice-work. She stood tense, with white face upraised.

The Rajah was wholly forgotten by her, and he stepped silently away to join another of his guests. The new English girl presented an enigma to him, but it was one in which he did not take much interest. All her fairness notwithstanding, she was not even pretty, according to his standard, and he had seen a good many pretty women.

Again through the dimness the clear voice came. It held a hint--a very carefully restrained hint--of passion.

"Or were I in the wildest waste,
 Sae black and bare, sae black and bare,
The desert were a paradise
 If thou wert there, if thou wert there.
Or were I monarch o' the globe,
 Wi' thee to reign, wi' thee to reign,
The brightest jewel in my crown
 Wad be my queen, wad be my queen."

The song was ended; the banjo throbbed itself into silence. Olga's hands went up to her face. She wanted to keep the silence, to hold it fast, while she chased down that elusive phantom that dodged her memory.

Ah! A voice beside her, Nick's arm through hers! She raised her face. The phantom had fled.

"After that serenade, I move that we take our departure," said Nick. "The youngster has a decent voice, so far as my poor judgment goes. Are you ready?"

Yes, she was ready. She longed to be gone, to get away from the careless, chattering crowd, to work out her problem in solitude and silence.

With scarcely a word she went with him, and they made their farewells together.

At the last moment Noel, his eyes very bright and coaxingly friendly, caught her hand and boldly held it.

"Did you catch it?" he asked.

She looked at him uncomprehendingly. "Catch what?"

He laughed. The pressure of his fingers was intimately close. "That glimpse I promised you," he said.

"Ah!" Understanding dawned in Olga's eyes, and in the same instant she removed her hand. "No, I'm afraid I didn't. I was thinking of something else. Good-bye!"

"Oh, I say!" protested Noel, actually crest-fallen for once.

Nick swallowed a chuckle, and clapped him on the shoulder. "Good-night, minstrel boy! Mind you bring the harp along to my Christmas picnic! We are not all so unappreciative as Olga."

Noel looked for a second as if he were on the verge of losing his temper, but the next he changed his mind and laughed.

"You bet I will, old chap!" he said, and wrung Nick's hand with cordiality.

Nick's chuckle became audible as they drove away. "He can't accuse you of encouraging him anyhow, Olga mia," he remarked. "If you keep it up at this pace, you'll soon choke him off."

Olga's answer was to draw very close to him, and to utter a great sigh.

"Wherefore?" whispered Nick.

She was silent for a moment, then: "I sometimes wish you were the only man in the world, Nick," she said, with quivering emphasis.

"Gracious heaven!" said Nick. "Don't make me giddy!"

She laughed a little, but there was a sound of tears behind. "Men are so silly," she said.

"Abject fools!" said Nick. "There's never more than one worth crying about."

"What do you mean, Nick?"

"Nothing--nothing!" said Nick. "I was just demonstrating my foolishness, that's all."

Whereat she laughed again in a somewhat doubtful key, and asked no more.

CHAPTER V
THE EVERLASTING CHAIN

It was a very thoughtful face that met Nick at the breakfast table on the following morning. But Nick's greeting was as airy as usual. He made no comments and asked no questions.

The day was Sunday, a perfect day of Indian winter, cloudless and serene. The tamarisks in the compound waved their pink spikes to the sun, and in the palm-trees behind them bright-eyed squirrels dodged and flirted. A line of cypresses bounded the garden, and the sky against which they stood was an ardent blue.

"What is the programme for to-day?" said Nick, when the meal was nearly over.

Olga leaned her chin on her hand, and looked across at him. "Shall you go to church, Nick?"

The cantonments boasted a small church and a visiting chaplain who held one service in it every Sunday.

Nick considered the matter in all its bearings while he stirred his coffee.

"No," he said finally; "I think I shall stay at home with you this morning."

"How do you know I am not going?" said Olga.

Nick grinned. "I'm awfully good at guessing, Olga mia."

She smiled rather wanly. "Well, I'm not going, as a matter of fact. I had a stupid sort of night."

Nick nodded. "I shan't take you out to dinner again for a long time."

"It wasn't that," she said. "At least, I don't think so. It was that song. Why did Noel sing it?"

"For reasons best known to himself," said Nick, taking out his cigarette-case.

She rose and went round to his side to strike a match for him, but reaching him she suddenly knelt and clasped her arms about his neck.

"Nick," she whispered, "I'm frightened."

His arm went round her instantly. "What is it, my chicken?"

She held him closely for a while in silence; then, her face hidden, she told him of the trouble at her heart.

"That song has been haunting me all night long. I feel as if--as if--someone-- were calling me, and I can't quite hear or understand. Nick, where--where is Violet?"

It had come at last. Once before she had confronted him with that question, and he had turned it aside. But to-day, he knew that he must face and answer it.

He laid his cheek against her hair. "Olga darling, I think you know, but I'll tell you all the same. She has--gone on."

Very gently he spoke the words, and after them there fell a silence broken only by the scolding of a couple of parroquets in a mimosa-tree near the verandah.

Nick did not stir. His lips twitched a little above the fair head, and his yellow face showed many lines; but there was no tension in his attitude. His pose was alert rather than anxious.

Olga lifted her face at last. She was very white, but fully as composed as he.

"That," she said slowly, "was the thing I couldn't remember."

He nodded. "It was."

Her hands clasped the front of his coat with nervous force. She looked him straight in the face.

As of old, the flickering eyes evaded her. They met and passed her over a dozen times, but imparted nothing.

"Nick," she said, "will you please tell me how it happened? I am strong enough to bear it now, and indeed--indeed, I must know."

"I have been waiting to tell you," Nick said. "Put on a hat, and we will go in the garden."

She rose at once. Somehow his brief words reassured her. She felt no agitation, was scarcely aware of shock. In his presence even the shadow of Death became devoid of all superstitious fears. In some fashion he made fear seem absurd.

Nick waited for her on the verandah with his face turned up to the sky. He scarcely looked like a man bracing himself for a stiff ordeal, but it was not his way to stoop under his burdens. He had learned to tread jauntily while he carried a heart like lead.

When Olga joined him, he put his hand through her arm and led her forth. The path wound along between the tangle of shrubs and lower growth till it reached the cypresses, and here was a shady stretch where they could pace to and fro in complete privacy.

Arrived here, Nick spoke. "It wasn't altogether news to you, was it?"

She passed her hand across her eyes in the old, puzzled way. "I didn't remember," she said, "and yet I wasn't altogether surprised. I think somehow at the back of my mind--I suspected."

"You remember now," said Nick.

She looked at him with troubled eyes. "No, I don't, dear. That's just it. I--I can't remember. It--frightens me." She clasped his hand with fingers that trembled.

"No need to be frightened," said Nick. "You were ill, you know; first the heat and then the shock. After brainfever, people very often do forget."

"Ah, yes," she said, with a piteous kind of eagerness. "But it is coming back now. I only want you to help a little." She stood suddenly still. "Nick, you are not afraid of Death, I know. Wasn't it you who called it the opening of a Door?"

"It is--just that," said Nick.

"But the body," she said, "the body dies."

"The body," he said, "is like a suit of clothes that you lay aside till the time comes for it to be renovated and made wearable again."

"Ah! She couldn't die, could she, Nick?" Olga's eyes implored him. "Not she herself!" she urged. "She was so full of life. I can't realize it. I can't--I can't! Tell me how it happened! Surely I never saw her dead! Whatever came after, I never could have forgotten that!"

"Tell me how much you do remember, kiddie," Nick said gently. "And I will fill in the gaps."

Her forehead contracted in a painful frown. "It's so difficult," she said, "so disjointed--like a dreadful dream. I know she was horribly afraid of Max. And then there was Major Hunt-Goring. I can't believe she ever liked him. It was only because he--flattered her, and gave her those dreadful cigarettes."

"Probably," said Nick.

"That morning when he invited us to go on his yacht is the last thing I can remember clearly," she said. "I didn't want to go, but--she--insisted. After that, my mind is just a jumble of impressions that don't fit into each other. I seem to remember being on the yacht, and Major Hunt-Goring and Violet laughing together. And then he came and told me an awful thing about her mother. He wanted me to say I would marry him, and I wouldn't because I hated him so. And after that he was so furious, he went and told her too."

Olga stopped with horror in her eyes. The effort to remember was plainly torturing her, yet Nick made no effort to help her.

"And after that?" he said.

"Oh, after that, there seems to come a blank. I remember her face, and how I held her in my arms and tried to comfort her. And then--oh, it's just like a dreadful dream!--I was running in the sun, running, running, running, never seeming to get anywhere. The next thing I really remember is being at the Priory and having lunch in that awful storm, and Max coming--do you remember?--do you remember? And how I kept him away from her? Poor child, he terrified her so." Olga was shuddering now from head to foot. Her eyes were wide and staring, as though fixed upon some fearful vision.

Nick did not attempt to interrupt her. He waited, alert and silent, for the vision to come to an end.

The end was not far off. She went on speaking rapidly, as if more to herself than to him. She seemed indeed to have forgotten him for the moment.

"What a frightful storm it was! That flash of lightning--how it shone through the east window--and the floor was all red as if--as if--" She broke off; her hand clenched unconsciously upon Nick's. "Did you see her?" she whispered. "Or was it only a nightmare? She--was trying--to--to--kill Max--in the dark!"

"She was not herself," said Nick. His voice was low and soothing; he spoke as if he feared to awake her.

"No--no! She was mad--like her mother. Oh, Nick, how beautiful she was!"

Suddenly the tension passed. Olga covered her face and began to cry.

His arm tightened about her; he drew her on up the shady walk. "And that is all you remember, kiddie?" he said.

She slipped her arm round his neck as they walked. "No, I remember two things more." She forced back her tears to tell him. "I remember Max's arm all soaked with blood. It stained my dress too. And I remember his saying that--that it was a hopeless case, and that she--Violet--was as good as dead. After that--after that----"

Nick waited. "After that?" he said.

She turned to him, her face anguished, piteous, appealing. "I can't get any further than that, Nick. It's just a dreadful darkness that makes me afraid. I think I begged him not to go to her. But I know he went, because--when he came down again"--her voice faltered; bewilderment showed through her distress--"when he came down again--" she repeated the words like a child conning a lesson, then stopped, staring widely. "Ah, I don't remember," she cried hopelessly. "I don't remember--except that I think--when he came down again--it was all over. And he seemed to be angry with me. Why was he angry with me, Nick? Why? Why?"

She began to tremble violently; but Nick's arm, strong and steadfast, drew her on.

"He wasn't angry," said Nick. "Up to that point you are all right, but there your imagination runs away with you. It's not surprising. He looks grim enough when he's on the job. But that's his way. We know too much of him, you and I, to take him over seriously."

"Then he really wasn't angry?" Olga said, relief struggling with doubt in her voice.

Nick began to smile. "He really wasn't," he said.

She gave a sharp sigh. "I've been so afraid sometimes. But why--why did he look so strange?"

"Doctors don't like being beaten," said Nick.

"But then, he knew it was hopeless--he said so. Was he angry because of his arm? Was he angry with her, do you think? Oh, Nick, my brain--my brain! It does whirl so! It won't let me think quietly."

"There is no need to make it think any more," said Nick, with quick decision. "Give it a rest! You've got hold of the main points, and that's enough for anyone. You mustn't fret either, dear. Remember, we are all going the same way. God knows why we take these things so hard. I suppose it's our silly little minds that won't let us look ahead."

"If we only could look ahead!" murmured Olga. "If we could only know!"

Nick's eyes sent a single flashing glance over the cypresses. His arm clasped her closely and very tenderly. "That's just where the trick of believing comes in," he said. "I don't see how those who honestly believe in the love of God can help believing that all is well with those who have gone on. To my mind it follows as the inevitable sequence. Those who doubt it are putting a limit to the Illimitable and placing a lower estimate on the love of God than they place upon their own. But we are all such wretched little pigmies--even the biggest of us. We are apt to forget that, don't you think? Horribly apt to try and measure the Infinite with a foot-rule. And see what comes of it! Only a deeper darkness and a narrowing of our own miserable limitations. We never get any further that way, Olga mia. Speculating and dogmatizing don't help us. We are up against the Unknown like a wall. But the love of God shines on both sides of it; and till the Door opens to us also, that's as much as we shall know."

He paused. Olga was listening with rapt attention. Her tears were gone, but the clasp of her hand was feverishly tense. Her breath came quickly.

"Go on, Nick!" she whispered. "Tell me more of the things you believe!"

He smiled whimsically. "My dear, I'm afraid I'm not over-orthodox. You see, I've knocked about a bit and seen something of other men's beliefs. The love of God is the backbone of my religion, and all that doesn't go with that, I discarded long ago. If Christianity doesn't mean that, it doesn't mean anything. I've no use for the people who think that none but their own select little circle will go to heaven. Such Gargantuan smugness takes one's breath away. It is almost too colossal to be funny. One wonders where on earth they get it from. I suppose it's a survival of the Dark Ages, but even then surely people had brains of some description."

"But death, Nick!" she said. "Death is such a baffling kind of thing."

"Yes, I know. You can't grasp it or fathom it. You can only project your love into it and be quite sure that it finds a hold on the other side. Why, my dear girl, that's what love is for. It's the connecting link that God Himself is bound to recognize because it is of His own forging. Don't you see--don't you know it is Divine? That is why our love can hold so strongly--even through Death. Just because it is part of His plan--a link in the everlasting Chain that draws the whole world up to Paradise at last. It's so divinely simple. One wonders how anyone can miss the meaning of it."

Olga's rapt face relaxed. She smiled at him--a very loving, comprehending smile. "Yes, I see it when you put it like that, Nick, of course. It is only just at first Death seems so staggering--such a plunge into the dark."

"But there is nothing in the dark to frighten us," Nick said. "If some of us died and some didn't, it would be terrible, I grant. But we are all going sooner or later. No one is left behind for long. To my mind there's a vast deal of comfort in that. It doesn't leave much time for grousing when we simply can't help moving on."

She squeezed his hand. "I wonder where I'd be without you, Nick."

Nick's grin flashed magically across his face. "I'm only a man, kiddie," he observed, "and I seem to have been gassing somewhat immoderately. However, them's my sentiments, and you can take 'em or leave 'em according to fancy."

Thereafter for a space they talked of Violet, touching no tragic note, recalling her as an absent friend. Olga dwelt fondly upon the thought of her, scarcely realizing her loss. The new life she had entered had done much to soften the blow when it should fall. Here in a strange land she did not feel her friend's death as she would inevitably have felt it at Weir. Circumstances combined with Nick's sheltering presence to lift the weight which otherwise must have pressed heavily upon her. Moreover, the longer she contemplated the matter, the more completely did she realize that it had not come to her with the force of a sudden calamity. Deep within her she had carried a nameless dread that had hung upon her like an iron fetter. She had longed--yet trembled--to know the truth. Now that burden seemed lifted from her, and she was conscious of relief. Before, she had feared she knew not what; but now she feared no longer. She was weary beyond measure, too weary for grief or wonder, though she did ask Nick, faintly smiling, why they had kept the truth from her for so long.

"I should have found it easier if I had known," she said.

But Nick shook his head with the wisdom of an old man. "You weren't strong enough to know," he said.

She did not contest the point, reflecting that Nick, with all his shrewdness, was but a man, as he himself admitted.

She asked him presently, somewhat haltingly, if he would give her the details of her friend's death. "Max was there, I know. But he never tells one anything. It was one of the reasons why I never got on with him."

A hint of the old resentment was in her tone, and Nick smiled at it. "Poor old Max! You always were down on him, weren't you? But there is really nothing to tell, dear. She just went to sleep, and her heart stopped. They said it was not altogether surprising, considering her state of health."

"Who said?" questioned Olga.

"Sir Kersley Whitton and Max. Max sent for him, you know."

"Oh, did he? Yes, I remember now. I saw him just for a moment." Again her brow contracted. "Oh, I wish I could remember everything clearly, Nick!" she said.

"Never mind, my chicken! Don't try too hard!" Cheery and reassuring came Nick's response. "Don't you think you have thought enough for one day? Shall we tell Kasur to order the horses, and go for a canter?"

She turned beside him. "Yes, I shall like that. But--why did you say I was always hard on Max?"

"The result of observations made," he answered lightly.

She smiled with a hint of wistfulness, and said no more. The child Olga would have argued the point. The woman Olga held her peace.

Undoubtedly Nick had stepped off his pedestal that day. She loved him none the less for it, but she wondered a little.

And Nick, philosopher and wily tactician, grinned at his fallen laurels and let them lie. He had that day accomplished the most delicate task to which he had ever set his hand. Behind the mask of masculine clumsiness he had subtly worked his levers and achieved his end. And he was well satisfied with the result.

Let her pity his limitations after a woman's immemorial fashion! How should she recognize the wisdom of the serpent which they veiled?

CHAPTER VI
CHRISTMAS MORNING

It was the strangest Christmas Day Olga had ever known, but she certainly had no time to be homesick.

She was roused by Nick scratching seductively at her window from the verandah, and, admitting him, she found him waiting to present a jeweller's box which contained a string of moonstones exquisitely set in silver. It was one of the most beautiful things she had ever seen, and she was delighted with it.

Through the medium of her ayah she had purchased a carved sandal-wood box from the bazaar for Nick, which she now presented, modestly hoping he didn't hate the smell.

"I adore it," declared Nick, sniffing it loudly. "It's just the East to me. I shall steep my ties in it. Many thanks, Olga mia!khitayah softly opened the door. "Shall I remove myself?"

"Of course not, Nick! Smoke a cigarette while I open them. They can't be anything very much."

The ayah, smiling broadly, laid two parcels on the table by Olga's bedside. A third one, which was very small, she dropped with a mysterious gesture into her hand.

"What can this be?" questioned Olga. "Sambaji, what is it?"

But Sambaji shook her head. "Miss sahib, how should I know?"

Olga suddenly turned crimson. She held out the tiny packet to Nick.

"You open it!" she said. "I'm sure it's something I don't want."

Nick made no movement to take it! "Sorry, dear. Two hands are better than one," he said.

Sambaji withdrew, still smiling.

Olga looked at the thing in the palm of her hand. She was trembling a little. "I don't want it, Nick," she said almost piteously.

Nick was heartless enough to laugh.

"Don't!" she pleaded, real distress in her tone. "Can't I send it back unopened?"

"Whom do you propose to send it to?" asked Nick, still chuckling.

She smiled faintly in spite of herself. "It's pretty certain where it comes from, isn't it?"

"Is it?" said Nick.

"Well, isn't it?" she persisted, still dubiously eyeing the unwelcome gift.

"I really can't say. But I don't see why you should be afraid of it in any case. To judge by the size of it, I shouldn't say it could be a very dangerous explosive."

She smiled again with obvious reluctance, and began to study the address on the packet. It was written in a very minute hand.

There followed a pause; then with abrupt resolution Olga's fingers began to work at the outer covering.

Nick watched her, amusement on his yellow face. "I'm not quite sure that two hands are better than one when they shake like that," he observed. "Ah, here comes the dedication!" as a tiny strip of paper fluttered from Olga's fingers. "It reminds me--vividly--of my own courtship. Quite sure you don't want me to go?"

"Nick!" she protested, with burning cheeks. "It's very horrid of you to laugh. Do you know what it is?"

"I can almost guess," he said, as a small leather case emerged from the paper. "I've seen 'em before."

Olga opened the case. It was lined with white velvet, and in the centre of it there flashed and glittered a diamond and emerald ring.

"Hullo!" said Nick.

Olga looked up at him with gleaming eyes. "Nick! How--how dare he!"

"It is pretty daring certainly," agreed Nick. "It's a valuable trifle--that."

Olga closed the case with a resolute snap. "I shall send it back at once."

"Hadn't you better read the dedication?" suggested Nick.

She took up the strip of paper, stretched it out, frowned at it. The writing on this also was minute. After a moment she read it out. "'Dum spiro spero. N.W.' Just as I thought!"

"Do you know what it means?" asked Nick.

She shook her head vigorously. "And I don't want to know."

"Oh, that's a pity," he said. "Pray let me enlighten your ignorance. It means, 'While I breathe I hope'--a very proper sentiment which does the young man infinite credit."

"I can't imagine how you can laugh," said Olga fierily, tearing the strip to fragments. "Can't you see I'm really angry?"

"My dear child, that's why!" chuckled Nick. "It's the best thing I've seen for a long time. The young man has all my gratitude. He has done more for my little pal than I with the best intentions could ever do myself."

She stretched out her hand to him then with a little smile. "Nick, you silly old boy! Well, tell me what to do!"

"Quite sure you don't like him?" questioned Nick.

"No. I do like him." Olga's smile deepened. "But I think it was outrageous of him to send me this thing. And I shall have to tell him so."

"I should," said Nick. "You will have ample opportunities when we get to Khantali. Take the thing with you and give it back to him there. Afterwards, if it seems necessary, I'll tell him to moderate the pace if you like. But the boy's a gentleman. I don't think it will be necessary." He smiled at her quizzically. "I knew it was coming, Olga mia. I can smell a love affair fifty miles away. But I shouldn't be persuaded to have him if I were you. He's altogether too young for matrimony by about ten years. Let him wait for Peggy Musgrave to grow up. He will be of a marriageable age by that time."

Olga laughed, and turned to her other parcels. Nick's worldly wisdom struck her as being a little funny when she knew herself to be so infinitely wiser than he.

She found the two remaining packets to contain presents from the Musgraves, some beautiful Indian embroidery from Daisy and a pair of little Hindu gods in carved ivory from Will. Nick stopped to admire these, and then betook himself to his own room to dress.

Left alone, Olga took up the ring-case once more, and slowly opened it. The stones glinted in the morning light, the diamonds white and intense, the emeralds piercingly green. She wondered why he had chosen emeralds; they seemed to her to belong to something in which he had no part. At the back of her mind there hovered a vague, elusive something like an insect on the wing. Suddenly it flashed into her full consciousness, and her eyes widened and grew dazed. She saw not the shimmering iridescence of the stones, but a darting green dragon-fly which for one fleeting instant poised before her vision and the next was gone. A sharp shudder assailed her. She closed the case....

When she met Nick again there was no trace of agitation about her. She seated herself behind the coffee-pot, and told him she had decided to go to church.

"I congratulate you," said Nick. "So have I."

They were half-way through breakfast when there came the ring of spurred heels on the verandah.

"Hullo!" said Nick. "Enter amorous swain!"

The colour leaped to Olga's face. She said nothing, and she certainly did not smile a welcome when Noel's brown face peered merrily in upon them.

"Happy Christmas to you, good people! May I come and break my fast, with you? I've been all round the town and this is the last port of call."

"Come in by all means!" said Nick. "Have you brought your harp?"

Noel clapped a free and easy hand upon his shoulder. "No, I haven't. I can't harp on a full heart alone. I've tied the Tempest to your garden palings. I hope he won't carry 'em away, for I can't pay any damages, being broke in every sense of the word! Good-morning, Olga! I'm calling everyone by their Christian names this morning in honour of the day. It's my birthday, by the way; hence my romantic appellation."

He dropped into a bamboo-chair and stretched out his arms with a smile of great benignity.

"I've even been to see Badgers," he said. "He was in his bath and didn't want to admit me. However, I gained my end, I generally do," said Noel complacently, with one eye cocked at Olga's rigidly unresponsive face.

"Who is Badgers?" asked Nick.

"Why, the C.O. of course. I didn't find him in at all a Christmas spirit; but it was beginning to sprout before I left. I say, I hope you are providing lots of beef for our consumption, Nick. It's the first Christmas I've spent out of England, and I don't want to be homesick. Any form of indigestion rather than that!" He turned suddenly upon Olga. "Why does the lady of the ceremonies preserve so uncompromising an attitude? I feel chilled to the marrow."

She controlled her blush before it could overwhelm her, and very sedately she made answer. "I am not feeling very pleased with you; that's why."

"Great heaven!" said Noel. "What on earth have I done?"

"You might have the decency to let me finish my breakfast in peace," protested Nick. "My appetite can't thrive in a stormy atmosphere."

Noel turned to him, smiling persuasively. "Can't you take your breakfast into the garden, old chap? I want to thresh this matter out at once. I'm sure you have your niece's permission to retire."

But at that, Olga rose from the table. "Suppose we go into the garden, Mr. Wyndham," she said.

Noel sprang up with a jingle of spurs. "By all means!"

"Get a hat, Olga!" said Nick.

She threw him a fleeting smile and departed.

Noel propped himself against the window-frame and waited. He did not appear greatly disconcerted by the turn of events. Without an effort he conversed with Nick on the chances of the forthcoming polo-match.

When Olga came along the verandah a minute later he stepped out and joined her with a smile.

They passed side by side down the winding path that led to the cypress walk. Olga's face was pale. She looked very full of resolution.

"I am quite sure you know what I am going to say," she said very quietly at length.

"You haven't wished me a happy Christmas yet," remarked Noel, still smiling his audacious smile. "Can it be that?"

Olga's face remained grave. "No," she said. "I don't feel friendly enough for that."

"I say, what have I done?" said Noel.

She stopped and faced him, and he suddenly saw that she was very nervous. She held out to him a little packet wrapped in tissue-paper.

"Mr. Wyndham," she said, speaking rapidly to cover her agitation, "you couldn't seriously expect me to accept this, whatever your motive for sending it. Please take it back, and let me forget all about it as quickly as possible!"

Noel's hand clasped hers instantly, packet and all. "My dear girl," he said softly, "don't be upset,--but you're making a mistake."

She looked up, meeting the Irish eyes with a tremor of reluctance. In spite of herself, she spoke almost with entreaty. For there was something about him that stirred her very deeply. "Please don't make things hard!" she said. "You know you have no right. I never gave you the smallest reason to imagine I would take such a gift from you."

Noel was still smiling; but there was nothing impudent about his smile. Rather he looked as if he wished to reassure her. "How did you know where it came from?" he said.

The colour she had been so studiously restraining rushed in a wave over her face. "Of course--of course I knew! Besides, there was a line with it."

"May I see the line?" said Noel.

She stared at him, her agitation increasing. What right had he to be so cool and unabashed?

"I tore it up," she said.

"What for?" said Noel.

Her eyes gleamed momentarily. "I was angry."

"Angry with me?" he questioned.

"Yes."

"Does it make you angry to know that a man cares for you?" he said.

Her eyes fell before the sudden fire that kindled in his with the words. "Don't!" she said rather breathlessly. "Please don't!"

"You ought to be sorry for me," he whispered, "not angry."

She turned her face aside. "Of course--that--would not make me angry. Only--only--you had no right to--to send me--a present--a valuable present."

"And if I didn't?" said Noel.

She looked at him in sheer astonishment. He still held her hand with the packet clasped in it.

"What if I am not the delinquent after all?" he said.

"What do you mean?" Her eyes met his again, wide and incredulous.

"What if I tell you that this packet--whatever it contains--did not come from me?"

He asked the question with a faint smile that set some chord of memory vibrating strangely in her soul. But she could not stop to wrestle with memory then. His words demanded her instant attention.

"Not come from you!" she repeated, as one dazed. "But it did! Surely it did!"

"Most surely it didn't!" said Noel.

She freed her hand and opened it, gazing at the subject of their discussion almost with fear. "Mr. Wyndham!"

"Call me Noel!" he said. "There's nothing in that. Everybody does it. And don't be upset on my account! It was a perfectly natural mistake. I'm deeply in love with you. But--all the same--this present did not come from me."

"It had your initials," she said, still only half believing.

"Then it was probably a hoax," said Noel.

"Oh, no! That's not possible. It--it--you see, it's valuable." Olga's voice was almost piteous.

"I say, don't mind!" he said. "It's just some other fellow's impudence. I'll kick him for you if I get the chance. You're quite sure about my initials?"

"Quite," she said.

"And what else was there?"

She frowned, "Only a Latin motto."

"Tell me!" he said persuasively.

She continued to frown. "It was 'Dum spiro spero.'"

"Great Scott!" he said. "Do you think I should have been as presumptuous as that? I should have just said, 'With Noel's love,' and you wouldn't have had the heart to fling it back again."

She smiled, not very willingly. "I can't understand it at all."

"I can," he said boldly. "I've known there was another fellow, ever since the first night I met you. But I've been hoping against hope that he didn't count. Does he count then?"

Olga turned sharply from him. She was suddenly trembling. "No!" she whispered.

He drew a step nearer to her. "Olga--forgive me--is that the truth?"

She controlled herself and turned back to him. "There is no one in India who would have sent me this," she said. "I can't account for it--in any way. Please forgive me for accusing you of what you haven't done. And--and--"

She stopped short, for he had caught her hands in an eager, boyish clasp. "Olga, don't--there's a dear!" he begged with headlong ardour. "I don't love you any the less because I didn't do it. I believe myself it's a beastly hoax, and I'm just as furious as you are. But, I say, can't we found a partnership on it? Is it asking too much? Pull me up if it is! I don't want to be premature. Only I won't have you sick or sorry about it, anyhow so far as I am concerned. You were quite right in thinking that I loved you. I do, dear, I do!"

"But you mustn't!" she said. She left her hands in his, but the face she raised was tired and sad and unresponsive. "I feel a dreadful pig, Noel," she said, speaking as if it were an effort. "I almost made you say it, didn't I? And it's just the one thing I mustn't let you say. You're so nice, so kind, such a jolly friend. But you're not--not--not--"

"Not eligible as a husband," suggested Noel.

"Don't use that horrid adjective!" she protested. "You make me feel worse and worse."

He laughed, his sudden, boyish laugh. "No, but there's nothing to feel bad about, really. And you didn't make me say it. I said it because I wanted to. Also, you're not bound to take me seriously. I'm not always in earnest--as you may have discovered. Look here, you've warned me off. Can't we talk about something else now?"

"If you're sure you don't mind," she said, smiling rather wistfully.

He cocked his eyebrows humorously. "Of course I mind. I mind enormously. But that's of no consequence. By the way, I suppose your funny little uncle isn't given to playing practical jokes?"

"Nick? Why no!" Olga surveyed him in astonishment. "Nick is the soul of wisdom," she said.

"Is he though?" Noel looked amused. "I must get him to give me a few hints," he observed. "I wonder if he has left any breakfast. You know, I haven't had any yet."

"Oh, let us go back!" said Olga turning. "And please do forget all about this tiresome misunderstanding! Promise you will!"

He waved his hand. "The subject is closed and will never be reopened by me without your permission. At the same time, let me confess that I have presumed so far as to procure a small Christmas offering for your acceptance. You won't refuse it, will you?"

Olga looked up dubiously; but the handsome young face that looked back would only laugh.

"What is it?" she said at length.

Gaily he made answer. "It's a parrot--quite a youngster. I picked him up in the bazaar. He isn't properly fledged yet, but he promises well. I'm keeping him for a bit to educate him. But if you won't have him, I shall wring his neck."

"I'm sure you wouldn't!" she exclaimed.

He continued to laugh, though her face expressed horror. "And you will be morally responsible; think of that! It's tantamount to being guilty of murder. Horrible idea, isn't it? You--who never in your life killed so much as a moth! Hullo! What's up?"

For Olga had made a sudden, very curious gesture, almost as if she winced from a threatened blow. Her face was white and strained; she pressed her hands very tightly over her heart.

"What's up?" he repeated, in surprise.

She gazed at him with the eyes of one coming out of a stupor. "I don't know," she said. "I had a queer feeling as if--as if--" She paused, seeming to wrestle with some inner, elusive vision. "There! It's gone!" she said, after a moment, disappointment and relief curiously mingled in her voice. "What were we talking about? Oh, yes, the parrot! It's very kind of you. I shall like to have it."

"I've christened it Noel," he remarked, with some complacence. "It's a Christmas present, you see."

"I see," said Olga, beginning to smile. "And you are teaching it to talk?"

"I'm only going to teach it one sentence," he said.

"Oh, what is it?"

He gave her a sidelong glance. "I don't think I'd better tell you."

"But why not?"

"It'll make you cross."

Olga laughed. Somehow she could not help feeling indulgent. Moreover, the interview was nearly at an end, for they were nearing the bungalow, and Nick's white figure was visible on the verandah.

"In that case," she said, "you had better not educate it any further."

"Oh, it won't make you cross on the bird's lips," Noel assured her.

"Has it got lips?" she asked. "What a curious specimen it must be!"

"I say, don't laugh!" he besought her, with dancing eyes. "It's not a joke, I assure you. I'll tell you what I'm teaching it to say if you like. But I shall have to whisper it. Do you mind?"

Again she found him hard to resist, albeit she did not want to yield. "Well?" she said.

They were close to the bungalow now. Noel came very near. "Of course you can wring the little brute's neck if it displeases you," he said, "but it's a corky youngster and I don't much think you will. He's learning to say, 'I love you, Olga.'"

Olga looked up on the verge of protest, but before she could utter it Nick's gay, cracked voice hailed them from above; and Noel, briskly answering, deprived her of the opportunity.

CHAPTER VII
THE WILDERNESS OF NASTY POSSIBILITIES

When Nick heard of the mistake that had been made, he raised his eyebrows till he could raise them no further and then laughed, laughed immoderately till Olga was secretly a little exasperated.

They did not have much time for discussing the matter, and for some reason Nick did not seem anxious to do so. If he had his own private opinion, he did not impart it to Olga, and, since he seemed inclined to treat the whole affair with levity, she did not press him for it. For she herself was regarding matters very seriously.

Noel's candid adoration was beginning to assume somewhat alarming proportions, and she had a feeling that it was undermining her resolution. She was not exactly afraid, but she did not feel secure. He appealed, in some fashion wholly inexplicable, to her inner soul. His very daring attracted her. By sheer audacity he weakened her powers of resistance. And yet she knew that he would not press her too hard. With all his impetuosity, he was so quick to understand her wishes, so swift to respond to the curb. No, he would not capture her against her will. But therein she found no comfort. For he was drawing her by a subtler method than that. His boyish homage, his winning ardour, these were weapons that were infinitely harder to resist. There was scarcely a woman in Noel Wyndham's acquaintance who had not at one time or another felt the force of his fascination. He exerted it instinctively, often almost unconsciously, and now that he had deliberately set himself to attract he wielded his power with marvellous effect. His warmth, his gaiety, his persistence, all combined to make of him a very gallant knight; and Olga was beginning to find that it hurt her to resist the magnetism by which he held her. And yet--and yet--deep in the soul of her she knew how little she had to give. That haunting memory which yet invariably eluded her made her vaguely conscious that far down in the most secret corner of her heart was a locked door which would never open to him. She herself scarcely knew what lay behind it, but none the less was it sacred. Not even to Nick--trusted counsellor and confidant--would that door ever open; perhaps to none....

The Christmas service roused her somewhat from the contemplation of her perplexities, and after it there were friends to greet--Colonel Bradlaw and his merry little wife, Will Musgrave, Daisy, and the radiant Peggy.

They made a cheery crowd as they assembled in the hot sunshine before Nick's bungalow a little later and discussed their final arrangements for the picnic at Khantali.

The Bradlaws had a waggonette, and Daisy and Peggy were to drive with them. Noel had a dog-cart in which he boldly announced that Olga must accompany him.

Olga wanted to ride, but Nick declared that this would overtire her, adding with a grin that he would occupy the back seat in the dog-cart if Noel had no objection.

Noel grinned also, and expressed his delight; but at the last moment a couple of his brother-subalterns came up and took forcible possession of Nick, protesting that such a celebrity could not be permitted to take a back seat and insisting that he should travel in the place of honour in their dog-cart. Nick, finding himself outnumbered, submitted with no visible discomfiture, and the procession, being completed by about a dozen equestrians, finally started with much laughter and badinage upon the long, rough journey through the jungle to Khantali.

The khitmutgarsahibs' heads already. Perhaps he wondered in what condition they would return.

"I say, you don't mind?" said Noel coaxingly, as they drew ahead along the dusty road.

And Olga answered lightly, "I'm not going to mind anything or think of anything serious all day long."

He laughed. "I'm with you there. It's a jolly world, isn't it? And it's a shame to spoil it. As a matter of fact, I tried to get Peggy for a companion, but her mother wouldn't hear of it. I am too headlong and Peggy is too precious."

Olga laughed. "The Rajah was talking about a man-eating tiger at Khantali only the other day."

"Oh, yes, there is one too. But I'm afraid we are not very likely to come across him."

"Afraid! Do you want to then?"

Noel's eyes shone with enthusiasm. "I'm just aching to get a shot at one of these creatures. I've never so much as seen one in the wild yet. If the Rajah gets up an expedition I hope he'll take me along."

"He asked me if I would go," said Olga.

"Did he though? Very affable of him! I hope you said No!"

She laughed at his tone. "Well, yes, I did. But it was only because I didn't think I should like it."

"Not like a tiger-hunt!" ejaculated Noel.

She coloured a little. "Do you really like seeing things die?"

"Oh, that!" said Noel. "You're squeamish, are you? No, I'm never taken that way myself. That is in great part why I came here. I hoped--everyone thought--there was going to be some sort of shindy. But--I suppose it's the result of your clever little uncle's tactics--it seems to have fizzled out. Very satisfactory for him no doubt, but rather rough luck on us."

"Was there really any danger?" Olga asked.

"Oh, rather! The city was simply swarming with budmashes, and it was said that the priests had begun to preach a jehadraj. Then there was a bomb found on the parade-ground one night, close under the fort. It would have blown a good many of us sky-high if it had exploded, and damaged the fort as well. Badgers was quite indignant. You see the fort has just been painted and generally smartened up in anticipation of General Bassett coming this way. He is expected on a tour of inspection in a few weeks, and we naturally want to look our best when the officer commanding the district is around. Hence the righteous wrath of Badgers!"

"I never heard of all this," said Olga, from whose ears the seething unrest of the State had been studiously kept by Nick.

"No?" said Noel. "Well, there's no chance now of any fun here. I'm pinning all my hopes on the possibility of a shine on the Frontier."

Olga looked at his brown, alert face with its restless Irish eyes, and understood.

"You never think of the horrid part, do you?" she said.

He laughed, and flicked his whip at a wizened monkey-face that peered at them round the bole of a tree. "What do you mean by the horrid part?"

She hesitated.

He turned his gay face to her. "Do you mean the hardships or the actual fighting?"

She gave a little shudder. Even in that brilliant warmth of sunshine she was conscious of a sense of chill. "I mean--the killing," she said. "It seems to me one could never forget that. It--it's such a frightful responsibility."

"It's all part of the game," said Noel. "I couldn't kill a man on the sly. But when the chances of being killed oneself are equal--well, I don't see anything in it."

"I see." Olga was silent a moment; then, with a curious eagerness: "And was that what you were thinking of that night when you told Peggy that sometimes it was the only thing to do?" she asked. "Forgive my asking! But I've wondered often what you meant by that."

"Great Scott!" said Noel, with a frown of bewilderment. "What night? What were we talking about?"

She explained with a touch of embarrassment. "It was the night I arrived. Don't you remember I came upon you hearing her say her prayers?--in fact you were saying them with her. I liked you for doing that," she said simply.

"Thank you," said Noel with equal simplicity. "I remember now. The kiddie said something about it being wicked to kill people, didn't she?"

"Yes. And you said--it was just before I interrupted you--you said that sometimes it was the only thing to do."

Noel nodded. "I remember. Well, can't you imagine that? Don't you agree that when a man is fighting for his country, or in defence of someone, he is justified in slaying his enemies?"

Olga was frowning also, the old, troubled frown of perplexity. "Oh, of course, when you put it like that," she said; then put her hand to her head with a puzzled air. "But that wasn't quite what I meant."

"What did you mean?" said Noel.

She shook her head. "I don't quite know. It's difficult to express things. Whenever I try to discuss anything I always seem to lose the thread."

Noel grinned boyishly. "Good for me! You'd jolly soon floor me if you didn't. Look at that parroquet, I say! He flashes like an emerald, and see that imp of a monkey! He's actually daring to rebuke us for trespassing. I call this road a disgrace to the State, don't you? If I were the Rajah--by the way, the Rajah isn't coming, is he?"

Olga thought it possible. She knew he had been asked, but he had not returned any definite reply. She hoped he would be prevented.

"Oh, don't you like him?" said Noel. "I detest him myself. That's partly why I'm so keen on smashing his team to-morrow. He's a slippery customer, he and that wily old dog Kobad Shikan. They'd erupt, the two of them, if they dared and overwhelm us all. But--they daren't!" And Noel turned his face upwards, and laughed an exceeding British laugh.

"I wonder how you know these things," said Olga, watching him.

"What? I don't know 'em of course. I'm only assuming," said Noel. "I only play about on the surface, as it were, and draw my own conclusions as to the depths. It's quite a fascinating game, and nobody's any the worse or the wiser."

"And you think Kobad Shikan untrustworthy?" questioned Olga.

"My dear girl, could anyone with any sense whatever think him anything else? Could he have run the show for so many years if he had been anything less than a crafty old schemer? Oh, you bet he hasn't been Prime Minister and Lord High Treasurer all this time for nothing. What does Nick think of him?"

"Nick never discusses any of them." Olga was considerably astonished by these revelations. "I thought it was fairly plain sailing," she said.

"Did you though? Well, Nick is a genius, as everyone knows. He is probably in the thick of everything, and knows all that goes on. He'll be a C.S.I. before he's done."

"Oh, do you think so?" said Olga, with shining eyes.

"Rather! It's pretty evident. You wait till old Reggie comes along, and ask him. He is a great backer of Nick's. So am I," said Noel modestly. "I'd back him against all the Kobad Shikans in the Empire."

This, as Noel had doubtless foreseen, proved a fruitful topic of conversation and lasted them during a considerable part of their drive. Nearly the whole of the way lay through the jungle, here and there narrowing to little more than a track over which great forest-trees stretched their boughs. It was all new country to Olga, and the quiet, sunless depths as they advanced, held her awe-struck, spellbound. She gazed into the thick undergrowth with half-fearful curiosity. Once, at a sudden loud flapping of wings, she started and changed colour.

"There must be so many wild things there," she said.

"Teeming with 'em," said Noel. "We've come along at a rattling pace. Shall we pull up and wait for the rest to turn up?"

But Olga did not want to linger on the jungle-road. "Besides we've got most of the provisions," she pointed out. "And I want to get things arranged a little before anyone comes."

They pressed on, therefore, past glades, obscure and gloomy, where the flying-foxes hung in branches from the trees, and the little striped squirrels leaped and scuttled from bough to bough, where the blue jays laughed with abandoned mirth and the parroquets squabbled unceasingly, and cunning monkey-faces peered forth, grimaced, and vanished.

"This place is full of critics," declared Noel. "Can't you feel the nasty remarks they're making?"

Olga laughed and slightly shivered. "It isn't a very genial atmosphere, is it? But I think we must be nearly there. Doesn't that look like a break in the trees ahead?"

She was right. They were coming to a clearing in the jungle. Gradually it opened before them. The trees gave place to shrubs, and the shrubs to tall kutcha-grass which Olga viewed with deep suspicion.

"How easily a tiger could hide there!" she said.

Noel laughed aloud. "I daresay the brute's a myth, but in any case they never come out in the day-time. Are you really nervous, or only pretending?"

She was not pretending, but she did not tell him so. The kutcha-grass was very thick, quite impenetrable. It stretched like a solid wall on each side of them for a considerable distance--a choked wilderness of coarse weed that grew higher than their heads.

"I say, what a charming spot!" said Noel. "Did Nick choose it for the scenery, do you think, or the excellence of the road?"

They were bumping in and out of dusty holes with a violence that threatened repeatedly to overturn them altogether.

Olga laughed rather hysterically. "I'm sure the champagne will be quite un-manageable after all this shaking up. And just look what a lather your horse is in!"

"It's a case of the wicked uncle and the lost babes over again," declared Noel. "It also smacks of The Pilgrim's Progress. Old Bunyan would have made some good copy out of this. He'd have dubbed you Mistress Timorous and me Master Over-bold."

Olga laughed again more naturally. Noel could be very wholesome and reas-suring when he liked.

"And this beastly jungle-grass," he proceeded, "is the Wilderness of Nasty Pos-sibilities. Hold up, Tinker, my lad, and get out of it as fast as you can!"

Tinker was obviously most anxious to comply. He bent all his sweating ener-gies to the task. The road--if such it could be called--bent in a wide curve through the high grass. As they gradually rounded this, it became evident that that stage of the journey was nearly over. The thick walls opened out. They had a glimpse of wider country ahead dotted with mango-trees.

"Hooray!" sang out Noel. "We return to civilization!"

But it was not a very populous civilization which they were approaching. They came within view of a domed temple indeed, but it was a temple set among ruins. There was no sign of any inhabitant, near or far.

"There's a well somewhere," said Olga. "Nick said we were to camp there."

"So be it!" said Noel. "It's Nick's funeral. Let us find his precious well!"

They emerged from the jungle-road with relief, and approached a group of mango-trees. These led in a somewhat broken grove to the temple which stood amidst stunted palms and cypresses. The mid-day sun was fierce, and the shade of the mangoes was welcome. For about a hundred yards they travelled over a road that was nearly choked by stones and grass, and then somewhat unexpectedly they discovered the well.

It was plainly very ancient, its round stone mouth crumbling with age. All about it and over its edges grew the coarse grass. It must have been many years since native women had foregathered there to discuss the affairs of forgotten Khantali. Above it, on rising ground, stood the temple, domed, mysterious, deserted.

"A place for satyrs to dance in, what?" suggested Noel. "We ought to have come here by moonlight. Let's get down and investigate. The others can't be far behind."

"Yes, let us fix on a place before they come!" said Olga. "It will save such a lot of discussion."

"Excellent notion! I'll tie up Tinker to one of these trees. I don't call this a very promising site for a bean-feast," said Noel, wrinkling his nose. "It's so beastly stuffy."

"Yes, we will try the temple first," said Olga. "It stands higher. There will be much more air there."

They descended. There was still no sign of the rest of the party. "I expect they gave us a start to keep out of the beastly dust," said Noel. "They'll be here directly. Nick has pitched on a secluded corner anyhow. I shouldn't think the foot of man had trodden it for a thousand years."

Olga laughed. "I wonder. It's better than the jungle, isn't it? I don't feel nearly so creepy here."

"What price tigers?" grinned Noel.

"Oh, I've got over that," she declared. "But I didn't like your Wilderness of Nasty Possibilities."

He flashed her a merry look. "You ought not to be afraid with Master Overbold by your side. As for the tiger, we may meet him yet."

"Oh, no, we shan't!" she asserted with confidence. "It would be too ludicrously like a fairy-tale."

"Horribly ludicrous!" said Noel. "Well, come along and look for him!"

So side by side they started.

CHAPTER VIII
THE SOUL OF A HERO

The way was exceedingly rough and here and there almost overgrown with coarse weeds. Near the temple, the ground ascended fairly steeply, and the path narrowed so that it was impossible to walk abreast.

"Wonder if there are any of those jolly little karaits about," speculated Noel. "If you don't mind, I'll go first."

"I believe I saw a scorpion!" said Olga, as he took the lead.

He laughed at her over his shoulder. "Or a lizard! Stick to it, Mistress Timorous! You'll develop a taste for adventure soon."

"Oh, I'm not a coward really," she protested. "At least I never used to be!"

"You are the sweetest girl in the world," said Noel, in a tone that reduced Olga to instant and uncompromising silence.

She could not refuse his hand, however, when he paused to help her over the rough places. It was an utter impossibility to be ungracious to Noel for long. He was far too seductive.

They reached the top of the ascent and found themselves close to the temple. The place was a ruin. Blocks of stone, that once had been part of its structure, were scattered in all directions; and, advancing, they presently stumbled upon the monstrous head of a broken idol.

"This is the temple of Dagon," said Noel dramatically. "I don't think it's a very suitable place for a picnic. One might find bits of human sacrifices about and that would spoil the appetite."

"Oh, don't be gruesome!" Olga besought him. "Let's go in, as we are here."

They crossed the stone-strewn space through the shadowy cypresses, and entered under the dome. The place was dark and very eerie. Their footsteps echoed weirdly, and instantly there ensued a wild commotion overhead of owls and flying-foxes.

Olga started violently, and Noel looked upwards with a laugh that echoed and echoed in sinister repetition.

"What a ghastly place!" whispered Olga, as it died away at last.

The whisper was taken up and repeated from wall to wall till the further darkness swallowed it. Olga's hand went out instinctively and closed upon Noel's arm. Her nerves were not strung to this.

Almost before she knew it, he had drawn her to him, and slipped the arm about her. She looked up swiftly to protest, but the words were never spoken. They died upon her lips. For even as she opened them to speak there came an awful sound from the darkness.

It began deep and low, swelling in volume till it filled the building, reverberating from stone to stone, vibrating along the broken floor--a growl rising to a furious snarl--the unmistakable voice of an angry beast.

Olga stood as one petrified, feeling the arm around her tighten to a grip, but too lost in horror to take any note thereof. Staring widely into the darkness before them, she saw two points of light, red, ominous, advancing as it were by swift stealth out of the deep shadow.

At the same moment, Noel by a sudden, wholly unexpected movement thrust her behind him.

"Go!" he said. "Go for your life! Get back to Tinker and warn the rest! I'll keep the brute from following you."

His voice was short and authoritative; it held compulsion. In that moment of emergency he was a boy no longer, but a man, cool and strong and undismayed--a man to command obedience.

"Go quickly!" he said. "Remember it's up to you to warn them. This other is my job. Good-bye!"

He spoke without turning his head; yet the very brevity of his speech seemed to give her strength. Mechanically, she moved to obey.

Later she never remembered passing out of that place of horror. She went, hardly knowing what she did. The sudden smiting of the sunshine between the cypress boughs was the first she knew of having left the temple behind her. As one stricken blind, she moved, too stunned for panic.

And then--how it happened she was utterly unable to realize--as if he had dropped from the sky a man stood suddenly in her path.

He wore a pith helmet dragged forward over his eyes, and she was too dazzled by the sun to see his face. But there was something--something in his gait, his fig-ure, his attitude--that sent a wild thrill through her, waking her to vivid, pulsing life. With an incoherent cry she clutched him by the arm.

"The tiger!" she gasped. "The tiger!"

"Where?" he said.

She pointed back over her shoulder, her eyes dilated, anguished. "In the temple,--and Noel is there! He will be killed!"

In a single movement he had freed his arm and was gone. She heard his feet racing over the stones, and she turned up her face to the blinding sunshine and frantically prayed....

Minutes--or could it have been only seconds?--passed. From below her came Tinker's frightened neigh. She could hear him stamping in the undergrowth. But she had no further thought of going to him. That spot with all its terrors held her chained.

Suddenly from behind her there came a loud report--a nerve-shattering sound. She whizzed round. He had a gun, then. She had not seen that he had a gun.

But what had happened? What? What? She was trembling so that she could barely stand, yet she forced her quaking limbs to move. Back she stumbled, back through the glaring sunlight. Once she fell, and saw a lizard--or was it a scorpion?--flick from her path. And then she was up again, panting, sobbing, utterly unnerved, but struggling with all her failing strength to reach the ruined temple, to see for herself what lay there.

An awful silence brooded across the stony space. It was as though a curse had fallen upon it. She tried to lift her voice, to call to Noel, to make some sound in the stillness. But her throat was powerless.

She thought he must be dead. She thought that her brain had tricked her, that she had only dreamed of the coming of the second man, had dreamed of the gun-shot, had dreamed all but those dreadful gleaming eyes coming stealthily nearer and nearer out of the dark.

Again she tried to call, and again piteously she failed. She reached the temple staggering, her hands stretched gropingly before her. And even as she did so, the silence was rent by a sound that convinced her wholly that she was indeed dreaming--a sound that echoed and echoed through the gloom, making her pulses leap again in spite of her--the sound of a ringing British laugh.

She fell against the broken marble of the doorway, her hands pressed fast over her face. She was struggling with herself, consciously striving to nerve herself to go in and find his dead body. Of any personal danger she was past thinking. Had the tawny body of their enemy sprung out upon her then she would scarcely have known fear.

And so when Noel came suddenly to her, caught her hands into his own, making her look up, his brown face bent close to hers, she simply gazed at him uncomprehendingly, not believing that she saw him.

Swift concern flashed into his eyes. He drew her to him and held her in his arms. "Olga,--Olga dear, don't you know me?" he said. "You've had a beastly fright, haven't you? But the brute's dead, and no one else is any the worse. There, there! It's all right. Did you think I was killed and eaten?"

He was holding her closely now. His voice came softly, on a winning note of tenderness, into her ear. "And would you have cared--would you have cared--darling--if I had been?"

But she leaned against him quivering and speechless, unresisting, unresponding.

He held her for a space in silence, patting her shoulder reassuringly. But it was not in him to be silent for long. After a few seconds he was speaking again with cheery confidence.

"Let's get out of this ghastly place! The rest of the party must be coming along now. It was a nasty experience, wasn't it? But you're getting better, eh? That chap with the gun came up just in time to save my bacon. You saw him, didn't you?"

"Yes," she whispered feebly.

His arms relaxed a little. He looked down into her face. "Better now?"

With an effort she answered him. "Yes,--getting better."

"Can you walk?" he said. "Or shall I carry you?"

That roused her somewhat. "Oh, let me walk!" she said; and, after a moment:

"Forgive me for being foolish! It--it was the shock. I shall be all right now. Just let me hold your arm."

He gave it, still looking at her in a fashion which she was at no loss to understand. Instinctively she sought to divert his attention. "Tell me what happened! Who--who was the man with the gun?"

His expression changed a little. A momentary shadow crossed his face. He answered her with a touch of restraint. "Oh, he's a fellow I've met before. You'll see him again, I daresay. He has been chasing around after this infernal tiger since early morning. Had a shot at the brute once and wounded him. Been hunting for him ever since."

"All alone?" asked Olga in amazement.

Noel nodded. "Cracked thing to do, but as he's bagged his game I suppose he'll do it again."

"And what is he doing now?" asked Olga, as they descended the narrow path.

"Oh, he was going to clear out. He was awfully disgusted that the skin wasn't worth having. And there wasn't much of the head left." Noel made a face. "I shouldn't advise any of our picnic party to go near that beastly temple. It's a deal too sacrificial just now. Hullo! Here come some of 'em at last! You'll be glad to get back under Nick's wing."

He smiled at her quizzically, and Olga smiled back reassured. But reaching the lower ground, she detained him for an instant.

"Noel," she said rather haltingly, "there are some things beyond words, and--and I think this is one of them. But I shall never forget what you did. It--it was--magnificent."

"Great Scotland!" said Noel. He spoke banteringly, but she could not meet his eyes. "And you think I could have done anything else?"

She smiled rather wistfully. "Not you--perhaps," she said. "But it was fine of you all the same."

"And you're--not sorry--I wasn't eaten?" he suggested.

She gave him her hand with a gesture half-appealing. "We won't talk about it," she said. "It just won't bear talking about."

Her voice trembled a little but she was plainly anxious that he should not notice it. He stood a moment silent, holding her hand. From the direction of the jungle-road there came the sounds of the approaching party--the rattle of hoofs and jingle of bells mingling with laughing voices and gay shouts. It seemed incredible that a bare ten minutes had elapsed since their own arrival upon the scene.

Noel's hand tightened a little upon hers. He bent with a certain serious gallantry that became him well, and carried it to his lips.

"My lady's wishes shall be obeyed always," he said gravely.

She knew that he meant her to ascribe a full meaning to his words. And she let herself be reassured, for that she knew him now to possess the soul of a hero.

CHAPTER IX
THE MAN WITH THE GUN

In after-days when Olga looked back upon the rest of that Christmas picnic, she could remember very little in detail of what took place. Her mind was so fully occupied with the adventure in the ruined temple that the events immediately following it made but a slight impression upon her.

That they lunched at length by the ancient well, that Nick and the Musgraves petted and made much of her, that Noel considerately amused himself with the care and entertainment of Peggy, all these things she was able afterwards vaguely to recall, but none of them remained vividly in her memory.

During the afternoon she rested, with Daisy sitting by her side and Nick smoking a few yards away, until presently the Rajah rode up unescorted and occupied Nick's attention for the remainder of the time. He came and shook hands with Olga later and congratulated her on her escape, but his manner seemed to her perfunctory and somewhat absent. Remembering Noel's words, she wondered what schemes were developing behind those dusky eyes.

Her thoughts, however, did not dwell on him; they were curiously active in another direction. Over and over again she saw herself stumbling over the stones under the cypresses and finding herself all-suddenly face to face with a man in a pith helmet. She was haunted by the thought of him, though she had not in the glare discerned him fully. She had seen him as one sees a shadow on a sheet, a momentary impression, suggestive but wholly elusive, capable of stirring her to the depths but yet too vague to grasp.

Even to her own secret heart she could not account for the wild suspicion to which that lightning glimpse had given birth. The man was probably a very ordinary Briton under ordinary circumstances. That he had a breadth of shoulder that imparted the impression of power and somewhat discounted his height, that his first appearance had been so leisurely that he might have been strolling in an English garden--the sauntering vision flashed across her as she had often seen it, hands deep in pockets, and stubby brier-pipe between his teeth--that his brevity of speech had impelled her to clearness of brain and prompt reply--all these were but incidents that might have characterized the coming of any stranger. And yet whenever she recalled any one of these details, she found her heart beating up against her throat as though it would choke her.

And why had he disappeared so suddenly, this stranger with the gun? How she wished she had had the presence of mind to turn back into the temple to find him! Why had Noel spoken of him with such evident restraint? Had he been under orders so to speak? She almost resolved to ask him, but realized immediately that for some reason she could not. Besides, had he not said she would see him again? And when she saw him--when she saw him--again she had to still the tumult of her heart--doubtless she would tell herself how utterly unreasonable her agitation concerning him had been. She would make the acquaintance of a total stranger and wonder how he had ever reminded her of the one man in her world who alone had had the power to move her thus.

So, over and over again she reassured herself, considering the matter and dismissing it, only to admit it over and over again for further consideration.

Nick made unflattering comment upon her jaded appearance when the time came to return, and bundled her unceremoniously into the Musgraves' dog-cart before Noel could put in a claim. Olga was in some sense relieved, for she did not want to talk, and Daisy fully understood and left her in peace during the drive back to Sharapura.

The brief twilight came upon them just before they reached their destination, and when they stopped before the bungalow it was nearly dark. The stately khitmutgar was waiting for them, and helped Olga to descend. He stood by with massive patience while the Musgraves bade her farewell and drove away; then with extreme dignity he addressed her.

"There is a strange sahib sahib," he said.

Olga's heart gave a wild bound. "To see me? What name, Kasur?"

"Miss sahib, he gave no name. 'She knows me,' he said. 'I will announce myself.'"

Olga turned to the verandah steps, as if drawn thereto by some unseen magnetic force. Sedately Kasur followed.

"Will the Miss sahibsahib?" he suggested decorously.

She turned at the head of the steps. Her eyes were alight, feverish. She was strung to so high a pitch of excitement that she scarcely knew what she did.

"No, I can't wait," she threw back to him. "But Ratcliffe sahib will be in directly. Tell him when he comes." And with that she was gone, running swiftly, as one who obeys an urgent call.

The lamps were alight in the drawing-room and the glare streamed out across the verandah. It dazzled her as she entered, but yet she did not pause. Not till that moment did she realize how great a void the absence of one man had made in her life. Not till that moment did she understand the reason of the crushing sense of loss which for so long had been with her. Perhaps she did not fully understand it then, but there was no hiding the sudden rapture of gladness at her heart. It pierced her almost with a sense of pain, and with it came a stabbing certainty that this was no new thing--that sometime, somewhere, she had felt it all before.

He was on his feet lounging against the mantelpiece as she entered, but he straightened himself to meet her, and dazzled though she was, she saw his outstretched hand.

As it closed upon her own, she found her voice, though panting between tears and laughter. "Max! You--you!"

"A happy Christmas to you!" said Max.

He grasped her hand very firmly. How well she remembered that strong restraining grip! How often had she felt the controlling magic of it! Once she had even hotly resented it; but to-day--to-day--

She saw his mouth go up at one corner in the old, quizzing way. "'If my heart by signs can tell--'" he began, and ended, openly smiling, "I should almost dare to fancy you were--well, shall we say not annoyed?--to see me."

"Annoyed!" she laughed, still struggling with an outrageous desire to cry.

He looked at her critically. "You haven't grown any plumper since I saw you last, fair lady. Do you live on air in these parts? You will be flattered to hear that your resemblance to the great Nick is more pronounced than ever. Where is he, by the way? I hope he hasn't been eaten by a tiger, though I scarcely think any tiger, would be such a fool as to expect to find any nourishment in him."

"Oh, don't be horrid!" she said, laughing more naturally. "That's too gruesome a joke after what happened this afternoon."

"I wasn't joking," said Max. "I'm a serious-minded person. And what did happen this afternoon--if it isn't indiscreet to ask?"

She raised her eyes to his in astonishment. "But you were there!" she said.

"Who told you so?" demanded Max.

"I saw you myself, I spoke to you. I told you about--about Noel being in the temple--with the tiger." She halted a little over the explanation.

Max smiled at her--a curious smile that seemed to express relief. "I didn't think you recognized me in a helmet," he said. "Yes, I was there. I'd been on the brute's track since daybreak. I'm told that it's the proper thing to let natives do all the stalking in this country. But to my mind that's half the fun. Gives the tiger a sporting chance, too."

"You were actually hunting it all by yourself!" said Olga, with a quick shudder.

Her hand still lay in his; he gave it a sudden sharp squeeze. "Don't shiver like that! It's a sign of too vivid an imagination. Yes, I was all on my own, and enjoyed it. It was my first tiger too. I've learned quite a lot about the Indian jungle to-day. What made Nick choose the haunts of a man-eater for his Christmas party? Was it one of his little jokes?"

"We didn't believe in the man-eater," said Olga, beginning to make subtle efforts to recover possession of her hand. "There hadn't been one so near for years, and Nick said he thought it was bunkum."

"There," said Max, "he did not display his usual shrewdness of intelligence. Where is the little god by the way?"

"He's following on with Noel. They stopped behind to finish packing."

Max's fingers closed more firmly upon hers, so that without open resistance she could not free herself. "Noel seems to have developed into quite a picturesque cavalier," he observed impersonally.

He was watching her, she knew; and over her face there ran a great wave of colour. She was furiously aware of it even before she saw his faint smile. Desperately she sought to turn the subject.

"Why didn't you come back to us when the tiger was dead?" she said. "Why didn't you let Noel tell me you were there?"

She caught the old glint of mockery in his eyes as he made reply. "As you have foreseen, fair lady," he observed, "one answer will suffice for both questions. It was not my turn just then. Moreover, you knew I was there."

"I wasn't absolutely sure," she protested quickly. "I thought it probable that I had made a mistake."

"Didn't you expect to see me?" he asked her coolly.

She stared at him. "How could I? I never dreamed of your being in India."

He passed the question by. "And yet you were the only person in India whom I took the trouble to inform of my arrival."

Her eyes widened. "What can you mean?"

"Didn't you get a message from me this morning?" he asked.

"From you?" she said incredulously.

"I sent you a message," said Max.

Her hand leaped suddenly in his. So that was the explanation! She began to tremble. "I--didn't understand," she said piteously.

She wished he would turn his eyes from her face, but he kept them fixed upon her. "I wonder who got the credit for it," he said.

She turned from his scrutiny in quivering silence. But her hand remained in his.

He took her gently by the shoulder. "Olga, tell me!" he said.

"I didn't know it came from you," she whispered.

"Why not? I wrote a line with it."

"Yes, but--but--"

"But--" said Max, with quiet insistence.

She tried to laugh. "It was very absurd of me. The initials weren't very clear. I thought they were--someone else's."

"Noel's?" he said.

She nodded.

There was a brief silence, during which she dared not look round. Then he spoke, his voice drily humorous. "I suppose you thanked him for it then?"

"No, I didn't," she said. "At least--at least--I was vexed, but I didn't want to hurt his feelings."

"No?" said Max, in the same cynical tone.

Her hand slipped free at last. She spoke more firmly. "I told him I couldn't accept it."

"Poor Noel!" observed Max. He took his hand from her shoulder also, and she knew that he thrust it into his pocket. "And what did he say to that?"

She hesitated. "Well, of course he--he explained--that he hadn't sent it."

"And you believed him?"

"Of course I did. He--we thought perhaps it was a hoax."

Max grunted; she wondered if he were seriously displeased. And then abruptly he turned her thoughts in another direction. "Well, now that you know the truth,--what are you going to do about it?"

The question came with the utmost coolness, but yet in some fashion it sounded like a challenge. She felt compelled to turn and face him.

Thick-set and British, he confronted her. "Before you decide," he said, "there's just one little thing I should like you to remember. You may not have been in love with me--I don't think you were; but you engaged yourself to me quite a long time ago."

Olga's hands were locked together. But she met the challenge unflinching, unafraid. Quite suddenly she knew how to answer it. Yet she waited, not answering, her pale eyes shining, her whole being strung to throbbing expectation.

He came a step nearer to her, looking at her very intently. "Well?" he said.

She made a little fluttering movement with her clasped hands. Her face was raised unfalteringly to his. "I haven't forgotten," she said.

"But you thought I had," said Max.

Her lips quivered. "So many things have happened since then," she said, in a low voice.

"What of that?" he said, and suddenly there was a deep note in his voice that she had never heard before. "Do you think that so long as the world holds us both I would be content without you?"

The words were few, but they thrilled her as never had she been thrilled before. There came again to her that breathless feeling as though an immense wave had suddenly burst over her. She raised her face gasping, half-frightened. She even had a wild impulse to turn and flee.

But it was gone on the instant, for very suddenly Max Wyndham's arms closed about her, holding her fast, and she had no choice but to surrender. With a sob she yielded herself to him, clinging very tightly, her face hidden with a desperate shyness against his shoulder.

He spoke no word of love, simply holding her in silence during those first great moments. But at length his hand came up and lay quietly, reassuringly, upon her head. She quivered under it for a little. He waited till she was still.

"Olga," he said then, speaking very softly, "will you tell me something?"

"Perhaps," she whispered back.

"Why are you afraid of me? You never used to be."

She clung a little closer to him and was silent.

"Don't you know?" he said.

"Not altogether." Tremulously she made answer.

"I've had a feeling--all this time--that you were angry with me for some reason."

"For what reason?" he said.

"That's what I never could remember."

The hand upon her head moved and lightly stroked her cheek; then very gently but with evident determination turned her face upwards. His eyes, green and piercing, looked straight into her soul.

"You think that still?" he asked.

"No." Panting, she answered him; for deep within her, memory stirred afresh. The phantom of her dread lurked once more darkly in the background. The last time those eyes had searched her thus, her soul had been in agony. Wherefore? Wherefore? She struggled to remember.

And then in a flash all was gone. The past went from her. She was back again in the present, with the throbbing consciousness of Max's arms enfolding her, and the overwhelming knowledge that Max loved her filling all her world.

"You're not afraid now," he said.

"No," she answered softly.

"Then--" he set her free, bending to her, his face close to hers--"I may go on 'breathing and hoping,' may I, without running any risk of scaring you away?"

She laughed--a faint, sweet laugh more eloquent than words, realizing fully that, albeit her defences were down, he would not enter her citadel until she gave him leave.

His chivalrous regard for her went straight to her heart. In Noel it would not have surprised her, but in Max it was so unexpected that for a moment she hardly knew how to meet it.

He waited with the utmost patience, his smile, subtly softened but still unmistakably humorous, hovering at the corner of his mouth.

And so after a moment, half-laughing, with a face on fire, she reached out, took the red head between her hands, and bestowed a very small, shy kiss upon his cheek.

The next instant he held her crushed against his heart while his lips pressed hers with all the fiery passion of a man's worship....

It must have been several minutes later that a cracked voice was suddenly uplifted in the verandah singing a plantation love-song with more of pathos than tunefulness.

Olga started at the sound, started violently and guiltily, and slipped out of reach with a scarlet countenance.

"Nick!" she whispered.

Max glanced at the open window, raised his brows, shrugged his shoulders, and strolled across to it. Nick it was, stationed at a discreet distance, but dimly discernible in the darkness.

"Let me go to him first!" murmured Olga.

She passed Max with a touch of the hand and a fleeting smile, and was gone.

Nick's plaintive lament came to an abrupt conclusion two seconds later, and Max turned back into the room with his hands thrust deep in his pockets, and one side of his mouth cocked at an angle expressive of extreme satisfaction. He had dared a good deal that day, far more than Olga vaguely dreamed, and events had proved him more than justified.

CHAPTER X
A TALK IN THE OPEN

Noel dined with the Musgraves that night. His mood was hilarious throughout, but he seemed for some reason unwilling to discuss the adventure he had shared with Olga in the temple, and of their rescuer he scarcely spoke at all. He seemed in fact to have practically dismissed the whole matter from his mind, and when he bade them farewell at the end of the evening Daisy acknowledged to her husband that she was disappointed.

"I felt so sure he had begun to care for Olga," she said. "He doesn't often miss his opportunities, that boy."

"Perhaps Olga doesn't chance to care for him," suggested Will, with his arm round his wife's waist. "That does happen sometimes, you know."

She smiled, her cheek against his shoulder. "I can't imagine any girl resisting Noel's charms if he were the first comer--as I fancy he must be," she said.

"I wonder if he is," said Will. "She told me the other night she had never been in love, but she seemed to know so much about the disease that I rather doubted her veracity."

"Fancy your living to call it a disease!" said Daisy, with a faint sigh.

He stooped and kissed her. "Oh, I'm not a cynic, my dear," he said. "Shall we call it an incurable affection of the heart instead?"

"That's almost as bad," she protested.

"I said incurable," pleaded Will. "I ought to know, for I fell a victim to it long ago."

She laughed softly against his shoulder. "Well, if you will have it so, it's very infectious, you know. And I am a victim too."

His arm tightened. "Mine was always a hopeless case, Daisy," he murmured half wistfully.

She turned her lips up to his. "When it attacks old folks--like you and me, dear--it always is," she said.

He kissed her again, lingeringly and in silence. There had been a time of which neither ever spoke when Will's love for his wife had been to her a thing of little value. He had not been the first comer. That time had passed long since, and with it the last of their youth. But though for them romance was no more, they had become lovers in a sense more true. Their lives were bound up together and woven into one by the Loom of God.

Whatever opportunities Noel might have missed that day, he certainly did not permit the thought of them to depress him. With his customary jauntiness, he took his departure; but he did not return straight to his quarters at the cantonments. He turned his steps in the direction of the dak-bungalow, whistling in the starlight as he went.

A chilly wind was blowing, and the dust swirled about his feet. The road gleamed white and deserted before him. He swung along it, erect and British, caring nothing for dust or cold. From far away, in the direction of the jungle, there came the desolate cry of a jackal; but near at hand there was no sound but the rush of the wind past his ears and the swish of the dust along the way.

He came at length within sight of the dak-bungalow and saw beyond it the lights of the native city. Nick's bungalow, tucked away amongst its trees, was not visible.

"They're horribly near that treacherous hound," he murmured to himself, as he strode along. "I wonder if Nick realizes the risk. They might be murdered in their beds any night, and none of us down at the cantonments any the wiser. The Rajah and old Kobad Shikan would be horrified of course. It's so easy to be horrified--afterwards."

Unconsciously he quickened his steps. Somehow the danger had always seemed remote until that night. Had the day's adventure unsettled his nerves, or had he hitherto always underrated it? How ghastly it would be if--His thoughts broke off short. A figure had detached itself from the vagueness in front of him, and a whiff of rank tobacco smoke came suddenly to his nostrils.

Noel straightened himself and quickened his stride. He had the soldier's instinct for making the most of his height. The square, lounging figure that sauntered towards him looked almost short by comparison.

They met about fifty yards from the dak-bungalow. "Hullo!" said Max.

His tone was coolly fraternal, but his hand came out at the same time and Noel remembered the grip of it for some minutes after.

"What on earth have you come out here for?" he said.

Max smoked a pipe in one corner of his mouth and smiled with the other. "Like the girls," he said, "I've come out to get married."

"You're not going to marry Olga!" said Noel quickly and fiercely.

"That's just what I want to talk to you about," said Max. "Shall we walk?" He took his brother by the arm and led him forward. "I thought a talk in the open would be preferable. My hutch in this beastly little inn is not precisely inviting. I go to Nick's bungalow to-morrow."

"The devil you do!" said Noel.

The hand on his arm was not removed. It closed very slowly and surely. "Look here, old chap," Max said, "say what you like to me and welcome, if it does you any good. But there is no actual necessity for you to express your feelings. For I know what they are; and--I'm infernally sorry."

The words were quietly uttered, but they sent a shock of amazement through Noel. He stood still and stared. He had never heard anything of the kind from Max before.

Steadily Max drew him on. "When I wrote you that letter in the autumn, I meant you to do exactly what you have done. I didn't of course anticipate playing such a heathen trick on you as cutting you out. I regarded myself at that time as out of the running. Circumstances which there is no need to discuss had set dead against me, and I had reason to believe that she might need an able-bodied man's protection. Nick is all very well as a moral force, but physically he is a negligible quantity. I didn't fancy the idea of her coming out here with the chance of the aforementioned danger cropping up."

"What danger?" said Noel, abruptly.

Max hesitated a moment. "It's rather a long story. There was another fellow--a great hulking bounder. I was half afraid he might follow her out here and make himself objectionable. I thought you would probably get friendly with her, and she might turn to you for help if she needed it. You're the sort of chap a woman would turn to. And anyhow, I know you're sound fundamentally."

"Do you?" murmured Noel.

Max went on. "At that time I never thought of coming out here myself. It was Nick who first suggested it at a time when I believed my chances to be nil. And gradually the idea took hold of me. We had been almost engaged before. And though I didn't believe in my luck any longer, I thought I would have one last shot. Kersley backed me as usual. I am to go into partnership with him when I get back. He urged me to come, even said I owed it to her. I wasn't so sure of that myself, but events have proved him justified. I thought in any case I should only hurt myself and that wouldn't matter much. Afraid I behaved like a selfish ass. But I didn't know how far matters had gone, or even if they were likely to move at all. She isn't the sort of girl that attracts at first sight. It never occurred to me to be attracted till I found out how badly she disliked me. Then I used to bait her, and I liked her spirit. After that--" an odd, tender note had crept into his voice; he stopped abruptly.

Noel set his teeth and tramped along in dogged silence.

For a few seconds Max followed his example; then took up his discourse at the final point. "So I chanced a final throw and came out here; I thought at the worst she could only send me away again, and I should be no more badly off than I was before. Well, I got here, and the first thing. I heard was that Nick was giving a picnic at Khantali, and that there was a man-eater there. My informant was a native groom at the inn. He seemed to believe in the man-eater, and as I had equipped myself with a Winchester with the idea of solacing myself with big game when I had been given my conge, I armed myself and went to have a look for him. You know the rest. I must admit I was nearly as staggered as she was when I saw her come out of the temple. As soon as I had a moment for thought, it occurred to me that I should be probably one too many if I presented myself then. It was your chance, not mine; so I decided with your connivance to lie low. This evening I called to see the result. I fully expected to be told that you and she were engaged, and I went prepared to congratulate. But directly I saw her, I knew that it was otherwise. And I realized that my luck had turned."

"She accepted you?" Curt and straight came the words.

"She did." Calmly and deliberately Max made answer. "I had sent her a ring earlier in the day, which little attention, it seems, she had attributed to you."

"Yes; she tried to return it this morning." Noel spoke with his eyes fixed straight ahead.

"She is wearing it to-night," said Max.

Noel tramped on again in silence.

Suddenly he stopped, facing round upon his brother with a gesture that was openly passionate. "Damn it, Max! You're deuced cool, I must say! Aren't there girls enough in England without your posting out here to take the one I want? She's half in love with me already. I'd have won her over in another week--in less! Very likely to-morrow!"

Max stood still. They had nearly reached the gate that led into Nick's compound. The rustle of the cypresses in the night-wind came to them as they faced each other. Noel's hands were clenched, Max's well out of sight in the depths of his pockets.

He did not speak at once, but there was no hint of irresolution in his attitude.

"Yes," he said, after a moment. "You jolly nearly died for her, and if anyone has a right to her, you have. But, my dear chap, you can't get away from the fact that she was mine before you ever met her. I know that now. I didn't before to-night, though so far as I am concerned, she has been the only girl in the world for a very long time. Not knowing it, I'd have been quite ready--I'd be ready now--for you to have her; glad even. But knowing it--well, it rather alters the case, doesn't it? You see," his mouth twisted a little in the old cynical curve, "we can't hand her about and barter for her like a bale of goods. She's a woman; and--whether we like it or not--in these things the woman must have the casting vote."

"It's so beastly unfair!" Noel broke in hotly, boyishly. "Why the devil couldn't you stay away a little longer?"

"And suppose I had!" For the first time Max spoke sternly. "Suppose I had!" he repeated, with eyes that suddenly shot green in the starlight. "Suppose you had won her before I came--suppose you'd been engaged, and I had come along afterwards! What then?"

"You'd have been too late," said Noel, the dogged note in his voice.

"You wouldn't have set her free?" Max flung the question with brief contempt.

"No!" Noel flung back the answer fiercely.

"Not if you had known she cared for me first?" Max's voice was suddenly quiet and chill. It expressed a cold curiosity, no more.

Noel writhed before it. "Confound you, no!" he cried violently.

There fell a sudden deep silence. Max stood quite motionless during the passage of seconds, watching, waiting, while Noel stood before him, fiercely threatening.

Then, very abruptly, as if he had suddenly discovered that there was nothing to wait for, he turned on his heel.

"Good-night!" he said, and walked away.

He went with his customary, sauntering gait, but there was absolute decision in his movements. It was quite obvious that he had no intention of returning.

And Noel made no attempt to call him back. He stood with his black brows drawn, and dumbly watched him go.

At the end of thirty seconds, he wheeled slowly round, and turned his sullen face towards Nick's bungalow. As he did so, there was a slight movement near the gate as of someone stealthily retreating.

Instantly suspicion leaped, keen-edged with anxiety, into his brain. In a flash his former fears rushed back upon him. They were so horribly near the native city, so horribly undefended. He remembered the bomb on the parade-ground, and felt momentarily physically sick.

In another instant he was speeding to the open gate. He turned sharply in between the cypresses, and was met by a white-clad, cringing figure that bowed to the earth at his approach.

Noel stopped dead in sheer astonishment. So sudden had been the apparition that he scarcely restrained himself from running into it. Then, being in no pacific mood, his astonishment passed into a blaze of anger.

"What the devil are you sneaking about here for?" he demanded. "What are you doing?"

The muffled figure before him made another deep salaam. "Heaven-born, I am but a humble seller of moonstones. Will his gracious excellency be pleased to behold his servant's wares?"

It was ingratiatingly spoken--the soft answer that should have turned away wrath; but Noel's tolerance was a minus quantity that night. Moreover, he had had a severe fright, and his Irish blood was up.

"You may have moonstones," he said, "but you didn't come here to sell them. The city's full of you infernal budmashes. It's a pity you can't be exterminated like the vermin you are. Be off with you, and if I ever catch you skulking round here again, I'll give you a leathering that you'll never forget for the rest of your rascally life!"

The moonstone-seller bowed again profoundly. "Yet even a rat has its bite," he murmured in a deferential undertone into his beard.

He turned aside, still darkly muttering, and shuffled past Noel towards the road.

Noel swung round on his heel as he did so, and administered a flying kick by way of assisting his departure. Possibly it was somewhat more forcible than he intended; at least it was totally unexpected. The moonstone-seller stumbled forward with a grunt, barely saving himself from falling headlong.

A momentary compunction pricked Noel, for the man was obviously old, and, by the peculiar fashion in which he recovered his balance, he seemed to be crippled also. But the next moment he was laughing, though his mood was far from hilarious. For, with an agility as comical as it was surprising, the moonstone-seller gathered up his impeding garment and fled.

He was gone like a shadow; the garden lay deserted; Noel's bitterness of soul returned. He glanced towards the darkness of the cypresses where they had walked only that morning, and a great misery rose and engulfed his spirit. A second or two he stood hesitating, irresolute. Should he go in and see her? Vividly her pale face came before him, but glorified with a radiance that was not for him. No, he could not endure it. By to-morrow he would have schooled himself. To-morrow he would wish her joy. But to-night--to-night--he drained the cup of disappointment for the first time in his gay young life and found it bitter as gall.

With a fierce gesture he flung round and tramped away.

CHAPTER XI
THE FAITHFUL WOUND OF A FRIEND

All the social circle of Sharapura and most of the native population usually assembled on the polo-ground to witness the great annual match between the Rajah's team and the officers stationed at the cantonments. It was to be followed by a dance at the mess-house in the evening, to which all English residents far and near had been bidden, and which the Rajah himself and his chief Minister, Kobad Shikan, had promised to attend.

The day was a brilliant one, and Olga looked forward to its festivities with a light heart. The thought of Noel was the only bitter drop in her cup of happiness, but instinct told her that his wound would be but a superficial one. She was sorry on his behalf, but not overwhelmingly so. As Nick had wisely observed, it would be far more fitting for him to wait and marry Peggy Musgrave. They were eminently well suited to each other, and would be playfellows all their lives.

She expected Max to present himself in the course of the morning, and he did not disappoint her. He made his casual appearance soon after Nick had departed for the Palace, and found her in the garden. Not alone, however, for Daisy had arrived before him to see how Olga fared after the previous day's adventure.

Max, strolling out to them, was met by Olga in a glowing embarrassment which he was far from sharing, and introduced forthwith to Daisy as "Noel's brother."

Daisy, who had just been listening to a somewhat halting account of his unexpected arrival the day before, marked her very evident confusion and leaped to instant comprehension. So this was the cause of Noel's reticence! She shook hands with Max with a very decided sense of disappointment, resenting his intrusion on Noel's behalf, and with womanly criticism marvelling that this thick-set unromantic Englishman could ever have held the girl's fancy when Noel, the handsomest officer in the district, had been so obviously at her feet.

She heaved a little sigh for Noel even while she said, smiling, "I have just been hearing of your dramatic arrival yesterday, Dr. Wyndham. You could scarcely have chosen a more thrilling moment."

He smiled also, with slight cynicism. "Yes, there were plenty of thrills for all of us," he said. "Have you heard the latest?"

Daisy's eyes travelled from him to Olga, who stretched out her left hand, bearing Max's ring upon it, and said, very sweetly and impulsively: "Oh, Mrs. Musgrave, I was just going to tell you about it. Please don't think me deceitful! It--it--it only happened last night."

"My darling child!" Daisy said. She took the outstretched, trembling hand and folded it in a soft, warm clasp. Her eyes went back to Max, whose expression became more ironical than ever under her scrutiny. It was as if he observed and grimly ridiculed her jealousy on his brother's behalf. And Daisy's resentment turned to a decided sense of hostility. She discovered quite suddenly but also quite unmistakably that she was not going to like this young man.

She was sure the green eyes under their shaggy red brows saw and mocked her antipathy. There was even a touch of insolence about him as he said: "I'm afraid it's taken your breath away, but it is not such a sudden arrangement as it appears. Strange to say all women don't fall in love with me at first sight. Olga, for instance, did quite the reverse, didn't you, Olga?"

His eyes mocked Olga now openly and complacently. Daisy told herself indignantly that she had never in her life witnessed anything so disgustingly cold-blooded. He positively revolted her. She saw him as a husband, selfish, supercilious, accepting with condescension his young wife's eager devotion, and her congratulations died on her lips. For Daisy was a woman with whom a man's homage counted for much. She had been accustomed to it all her life and its absence was an offence unpardonable. And then suddenly Olga overcame her shyness, and boldly came to the rescue.

"Max, don't make Mrs. Musgrave think you a beast! It isn't fair to me. He isn't a bit like this really," she added to Daisy. "It's all affectation. Nick knows that."

Daisy laughed. The girlish speech helped her, if it did not remove her doubts. She gave her free hand to Max, saying, "I suppose we are none of us ourselves to strangers, but, since you are engaged to Olga, I hope you will not place me in that category. You are very, very lucky to have won her, and I wish you both every happiness."

Max bowed, still with a hint of irony. "It's nice of you not to condole with Olga," he said. "I feel inclined to myself. Perhaps, if I am not wanted, I may be allowed to go and have a smoke on the verandah. I am expecting my traps to turn up directly," he added to Olga.

"Oh, we must come and see about them," she said. "The khit will show you your room. Max is going to put up with us now," she told Daisy, with a smile that pleaded with her friend to be lenient.

Daisy's hand still held hers. "That is nice, dear," she said. "I must be getting back to Peggy. Is your fiance coming to the regimental dance to-night?"

"Oh, Max,"--Olga's eyes shone upon him,--"you will, won't you? But of course you will. Noel will have settled that."

The corner of Max's mouth went down. "Noel is not in the habit of settling my affairs great or small," he observed. "If I go at all, it will be in the little god's train and under his auspices alone. But I warn you I'm not much of a dancer."

"What nonsense!" said Olga. "All doctors dance. It's part of their hospital training."

"Is it?" said Max. "Then my medical education is incomplete. My partners generally prefer to sit out after the first round."

"I shan't sit out with anyone," declared Olga. "It's such a waste of time. One can do that any day."

"So one can," said Max. "I hope you are not hurrying away on my account, Mrs. Musgrave. My business here is not urgent. It will very well wait."

He was evidently in an incurably cynical mood, and Olga gave him up in despair. She went with Daisy to the gate, and, with her arms round her neck, besought her, half-laughing, not to be misled by appearances.

"I was myself," she confessed. "I actually hated him once. But now--but now--"

"But now it's all right," smiled Daisy. "Run back to him, dear child! I should imagine he is the sort of young man who doesn't like to be kept waiting."

That was all the criticism she permitted herself, but Olga, returning slowly to

Max on the verandah, was regretfully aware that the impression he had made upon this friend of hers was far from favourable.

"It isn't nice of you, Max," she began, as she reached him. "It really isn't nice of you."

But she got no further than that for the moment, for Max literally lifted her off her feet, holding her fast in his arms while he kissed the colour into her white face, finally lowering her into Nick's favourite hammock and dexterously settling her therein.

"You shouldn't!" she protested feebly. "You shouldn't! And indeed I'm not going to lie here."

"You are going to do as you are told, fair lady," he responded grimly. "What have you been lying awake half the night for?"

"I didn't," she began. "At least--" seeing his look of open incredulity--"it couldn't have been so long as that. And I--I had a lot of things to think about. No, Max, you're not to feel my pulse! Max, I won't have it!"

She pulled desperately, and freed herself. Max thrust his hands into his pockets, faintly smiling, and stood over her, contemplating her.

"Well, tell me all the things you had to think about!" he said.

She shook her head, flushed still and slightly distressed. "No, Max."

He stooped over her, searching her face. "Do you like being engaged, Olga?" he asked.

She sat up quickly and leaned against him, her hands clasped upon his arm.

"I'm happy enough to--to want to cry," she said, a slight catch in her voice.

He held her closely again, her head against his heart. "No, that's not the reason," he said softly into her ear. "Something is bothering you, isn't it?"

She swallowed once or twice and nodded. "I'm--foolish," she managed to utter after a moment.

"Never mind if you can't help it!" he said. "Tell me what it's about!"

But she was silent.

"Afraid I shan't understand?" he questioned.

Her hand nestled into his, but she kept her face down. "I wrote a long, long letter to Dad last night," she remarked irrelevantly, after a pause. "He--I'm afraid he'll be rather surprised."

"I wonder," said Max.

She glanced up for an instant. "Did he know you were coming out here to me?" she asked.

"He did." There was a queer note of dry exultation in Max's reply.

"Oh, Max!" Her head went back to its resting-place. "He thought I didn't like you, you know. What--what did he say?"

"He told me I was a fool," said Max.

Olga laughed. "Dear Dad! I suppose he thought you were wasting your time over a wild goose chase."

"Yes; he didn't anticipate my catching my wild goose, I admit. Kersley on the other hand was so confident that he practically hoofed me out of England. He wants a married partner, you know, so perhaps he was not altogether disinterested."

Again the complacent note sounded in Max's voice.

Olga's fingers closed tightly on his hand. "Is that why you are so anxious to get married?" she asked, in a muffled voice.

Max's fingers responded so swiftly and so mercilessly that she cried out with the pain. "Max! How brutal!"

"You deserved it," said Max without compunction.

"But I didn't! I only asked a simple question," she protested.

"No, you didn't; it was a compound one." He opened his hand and sternly regarded the crushed fingers. "If you develop claws, Olga," he said, "you must expect trouble."

She laughed again. "It isn't a question of developing: they're there--full-grown. Do you remember that day I stabbed you with my darning-needle?"

"I do," said Max. He turned his hand over and showed her a small white scar on the back. "I suppose you never realized that that was the beginning of everything?"

"It wasn't with me!" declared Olga. "I could have slain you that night!"

"Because I told you you ought to be whipped," said Max. "It was quite true, you know. Dr. Jim would have said the same. He would probably have done it too."

"I'm sure he wouldn't!" Olga lay back in the hammock with the scarred hand between her own. "Dad is very just. He would have realized that you were quite insufferable."

"That wouldn't have justified you, my child," maintained Max.

She snapped her fingers at him. "I'd do it again to-day if you were as horrid as you were then."

"Not you!" said Max.

She opened her eyes. "You think I wouldn't dare?"

He looked back at her with composure. "It is more a matter of caring than daring, my dear," he said. "Your heart wouldn't be in it. But you are afraid of me all the same."

She coloured and turned the subject. "When is Sir Kersley going to make you his partner?"

"Directly I return," said Max.

"And when will that be?"

He considered a moment. "I expect to reach England in a month from now."

"Max!" She sat up again quickly. "Oh, you're not going so soon!" she said.

He put his arm round her shoulders. "But you will be coming back yourself in April. Nick told me so."

"In April! But that's aeons away!" protested Olga.

His eyes looked down into hers, and the old gleam which once she had taken for mockery hovered there. Her own eyes flickered and sank before it. There was something quick and fiery in it that she could not meet.

"I'll take you back with me," he said, "if you will come."

She started a little. "Oh, no!" she said.

"Why 'Oh, no'?" he enquired.

She was silent for a moment, her face downcast. "I couldn't leave Nick--possibly--out here," she said then.

"Why not? Can't the little god take care of himself?"

"No. And I wouldn't let him if he could. I shouldn't feel easy about him. He--he--I feel as if he is trying to walk a tight rope every day."

"It's a sort of thing he ought to do very well, I should say," observed Max. "But what is he doing it for?"

She looked up. "He thinks he is getting on splendidly," she said. "He and the Rajah are such friends! But the Rajah isn't everybody, and I'm not sure even of him. Someone tried to blow up the fort with a bomb not so very long ago."

"Oh, that's the game, is it?" said Max. "You think a similar little joke might be played on Nick, and if so you want to be there to see."

She smiled faintly, in a sense relieved that he did not treat the matter too seriously. "It makes one a little nervous for him," she said, "though of course there may be no reason for it."

"I see," said Max. "It's just a nightmare, is it?"

He was watching her intently, and under his look her heart quickened a little.

"It may be all nonsense, yes," she admitted. "But in any case I won't leave Nick out here. He is in my special charge."

He laughed. "Well, there's no appealing against that. You will be home in April then. Will you marry me on Midsummer Day?"

Olga's eyelids flickered and fell. "I must think about it," she said.

He pinched her cheek. "Say Yes," he said.

She turned her face impulsively; her lips just touched his hand. "I wonder if I shall, Max," she said.

"Say Yes," he repeated, still softly but with insistence.

She leaned her head against him. "I'd like to say Yes," she said. "But somehow--somehow--I have a feeling that--that--"

"My dear," said Max very practically, "don't be silly!"

She turned and clung to him very tightly. "Max, I--I've got something--on my mind."

His arm, very steady and strong, grew close about her. "Tell me!" he said.

Haltingly she complied. "You will think me morbid. I can't help it. Max, all last night--all last night--I felt as if--as if a spirit were with me--calling--calling--calling, trying to make me understand something, trying to--to warn me--of some danger--I couldn't see."

She broke off in tears. It seemed impossible to put the thing into words. It was so intangible yet in her eyes so portentous. Max's hand was on her head, stilling her agitation. She wondered if he thought her very absurd, but he did not leave her long in doubt.

"There's nothing to cry about, my dear," he said. "Your nerves were a bit strung up after the tiger episode, that's all. They will quiet down in a day or two. All the same"--his hand pressed a little--"I'm glad you told me. A trouble shared is only half a trouble, is it? And I have a right to all your troubles now."

He took her handkerchief, and dried her eyes with the utmost kindness; then turned her face gently upwards.

"Is that quite all?" he asked.

She tried to smile, with quivering lips.

"Not quite?" he questioned. "Come, I may as well know, mayn't I?"

"I don't know that there is anything gained by telling you," she said. "You never liked talking about your cases to me."

He frowned a little. "My dear girl, what particular case is it you have on your mind?"

She hesitated. "You won't be vexed?"

"Vexed? No!" he said; but he continued to frown slightly notwithstanding.

"I hope you won't be," Olga said, "because I simply can't argue about it. Max, I sometimes think to myself that if--you hadn't known--and Violet hadn't come to know--about--about her mother--things might have been--very different."

"Meaning I should have fallen in love with her?" said Max.

She nodded. "It may be a breach of confidence, but--I think I'll tell you now. Max, she cared for you."

She spoke the words with an effort, her eyes turned from him. Perhaps she was afraid that she might encounter cynicism in the vigilant green eyes, and she could not have endured it at that moment.

But at least there was none in his voice when he said: "Yes, I know she did. That was what made her hate me so badly afterwards. I am very sorry, Olga; but, for your comfort let me tell you this. I should never--under any circumstances--have come to care for her. You won't like me for saying it, but she was never more to me than a very interesting case, and, apart from medical investigation, she would simply not have existed so far as I was concerned. She didn't appeal to me."

Olga winced a little. "Oh, Max, but she was so beautiful!" she urged wistfully.

He made a slight gesture of impatience. "I don't dispute it. But what of it? My brain is not the sort to be turned by beauty. There was too much of it for my taste. She was exotic. That type of beauty gives me indigestion."

Olga looked at him reproachfully. "You didn't like her, Max?"

"Not much," said Max.

She made a movement as if she would withdraw herself from him, but he quietly and very resolutely held her still. "Although you knew she cared for you!" she said.

"Yes, in spite of that;" said Max. "In fact, I felt a bit vexed with her for complicating matters in that fashion. Goodness knows I never gave her the smallest reason for it!"

Olga laughed faintly, with an unwonted touch of bitterness. "It's a pity women are such doting fools," she said.

He looked at her attentively. "Did you say that?" he asked.

She met his look, not without defiance. "Yes, and I meant it too. It's such a wicked waste. And I think--- I think--in her case it was something far worse. I believe it was that which in a very great measure helped to unhinge her mind."

"How could I help it?" demanded Max almost fierily. "I never wanted her to care."

"That was just the cruel part of it," said Olga. "It was just your utter indifference that broke her heart."

"Good heavens!" said Max.

He let her go very abruptly and leaned against one of the verandah posts as if he needed support.

Olga tilted herself over the side of the hammock and stood up. "You couldn't help not caring," she said. "But--you might have been a little kinder. You needn't have made her hate and fear you."

Max surveyed her grimly from under drawn brows. "My dear," he said, "you simply don't know what you are talking about."

That fired her. A quiver of passion went suddenly through her. She faced him as she had faced him in the old days with a courage that sustained itself.

"Indeed, I know!" she said. "Better than it is in your power to understand. Oh, I know now what made her--hate you so."

The last words came with a rush, almost under her breath; but they were fully audible to the man lounging before her.

He did not speak at once, and yet he did not give the impression of being at a loss. He continued to lounge while he contemplated her with eyes of steady inscrutability.

He spoke at length with extreme deliberation. "And so you want to take me to task for breaking her heart, do you?"

"She was my friend," said Olga quickly.

He stood up slowly. "And would you have liked it better if I had made love to her?"

She flinched as if that stung. "No--no! But you might have been kind--you might have been kind--since you knew she cared. If you hadn't made such a study of her, she would never have looked your way. That was the cruel part of it--the dreadful, cold-blooded part."

"What do you mean by kind?" said Max. "You don't seem to realize that the poor girl was mad. If I had been soft with her she would have been beyond my control at once."

"Oh, but she wasn't mad then," Olga's hands clasped each other tightly. "Max," she said, and there was no longer indignation in her voice--it held only pain, "I'm afraid you and I have a good deal to answer for."

"Perhaps," said Max. He was frowning still; but he did not appear angry. She did not wholly understand either his look or tone. "I suppose she thought I treated her badly," he said.

Olga nodded silently.

"She told you so?" His voice sounded stern; yet, still he did not seem to be angry.

"No, never." Almost involuntarily she answered him. "But she did say--once--that you cared only for your profession, that it was not in you to--to worship any woman."

"And you think that too?" he said.

His voice was softer now; it moved her subtly. She turned her face away from him and stifled a sob in her throat.

"No; but, Max--to build our life-happiness on--on the ruin of hers; that--that--is what troubles me."

"But my dear girl!" he said. He took her two hands clasped into his. "I can't reason with you, Olga," he said. "You are quite unreasonable, and you know it. If you were any other woman, I should say that you felt in the mood for a good cry and so were raking up any old grievance for a pretext. As you are you, I won't say that.

But I absolutely prohibit crying in my presence. If you want to indulge in tears, you must wait till I am out of the way."

She smiled at him faintly. "Max, I--I loved her-so; and I wasn't even with her--when she died."

Max was silent, suddenly and conspicuously silent, so that she knew on the instant that he had no sympathy to bestow on this point.

Yet an inner longing that was passionate urged her to brave his silence. Pleadingly she raised her face to his.

"Max, you were there, I know. Tell me--tell me about it!"

But he looked straight back at her with eyes that told her nothing, and she saw that his face was hard. For a little she tried to withstand him, mutely beseeching him; but at length her eyes fell before his.

And then Max spoke, briefly yet not unkindly. "My dear Olga, believe me, in nine cases out of ten it is better to forget those things that are behind; and this is one of the nine. I can't tell you anything on that subject, so we had better regard it as closed."

It was a bitter disappointment to her; but she saw that there was no appealing against his decision. She made as though she would turn away.

But he stopped her with quiet mastery. "No, I won't have that," he said. "I am not so cold-blooded as you think. I haven't hurt you--really, Olga!"

A note of tenderness sounded in his voice. She yielded to him, albeit under protest.

"But you have!" she said.

He held her in his arms again. He kissed her drooping lips. "Well, if I have," he said, "it's the faithful wound of a friend. Can't you forgive it?"

That Max should ever ask forgiveness was amazing. Her bitterness went out like the flare of a match. She laid her head against his neck.

"Max--dear, I didn't mean to be horrid!"

"You couldn't be if you tried," he said.

She clung faster to him. "How can you say so? I've hardly ever been anything else to you."

"When are you going to reform?" said Max, with his lips against her forehead.

"Now," said Olga into his neck.

"Really?" Max's voice came down to her very softly. "Then--won't you say Yes to the Midsummer Day project?"

She was silent for a little, as if considering the matter or summoning her resolution. Then with sudden impulse she lifted her face fully to his.

"Yes, Max," she said.

CHAPTER XII
A LETTER FROM AN OLD ACQUAINTANCE

It was universally acknowledged that the Rajah's Prime Minister, Kobad Shikan, was the most magnificent figure on the polo-ground that afternoon. The splendour of his attire was almost dazzling. He literally glittered with jewels. And his snow-white beard added very greatly to the general brilliance of his appearance. It was not his custom to attend social gatherings at all. Unlike the Rajah, he was by no means British in his tastes; and he never wore European costume. At the same time no one had ever detected any anti-British sentiments in him. He walked with such extreme wariness that no one actually knew what his sentiments were.

Why he had decided to grace the occasion with his presence was a matter for conjecture. Owing possibly to his habitual reticence, he was no favourite with the English portion of the community. Daisy Musgrave had nicknamed him Bluebeard long since, and Peggy firmly believed that somewhere in the depths of the Rajah's Palace this old man kept his chamber of horrors.

"What on earth has he come for, Nick?" murmured Olga, as they found places in the pavilion.

Nick laughed, a baffling laugh. "I asked him to come," he said.

"You, Nick! Why?"

He frowned at her. "Don't ask questions, little girl! Ah, that's a fine pony down there! Ye gods! What wouldn't I give to have another fling at the game!"

"Oh, but you never must!" said Olga quickly. "I couldn't bear you to take that risk indeed."

"You'd like to wrap me up in cotton-wool and seal me in a safe," laughed Nick.

"No; but, Nick, you are so reckless," she said, with loving eyes upon him. "It would be madness, wouldn't it, Max?"

Max's shrewd look rested for a moment on his host. "Little gods sometimes accomplish what mere mortals would never dream of attempting," he said. "How soon do you expect to be Viceroy, Nick?"

"Oh, not for a year or two," said Nick. "I haven't talked it over with my wife yet. There's no knowing. She may object. Wives are sometimes hard to please, you know." He flung a humorous glance at Max, and turned to leave them. "You will excuse me, I am sure, with the utmost pleasure. I am going to play spelicans with Kobad Shikan."

He was gone, and Olga turned to Max, smiling somewhat uneasily. "I wish he wouldn't," she said.

"What? Play spelicans? I should think he might prove as great an adept at that as walking the tight rope," said Max. "Ah, here comes your friend Mrs. Musgrave! She went home and told her husband this morning that I was the most objectionable young man she had ever met."

Olga's eyes widened with indignation. "Max, I'm sure she didn't, and if she did it was entirely your own fault. I believe you wanted her to think so."

"Some people have an antipathy to red hair," observed Max. "You had yourself at one time, I believe. Hullo! Is that our gallant Noel in polo-kit? What a magnificent spectacle!"

It was Noel following Daisy, whose rickshaw he had just spied, and bearing the proud Peggy on his shoulder.

He came straight to Olga, smiling with supreme ease, lowered Peggy from her perch, and dropped into the vacant seat beside her. Daisy passed on with a smile to join the Bradlaws. Peggy remained, glued to her hero's side.

"I say," said Noel, "I hope you haven't been thinking me beastly rude, Olga. I've been wishing you happiness with all my heart all the morning, but I simply couldn't get round to tell you so."

It was charmingly spoken. Her hand lay in his while he said it. He did not seem to observe his brother on her other side. But Peggy observed him and clung to Noel's shoulder with wide, fascinated eyes fixed upon the stranger.

"Noel," cut in the high, baby voice, "isn't that an ugly man? Who's that ugly man, Noel?"

Noel squeezed Olga's hand and set it free to lift the small questioner to his knee.

"That handsome gentleman, Peggy, is my brother, and he is going to marry this pretty lady--whom you know. Any more questions?"

Peggy stared at Olga very seriously. "Do you want to marry him, Miss Ratcliffe?" she asked.

"Of course she does," said Max. "Everyone wants to marry me. It's a sort of disease that spreads like the plague."

Peggy's eyes returned to him and fixed him with grave attention.

"I don't want to marry you," she announced with absolute decision.

"You'd rather have the plague, eh?" suggested Noel.

"No," said Peggy, and turned to him with her sweet, adoring smile. "But I'm goin' to marry you; aren't I, Noel?"

"Hear, hear!" said Noel with enthusiasm.

"Highly suitable," said Max.

"I hope you will both be very happy," said Olga, with a touch of earnestness that she emphasized with a secret pressure of Noel's arm.

"We shall be as happy as the day is long," said Noel, smiling straight into her eyes. "Now, little sweetheart," turning to Peggy, "I must be off. We've got some tough work in front of us."

"I hope you'll win," said Olga.

He stood up, looking very straight and handsome. His dark eyes, laughing downwards, seemed to challenge her to detect any shadow of disappointment in them.

"Win! Why, of course we shall. We're going to lick Akbar & Co. into the middle of next week--for the honour of the Regiment and Badgers."

He cast an impudent glance over his shoulder towards his commanding officer, with whom, however, he was a supreme favourite; smiled again at Olga while wholly over-looking Max, then swung around on his heel and departed.

Peggy stood for a moment watching him go, then with sudden resolution put aside the arm Olga had passed around her and ran after him.

"Highly suitable," Max said again.

Olga turned to him. "That's what Nick says. But it's such a long while for him to wait, poor boy."

"That wouldn't hurt him," said Max. "Do him all the good in the world, in fact. He's too much of a spoilt darling at present."

"Oh, Max, how can you say so? He is so splendid."

Max's mouth curved downwards. He said nothing.

"Max!" Olga's voice was anxious; it held a hint of pleading also, "you haven't-- quarrelled, have you?"

Max turned deliberately and looked at her. "I never quarrel," he said.

"But you don't seem to be on very good terms," she said.

"The boy is such a puppy," Max said.

"Oh, he isn't!" she protested, flushing swiftly and very hotly. "He--he is the very nicest boy I know."

He laughed a little. "I believe you would have married him if I hadn't come along just in time."

Olga turned her burning face to the field. She was silent for a space, studying the mixed crowd assembled there, till, feeling his eyes persistently upon her, she was at length impelled to speak.

"It is quite possible," she said in a low voice.

"Really? You like him well enough for that?" Max's voice was quite calm, even impersonal. He spoke as one seeking information on a point that concerned him not at all.

Again for a time Olga was silent while the deep flush slowly died out of her face. At last with a little gesture of confidence only observable by him, she slipped her hand under his arm. "I wasn't in love with him, Max," she whispered. "But--I think--perhaps I could have been."

He pressed her hand to him with no visible movement. "And now?" he said.

"Ah, no, not now," she murmured, half-laughing. "You have quite put an end to that."

They were interrupted. Colonel Bradlaw had just heard of their engagement from Daisy, and came up to make Max's acquaintance and to offer his pompous felicitations.

Before these were over the game began, greatly to Olga's relief. She took a keen interest in it, and marked the adroit celerity with which the Rajah's team took the field with anxiety. The Rajah himself was an excellent player, and he was obviously on his mettle. Moreover, his ponies were superior to those of the British team; and the odds were plainly in his favour.

"Oh, he mustn't win; he mustn't!" said Olga feverishly.

"Don't get excited!" Max advised. "Follow the example of Nick's Oriental friend in front of us. He doesn't look as if red-hot pincers would make him lose his dignity."

"Horrid old man!" breathed Olga.

And yet Kobad Shikan was conversing with Nick with exemplary courtesy, giving no adequate occasion for such criticism.

"Is he another bete-noir of yours then?" asked Max.

She laughed a little. "Yes, I think he is detestable, and I believe he hates us all."

"Poor old man!" said Max.

All through that afternoon of splendid Indian winter, they watched the polo, talking, laughing, or intimately silent. All through the afternoon Nick remained with Kobad Shikan, airily marking time. And all through the afternoon Noel distinguished himself, whirling hither and thither, hotly, keenly, untiringly pressing for the victory. If the Rajah were on his mettle, so undoubtedly was he. He had never played so brilliantly before, and the wild applause he gained for himself should have been nectar to his soul. Yet to many it almost seemed that he did not hear it. He laughed throughout the game, but it was with set teeth, and once in a close encounter with the Rajah his eyes flamed open fury into the face of the Oriental as the latter swept the ball out of his reach.

It was a splendid fight, but the British team were outmatched. In the end, after a fierce struggle, they were beaten by a single goal.

Victors and vanquished came to the pavilion later and had tea with their supporters. But Noel did not return to Olga's side. He kept at a distance, surrounded by an enthusiastic group of fellow-subalterns.

Peggy, restrained by her mother from joining him, watched him with longing eyes; but she watched in vain. Noel did not so much as glance in their direction, and very soon he departed altogether with a brother-officer.

"Wyndham seems down on his luck," observed Major Forsyth, Noel's Major, to Daisy, to whom he had just brought tea. "He's no need to be. He played like a dozen devils."

She smiled with that touch of tenderness that all women had for Noel. "I expect he doesn't like being beaten, poor boy."

"He hasn't learned the art of taking it gracefully," said the Major. "But he shouldn't show temper. It's a sign of coltishness that I don't care for."

"Ah, well, he's young," said Daisy, with a sigh. "He'll get over that."

Her thoughts dwelt regretfully upon the young officer as she returned with Peggy. She believed that she understood Noel better than anyone else did just then.

Peggy did not understand him at all, and was deeply hurt by her cavalier's defection. She did think he might have said good-bye to her before he went.

Will, meeting them at the gate of their own compound, laughed down his small daughter's grievance. "Do you really suppose he could remember a midget like you?" he asked, as he tossed her on to his shoulder. "You expect too much of us, my baby."

"You wouldn't have goed away like that, Daddy," she protested, locking her small fingers lovingly under his chin.

"Ah, well, I'm old, you see," said Will. "I've learned how to please--or should I say how not to displease?--you sensitive ladies."

"Did Mummy teach you?" asked Peggy with interest.

Will laughed with his eyes on his wife's face. "On that subject," he said, "she taught me absolutely all I know."

Daisy smiled in return. "I set you some hard lessons, didn't I, Will?" she said. "Why, how late we are! I had no idea the evening mail was in. Peggy, run to ayah, darling! Only one letter for me! Who on earth is it from?"

She took it up and inspected the handwriting on the envelope.

"It's a bold enough scrawl," said Will. "Some male acquaintance apparently."

"No one interesting, I am sure," said Daisy.

She opened the envelope as she stood, withdrew the letter, and glanced at the signature.

The next instant she flushed suddenly and hotly. "That man!" she ejaculated.

"What man?" said Will.

She turned to the beginning of the letter. "Oh, it's no one you know, dear. A man I met long ago at Mahalaleshwar--that time you were at Bombay, soon after we married. He was a shocking flirt. So was I--in those days. But he got too serious at last, and I had to cut and run. I daresay there wasn't any real harm in him. It was probably all my own fault. It always is the woman's fault, isn't it?"

She twined her arm in his, looking up into his face with a little smile, half-mocking, half-wistful.

He stooped to kiss her. "Well, what does the bounder want?"

"Oh, nothing much," she said. "Simply, he finds himself in this direction after big game, and, having heard of our being here, he wants to know if we will put him up for a night or two--for the sake of old times, he has the effrontery to add."

"Do you want him?" asked Will, the echo of a fighting note in his voice.

She smiled again as she heard it. "No, not particularly. I am really indifferent. But I think it would look rather silly to refuse, don't you? Besides, it would be good for him to see how old and staid I have become."

Will looked slightly grim. Nevertheless, he did not argue the point. "All right, Daisy. Do as you think best!" he said.

She returned to her letter, still holding his arm. "That's very wise of you, Will," she said softly. "Then I suppose I shall write and tell him to come."

"What's the fellow's name?" asked Will.

Daisy turned again to the signature. "Merton Hunt-Goring. He was a major in the Sappers, but he has retired now, he says. He can't be very young. He was no chicken in those days. I didn't really like him, you know; but he amused me."

Will smiled. "Poor darling! Your bore of a husband never did that."

She rubbed her cheek against his shoulder. "Dear old duffer! When are we going for that honeymoon of ours? And what shall we do with Peggy? Don't say we've got to wait till she is safely married to Noel!"

Will's eyes opened. Never since Peggy's birth had Peggy's mother tolerated the possibility of leaving her. He had always believed that her whole soul centred in the child, and he had been content to believe it; such was the greatness of his love.

"You would never bear to leave Peggy behind," he said.

She laughed at him, her soft, mocking laugh of mischievous, elusive charm.

"Do you suppose I shall want a child to look after when I am on my honeymoon? Of course I should leave her behind--not alone with ayah, of course. But that could be arranged. Anyhow, it is high time she learned to toddle alone on her own wee legs for a little. She is very independent already. She wouldn't really miss me, you know."

"Wouldn't she?" said Will. "But what of you? Your heart would ache for her from the moment you left her to the moment of your return."

She laughed again, lightly, merrily, her cheek against his sleeve.

"Not with my own man to keep me happy. There were no Peggies in the Garden of Eden, were there?" Then, as he still looked doubtful, "Oh, Will,--my own dearest one--how blind--how blind thou art!"

That moved him, touching him very nearly. He suddenly flushed a deep red. His arm went swiftly round her. "Daisy, Daisy--" he whispered haltingly, "I am not--not more to you than our child?"

She turned her face up to his; her eyes were full of tears though she was smiling still. "More to me than all the world, dear," she whispered back; "dearer to me than my hope of heaven."

She had never spoken such words to him before; he had never dreamed to hear them on her lips. It was not Daisy's way to express herself thus. In the far-off days of their courtship she had ever, daintily yet firmly, kept him at a distance. Since those days she had suffered shipwreck--a shipwreck from which his love alone had delivered her; but though the bond between them had drawn them very close, he had never pictured himself as ruling supreme in his wife's heart.

He was strongly moved by the revelation; but it was utterly impossible to put his feeling into words. He could only stoop and kiss her with a murmured, "God bless you, Daisy!"

They parted then, she to follow Peggy and superintend the evening tub, he to return to his desk and his work.

But his work did not flourish that evening; and presently, waxing impatient, he rose and went to seek her, drawn as a needle to a magnet.

He found her dressed for the regimental ball, and such was the witchery of her in her gown of shimmering black that he stood a moment in the doorway of her room as though hesitating to enter.

She turned from her table smiling her gay, sweet smile. Her silvery hair shone soft and wonderful in the lamplight.

"Ah, my dear Will," she said, "are you coming to for once? I wish you would. Do leave that stuffy old work--just to please me!" She went to meet him, with hands coaxingly outstretched. "It's getting late," she said, "I'll help you to dress."

He took the hands, gazing at her as if he could not turn his eyes away. "There's not much point in my trying to work to-night," he said, his voice very deep and a trifle husky. "I see and think of nothing but you. Great heavens, Daisy, how lovely you are!"

She laughed at him with tender raillery. "Dearly beloved gander, there is no one in the world thinks so but you."

"You've turned my head to-night," he said, still gazing at her. "By Heaven, I believe I'm falling in love with you all over again."

"Ah, well, it's to some purpose this time," she laughed, "for I'm very badly smitten too."

He did not laugh; he could not. "Daisy," he said, "we will have that honeymoon."

She pressed towards him with eagerness none the less because she pretended it to be half-feigned. "Will, you darling! When? When?"

His arms clasped her. His chest was heaving. "Very soon," he said, speaking softly down into her upraised face. "I've been thinking, dear--thinking very hard, ever since you asked me. I can get long leave in about three months--if I work for it. We'll go Home for the summer, you and I and the kiddie. If you are sure you can bear it, we will take her to Muriel Ratcliffe--and leave her in her charge."

He paused.

"Go on!" breathed Daisy. "And then?"

"Then we will go away together--you and I--you and I--right away into the country, and be--alone."

Daisy drew a deep breath. Her eyes were shining. She spoke no word. Only, after a moment, her hands stole upwards and clasped his neck.

"Will it do?" said Will.

She nodded mutely.

He held her closely. "Daisy, forgive me for asking--it won't hurt you to go back to England?"

Her eyes met his with absolute candour. "No, dear," she said.

"I was thinking," he said, stumbling a little, "sometimes old scenes, you know--they bring back--old heartaches."

"My heart will never ache--in that way," she answered gently, "while I have you." She paused a moment; then: "I'd like you to understand, Will," she said. "It isn't that I have forgotten. I have simply passed on. One does, you know. And I think that is--sometimes--how the last come to be first. It doesn't hurt me any longer to remember my old love. And it mustn't hurt you either. For it isn't a thing that could ever again come between us. Nothing ever could, Will. We are too closely united for that. And it is your love, your faith, your patience, that have made it so."

She ended with her head back, her lips raised to his, and in the kiss that passed between them there was something sacred, something in the nature of a bond.

Yet in a moment she was smiling again, the while she slipped from his close embrace. "And now you are going to dress for the ball. Come, you won't refuse me just for to-night--just for to-night!"

She pleaded with him like a girl and she proved irresistible. Half dazzled by her, he surrendered to her wiles.

"I will come if you like, Daisy; but I'm afraid I shall only be in the way. My dancing has grown very rusty from long disuse."

"What nonsense!" she protested. "Why, I only married you for the sake of your dancing. If you don't come, I shall spend the whole evening dancing with Nick."

"Oh, I'm not afraid of Nick!" said Will. "He is as safe as the Bank of England."

"Is he?" said Daisy. "You wait till you catch us alone some day. I tell you frankly, Will, I've kissed Nick more than once!"

"My dear," he said, "your frankness is your salvation. You have my full permission to do so as often as you meet."

She made a face at him, and finally freed herself. "Many thanks! But you wouldn't like me to create a scandal by dancing with him all the evening, I am sure. So," giving him a small, emphatic push, "go at once and dress your lazy self, and do your duty as a husband for once!"

"Shall I be adequately rewarded for it?" questioned Will, looking back as he turned to go.

She blew him an airy kiss. "Yes, you shall have half my waltzes."

He still lingered. "And the other half?"

"The other half," said Daisy, "will be divided equally between Nick and my prospective son-in-law."

And at that Will laughed like a merry boy and moved away. "I know I can cut out Noel," he said as he went. "As for Nick, he is welcome to as many as he can get."

CHAPTER XIII
A woman's prejudice

The evening was marked for ever in Olga's calendar as the merriest of her life. She was positively giddy with happiness, and she danced as she had never danced before. No one deemed her colourless or insignificant that night. She was radiant, and all who saw her felt the glow.

The only flaw in her joy was a slight dread of Noel; but this he very quickly dispelled, singling her out at once to plead for dances.

"You've saved a few for me, I know," he said, in his wheedling Irish way, and she saw at once that, whatever his inner feelings, he had no intention of wearing his heart on his sleeve.

She showed him her programme. "Yes, I've kept quite a lot for you to choose from," she said.

He flashed her a glance from his dark eyes that made her drop her own. "All right then," he said coolly. "I'll take 'em all."

She raised no protest though she had not quite expected that of him. She felt she owed it to him--as if in short she ought to give him anything he asked for to make up for what she had been compelled to withhold.

Max, sauntering up a little later, took her programme and looked at it with brows slightly raised. He gave it back to her, however, without comment.

Noel was the best dancer in the room, and Olga fully appreciated the fact. She loved Nick's dancing also, but it always brought to notice his crippled state, a fact which he never seemed to mind, but which she had never wholly ceased to mourn.

It was a great surprise to her to see Will Musgrave on the scene. When he came to her side her programme was full.

"Oh, knock off one of Nick's!" he said. "I owe him one."

But she would not do this till Nick's permission had been obtained and Nick had airily secured Daisy as a substitute.

Her dances with Max were spent chiefly in a very dark corner of the verandah, as he maintained that she was in a highly feverish condition and rest and quiet were essential. There was certainly some truth in the assertion though she indignantly denied it, and the intervals passed thus undoubtedly calmed her and kept her from reaching too high a pitch of excitement.

Max was exceedingly composed and steady. He danced with Daisy Musgrave, and provoked her to exasperation by his sang-froid.

"He is quite detestable," she told her husband later. "What on earth Olga can see to like in him is a puzzle I can never hope to solve. Noel is worth a hundred of him."

At which criticism Will laughed aloud. "There is no accounting for woman's fancies, my dear Daisy. And I must say I think young Noel would prove something of a handful."

"Anyhow he is human," retorted Daisy. "But this young man of Olga's is as self-contained and unapproachable as a camel. I'd rather deal with a sinner than a saint any day."

"Is Dr. Wyndham a saint?" questioned Will.

She laughed with just a touch of hardness. "A very scientific one, I should say. He has the most merciless eyes I ever saw."

She expressed this opinion a little later to Nick who took her in to supper, and for once found him in disagreement with her.

"Dearest Daisy," he said, "you can't expect a genius to look and behave like an ordinary mortal. That young man is already one of the most brilliant members of his profession. He has practically the world at his feet, and he'd be a fool if he didn't know it. I quite admit he may be merciless, but he is magnetic too. He can work with his mind as well as his hands, and he is never at a loss. Now that is the sort of man I admire. I think Olga has shown excellent taste."

"I don't!" declared Daisy emphatically. "I simply can't understand it, Nick. He may be an excellent match for her from a worldly point of view, but from a romantic standpoint--" She broke off with an expressive gesture--"I suppose it is a love-match?"

Nick laughed, blinking very rapidly as her eyes sought his. "Look at the kiddie's face if you want to know! She is as happy as a lark. Also, I seem to remember some-one once saying to me that there wasn't a man in the universe that some woman couldn't be fool enough to love."

Daisy smiled in spite of herself. "I know I did. But some attachments are quite unaccountable all the same. I suppose if you are satisfied, I ought to be; but, you know, there is something about that young man that puts me in mind of a destroy-ing angel. There's a tremendous power for shattering things hidden away in him somewhere. He may be a genius. I daresay he is. But one feels he wouldn't stick at anything that came in his way. If he failed he would simply trample his failure un-derfoot without scruple and go on. He is ruthless, Nick, or he couldn't have cut out poor Noel so overwhelmingly. I always thought till yesterday that Noel's chances were very good."

"I never favoured Noel's addresses," said Nick lightly. "He wants more ballast, to my mind. Whatever Max may be, at least he's solid. He wouldn't capsize in a gale."

Daisy laughed. "I see you are not to be influenced by a woman's prejudice. I daresay you are right, but there is also something in what I say or my instinct is very seriously at fault."

"On that point," said Nick politely, "chivalry does not permit me to express an opinion. Also, you are far too lovely to thwart, if I may use an old friend's privilege to tell you so."

She laughed carelessly enough though her cheeks flushed a little. "You are a gross flatterer, Nick."

"On the contrary," he said, "I worship at the shrine of Truth. You are more beautiful to-night than I have ever before seen you."

She laughed again with a hint of something that was not careless. "I'm glad you think so." She paused a moment; then: "Nick," she said softly, "dear old friend, Will and I are going for our second honeymoon this year!"

Carefully subdued though it was Nick heard the note of exultation in her voice. His own magic smile flashed across his face. Under the table his hand gripped hers.

"Thanks for telling me, dear!" he said, in a rapid whisper. "Long life and happiness to you both!"

For the rest of his time with her, he was gay and inconsequent. Very thorough was the understanding between them. They had been pals for many years.

When he left her, it was to go in search of Olga whose name was the only one left on his programme.

He found her with Noel on the verandah whither they had just betaken themselves for some air after the heat of the supper-room. He broke in upon them without ceremony.

"Look here, Olga mia! I've got to go. I'm afraid I shall have to cut our dance. You can give it to Max with my love. Daisy will take care of you here, and he can bring you home."

"Got to go, Nick! Why?" She turned to him in surprise. "You're not going to the Palace at this time of night surely! Why, the Rajah is still here, isn't he?"

"Great Lucifer, no!" said Nick. "But I've got some business to see to that won't keep. You'll be all right with Max to take care of you. Good-night!" He kissed her lightly. "See you in the morning! Don't overtire yourself, and don't get up early! Good-night, Noel!"

He would have departed with the words, but Noel detained him. "I say, Nick! I've been wanting a word with you all day, but couldn't get it in. If I lived where you do, I should keep a pretty sharp look-out. I caught an old brute of a moonstone-seller (at least that's what he called himself) prowling about your place only last night, and kicked him off the premises."

Nick stood still. His eyes flickered very rapidly as he faced Noel in the dimness. "Awfully obliged to you, my son," he said, and in his cracked voice there sounded a desire to laugh. "But that poor old seller of moonstones happens to be a very particular friend of mine. You needn't kick him again."

"What?" said Noel. "That mangy old cur a friend of yours?"

"He isn't mangy," said Nick. "And he's been very useful to me in one way and another; will be again, I daresay."

"My dear chap," Noel protested, "you don't mean to say you trust those people? You shouldn't really. It's madness. They are treachery incarnate, one and all."

Nick laughed flippantly. "Even treachery is a useful quality sometimes," he declared, as he turned to go. "Don't you worry yourself, my boy. I can walk on cat's ice as well as anyone I know."

He was gone, humming his favourite waltz as he departed; and Noel turned back to his partner with a grunt of discontent.

"He'll play that game once too often if he isn't careful," he said.

"Is there really any danger?" Olga asked.

"I should say so," he answered, "but it seems I am of no account."

"Oh, he didn't mean that," she said quickly.

He looked at her. "He is not the only person who thinks so, Olga."

She slipped a friendly hand on to his arm. "Noel," she said, "you don't think I think so, do you?"

He laid his hand on hers and pressed it silently. They stood together in the semi-darkness, isolated for the moment, very intimately alone.

"Noel," Olga whispered at length, a tremor of distress in the words, "you mustn't think that; please--please, you must never think that!"

He moved a little, stooped to her. "Olga," he said, speaking quickly, "I'm not blaming you. You couldn't help it. It's just my damned luck. But--if I'd met you--first--I'd have won you!"

The words came hot and passionate. His hand gripped hers with unconscious force. She made no attempt to free herself. Neither did she contradict him, for she knew that he spoke the truth.

Only, after a moment, she said, looking up at him, "I'm so dreadfully sorry."

"You couldn't help it," he reiterated almost savagely. "Anyhow you're happy; so I ought to be satisfied. I should be too, if I didn't have a sort of feeling that you'd have been happier with me. P'raps I'm a cad to tell you, but it's hit me rather hard."

He broke off, breathing heavily. She drew nearer to him, stroking his shoulder softly with her free hand. "Dear Noel, I love you for telling me," she said. "I feel dreadfully unworthy of your love. But I'm very, very grateful for it. You know that, don't you? And I--I'd marry you if my heart would let me, but,--dear, it won't."

He forced a laugh. "I know you would. That's just the damnable part of it. Life is an infernal swindle, isn't it? It's brimful of this sort of thing." He stood up with a jerk, and pulled himself together. "Forgive me, Olga! I didn't mean to let off steam in this way. I'm a selfish hound. Forget it! Only promise me that if you ever want a friend to turn to, you'll turn to me."

"Indeed I will!" she said very earnestly.

He held her hands very tightly for a moment and let them go; but they clung to his. She looked up at him appealingly.

"Noel," she said, with slight hesitation, "please--for my sake--be friendly with Max!"

He drew back instantly with a boyish gesture of distaste. "Oh, all right," he said.

She saw that he would not endure pressure on this point, and refrained from pursuing it; but his reception of her request was a disappointment to her. Somehow she had come to expect greater things from Noel.

The rest of the evening slipped away magically. She danced a great many dances without any sense of fatigue; but when it was all over at last a great weariness descended upon her. She drove back with Max, so utterly spent that she could hardly speak.

Yet, as they entered Nick's bungalow, she roused herself and turned to him with her own quick smile. "It's been the happiest evening of my life," she said.

"Really!" said Max.

She slipped the cloak from her shoulders and went close to him. The love in her eyes gave them a glory that was surely not of earth. She took him by the shoulders, those clear, shining eyes raised to his.

"I'm afraid you've had a dull time," she said. "I hope you haven't hated it."

"Not at all," said Max.

Yet a hint of cynicism still lingered about him as he said it. He stood passive within her hold.

She pressed a little nearer to him. "Max, you didn't mind my giving all those dances to Noel? You--understood?"

He began to smile. "My dear girl, yes!"

"You are sure?" she insisted.

He took her upraised face between his hands. "I have always understood you," he said.

"I can't help being sorry for him, can I?" she said wistfully.

He bent and kissed her. "It's a wasted sentiment, my child; but if it pleases you to be sorry, I have no objection."

"He is much nicer than you think," she pleaded.

He laughed at that. "I've known him from his cradle. He's a typical Wyndham, you know. They are all charming in one sense, and all rotten in another."

"Oh, Max!" she protested.

"I'm an exception," he said; "neither charming nor rotten. Now, my dear, since your estimable little chaperon has deserted you it's up to me to send you to bed. Do you want a drink before you go?"

She leaned her head against his shoulder. "No, I don't want anything. I feel as if I had had too much already. I don't want to go to bed, Max. I don't want to end this perfect day."

"There is always to-morrow," he said.

"No; but to-morrow won't be the same. And the time goes so fast. Very soon you will be going too."

"It will soon be Midsummer Day," smiled Max.

She gave a sudden, sharp shiver. "Lots of things may happen before then."

He held her closely to him for a moment, and in the thrilling pressure of his arms she felt his love for her vibrate; but he made no verbal answer to her words.

Slowly at length she released herself. "Well, I suppose I must say good-night. I hope you will be comfortable. You are sure you have all you want?"

"Quite sure," he said.

"Then good-night!" She went back for a moment into his arms. "I wonder Nick isn't here. Do you think he can have gone to bed?"

"Haven't an idea," said Max. "Anyhow I don't want him. And it's high time you went. Good-night, dear!"

Again closely he held her; again his lips pressed hers. Then, his arm about her, he led her to the door.

They parted outside, she glancing backward as she went, he standing motionless to watch her go. At the last she kissed her hand to him and was gone.

He turned back into the room with an odd, unsteady smile twitching the corner of his mouth.

The hand with which he helped himself to a drink shook slightly, and he looked at it with contemptuous attention. His favourite briar was lying in an ash-tray, where he had left it earlier in the day. He took it up, filled and lighted it. Then he sauntered out on to the verandah, drink in hand.

The night was dark and chill. He could barely discern the cypresses against the sky. He sat down in a hammock-chair in deep shadow and proceeded to smoke his pipe.

From far away, in the direction of the jungle, there came the haunting cry of a jackal, and a little nearer he heard the weird call of an owl. But close at hand there was no sound. He lay in absolute stillness, gazing along the verandah with eyes that looked into the future.

Minutes passed. His pipe went out, and his drink remained by his side forgotten. He wandered in the depths of reverie....

Suddenly from the compound immediately below him there came a faint rustle as of some living creature moving stealthily, and in a second Max was back in the present. He sat up noiselessly and peered downwards.

The faint rustle continued. His thoughts flashed to the tiger he had slain the day before at Khantali. Could this be another prowling in search of food? He scarcely thought so, yet the possibility gave him a sensation of bristling down the spine. He remained motionless in his chair, however, alert, listening.

Softly the intruder drew near. He heard the tamarisk bushes part and close again. But he heard no sound of feet. It was a cat-like advance, slow and wary.

He wondered if the creature could see him there in the dark, wondered if he were a fool to remain but decided to do so and take his chances. Max Wyndham's belief in his own particular lucky star was profound.

Nearer and nearer drew the unseen one, came close to him, seemed to pause,--and passed. Max was holding his breath. His hands were clenched. He was strung for vigorous resistance.

But as he realized that the danger--if danger there had been--was over, his muscles relaxed. A moment later with absolute noiselessness he rose and leaned over the verandah-rail, intently watching.

Seconds passed thus and nothing happened. The rustling sound grew fainter, faded imperceptibly at length into the stillness of the night. Could it have been a jackal, Max asked himself?

He stood up and looked once more along the verandah. Nick's room was just round the corner of the bungalow. The nocturnal visitor had gone in that direction. With noiseless tread he followed.

He reached the corner. The soft glow of a night-lamp lay across the verandah. The window was open. He paused a second, then strode softly up and looked in.

A bamboo-screen was pulled across the room, hiding the bed. The lamp was burning behind it. As Max stood at the window, a turbaned figure came silently round the screen. It was the figure of an old man, grey-bearded, slightly bent, clad in a long native garment. For a moment he stood, then stepped to the window and closed it swiftly in Max's face. So sudden and so noiseless was the action that Max was taken wholly by surprise. He did not so much as know whether his presence had been observed.

Then the blind came down with the same noiseless rapidity, and he was left in darkness.

Mindful of the mysterious visitor in the compound, he turned about and felt his way back to the corner of the bungalow, deciding that the lighted drawing-room was preferable to the dark verandah.

Reaching the corner and within sight of the lamplight, he stopped again and listened. But the compound was still and to all appearance deserted. He waited for a full minute, but heard no sound beyond a faint stirring of the night-wind in the cypresses. Slowly at length he turned and retraced his steps, contemptuously wondering if the mysterious East had tampered with his nerves.

It was evident that his host had retired for the night with the assistance of his bearer, and he decided to follow his example. He closed and bolted the windows and went to his own room.

CHAPTER XIV
SMOKE FROM THE FIRE

It always used to be regarded as anything but a model State," smiled Major Hunt-Goring, as he lay in a long chair and watched Daisy's busy fingers at work on a frock for Peggy. "I suppose our friend Nicholas Ratcliffe has changed all that, however. A queer little genius--Nick."

"He is my husband's and my greatest friend," said Daisy.

"Really!" Hunt-Goring laughed silkily. "Do you know, Mrs. Musgrave, that's the fifth time you have mentioned your husband in as many minutes? If I remember aright, he used not to be so often on your lips."

Daisy glanced up momentarily. "And now," she said, "he is never out of my thoughts."

"Really!" Hunt-Goring said again. He looked at her very attentively for a few seconds before he relaxed again with eyes half-closed. "That is tres convenant for you both," he observed. "I enjoy the unusual spectacle of a wife who is happy as well as virtuous."

Daisy stitched on in silence. Privately she wondered how she had ever come to be on intimate terms with the man, and condemned afresh the follies of her youth.

"Have you been Home since I had the pleasure of your society at Mahalaleshwar I will not say how many years ago?" asked Hunt-Goring, after a pause.

"I went Home the following year," said Daisy. "We thought--we hoped--it would make our baby boy more robust to have a summer in England."

"Oh, have you a boy?" said Hunt-Goring, without much interest.

"He died," said Daisy briefly.

Hunt-Goring looked bored, and the conversation languished.

Into the silence came Peggy, fairy-footed, gay of mien. She flung impulsive arms around her mother's neck and pressed a soft cheek coaxingly to hers.

"Mummy, Noel is comin' to teach me to ride this morning. I may go, mayn't I?"

"My darling!" said Daisy, in consternation. "He never said anything to me about it."

Peggy laughed, nodding her fair head with saucy assurance. "He promised, Mummy."

"But, dearie," protested Daisy, "you can't ride Noel's horse. You'd be frightened, and so would Mummy."

Peggy laughed again, the triumphant laugh of one who possesses private information. "Noel wouldn't let me be frightened," she said, with confidence.

"Who is Noel?" asked Hunt-Goring.

Peggy looked at him. She was not quite sure that she liked this friend of her mother's, and her look said as much. "Noel is an officer," she said proudly. "He's the pwettiest officer in the Regiment, and I love him."

"Ha!" Hunt-Goring laughed. "You inherit your mother's tastes, my child." He looked across at Daisy. "She always preferred the pretty ones."

"I know better now," said Daisy, without returning his look.

He laughed again and stretched himself. "What became of that handsome cousin of yours who paid you a visit in the old M'war days?"

"Do you mean Blake Grange?" Daisy's voice suddenly sounded so remote and cold that Peggy turned and regarded her in round-eyed astonishment.

"Yes, that was the fellow. He got trapped at Wara along with General Roscoe and Nick Ratcliffe. What happened to him? Was he killed?"

"No, not then." Slowly Daisy lifted her eyes; slowly she spoke. "He gave his life in England the following year to save some shipwrecked sailors."

"Did he, though? Quite a hero!" Hunt-Goring's eyes met hers and insolently held them. "Were you present at the sacrifice?"

"Yes," she answered him briefly, but there was tragedy in her eyes.

"Ah!" said Hunt-Goring softly. "That made a difference to you."

She did not answer; she leaned her cheek against Peggy's fair head in silence.

"My dear lady," said Hunt-Goring, "you always took things too seriously."

She gave a brief sigh, and took up her work again. "Life is rather a serious matter, I find," she said, with a smile that was scarcely gay.

"Nonsense!" said Hunt-Goring.

"Don't you find it so?" Daisy did not look up again; she stitched on rapidly with the child leaning against her knee.

"I?" he said. "Oh, sometimes it seems so, when things don't fit. But I don't care, you know. I have a volatile mind, I am glad to say."

"Are you never afraid of growing old?" asked Daisy.

He laughed his soft, self-satisfied laugh. "Oh, really, you know, I don't think they will let me do that at present."

"You never think of getting married?" asked Daisy.

Hunt-Goring's smile changed a little, grew subtly harder. "Most people think of it at one time or another." he observed. "But personally I do not regard myself as a marrying man."

"And you are never lonely?" she said.

"I am seldom alone, my dear Mrs. Musgrave," he said.

She turned the conversation. "Where have you been living since your retirement?"

"I took a place in England in the hunting-country--quite a decent place."

"Ah? Where?"

"About two miles from a little town called Weir." Hunt-Goring spoke deliberately, still watching his hostess's slim fingers at work.

"Why!" Swiftly Daisy looked up. "That is where the Ratcliffes live--Jim Ratcliffe and Olga. Olga is out here now with Nick. Did you know?"

Hunt-Goring nodded to each sentence. "I know it all. I know Jim Ratcliffe, and a burly old monster he is. I know Nick of Redlands--also the sedate Mrs. Nick. And, last but not least, I know--Olga."

He spoke mockingly; his look was derisive.

"I had no idea you had been living there," said Daisy.

"I was the hornet in the hive," said Hunt-Goring with his lazy laugh. "It's rather a hole of a place, though I liked The Warren well enough. I'm not going back there. You can tell Olga so with my love."

"She and Nick are dining here to-night," observed Daisy, "so you will be able to tell her yourself."

"What! To meet me!" It was Hunt-Goring's turn to look surprised. He did so with an accompanying sneer. "How did you describe me, I wonder? You couldn't have mentioned my name."

Daisy regarded him steadily for a moment. "Is there any reason why she should not meet you?" she asked.

"None whatever," said Hunt-Goring, with a shrug. "Needless to say, I shall be quite charmed to meet her."

At this point the conversation was interrupted by the sudden appearance of Noel. He came out through the French window of the drawing-room with his habitual air of cheery assurance, and was instantly pounced upon by Peggy who hailed him with delight.

He caught her up in his arms. "Well, little sweetheart, are we going for our ride? What does Mummy say?" He laughed down at Daisy, the child mounted high on his shoulder.

Daisy laughed back because she could not help it. "Oh, Noel, you are incorrigible! I don't think I dare trust her to you. Why do you suggest these headlong things?"

"But, my dear Mrs. Musgrave," he protested, "does any harm ever come to her when she is with me? You know I would guard her with my life!"

"Yes, I know," smiled Daisy. "But I am not sure that that would be a very great safe-guard. You are so reckless yourself. By the way, let me introduce Major Hunt-Goring--an old friend. Major Hunt-Goring--Mr. Wyndham!"

Noel nodded careless acknowledgment. Hunt-Goring merely lifted his brows momentarily. He did not greatly care for the boy's familiarity with his hostess. It was a privilege which he did not wish to share.

"Well, shall we start?" said Noel. "I've brought one of my polo mounts for Peggy," he added to Daisy. "You know the Chimpanzee. He's as quiet as a lamb. Come and give us a send-off! Really you needn't be anxious."

He patted her arm coaxingly, reassuringly, and Hunt-Goring took out his cigarette-case. He was plainly bored to extinction.

Daisy left him with a smiling apology. She did not suggest that he should accompany them, and he did not offer to do so.

"I don't like that man," declared Peggy as Noel bore her away. "He looks so ugly when he smiles."

"Only the Daisies and Peggies of this world manage to look pretty always," observed Noel gallantly.

For which dainty compliment Daisy frowned upon him. "My vanity days are over," she said, "but do remember that hers are yet to come!"

They went round to the front of the bungalow where Noel had left the mounts; and after a good deal of discussion and many injunctions Peggy was, to her huge delight, perched astride the Chimpanzee, a creature of almost human intelligence who plainly took a serious view of his responsibilities, to Daisy's immense relief.

She watched them ride away together at length at a walking pace, Noel on his tall Waler leading the polo-pony, from whose back Peggy waved her an ardent farewell; and finally went back to her guest feeling reassured. Noel evidently had no intention of taking any risks with Peggy in his charge.

"It's very good of him," she remarked, as she sat down again on the verandah.

Hunt-Goring opened his eyes a quarter of an inch. "I beg your pardon?"

"Oh, nothing," said Daisy, feeling slightly annoyed. "He's a nice boy, that's all; and I am grateful to him for being so kind to my little Peggy."

"It probably answers his purpose," said Hunt-Goring, smothering a yawn.

Daisy took up her work again in silence.

Hunt-Goring finished his cigarette in dreamy ease before he spoke again.

She thought he was half-asleep when unexpectedly he accosted her, referring to the subject in which he had seemed to take but slight interest.

"Did you say that puppy's name was Wyndham?"

"He isn't a puppy," said Daisy, quick to defend her friend.

He smiled his tolerant amusement. "My dear little woman, that wasn't the point of my enquiry."

Daisy stiffened. She suddenly began to sew very fast indeed, without speaking. Her pretty lips were compressed, but Hunt-Goring seemed sublimely unconscious of the fact. He smiled to himself as at some inward thought.

"You did say his name was Wyndham, I think?" he said, after a moment.

"I did," said Daisy.

"There was a fellow of the same name who lived at Weir," observed Hunt-Goring. "He was the doctor's assistant; had to leave in something of a hurry, I believe. There was the beginning of a scandal, but it was hushed up--strangled at birth, so to speak."

"What?" said Daisy. She looked across at him swiftly, her dignity and work alike forgotten.

Hunt-Goring still smiled placidly. "I daresay it might be described as a regrettable incident. It concerned the sudden death of a young girl at which event the said Dr. Wyndham presided. I really shouldn't have mentioned it if it hadn't been for the familiarity of the name."

"They are brothers," said Daisy.

"Really! That is strange." Again Hunt-Goring barely concealed a yawn. "Olga Ratcliffe used to be somewhat smitten with the young man in what I might call her calf days. Doubtless she has got over that by now, especially as the girl who died was a friend of hers."

"But she can't know of that!" said Daisy quickly. "She has been very ill, you know--an illness brought on by the shock of it all."

"Indeed!" said Hunt-Goring, and became significantly silent.

Daisy continued to look at him. "She has not got over it," she said slowly at length, speaking as though uttering her thoughts aloud. "He is out here now, arrived only last week. And--they are engaged to be married."

"Chacun a son gout!" observed Hunt-Goring.

She made a sharp movement of impatience. "Oh, don't be so cold-blooded! Tell me--do tell me--the whole story!"

"My dear Daisy," said Hunt-Goring daringly, "there is practically nothing more to tell."

"But there must be," Daisy argued, ignoring side-issues. "How did the gossip arise? There is never smoke without some fire."

"True," said Hunt-Goring. "But for the truth of the gossip I will not vouch. It ran in this wise. The girl was beautiful--and gay. The man--well, you have had some experience of the species; you know what they are. Trouble arose; there was madness in the girl's family. She became demented; and a certain magic draught did the rest. It was risky of course; but it was a choice of evils. He chose the surest means of protecting his reputation--which, I believe, is considered valuable in his profession."

"Oh, it isn't possible!" protested Daisy. "It simply can't be. How did you hear all this?"

Hunt-Goring laughed. "How does one ever hear anything? I told you I didn't vouch for the truth of it."

"I wonder what I ought to do," said Daisy.

"Do?" He looked at her. "What do you contemplate doing? Is it up to you to do anything?"

Daisy scarcely saw or heard him. "I am thinking of little Olga. She is engaged to him. She--can't know of this evil tale."

"She probably does," said Hunt-Goring. "They were very intimate--she and Violet Campion."

"It isn't possible," Daisy said again. "Why, I believe she was actually with the poor girl when she died. Nick told me a little. He said it had been very sudden and a severe shock to her."

"I should say it was," said Hunt-Goring.

She looked at him. "You were there at the time?"

"I was at The Warren--yes." He spoke with an easy air of unconcern.

Daisy leaned towards him. "And Nick--do you think Nick knew?"

Hunt-Goring looked straight back at her. "I think," he said deliberately, "that I should scarcely trouble to tackle Nick on the subject. He knows exactly what it suits him to know."

"What do you mean?" Daisy spoke sharply, nervously.

"Merely that he and the young man are--and always have been--hand and glove," explained Hunt-Goring smoothly. "Nick is a very charming person no doubt, but--"

"Be careful!" warned Daisy.

He made her a smiling bow. "But," he repeated with emphasis, "he is not senti-mentally particular in a matter of ethics. He looks to the end rather than the means. Also you must remember he is a man and not a woman. A man's outlook is differ-ent."

"Do you mean that Nick would overlook a thing of this kind?" asked Daisy.

Hunt-Goring nodded thoughtfully. "I think he would condone many things that you would regard as inexcusable, even monstrous. Otherwise, he would scarcely have been selected for his present job."

Daisy was silent.

"And you must remember," Hunt-Goring proceeded, "that this young Wyndham is a rising man--a desirable parti for any girl. He will probably never make another blunder of that description. It is too risky, especially for a man who means to climb to the top of the tree."

"You really think it possible then that Nick knows?" Daisy still looked doubtful.

"I think it more than possible." Hunt-Goring spoke with confidence. "I am sorry if it shocks you, but, you know, he is really too shrewd a person not to know current gossip and its origin."

This was a straight shot, and it told. Daisy acknowledged it without argument.

"But Olga!" she said. "Olga can't know."

"Perhaps not," admitted Hunt-Goring. "And--in that case--it would be advisable to leave her in ignorance; would it not?"

He took out another cigarette with the words, flinging her a sidelong glance as he did it.

But Daisy was silent, looking straight before her.

"Surely," said Hunt-Goring, through a cloud of aromatic smoke, "whether there is anything in the tale or not, the fewer that know of it--the better."

"Oh, I don't know." Daisy spoke as if compelled. "No woman ought to be married blindfold. It is too great a risk."

Hunt-Goring leaned back again in his chair. "If I were in your place, I should maintain a discreet silence," he said.

"I don't think you would," said Daisy.

He inhaled a long breath of smoke. "If I didn't, I should approach the girl herself--find out what she knows--and, with great discretion, put her on her guard. I don't think you would gain much by opening up the matter in any other quarter."

"You mean it would be no good to discuss it with Nick?" said Daisy.

Hunt-Goring looked at the end of his cigarette. "Perhaps I do mean that," he said. "He would probably prevent it coming to Olga's knowledge if he had set his heart on the match."

"He couldn't prevent my telling her," said Daisy quickly.

"No?" Hunt-Goring gave utterance to his silky laugh. "Well," he said, "my experience of Nick Ratcliffe is not a very extensive one; but I should certainly say that he knows how to get his own way in most things. Perhaps you have never come into collision with him?"

Daisy coloured suddenly, and was silent.

Hunt-Goring laughed again. "You see my point, I perceive," he remarked. "Well, I leave the matter in your hands, but--if you really wish to warn the girl, I should not warn Nick Ratcliffe first."

He spoke impressively, notwithstanding his laugh. And Daisy accepted his advice in silence.

Much as she loved Nick, she knew but too well how a struggle with him would end, and she shrank from risking a conflict. Besides, there was Olga to be thought of. She resumed her sewing with a puckered brow. Certainly Olga must be warned.

There might be no truth in the story, but then rumours of that description never started themselves. And Max Wyndham--well she had been prejudiced against him from the beginning in spite of the fact that Nick was all in his favour. He was ruthless and unscrupulous; she was sure of it. How he had ever managed to win Olga was a perpetual puzzle to her. Perhaps he really was magnetic, as Nick had said. But she believed it to be an evil magnetism. As a lover, he was the coolest she had ever seen.

"Altogether objectionable," had been her verdict from the outset.

And now came this monstrous tale to confirm her previous opinion. Impulsively Daisy decided that Olga must not be left in ignorance. Marriage was too great a speculation for any risk of that kind to be justifiable. She felt she owed it to the girl to warn her--to save her from a possible life-long misery. These things had such a ghastly knack of turning up afterwards. And Olga was so young, so trusting--

"Are you going to take my advice?" asked Hunt-Goring.

She looked up with a start. "What advice?"

"As to maintaining a discreet silence," he said.

His eyes were half-closed; she could not detect the narrowness of his scrutiny.

"No," she answered. "I shall certainly speak to Olga. It wouldn't be right--it wouldn't be fair--not to do so." Her look was suddenly appealing. "There is a freemasonry among women as well as men," she said. "We must keep faith with one another at least."

Hunt-Goring closed his eyes completely, and smiled a placid smile. "Dear Mrs. Musgrave," he said, "you are a true woman."

And she did not hear the note of exultation below the lazy appreciation of his words.

CHAPTER XV
THE SPREADING OF THE FLAME

Certainly Major Hunt-Goring was the last person Olga expected to meet at the Musgraves' dinner-party that night, and so astounded was she for the moment at the sight of him that she came to a sudden halt on the threshold of the drawing-room.

"Hullo!" murmured Max's voice behind her. "Here's a dear old friend!"

Max's hand gently pushed her forward, and in an instant she had mastered her astonishment. She met the dear old friend with heightened colour indeed, but with no other sign of agitation. He smiled upon her, upon Max, upon Nick, with equal geniality.

"Quite a gathering of old friends!" he remarked.

"Quite," said Nick. "Have you only just come out?"

"No, I've been out some weeks. I came after tiger," said Hunt-Goring, with his eyes on Olga, who had passed on to her host.

"You won't find any in this direction," said Nick. "Wyndham bagged the last survivor on Christmas Day, and a mangy old brute it was."

"I daresay I shall come across other game," said Hunt-Goring, bringing his eyes slowly back to Nick.

Nick laughed. "It's not particularly plentiful here. You'll find it a waste of time hunting in these parts."

"Oh, I have plenty of time at my disposal," smiled Hunt-Goring.

Nick's eyes flickered over him. He also was smiling. "Perseverance deserves to be rewarded," he said.

"And usually is," said Hunt-Goring. He held out his hand to Max. "Ah, Dr. Wyndham, I'm delighted to meet you again. You will be gratified to hear that, thanks to your skilful treatment, my thumb has mended quite satisfactorily."

Max looked at the hand critically; he did not offer to take it. "I am--greatly gratified," he said.

Hunt-Goring withdrew it, still smiling. "May I congratulate you on your engagement," he said.

Max's mouth went down ironically. "Certainly if you feel so disposed," he said.

Hunt-Goring laughed easily. "You young fellows have all the luck," he said. "When do you expect to be married?"

"On Midsummer Day," said Max.

"Really!" Hunt-Goring's laugh was silken in its softness. "Your plans are all cut and dried then. Yet, you know, 'there's many a slip,' etc."

"Not under my management," said Max.

He looked hard and straight into the other man's eyes, and turned aside.

Nick had already joined his hostess, and was making gay conversation about nothing in particular.

Noel came in late, acknowledged everyone with a deep salaam, and attached himself instantly to Olga.

With relief she found that he was to take her in to dinner. He was in a mood of charming inconsequence, and under his easy guidance she gradually recovered from the shock of her enemy's appearance on the scene.

"I hear on the best authority that General Bassett is expected in a fortnight," he told her. "We are going to treat him royally. You ladies will have to work hard."

"Max will be on his way Home by then," said Olga, with a sigh.

He laughed. "Well, I shall be left, and I shan't let you grizzle. We must organize a fete week. You and I will be the head of the committee. I'll come round to-morrow, and we'll draw up a plan to submit to old Badgers; merely a matter of form, you know. He'll consent to anything. We will have a fancy-dress ball for one thing, and a picnic or two, and some races and gymkhanas. Perhaps we might manage some private theatricals."

"Oh, we couldn't possibly!" protested Olga. "We could never get anything up in time."

But Noel was not to be discouraged. He proceeded to sketch out a lavish pro-

gramme of entertainments with such energy and ingenuity that at length he managed to infuse her with some of his enthusiasm, and the end of dinner came upon
her as a surprise.

Will, Hunt-Goring, Max, and Nick sat down to play bridge when it was finally
over--at the suggestion of Hunt-Goring, who displayed not the smallest desire to
seek her out. It seemed as though all memory of their former relations had passed
completely from his mind. Neither by word nor look did he attempt to recall old
times.

And gradually Olga became reassured. His fancy for her had quite obviously
evaporated. He scarcely so much as glanced her way.

Could it have been mere coincidence that had brought him there? she began
to ask herself. Stranger things had happened; and he was plainly on intimate terms
with his hostess, rather more intimate than Daisy's manner seemed to justify. But
then familiarity with women was one of his main characteristics, as she knew but
too well. He had not been able to exercise this much at Weir. She suspected that
boredom alone had induced him to pursue her so persistently.

In any case, it was over. He cared for her no more and was at no pains to conceal the fact, which she on her part recognized with profound relief.

She went with Daisy to the drawing-room, leaving the card-players established
in Will's especial den. Noel airily accompanied them, and sang a few songs at the
piano, as much for his own pleasure as theirs. He was in a particularly charming
mood, and was evidently determined to enjoy himself to the utmost.

But he was not minded to give them too much of his society, and presently he
slipped away to take a peep at Peggy.

"I shan't wake her," he said; but apparently he found his small adorer awake,
for he did not return.

"He's a dear boy," said Daisy.

Olga assented warmly. "I shall love him for a brother."

Daisy smiled faintly. "Poor Noel! I'm afraid that is scarcely the sort of appreciation he wants."

Olga flushed. She was standing near the window, her girlish face outlined
against the dark. Very young and slender she looked standing there, scarcely more
than a child; and Daisy's heart went out to her in a sudden rush of almost passion-

ate tenderness. She rose impulsively and joined her. She slipped a warm arm round her waist.

Olga glanced at her in momentary surprise, then swiftly responded to the caress. She leaned her cheek against Daisy's shoulder.

"You see," she said, "I met Max first."

"I see, dear," said Daisy. She hesitated a moment. "And Max is your ideal of all that a man should be?" she asked then.

"Oh, no!" said Olga. She gave a little laugh. "No; Nick is that, and always has been. I don't think anyone could idealize Max, do you?"

"But you love him?" said Daisy.

Olga looked at her with clear, direct eyes. "Oh, yes, I love him. But I don't try to think he is nicer than he really is. Nice or horrid, I love him just the same."

"Do you know any horrid things about him, then?" Daisy asked.

Olga laughed again. "I knew the horrid part of him first," she said. "Why, I--I almost hated him once."

"And then you changed your mind," said Daisy.

The love-light glowed softly in Olga's eyes as she answered, "Yes, dear Mrs. Musgrave; he made me."

Daisy uttered a sharp, involuntary sigh. "I hope he is all you believe him to be," she said.

"But why do you say that?" questioned Olga. "I'm afraid you don't like him."

Daisy hesitated. "I am afraid I know too much about him," she said at length.

Olga looked at her in surprise. "Has Noel been telling you things?"

Daisy shook her head.

"Oh, then it's that detestable Major Hunt-Goring!" said Olga, adding quickly: "Please forgive me for running down your guest; but he really is a hateful man."

"I don't care for him myself, dear," said Daisy.

"He has only come here to make mischief," said Olga, with conviction. "I guessed it the moment I saw him. He hates me because--because--" she faltered a little--"because I wouldn't marry him. As if I possibly could!" she ended fierily. "And as if he would have really liked it if I had!"

"Oh, is that it?" said Daisy, in a tone of enlightenment.

Olga nodded. "He's a beast, Mrs. Musgrave. And what has he been telling you about Max?"

Daisy hesitated. She was assailed by sudden misgiving. Was it all a ruse? She did not trust Major Hunt-Goring. She believed him fully capable of vindictiveness, and yet, so subtle had been his strategy, he had not seemed vindictive. He had repeated the story idly in the first place, and, finding she took it seriously, he had advised her to hold her peace. No, she would do him justice at least. She was convinced that he had not been deliberately malicious in this case. It had not been his intention to work evil.

"Tell me what he said!" said Olga.

Her tone was imperative; yet Daisy still hesitated. "Do you know, dear, I don't think I will," she said.

"Please--you must!" said Olga, with decision. "It concerns me as much as it does him."

"I am not sure that it really concerns either of you," Daisy said. "It was just a piece of gossip which may--or may not--have had any foundation."

"Still, tell me!" Olga insisted. "Forewarned is fore-armed, isn't it? And things do get so distorted sometimes, don't they?"

"Well, dear--" Daisy was beginning to wish herself well out of the matter--"it is not a pretty story. You and Nick may possibly have heard of it. Quite possibly you know it to be untrue. Major Hunt-Goring told me it was sheer gossip, and he would not vouch for the truth of it. It concerned the death of your friend Violet Campion."

"Ah!" said Olga. She breathed the word rather than uttered it. All the colour went out of her face. "Go on!" she whispered. "Go on!"

"You know the tale?" said Daisy.

"Tell me!" said Olga.

Reluctantly Daisy complied. "It was whispered that there had been an understanding between them, that the poor girl went mad with trouble, and that--to protect himself from scandal--he gave her a draught that ended her life."

Briefly, baldly, fell the words, spoken in an undertone, with evident unwillingness. They went out into silence, a silence that had in it something dreadful, something that no words could express.

It was many seconds before Daisy ventured a look at the girl's face, though her arm was still about her. When she did, she was shocked. For Olga was gazing straight before her with eyes wide and glassy--the eyes of the sleep-walker who stares upon visions of horror which no others see.

As Daisy moved, she moved also, went to the window, stepped straight out into the night. Dumbly Daisy watched her. She had obeyed her instinct in speaking, but now she knew not what to say or do.

Slowly at length Olga turned. She came back into the room. The glassy look had gone out of her eyes. She appeared quite normal. She went to Daisy, and laid gentle hands upon her shoulders.

"You did quite right to tell me," she said. "It is something that I certainly ought to know."

Her face was deathly, but she smiled bravely into Daisy's troubled eyes.

"My dear, my dear," Daisy said in distress, "I do pray that I haven't done wrong."

"You haven't," Olga said. "It was dear of you to tell me, and I'm very grateful."

She kissed Daisy very lovingly and let her go. There was nothing tragic in her manner, only an unwonted aloofness that kept the elder woman from attempting to pursue the subject.

The return of Noel a few minutes later was a relief to them both. He came in full of animation and merriment, precipitating himself upon them with a gaiety that overlooked all silences. As Daisy was wont to say, Noel was the most useful person she knew for filling in tiresome gaps. He did it instinctively, without so much as seeing them.

In his cheery company the rest of the evening slid lightly by. Olga encouraged him to be frivolous. She seemed to enjoy his society more than she had ever done before; and Noel was nothing loth to be encouraged.

When the card-players joined them, they were busily engaged in drawing up a programme for what Noel termed "the Bassett week," and so absorbed were they that they did not so much as glance up till Nick came between them and demanded to know what it was all about.

Max, cynically tolerant, looked on from afar; and Daisy, who had been feeling somewhat conscience-stricken at his entrance, rapidly found herself detesting him more heartily than ever. She was glad when Major Hunt-Goring drifted to her side and engaged her in conversation, and she more nearly resumed her old intimacy with him in consequence than she had done before.

The party broke up late, as Olga, Noel, and Nick continued their discussion until their elaborate schemes were complete. By that time Max and his host had retired for a final smoke, and had to be unearthed by Nick, who declared himself scandalized to find anyone still up at such an immoral hour.

Olga was standing with Noel, dressed for departure, waiting to go, when Hunt-Goring sauntered up to her.

"Well, Miss Ratcliffe," he said conversationally, "and how do you like India?"

It was the first time he had deliberately accosted her. She glanced up at him sharply, and made a slight, instinctive movement away from him. At once, albeit almost imperceptibly, Noel moved a little nearer to her. She was conscious of his intention to protect, and threw him a brief smile as she made reply.

"I am enjoying it very much."

"Really!" said Hunt-Goring. "And you are engaged to be married, I hear?"

Olga did not instantly reply. It was Noel who answered shortly: "Yes, to my brother. No objection, I suppose?"

It was aggressively spoken. Noel had quite obviously taken a dislike to the newcomer, a sentiment which Olga knew to be instantly reciprocated by the calm fashion in which Hunt-Goring ignored his intervention.

She found him waiting markedly for her reply, and braced herself to enter the arena. "Is it news to you?" she asked coldly.

He laughed his soft, hateful laugh. "Well, scarcely, since you, yourself, informed me of the approaching event some months before it took place."

Noel made a slight gesture of surprise, and the colour rose in a hot wave to Olga's face; but she looked steadily at Hunt-Goring and said nothing.

He went on, smoothly satirical. "I used to think the odds were in favour of Miss Campion, you know. You will pardon me for saying that I don't think there are many girls who could have cut her out."

Olga's face froze to a marble immobility. "There was no question of that," she said.

"No?" Hunt-Goring's urbanity scarcely covered his incredulity. "I fancied she took the opposite view. Well, well, the poor girl is dead and out of the running. I consider Max Wyndham is a very lucky man."

He spoke with significance and Noel's eyes, jealously watching Olga's face, saw her flinch ever so slightly. A hot wave of anger rose within him; his hands clenched. He turned upon Hunt-Goring.

"If you have anything offensive to say," he said, in a furious undertone, "say it to me, you damned coward!"

Hunt-Goring looked at him at last. "I beg your pardon?" he said.

Noel was on the verge of repeating his remark when, quick as a flash, Olga turned and caught his arm.

"Noel, please, please!" she gasped breathlessly. "Not here! Not now!"

He attempted to resist her, but she would not be resisted. With all her strength she pulled him away, her hands tightly clasped upon his arm. And it was thus that they came face to face with Max, sauntering in ahead of his host.

He glanced at them both, but showed no surprise, though both Olga's agitation and Noel's anger were very apparent.

"Look here, you two," he said, "Nick and I can't be kept waiting any longer. We value our beauty-sleep if you don't. And Mr. Musgrave is longing to see the last of us."

"Not at all," said Will courteously. "But Nick has suddenly developed a violent hurry to be gone. My wife is trying to pacify him, but she won't hold him in for long."

"Let us go!" said Olga. She took her hand from Noel's arm, but looked at him appealingly.

"All right," he said gruffly. "I suppose I had better go too."

"High time, I should say," observed his brother. "Good-night!"

Noel did not look at him or respond. He turned aside without a word, and left the room.

Max made no further comment of any sort, but Olga was aware of his green eyes studying her closely. Like Noel she avoided them. She shook hands hurriedly with Will, and went out to Nick and Daisy.

As Max turned to follow her, she heard Hunt-Goring's smiling voice behind him. "Good-bye, Dr. Wyndham! Delighted to have met you again--you and your fiancee. I have just been congratulating Miss Olga on her conquest."

Max went out as though the sneering words had not reached him, but his face was so grim when he said good-bye to Daisy that she felt almost too guilty to look at him. She held Olga to her very closely at the last, and saw her go with a passionate regret. Whether she had acted rightly or wrongly she did not know; but she felt that she had wrecked the girl's happiness, and the spontaneity of Olga's answering embrace did not reassure her.

CHAPTER XVI
THE GAP

Now, my chicken, to roost!" said Nick.

He turned to give her his paternal embrace, but paused as Olga very slightly drew back from it.

They stood in the dining-room which they had entered on arrival. Max had lounged across to the mantelpiece, and propped himself against it in his favourite attitude. He looked on as it were from afar.

"Please," Olga said rather breathlessly, and she addressed Nick as though he were the only person in the room, "I want to ask you something before we say good-night."

"Something private?" asked Nick.

She put her hand to her throat; her face was ghastly. Her voice came with visible effort. "It concerns--Max," she said.

Max neither moved nor spoke. He was looking very fixedly at Olga. There was something merciless in his attitude.

Nick flashed a swift glance at him, and slipped his arm round the girl. She was quivering with agitation, yet she made as if she would free herself.

"Please, Nick!" she said imploringly. "I want to be strong. Help me to be strong!"

"All right, dear," he said gently. "You can count on me. What's the trouble? Hunt-Goring again?"

She shivered at the name. "No--no! At least--not alone. He hasn't worried me."

She became silent, painfully, desperately silent, while she fought for self-control.

Again Nick glanced across at Max. "Pour out a glass of wine!" he said briefly.

Max stood up. He went to the table, and very deliberately mixed a little brandy and water. His face, as he did it, was absolutely composed. He might have been thinking of something totally removed from the matter in hand.

Yet, as he turned round, the air of grimness was perceptible again. He held out the glass to Nick. "I think I'll go," he said.

"No!" It was Olga who spoke. She stretched out a detaining hand. "I want you--please--to stay. I--I--"

She faltered and stopped as Max's hand closed quietly and strongly upon hers.

"Very well," he said. "I'll stay. But drink this like a sensible girl! You're cold."

She obeyed him, leaning upon Nick's shoulder, and gradually the deadly pallor of her face passed. She drew her hand out of Max's grasp, and relinquished Nick's support.

"I'm dreadfully sorry," she said, and her voice came dull and oddly indifferent. "You are both so good to me. But I think one generally has to face the worst things in life by oneself. Nick, I asked you a little while ago to fill in a gap in my memory--to tell me something I had forgotten. Do you remember?"

"I do," said Nick. Like Max, he was watching her closely, but his eyes moved unceasingly; they glimmered behind his colourless lashes with a weird fitfulness.

Olga was looking straight at him. She had never stood in awe of Nick.

"You didn't do it," she said in the same level, tired voice. "You put me off. You refused to fill in the gap."

"Well?" said Nick. His tone was abrupt; for the first time in all her knowledge of him it sounded stern.

But Olga remained unmoved. "Would you refuse if I asked you to do it now?" she said.

"Perhaps," he answered.

She turned from him to Max. "You would refuse too?" she said, and this time there was a tremor of bitterness in her voice. "You always have refused."

"It happens to be my rule never to discuss my cases with anyone outside my profession," he said.

"And that was your only reason?" A sudden pale gleam shot up in Olga's eyes; she stiffened a little as though an electric current ran through her as she faced him.

"It is the only one I have to offer you," Max said.

He also sounded stern; and in a flash she grasped her position. They were ranged against her--the two she loved best in the world--leagued together to keep from her the truth. A quiver of indignation went through her. She turned abruptly from them both.

"You needn't take this trouble any longer," she said. "I--know!"

"What do you know?" It was Max's voice, curt and imperative.

He took a step forward; his hand was on her shoulder. But she wheeled and flung it from her with an exclamation that was almost a cry of horror.

"Don't touch me!" she said.

He stood confronting her, hard, pitiless, insistent. Of her gesture he took no notice whatever. "What do you know?" he repeated.

She answered him with breathless rapidity, as if compelled. "I know that you made her love you--that when you knew the truth about her you gave her up. I know that you ruined her first--and deserted her afterwards for me. I know that you terrified her into secrecy, and then, when--when her brain gave way and there was no way of escape for you--I know that you--that you--that you--"

Her lips stiffened. She could not say the word. For several seconds she strove with it inarticulately; then suddenly, wildly, she flung out her hands, urging him from her.

"Oh, go! Go! Go!" she cried. "Let me never see you again!"

He did not go. He stood absolutely still, watching her.

But she was scarcely aware of him any longer. For her strength had suddenly deserted her. She was sunk against the wall with her hands over her face, sobbing terrible, tearless sobs that shook her from head to foot.

Nick started towards her, but Max stretched out a powerful arm, and kept him back. "No, Nick," he said firmly. "This is my concern. You go, like a good chap. I'll come to you presently."

"I will not!" said Nick flatly.

He gripped the opposing arm at the elbow so that it doubled abruptly. But Max wheeled upon him on the instant and held him fast.

"Look here," he said, "I'm in earnest."

"So am I," said Nick.

They faced one another for a moment in open conflict; then half-contemptuously Max made an appeal.

"Don't let us be fools!" he said. "It's for her sake I want you to go. I'll tell you why later. If you butt in now, you will make the biggest mistake of your life."

"Take your hands off me!" said Nick.

He complied. Nick went straight to Olga. "Olga," he said, "for Heaven's sake, be reasonable! Give him a chance to set things straight!"

It was urgently spoken. His hand, vital and very insistent, closed upon one of hers, drawing it down from her face.

She looked at him with hunted eyes. "Nick," she said, "tell him--to go!"

"I can't, dear," he made answer. "You've made an accusation that no man could take lying down. You'll have to face it out now."

"But it's the truth!" she said.

"It's a damnable lie!" said Nick.

"Nick," it was Max's voice measured and deliberate, "will you leave me to deal with this?"

Olga's hand turned in Nick's and clung to it. "You needn't go, Nick," she said hurriedly.

"Yes, I'm going," said Nick. "You can come to me afterwards if you like. I shall be in my room."

He squeezed her hand and relinquished it. His yellow face was full of kindness, but she saw that he would not be persuaded to remain. In silence she watched him go.

Then slowly, reluctantly, she turned to Max. He was standing watching her with fixed, implacable eyes.

"Well?" he said, as she looked at him. "Do you really want me to deny this preposterous story?"

She leaned against the wall, facing him. She felt unutterably tired--as if she were too weary to take any further interest in anything. Neither his denial nor Nick's could make the tale untrue.

"It doesn't make much difference," she said drearily.

"Thanks!" said Max shortly.

And then, as if suddenly making up his mind, he came to her and took her almost roughly by the shoulders.

"Olga," he said, "how dare you believe this thing of me?"

She looked at him and her face quivered. "You have never told me the truth," she said.

"And so you are ready to believe any calumny," said Max. His hands pressed upon her; his red brows were drawn together.

At any other moment she would have deemed him formidable, but she was beyond fear just then.

"If you would only tell me what to believe--" she said.

"And if I won't?" He broke in upon her almost fiercely. "If I demand your trust on this point--as I have a right to demand it on every point--what then? Are you going to give me everything except that?"

She shook her head. "No, Max."

"What do you mean?" he demanded.

She answered him steadily enough. "I mean that unless you can tell me the truth--the truth, Max," there was a piteous touch in her repetition of the words--"I can never give you--anything."

"Meaning you won't marry me?" he said.

Steadily she answered him. "Yes, I mean just that."

He continued to hold her before him. His face grew harder, grimmer than before. "And you think I will suffer myself to be thrown over?" he said.

That pierced her lethargy, quickened her to resistance. "I think you have no choice," she said.

Max's jaw set itself like an iron clamp. "There you show your absolute ignorance," he said, "of me--and of yourself."

"You couldn't hold me against my will," she said quickly.

"Could I not?" said Max.

Something of fear crept about her heart, hastening its beat. But she faced him unflinching. "No," she said.

He was silent; but she had an inexplicable feeling that the green eyes were drawing her gradually, mercilessly, against her will. Yet she resisted them, summoning all her strength.

And then she became aware that his hold had tightened and grown close. She awoke to the fact very suddenly, as one coming out of a trance, and swiftly, nervously, she sought to free herself.

Instantly his arms were about her. He gathered her to him with a force that compelled. He crushed her lips with his own in kisses so fierce and so passionate that she winced from them in actual pain, not sparing her till she sank in his arms, spent, unresisting, crying against his shoulder.

He made no attempt to comfort her; his hold was sustaining, but grimly devoid of all tenderness. Later she knew that he had fought a desperate battle for her happiness and his own, and it was no moment for relaxation.

He spoke to her at last, curtly, over her bowed head, "And you think--you dare to think--that I have ever loved another woman."

"I don't know what to think," she whispered, hiding her face lower on his breast.

"Then think this," he said, and there was a ring of iron in his voice, "that for no slander whatever will I hold myself answerable, either to you or to anyone else. I shall not defend myself from it. I shall not deny it. And because of it I will not suffer myself to be jilted. Is that enough?"

He spoke with indomitable resolution, but there must have been some yielding quality in the last words, for she suddenly found strength to lift her head again and turn her face up to his.

"Max," she said imploringly, "I believe I have wronged you, and I do beg you to forgive me.--But, Max, there is one thing that--for my peace of mind--you must tell me. Please, Max, please!"

She set her clasped hands against him, beseeching him with her whole soul. He looked down into her eyes, and his own were no longer stern but quite impenetrable. He spoke no word.

"I have always known," she said, faltering a little under his look, "always felt that there was something--something strange about--Violet's sudden death. Max, tell me--tell me--she didn't--make away with herself?"

She uttered the question with a shrinking dread that seemed to run shuddering through her whole body. And because he did not instantly reply, her face whitened with a sick suspense.

"Oh, she didn't!" she gasped imploringly. "Say she didn't! I--I think it would break my heart if--if--if--that--had happened."

"You must remember that she was not responsible for her actions," Max said.

Olga was trembling all over. "Then she did?"

He avoided the question. "Her life was over," he said, "in any case."

"Then she did?" Again sharply she put the question, as though goaded thereto by an intolerable pain. "Max," she said, "oh, Max, I could bear anything better than that! I don't believe it of her! I can't believe it!"

"But why torture yourself in this way?" he said. "What do you gain by it?"

"Because I must, I must!" she answered feverishly. "I dream about her night after night--night after night. My mind is never at rest about her. She seems to be calling to me, trying to tell me something. And I never can get to her or hear what it is. It's all because I can't remember. And sometimes I feel as if I shall go mad myself with trying."

"Olga!" Briefly and sternly he checked her. "You are getting hysterical. Don't you think there has been enough of this? If you go any further, you will regret it."

"But I must know!" she said. "Max, was it so? Did she take her own life?"

"She did not!"

Quietly he answered her, so quietly that for a moment she could hardly believe that he had given a definite reply. She stared at him incredulously.

"You are telling me the truth?" she said piteously at length. "You won't try to deceive me any more?"

"I have told you the truth," he said.

"Then--then--" She still gazed at him with wide eyes, eyes in which a certain horror gradually dawned and spread. "I am sure she did not die a natural death," she said with conviction.

Max was silent, grimly, inexorably silent.

She disengaged herself slowly from him. Her forehead drew itself into the old painful lines. She passed an uncertain hand across it.

As if in answer to the gesture he spoke, bluntly, almost brutally. "If you will have it, you shall; but remember, it is final. Miss Campion was suffering from a hideous and absolutely incurable disease of the brain which had developed into homicidal madness. She might have lived for years--a blinded soul fettered to a brain of raving insanity. What her life would have been, only those who have seen can picture. But, mercifully for her--rightly or wrongly is not for me to say--her torment was brought to an early end. In fact, almost before it had begun, a friend gave her deliverance. She died--as you know--suddenly."

"Ah!" With a cry she broke in upon him. "It was--the pain-killer!"

"It was." He scarcely opened his lips to reply, and instantly closed them in a single unyielding line. His eyes never left her face.

As for Olga, she stood a moment, as one stunned past all feeling; then turned from him and moved away. "So it was--your doing," she said, in a curious, stifled voice as if she were scarcely conscious of speaking at all.

He did not answer her. The words scarcely demanded an answer.

She reached the table unsteadily, and sat down, leaning her elbow upon it, her chin on her hand. Her eyes gazed right away down far vistas unbounded by time or space.

"It isn't the first time, is it?" she said. "You did it once before. I suppose--" her voice dropped still lower; she seemed to be speaking to herself--"as a Keeper of the Door, you think you have the right."

"Will you tell me what you mean?" he said.

She did not turn her head. She still gazed upon invisible things. "Do you remember poor old Mrs. Stubbs? You helped her, didn't you, in the same way?"

"I?" said Max.

The utter astonishment of his voice reached her. She turned and looked at him. "She died in the same way," she said.

"But--great heavens above--not with my connivance!" he exclaimed.

She continued to look at him, but with that same far look, as though she saw many things besides. "Yet--you knew!" she said.

He made a curt gesture of repudiation. "I suspected--perhaps. I actually knew--nothing."

"I see," she said, with a faint smile. "She just slipped through--and you looked the other way."

"Nothing of the sort!" he said sternly. "I did my utmost--as I have always done my utmost--to prolong life. It is my duty--the first principle of my profession; and I hold it--I always have held it--as sacred."

"And yet--you let Violet's go," she said.

He swung round almost violently and turned his back. "I will not discuss that point any further," he said.

She looked at him with an odd dispassionateness. She still seemed to be searching the distant past. "You never liked her," she said at last slowly. "And she was horribly afraid of you--afraid of you!" A sudden tremor of awakening life ran through the words. The stunned look began to pass. Again the horror looked out of her eyes. "She was so afraid of you that--when she went mad--she tried to kill you. Ah, I see now!" She caught her breath sharply--"You--you were afraid too!"

He remained with his back turned upon her, motionless as a statue.

"And so--and so--" Her eyes came swiftly back to the present and saw him only. The horror in them had become vivid, anguished. She rose and stretched an accusing finger towards him. "That was why you ended her life!" she said. "It was--to save--your own!"

He wheeled round at that and faced her with that in his eyes which she had never before seen there--a look that sent the blood to her heart. "By Heaven, Olga," he said, "you go--rather far!"

He came towards her slowly. There was something terrible about him at that moment, something that held her fettered and dumb before him, though--so great was her horror--she would have given all she had to turn and flee.

He halted before her, looking down into her face with a curious intentness. "You really believe that?" he said. "You can't conceive such a thing as this--utterly and inexcusably wrong as I admit it to be--you can't conceive it to have been done from a motive of mercy?"

She shrank away from him as from a thing unclean. The impulse to escape was still strong upon her, urging her to a wild resistance. She met the pitiless eyes that watched her like a creature at bay. "You never did anything in mercy yet!" she said. "There is no mercy in you!"

"Indeed!" he said, and uttered a brief, grating laugh that made her shudder. "In that case, I'm afraid I can't help you any further. I'm at the end of my resources."

Olga drew herself together with a supreme effort, mustering all her strength. "It is the end of everything," she said. "I can never marry you now. I never want to see you again."

He met her look implacably, with eyes that seemed to beat down her own. "I have told you that I won't submit to that," he said.

She caught her breath with a convulsive movement of protest. Perhaps never before had she so clearly realized the ruthlessness of the man and his strength.

"I can't help it," she said. "I can never marry you. Even if--if we had been married, I could not have stayed with you--after this."

She saw his mouth harden to cruelty at her words, and instinctively she drew back from him; but in the same instant his hands closed upon her wrists and she was a captive.

"Doesn't it occur to you," he said, "that you are bound to me in honour--unless I set you free?"

He spoke with the utmost calmness, but her heart misgave her. She saw herself at his mercy, an impotent prisoner striving against him, vainly beating out her will against the iron of his. In that moment she realized fully that not by strength could she prevail, and desperately she began to plead.

"But you will set me free, Max! You wouldn't--you couldn't--hold me against my will!"

"Couldn't I?" said Max, and grimly smiled. "There is nothing whatever that I couldn't do with you, Olga,--with--or without--your will."

She shivered sharply and uncontrollably, not attempting to contradict him.

"And that being so," he said, "it is not my intention to set you free. There is no earthly reason why you should not marry me, and therefore I hold you to your engagement. That is quite understood, is it?"

His hold tightened upon her. She saw that he meant every word, and her heart died within her. Her strength was running out swiftly, swiftly. Very soon it would be utterly gone. She cast a desperate glance upwards, and made one last supreme effort. "But, Max," she pleaded, "I thought you loved me."

His face was set in iron lines, but she thought it softened ever so slightly at her words. Had she pierced the one vulnerable point in his armour at last? She wondered, scarcely daring to hope.

"Well?" he said.

Only the one word; but somehow, inexplicably, her heart cried shame upon her, as though she had put a good weapon to an unworthy use. She stood before him, trying vainly to drive it home. But she could not. Further words failed her.

"I see," he said at last. "You think out of my love for you I ought to be willing to give you up. Is that it?"

She nodded mutely, not daring to look at him, still overwhelmed with that shamed sense of doing him a wrong.

"I see," he said again. "And--if it would be for your happiness to let you go--I might perhaps be equal to the sacrifice." His voice was suddenly cynical, and she never guessed that he cloaked an unwanted emotion therewith. "But take the other view of the case. You know you would never be happy away from me."

"I couldn't be happy with you--now," she murmured.

He bent slightly towards her as if not sure that he had heard aright. "Do you really mean that?" he asked.

She was silent.

"Olga!" he said insistently.

Against her will she raised her eyes, and met his close scrutiny. Against her will she answered him, breathlessly, out of a fevered sense of expediency. "Yes--yes, I do mean it! Oh, Max, you must--you must let me go!"

But he held her still. "You have appealed to my love," he said. "I appeal to yours."

But that was more than she could bear; the sudden tension snapped the last shreds of her quivering strength. She broke down utterly, standing there between his hands.

He made no attempt to draw her to him. Perhaps he did not wholly trust himself. Neither did he let her go; but there was no element of cruelty about him any longer. In silence, with absolute patience, he waited for her.

She made a slight effort at last to free herself, and instantly he set her free. She sat down again at the table, striving desperately for self-control. But she could not even begin to speak to him, so choked and blinded was she by her tears.

A while longer he waited beside her; then at length he spoke. "If you really honestly feel that you can't marry me, that to do so would make for misery and not happiness; if in short your love for me is dead--I will let you go."

The words fell curt and stern, but if she had seen his face at the moment she would have realized something of what the utterance of them cost.

But her own face was hidden, her paroxysm of weeping yet shook her uncontrollably.

"Is it dead?" he said, and stooped over her, holding the back of her chair but not touching her.

She made a convulsive movement, whether of flinching from his close proximity or protest at his words it was impossible to say.

He waited a moment or two. Then: "If it isn't," he said, "just put your hand in mine!"

He laid his own upon the table before her, upturned, ready to clasp hers. His face was bent so low over her that his lips were almost on her hair. She could have yielded herself to his arms without effort.

But she only stiffened at his action, and became intensely still. In the seconds that followed she did not so much as breathe. She was as one turned to stone.

For the space of a full minute he waited; and through it the wild beating of her heart rose up in the stillness, throbbing audibly. But still she sat before him mutely, making no sign.

Then, after what seemed to her an eternity of waiting, very quietly he straightened himself and took his hand away.

She shrank away involuntarily with a nervous contraction of her whole body. For that moment she was unspeakably afraid.

But he gave her no cause for fear. He bore himself with absolute self-possession.

"Very well," he said. "That ends it. You are free."

With the words he turned deliberately from her, walked to the door, passed quietly out. And she was left alone.

CHAPTER XVII
THE EASIEST COURSE

I won't be a party to it," said Nick.

"You can't help yourself."

Bluntly Max made reply. He lounged against the window while his host dressed. The presence of the stately khitmutgar who was assisting Nick was ignored by them both.

"I can generally manage to help myself," observed Nick.

Max's mouth took its most cynical downward curve. "You see, old chap, this chances to be one of the occasions on which you can't. It's my funeral, not yours."

Nick sent a brief glance across. "You're a fool, Max," he said.

"Thanks!" said Max. He took his pipe from his pocket and commenced to fill it with extreme care. There was something grimly ironical about his whole bearing. He did not speak again till his task was completed and the pipe alight. Then very deliberately through a cloud of rank smoke, he took up his tale. "It is one of the most interesting cases that have ever come under my notice. I am only sorry that I shall not be able to continue to keep it under my own personal supervision."

Nick laughed, a crude, cracked laugh. "It seems a pity certainly, since you came to India for that express purpose. I suppose you think it's up to me to continue the treatment?"

"Exactly," said Max.

"Well, I'm not going to." Again Nick's eyes flashed a keen look at Max's imperturbable countenance. "I held my peace last night," he said, "because matters were too ticklish to be tampered with. But as to keeping it up-----"

Max thrust his hands deep into his pockets. "As to keeping it up," he said, "you've no choice; neither have I. It may be a matter for regret from some points of view, but a matter of the most urgent expediency it undoubtedly is. I tell you plainly, Nick, this is not a thing to be played with. There are some risks that no one has any right to take. This is one."

He looked at Nick, square-jawed and determined; but Nick vigorously shook his head.

"I am not with you. I don't agree. I never shall agree."

Max's cynical smile became more pronounced. "Then you will have to act against your judgment for once. There is no alternative. And I shall go Home by the first boat I can catch."

"And leave her to fret her heart out," said Nick.

Max removed his pipe, and attentively regarded the bowl. After nearly a minute he put it back again and stared impenetrably at Nick. "She won't do that," he said.

"I'll tell you what she will do," said Nick. "She will go and marry that wild Irish brother of yours."

Max continued to look at him. His mouth was no longer cynical, but cocked at a humorous angle. "I say, what a clever little chap you are!" he said. "Whatever made you think of that?"

Nick grinned in spite of himself. Disagree as he might with Max Wyndham, yet was he always in some subtle fashion in sympathy with him.

"I suppose she might do worse," he admitted after a moment. "He's a well-behaved youngster as a general rule."

"Given his own way, quite irreproachable," said Max "He's not very rich, but he's no slacker. If he doesn't break his neck at polo, he'll get on."

"Oh, he's brilliant enough," said Nick. "I suppose he can be trusted to look after her. He's full young."

"He'll grow," said Max.

A brief silence fell between them. Max continued to smoke imperturbably. There was not the faintest sign of disappointment in his bearing. He looked merely ruminative.

Nick was thoughtful also. He sat and watched his man fasten his gaiters with those flickering eyes of his that never seemed to concentrate upon one point and yet missed nothing.

"What are you going to do about Hunt-Goring?" he asked suddenly.

"Do about him?" Max sounded supremely contemptuous. He raised one eyebrow in supercilious interrogation.

"Well, he dealt this hand," said Nick.

"With Mrs. Musgrave's kind assistance," supplemented Max.

Nick made a grimace. "Who told you that?"

"No one." Max blew a cloud of smoke upwards. "You're not the only person with brains, Nick," he observed, with sardonic humour. "But look here! Your friend Mrs. Musgrave is not to be meddled with in this matter. You leave her alone and Hunt-Goring too! He's killing himself by inches with opium, so he won't interfere with anyone for long. And she will prove a useful friend to Noel if allowed to take her own way."

"You really mean to take this lying down?" said Nick.

"It's the easiest course," said Max.

"So far as you are concerned?" Nick abruptly turned in his chair; but his scrutiny was of the briefest. He did not seem to look at Max at all; nor did he apparently expect an answer to his query, for he went on almost immediately. "It's damnable luck for both of you. Old man, are you sure it's all right?"

There was no subtlety in the question. Nick had long since abandoned subtlety in his dealings with Max Wyndham, a fact which indicated that he held him in very high esteem.

Max's response expressed appreciation of the fact. He took his hand from his pocket and carelessly stretched it out. "I am absolutely sure," he said. "Make your mind easy on that point!"

Their hand-grip was silent and brief. It ended the discussion by mutual consent.

At once Max changed the subject. "Is that chap your khit or your valet or what?"

"He is all three combined," said Nick. "Why? Think I work him too hard?"

The Indian showed his teeth in a splendid smile, but said nothing.

"No, but where's the other fellow?" said Max.

"What other fellow?" Nick thrust his one arm with vigour into his riding-coat.

"The chap I saw here the other night--an old chap. I came along the verandah to tell you there was someone sneaking in the compound, and he shut the window in my face. I presumed he was head-nurse or bearer, or whatever you are pleased to call them in these parts."

"Oh, that fellow!" said Nick. "Quite a venerable old chap, you mean? Rather scraggy--not over-clean?"

"That's the man," said Max.

Nick laughed. "Great Scott! You didn't seriously, think he was my bearer, did you? No, he's an old moonstone-seller who comes to see me occasionally. He's not so disreputable as he looks. I find him handy in the matter of bazaar politics, with which I consider it useful to keep in touch."

Max received the information with a nod. His green eyes were watching Nick's lithe movements with thoughtful intentness.

"How long is this job going to last?" he asked abruptly.

"Heaven knows," was Nick's airy response.

Max was silent a moment; then: "You will send her away if it gets too hot?" he said.

Nick took up his riding-switch. "It's a tricky climate," he observed, "but I am keeping an eye on the weather. I don't anticipate anything of the nature of a heat-wave at present."

Max grunted. "Are you sure your barometer is a trustworthy one?"

Nick smiled. "I have every reason to believe so." He turned and clapped a kindly hand on Max's shoulder. "All right, old chap. Don't be anxious! I'll take care of her," he said.

Max looked at him. "You had better take care of yourself too," he said.

"Trust me!" laughed Nick.

There came a knock at the door, to which Kasur responded. It was Olga's ayah. A few whispered words passed between them, then the khitmutgar softly closed it and approached Nick.

"Miss sahibsahibs. She asks that you will go to her, sahib, before you leave."

Nick glanced at Max. "You had better come too."

But Max shook his head. "No. I'll be on the verandah if she wants me, but I don't think she will."

Nick went to the door in silence; but ere he reached it Max spoke again. "Nick!"

"Well?" Nick paused as if reluctant.

Very deliberately Max followed him. They stood face to face. "You will remember what I have said," Max said, with slow emphasis.

"I'm not very likely to forget it," said Nick.

"And you will abstain from interference in this matter?" Max's voice was emotionless, but it had a certain quality of compulsion notwithstanding.

Nick's eyes darted over him. His whole frame stiffened slightly. "If you think I am going to bind myself hand and foot by a promise, you're mistaken," he said.

"I am only asking you to let matters take their course," said Max, unmoved.

"Circumstances may make that impossible," said Nick.

"They may. In that case, you are free to act as you think fit. But I don't think they will--and--damn it, Nick, it isn't much to ask. It's for her sake."

A tinge of feeling suddenly underran his speech. He flushed slowly and deeply; but he stood his ground.

As for Nick, he turned again to the door with his switch tucked under his arm. "All right," he said. "I accept the amendment."

He was gone with the words, almost as though he feared he had already yielded too far. Probably to no other man would he have yielded a single inch.

The interview had ended in a fashion extremely distasteful to him, yet he entered Olga's presence cheerily, with no sign of discontent.

"Hullo, my chicken! Not riding this morning? Haven't you slept?"

He sat down on the bed with Olga's arms very tightly round his neck, and prepared himself to make the best of a very bad business.

The night before he had soothed her in the midst of her distress with all a mother's tenderness, but by daylight he discarded the maternal role and resumed his masculine limitations.

"Come!" he said coaxingly to the fair head pillowed against his shoulder. "You're going to be a sensible kiddie now? You're going to forget all yesterday's nonsense? Max won't say any more if you don't. You've just got to kiss and be friends."

Olga little dreamed that thus cheerily he made his last stand for a hope which he knew to be forlorn.

She raised her head and looked at him with eyes that shone with the brilliance which follows the shedding of many tears. "It's no good ever thinking of that, Nick," she said, speaking quickly and nervously. "I've been awake all night, thinking--thinking. But there's no way out. I can't marry him. I can't even see him again. And, Nick,--I want you, please, to give him back his ring."

"My dear, you're not in earnest!" said Nick.

"Yes, yes, I am, dear. And I can't argue about it. My head whirls so. Oh, Nick, why didn't you tell me when I asked you to fill in the gap? It's such a mistaken kindness--if you only knew it--to keep back the truth--whatever it may be."

Nick groaned melancholy acquiescence. "But can't you forgive him, sweetheart? Most women can forgive anything. And you never used to be vindictive."

"I'm not vindictive," she made swift reply. "It isn't that I want to punish him. Oh, don't you understand? He may have acted up to his lights. And even if--if he had been anything but a doctor, I think it would have been a little different. But he--he knew so exactly what he was doing. And oh, Nick, I couldn't possibly marry a man who had done--that. I should never forget it. It would prey on me so, just as if--as if--I had been a party to it!" A violent shiver went through her. She clung closer to him. The horror had frozen in her eyes to a wide and glassy terror.

"Easy, easy!" said Nick gently. "We won't get hysterical. But isn't it a pity to do anything in a hurry? You won't feel so badly in a week or a fortnight. Don't do anything final yet! Put him off for a bit. He'll understand."

But Olga would not listen to this suggestion. "I must be free, Nick!" she said feverishly. "I can't be bound to him any longer. Oh, Nick, do help me to get free!"

"My dear child, you are free," Nick assured her. "But take my advice; don't shake him off completely. Give him just a chance, poor chap! Wait six months before you quite make up your mind to have done with him. You'll be sure to want him back if you don't."

But still Olga would not listen. "Oh, Nick, please stop!" she implored him. "I've been through it all a hundred times already, and indeed I know my own mind. If it were to drag on over six months, I don't think I could possibly bear it. No, no! It must be final now. Nick--dear, don't you understand?"

He nodded. "Yes, I do understand, Olga mia; but I think you are making a big mistake. The horror of the thing has blinded you temporarily. You are incapable of forming a clear judgment at present. By and by you will begin to see better. That's why I want you to wait."

"But I can't wait," she said. "It--it is like a dreadful wound, Nick. I want to bind it up quick--quick, before it gets any worse,--to hide it,--to try and forget it's there. I can't--I daren't--keep it open. I think it would kill me."

There was actual agony in her voice, and Nick saw that he had made his last stand in vain. Yet not instantly did he abandon it. Once more he thrust past her defences, though she sought so desperately to keep him out.

"It's not for us to judge each other, is it?" he said. "Be merciful, Olga! Don't you think there may have been--extenuating circumstances?"

She looked at him with quivering lips, and dumbly shook her head.

"Listen!" he said. "When Muriel and I were flying from Wara, I killed a man with my hands under her eyes. It was a ghastly business. I did it to save her life and my own. But--like you--she didn't look at the motive--only at the deed. And in consequence I became a thing abhorrent in her sight. She didn't get over it for a long time. But she forgave me at last. Can't you be equally generous? Or don't you love him well enough?"

Olga's hands clasped one another very tightly. She answered him under her breath. "I expect that's it, Nick, I don't love him any more at all. It has killed my love."

"Then you never loved him," said Nick with conviction.

She made no attempt to contradict him. Only her strained white face seemed to implore him to torture her no further. He saw it, and his heart smote him.

"I hate to hurt you, my chicken," he said. "But, dear, you're making such a hideous muddle of your life. I hate that even worse."

She flung her arms about his neck; she pressed her lips to his yellow face. "Darling Nick, never mind about me, never mind!" she whispered. "I am doing simply what I must do. I can scarcely think or feel yet. Only I know that I must get free. It isn't that I'm hard. It's just that I have no choice. Your case was different. You had to do it. But this--" her words sank, became scarcely audible--"Nick, could anything extenuate--this?"

"God knows," said Nick. He paused a moment, then added: "I sometimes think, if the whole truth were known, there would be an extenuating circumstance for every mortal offence under the sun."

She did not argue the point. She seemed beyond argument. "Very likely," she said. "But really I have no choice. You see, we were such friends--such friends. And then she loved him, while he--he had nothing but a professional interest for her, till he found her case to be hopeless, and then he lost even that. That's what made it so horrible--so impossible. If he had loved her--even a little--I could have understood. But as it was--Oh, Nick, don't you see?"

Yes, he did see. It was useless to reason with her. She was like a captive bird beating wild wings for freedom and wholly unable to gauge its awful desolation when won.

For the second time he had to own himself beaten. For the second time he withdrew his forces from the field.

"Well, dear, I'm sorry," was all he said, but it conveyed much.

When he quitted her presence a little later he carried with him the ring that Max had given her and a brief and piteous message to her lover that he would not try to see her again.

Max received both in grim silence, and within half an hour of so doing he had gone.

CHAPTER XVIII
ONE MAN'S LOSS

O h, damn!" said Noel.

He had made the remark several times before that morning, but he made it with special emphasis on this occasion in response to the news that his brother was waiting to see him.

Hot and cross from the parade-ground, he rolled off his horse and turned towards his quarters. The animal looked after him with a faint whinny of hurt surprise, and sharply Noel flung round again.

The saice grinned, but was instantly quelled to sobriety by his master's scowl. The horse whinnied again, and tucked a confiding nose under the young officer's arm.

"All right, old man! Here you are!" said Noel.

He fished out a lump of sugar and stuffed it between the sensitive lips that nibbled at his sleeve, kissed the white star between the soft brown eyes, whispered an endearing word into the cocked ear, slapped the glossy neck, and finally departed.

His face resumed its scowl as he entered the room where Max sprawled in a bamboo chair with his feet on another and the petted terrier of the establishment seated alertly on his chest. Max smiled at sight of it and stretched forth a lazy hand.

"Excuse my rising! I daren't incur this creature's displeasure."

Noel took the creature by the neck and removed it. Max's hand remained outstretched, but that he ignored.

"What have you come for?" he demanded gruffly.

"I should have said, 'What can I do for you?'" observed Max to the ceiling. "If you are thinking of having a drink, perhaps you will allow me to join you."

Noel went to the door and grumpily yelled an order. After which he jingled back, unbuckled his sword, and flung it noisily on the table.

Max turned his head very deliberately and regarded him.

His scrutiny was a prolonged one, and Noel finally waxed impatient under it. "Well, what are you staring at me for?" he enquired aggressively.

With a sudden movement Max removed his feet from the second chair and sat up. "Sit down there!" he said.

The words fell curt and sharp, a distinct order which Noel obeyed almost before he knew what he was doing. He dropped into the chair and sat directly facing his brother, a kind of surly respect struggling with the evident hostility of his expression.

His dog, feeling neglected, sprang on to his knees and licked his sullen face.

Max uttered a short laugh that was not unfriendly. "Oh, stop being a silly ass, Noel!" he said. "What on earth do you want to quarrel with me for? It's the most unprofitable game under the sun."

Noel sat stiffly upright, holding the dog at arm's length. "It's no fault of mine," he said.

His eyes were obstinately lowered in a mule-like refusal to meet his brother's straight regard. He looked absurdly like a schoolboy brought up for punishment.

Max considerately stifled a second laugh. "All right, it's mine," he said. "And I've come to apologize. Understand? I've come to make unconditional restitution of my ill-gotten gains. I'm just off to Bombay, to shake the dust of this accursed country off my feet, and to leave you in undisputed possession of the spoil. How's that appeal to you, you sulky young hound?"

Noel's eyes shot upwards at the epithet, though the supercilious good-humour of its utterance made it somehow impossible to raise any furious protest.

The entrance of his servant with drinks helped very materially to save his dignity. He pulled the table to him without rising and began to pour them out.

"Lemon?" he asked briefly.

"No, thanks. I'll have a plain soda. And if you've no objection we will thresh this matter out at once as I have to be off in ten minutes. I suppose you took in what I said just now?"

Noel held out a glass to him, his brown hand not quite steady. "May as well be explicit," he said gruffly.

"Quite so. Then my engagement to Olga Ratcliffe is at an end. Is that plain enough for you?"

Again the boy's eyes glanced upwards, meeting the imperturbable green eyes opposite for the fraction of a second. "Really?" he said.

"Yes, really." Max took a slow gulp from his glass and set it down. "Pleased?" he enquired.

Noel did not answer. His own drink remained untouched at his elbow. "Whose doing is it?" he enquired.

"Hers."

"What! Doesn't she care for you after all?" There was a sudden quiver in the question that belied the studied calm of the speaker.

Max took up his glass and drank again. "She can't stand me at any price," he said.

"Then what have you been doing?" There was no attempt to disguise the fierceness of the query. Noel started forward in his chair with hands clenched, and his dog slid to the ground.

"Take it easy!" said Max. "I'm not going to let you into that secret. It wouldn't be good for your morals. Besides, there's no time to go into that now. All I want to say to you is that there's a clear road in front of you and the odds are all in your favour. Go straight and I believe you'll win!"

Noel leaned nearer. His face was a curious blend of eagerness and resentment. "Do you mean--you've found out--that she'd sooner have me after all?" he blurted out.

Max looked at him, and a queer, half-pitying smile curved his grim mouth. "Yes, I suppose it amounts to that," he said, after a moment.

"Oh, I say!" said Noel.

He got up abruptly, and walked to the end of the room. Coming back, he gave a sharp gasp as of one rising from deep water, and the next moment very suddenly he laughed.

"I say," he said again, speaking jerkily, "is it the sun--or what? I feel as if--you'd hit me between the eyes."

Max nodded towards the table. "Have your drink, boy, and pull yourself together! You haven't won her yet, remember. You've got some uphill work before you still."

Noel stopped at the table, and raised his glass. His hand shook palpably, and the smile on Max's face became almost one of tenderness. He watched him in silence as he drank, then lifted his own glass.

"Here's to your success!" he said.

Noel's eyes came down to him. They had the rapt look of a man who sees a vision. "Oh, man," he suddenly exclaimed, "you don't know how I worship her!"

And then abruptly he realized what he had said and to whom, and flushed darkly, averting his look.

Max got to his feet, and faced him across the table. "You've got to worship her always," he said, and in his voice there throbbed some remote echo as of an imprisoned passion deep in his hidden soul. "She'll need the utmost you can offer."

Noel looked back at him again, and the shamed flush died away. He leaned impulsively forward, suddenly, boyishly remorseful for his churlishness.

"Max! Max, old boy! I'm an infernal brute!" he declared. "I was actually forgetting that you--that you----"

"You're quite welcome to forget that," interposed Max grimly. He moved round the table, and clapped a friendly hand on the boy's shoulder. "I shall make it my business to forget it myself," he said. "But look here, don't be headlong! She isn't quite ready for you yet. I speak as a friend; go slow!"

Noel looked at him, and again the hot blood rose to his forehead. He gripped the hand on his shoulder, and held it fast. "I say, Max," he said, an odd sort of deference in his tone, "she doesn't know--does she--what a much better chap you are than I?"

The corner of Max's mouth went up. "Don't talk bosh!" he said.

"I'm not," persisted Noel. "You're doing what I hadn't the spunk to do. I think she ought to know that."

Max's smile passed from amusement to cynicism. "Do you seriously think a woman loves a man for his good points?" he said.

"No; but you've no right to put her off with an inferior article," persisted Noel.

"My good chap, I! I tell you it was her own choice." Max almost laughed.

"But you care for her?" Noel's dark eyes became suddenly intent and shrewd, and the boyishness passed from his face. "See here, Max, I won't take any sacrifices," he said. "I may be a selfish brute, but I'm not quite such a swine as that. You care for her."

"Which fact is beside the point," said Max. His fingers suddenly answered Noel's grip with the strength of a restraining force. "If there is any sacrifice anywhere," he said, "it's not offered to you, so make your mind easy on that head. As I said before, she won't have me at any price. If she would, I shouldn't be here now. You see," again his mouth twisted, "I'm not so ultra-generous myself. But I don't see why we should both be losers, especially as you had half won her before I came along. So go ahead and good luck to you!"

He disengaged his hand and lightly slapped Noel's shoulder as a preliminary to taking his departure. But Noel, with a swift return to boyhood, caught him by the arms. "I don't know what to say to you, old chap," he said, quick feeling in the words. "You've made me feel like a murderer."

"My dear chap, what rot!"

"No, it's not rot! I've hated you like the devil. I'm beastly ashamed--beastly sorry. I'll do anything to atone--anything under the sun. Give me something to do for you, Max, old boy! I can't stand myself if you go like this."

He spoke impulsively enough, but there was more than mere impulse in his speech. Hot-headed repentance it might be, but it was the real thing.

Max stood still, faintly smiling. "My dear lad, there's nothing you can do for me that you won't do twice as well for yourself," he said. "I'm glad you care for her, and I'm not sorry you hated me for getting in your way. You might let me know when it's time to congratulate. That's all I can think of at the present moment--except, yes, one thing!"

"What?" said Noel.

Max's face hardened somewhat. "That fellow Hunt-Goring," he said. "He's the chap I told you of. Keep clear of him!"

Noel stiffened. "I should like to kill him," he said.

"Yes, but you can't. He's more than a match for you. He once had some hold over Olga--something very slight. I never bothered to find out what. But she has broken away and he is an enemy in consequence. Watch out for him, but don't fall foul of him! He won't worry you for long. He is taking opium enough to kill an ox every day of his life."

"Is he though? Well, no one will weep for him."

"Unless it's Mrs. Musgrave," observed Max drily.

"She doesn't like the bounder," declared Noel with conviction. "Look here; sit down again! I've seen nothing of you yet."

"No, I can't stop, thanks. I've said good-bye to everyone else, and time is up. Don't go and get smashed up at polo! If she doesn't want you now, she will very soon. Bear that in mind!"

Noel's dark eyes shone. "The only risks I'm likely to take would be for her safety. I wish to Heaven Ratcliffe could be made to see the danger they are in."

Max smiled a little. "I've been talking to him. We touched on that point. He knows--rather more on the subject than we do."

"But he makes light of it," Noel protested. "The place is infested with bud-mashes and he rather encourages them than otherwise. I myself kicked an old blackguard of a moonstone-seller--or so he described himself--off his premises only the other night."

Max broke into a laugh. "Did you though?"

"Yes. What is there to laugh at? Wouldn't you have done the same? And when I told Nick the day after, he described the old beggar as a friend of his."

Max was still laughing. "What a devil of a fellow you are! I've seen the old gentleman myself. I rather think he is a friend. How did he take the kicking?"

"Oh, I don't know. He cursed a bit and went. What's the joke, I say?"

Noel's voice was imperious. He was always somewhat impatient of matters beyond his comprehension. But Max turned the subject off.

"You're such a peppery chap--always wanting to fight someone. Well, I must be gone. You'll remember not to fight Hunt-Goring?"

"No. I shan't fight the brute unless he interferes." Noel followed him to the door and stood a moment. "I say, Max," he suddenly said, "was this affair Hunt-Goring's doing?"

"What affair?" Max spoke as one bored with the subject.

But Noel persisted. "Was it thanks to Hunt-Goring that this split with Olga came about?"

Max faced about. There was a very peculiar smile in his green eyes. "Well," he said very deliberately, "I don't say Hunt-Goring's influence has been exactly a genial one. But that fact in itself would not have much difference. The main reason is the one I have given you. If you are not satisfied with that--then you will never be satisfied with anything--and you won't deserve to be." He held out his hand. "Good-bye, lad! And again--good luck!"

Noel wrung the hand. They looked each other in the eyes, and Noel spoke impulsively as his habit was, but with genuine feeling. "Good-bye, old chap! I hope you'll get to the tip-top of the tree and stay there." He added, seeing Max's mouth go down, "But I know very well there's a bigger thing than success in the world, and if I can ever help you to it--by God, old boy, I will!"

He said it hurriedly, expecting it to be received with irony. But there was no trace of cynicism left in Max's face as he gave him a final grip, and turned away with the one word: "Thanks!"

When he had gone, Noel returned to the room with sober gait, and paused in the middle of it to pick up his sword.

"I wonder if he cares much," he murmured half aloud.

He stood by the table with eyes absently fixed, going over in his mind the conversation that had just passed, recalling the leisurely, supercilious tones, the semi-ironical kindness with which his brother had revealed the situation. Why had he troubled himself to do so? For a space Noel wondered.

And then very suddenly the words, "You've got to worship her always," flashed through his mind. Those words were the key to everything. He realized that fully. And again he was conscious of shame. Yes, Max did care. That was beyond all questioning. He cared enough to do what he--Noel--had wholly failed to do. His love was great enough to efface itself, a form of love--the rarest and the highest--of which he himself was as yet incapable. He could stand between the girl and death without a second's hesitation; but he could not live and sacrifice his happiness to hers.

Again the hot blood mounted to his forehead and slowly sank again. And in those few moments Noel Wyndham stepped into manhood and faced his soul anew. If she loved him, he would marry her and give her all he had; withholding nothing. She should not be a loser because she had loved him better than Max.

He would give her a love as strong and as worthy. He would make her happiness his aim and his goal, his watch-word and his prize. No sacrifice should ever be too great for her. He would offer all he had.

No; never should she come to repent her preference--to regret the love she had refused. She had chosen him--the lesser before the greater; and she should not find him wanting. She should not be disappointed in him. Never, never now should his love fail her!

Impulsive as always, he lifted his sword and kissed the hilt with reverence. "So help me, God!" he swore.

CHAPTER XIX
A FIGHT WITHOUT A FINISH

It was not the same Olga who went back into the busy little Anglo-Indian community at Sharapura after the breaking of her engagement, though it was only those intimate with her who marked the change. To the rest of the world she was as she had ever been, quiet and gentle, perhaps a little colourless, possibly in the eyes of some even insignificant, --"too reserved to be interesting," according to Colonel Bradlaw who liked a woman to have plenty of vivacity and mirth in her composition.

To those who knew her best--to Nick, to Daisy, and to Noel--she was changed, though it was a change of which she herself was scarcely aware. Her re-awakened spontaneity had gone again. She asked sympathy of none. Even to Nick she made no confidences. She had become wholly woman, and she had learned as it were to stand alone. She preferred her solitude.

Of Noel she seemed a little shy at first, until by frank good-fellowship he overcame this. Noel's courtship was apparently at a standstill. He made no open attempt to further his cause with her, though every day he sought her out with cheery friendliness, never overstepping the mark, never giving her the smallest occasion for embarrassment. And thus every day her confidence in him grew. She came to rely upon him in a fashion that she scarcely realized, depending upon his consideration and unfailing chivalry more than she knew. She had never liked him better than she liked him then, in the first desperate bitterness of her trouble. He asked so little of her, was so readily pleased with her mere friendship, and though at the back of her mind she knew that this was only his pleasant method of marking time she was none the less grateful to him for his patience. He helped her through her dark hours without seeming in the least aware that she needed help. He demanded rather than offered sympathy, and in giving it she found herself oddly soothed. She was glad that Noel wanted her, glad that he regarded her co-operation as quite indispensable to his schemes. He occupied her thoughts at a time when private reflection was torture. The misery was there perpetually at her heart, but he gave her no time to dwell upon it. He carried her along with him with an impetus which she had no desire to resist.

Nick watched his tactics from afar with unwilling admiration, wryly admitting to himself that they were precisely the tactics he would have pursued. He saw that the fulfilment of his prediction was merely a matter of time, and prepared himself to yield to the inevitable with as good a grace as he could muster. He was in fact more in sympathy with Noel than with Olga just then. The boy was undoubtedly developing under this new influence. The spoilt side of his nature was giving place to a new manliness that was infinitely more attractive, and Nick found it impossible not to accept him with approval.

Sir Reginald Bassett's visit was to take place early in February, and great were the preparations in progress for his entertainment. Daisy Musgrave found herself swept into the vortex of Noel's energies, and she on her part did her best to interest her guest therein. It was a futile effort on her part. Hunt-Goring only laughed at her and paid her lazy compliments. Why he stayed on was a problem that she was wholly at a loss to solve. Quite privately she had begun to wish very much that he would go. She was heartily tired of being for ever on her guard, and she never dared to be otherwise with him. Not that she found it really difficult to keep him at a distance. He was too indolent for that. When she withdrew herself, he never troubled to pursue. His attentions were never ardent. But he never failed to take advantage of the smallest lapse on her part. She could never be at her ease with him.

Will Musgrave was inclined to smile at his wife's difficulties. Perhaps he was not wholly sorry that the follies of her youth should thus come home to her. He did not like Hunt-Goring much, but the man never gave offence.

"I suppose he'll go when he's tired of us," said Will philosophically.

"And meantime neither Olga nor Noel will come near the place with him in it," sighed Daisy. "I don't believe he will ever go."

He laughed at that and pinched her cheek. "We shall though, little wife. That honeymoon of ours comes nearer every day."

She smiled an eager, girlish smile. "Dear old Will!" she murmured softly.

It was on that same evening that Noel broke his rule and raced in to give Daisy some important information with regard to his schemes for what he termed "the Bassett week."

He was full of excitement and declared himself unable to remain for a single moment more than his business demanded.

"I'm going to dine with Nick," he told her. "In fact, I'm due there now."

"I never see anything of Nick nowadays," said Daisy.

"No; nor do I. He's at the Palace, morning, noon, and night. Can't see the attraction myself. But no doubt he thinks he's doing something great. By the way, you're coming round to old Badgers' to-morrow, I suppose? We are going to hold a meeting of the committee. Olga will be there of course."

"How is Olga?" asked Daisy.

"Oh, all right. Why don't you go round and see her?" Noel asked the question with some curiosity. He had begun to wonder lately if there could have been a disagreement between them.

Daisy smiled with a touch of wistfulness. She had scarcely seen Olga since the breaking of her engagement. "I seem to have so little time nowadays. The last time I went, she was busy too."

"Oh, she's sure to be busy till Bassett week," laughed Noel. "I'm seeing to that. It's good for her, you know."

"Yes, I know," said Daisy. She added in a lower tone, for Hunt-Goring was smoking on the verandah outside the window, "I am glad you are taking care of her, Noel. She needs that."

Noel coloured a little. "I do what I can. So does Nick. But I wish you would go and see her. She wants a pal of her own sex."

"I am not so sure of that," said Daisy. "Ah, here's Peggy! I thought you wouldn't escape without seeing her."

Peggy's entrance was of the nature of a whirlwind. It completely diverted the thoughts of both. She was scantily clad in a bath-towel which she held tightly gripped with both hands about her small person. Her feet left little wet dabs on the floor as she pattered in.

"Oh, Noel!" she cried. "You horrid, horrid Noel! I've been callin' you for ever so long. And I was in my bath. I thought you'd like to see me in my bath."

"Peggy!" exclaimed her mother, scandalized.

Peggy's ayah, also scandalized, hovered in the doorway.

Peggy, herself, from the safe shelter of Noel's arms, smiled securely upon both.

"You mustn't tickle me," she said to her protector, "or I shall come undone. Why hasn't you been to take me for another ride, Noel?"

"Sweetheart--" he began with compunction.

But Peggy interrupted very decidedly. "No, you needn't make excuses. And I'm not goin' to be your sweetheart any more--ever--not till you take me for another ride."

"Oh, don't be cruel!" besought Noel. "I've been so shockingly busy lately. It wasn't that I forgot you, Peggy. I couldn't do that if I tried. So give me a kiss, little sweetheart, and let's be friends! I vow I'll tickle you if you won't."

Peggy, however, was nothing daunted by this threat. She kept her face rigidly turned over his shoulder. "When will you take me for another ride?" she demanded imperiously.

"Peggy," her mother broke in again, "I can't have you behaving like this, dear. It isn't decent. Go back to ayah at once!"

Peggy peeped mischievously over Noel's shoulder. "If I get down again, I shall come all undone," she said.

"By Jove, what a calamity!" said Noel. "Haven't you got a pin or something to hold the thing together?"

She tightened her arms about his neck. "You carry me back!" she whispered ingratiatingly. "An' I'll give you three booful kisses!"

Noel succumbed at once. "Can't resist that!" he remarked to Daisy. "I'll take her back and slap her for you, shall I?"

"I wish you would," said Daisy.

"He daren't!" declared Peggy.

"Ho! Daren't he?" laughed Noel. "That's the rashest thing you ever said in your life. Come along, you scaramouch, and we'll see about that!"

He bore her away, with her draperies slipping from her, followed by the ayah whose open horror was surveyed by Peggy with eyes of shining amusement. A little later her shrill squeals announced the fact that Noel was carrying out his threat after a fashion which she found highly enjoyable, and Noel subsequently emerged in a somewhat heated and tumbled condition and bade Daisy a hasty farewell.

"I've chastised the imp, but she's quite unregenerate. Glad I'm not her mother. I've sworn a solemn oath to take her out on the Chimpanzee to-morrow. I haven't time, but that's a detail. I'll work it somehow, if you don't mind having her ready by ten. I'll race round after parade."

"I ought not to let her go," Daisy protested.

He laughed at that. "Yes, yes, you must. I've promised. Good-bye! Ten o'clock then!"

He shook her hand and departed, singing as he went.

Hunt-Goring from the verandah watched him all-unperceived.

"The whelp seems pleased with himself," he observed to Daisy, with a sneering smile. "I presume that Fortune--in the form of Miss Olga Ratcliffe--favours the brave."

"He's very handsome, isn't he?" said Daisy, smiling back not without a touch of malice. "Who could help favouring such an Adonis?"

"Not you, I'm sure," said Hunt-Goring, "or the charming Peggy either. But I'm a little sorry for the red-haired doctor, you know. I feel in a measure responsible for that tragedy."

"The responsibility was mine," said Daisy gravely.

He turned his lazy eyes upon her. "Ah, to be sure! You wanted an excuse to procure that young man his conge, I believe. I hope you realize that you are in my debt for just so much as the excuse was worth."

Daisy made a quick movement of exasperation. "Do you never give women credit for being sincere?" she said.

"Only when they are angry," said Hunt-Goring, taking out his cigarette-case. "Now join me, won't you? Sincerity is such a heating quality. I shouldn't cultivate it if I were you."

But Daisy declined somewhat curtly. It was quite evident that her patience was wearing very thin.

Hunt-Goring did not press her. He smiled and subsided with obvious indifference. Perhaps he deemed it wiser not to try her too far, or perhaps he lacked the energy to pursue the matter.

He had taken to spending most of his time on the verandah, smoking his endless cigarettes and dreamily watching the world go by. He seemed almost to have forgotten that he was a guest, and, her exasperation notwithstanding, Daisy could not bring herself to remind him of the fact. For the man was changed. Day after day she realized it more and more clearly. Day after day it seemed to her that he dropped a little deeper into his sea of lethargy. His interest flagged so quickly where once it had been keen. He grew daily older while she watched. And a curious pity for him kept her from actively disliking him, although his power to attract her was wholly gone. She found herself bearing with him simply because he cared so little.

It was quite otherwise with Noel, who was frankly disgusted to find himself confronted with him on the following morning when, true to his promise, he made his appearance with Peggy's mount. Hunt-Goring was just preparing to establish himself on the verandah when Noel came striding along it in search of his small playmate. They so nearly collided in fact that it was impossible for either to overlook the other's presence.

Noel drew back sharply with his quick scowl. They had not met since the evening on which he had so furiously challenged him to battle on Olga's behalf. For Olga's sake, and perhaps a little in deference to Max's warning, he had refrained from following up the challenge, but he was more than ready to do so even yet; and his attitude said as much as he stood aside in glowering silence for the other man to pass.

Hunt-Goring however was plainly in a genial mood. He paused to bestow his smiling scrutiny upon the young officer. "Let me see! Surely we have met before?"

"We have," said Noel bluntly.

"I fear the occasion has slipped my memory," said Hunt-Goring.

A wiser man would have passed on. But Noel had not yet attained to years of discretion. He stood his ground and explained.

"We met at dinner here. Captain and Miss Ratcliffe were here too--and my brother."

"Oh, ah! I remember now. Quite an amusing evening, was it not?" Hunt-Goring laughed gently. "You were rather vexed with me for chaffing her about her engagement. I have always thought a little chaff was legitimate on such occasions."

"When it isn't objectionable," said Noel gruffly.

Hunt-Goring laughed again. "Do you know why the engagement was broken off?"

Noel drew himself up sharply. "That, sir, is neither your affair nor mine."

Hunt-Goring took out his cigarette-case. "Well, it was mine in a way," he observed complacently. "I pulled the strings, you know."

"Ah!" It was an exclamation of anger rather than of surprise. The blood mounted in a great wave to Noel's forehead. He looked suddenly dangerous. "I guessed it was your doing," he said, in a furious undertone.

Hunt-Goring continued to smile. "He wasn't a very suitable parti for her, my dear fellow. There was a certain episode in his past that wouldn't bear too close an investigation. Very possibly you have not been let into that secret. Your brother was not over-anxious to have it noised abroad."

Noel's hands were clenched. He seemed to be restraining himself from a violent outburst with immense difficulty.

"My brother," he said with emphasis, "is the gentleman of our family. He has never yet done anything that couldn't have been proclaimed from the house-tops."

Hunt-Goring uttered his sneering laugh. "What touching loyalty! My dear fellow, your brother is the biggest blackguard of you all, if you only knew it."

"You lie!" Violently came the words; they were as the sudden bursting of the storm. Something electric seemed suddenly to have entered into Noel. He became as it were galvanized by fury.

But still Hunt-Goring laughed. "Oh, not on this occasion, I assure you. I have too little at stake. I wonder why you imagined the engagement was broken off. I suppose your brother gave you a reason of sorts."

Noel's eyes shone red. "He gave me to understand that you had had a hand in it. I guessed it in fact. I knew what an infernal blackguard you were."

"Order! Order!" smiled Hunt-Goring. "After all, my share in the matter was a very small one. Most men have a past, you know. When you have lived a little longer, you will recognize that. So he didn't tell you why he had been thrown over? Left you to make your own inferences, I suppose? Or perhaps she made the flatter-ing suggestion that she had bestowed her affections upon--someone more captivating? I fancy she is wisely determined to secure as good a bargain as possible--for which one can scarcely blame her. And a man with so lively a past as your brother's would scarcely be a safe partner for one who values peace and prosperity."

"How dare you make these vile insinuations in my hearing?" burst forth Noel. "Do you think I'm made of sawdust? Tell me what you mean, or else retract every single word you've said!"

Hunt-Goring held up a cigarette between his fingers and looked at it. The fury of Noel's attitude scarcely seemed to reach his notice. He leaned against the balustrade of the verandah, still faintly smiling.

"I would tell you the whole story with pleasure," he said, "only I am not quite sure that it would be good for you to know."

"Oh, damn all that!" broke in Noel, goaded to exasperation by his obvious indifference. "If you want to save your skin, you'd better speak out at once!"

"To save my skin!" Hunt-Goring's eyes left their contemplation of the cigarette and travelled to his face. They held a sneer that was well-nigh intolerable, and yet which somehow restrained Noel for the moment. "What a very headlong young man you are!" pursued Hunt-Goring, in his soft voice. "I've done nothing to you. I haven't the smallest desire to quarrel with you. Nor have I given you any occasion for offence. It was Mrs. Musgrave--not I--who imparted the regrettable tale of your brother's shortcomings to his fiancee. In some fashion she conceived it to be her duty to do so."

"You meant her to do it!" flashed back Noel.

"Ah! that is another story," smiled Hunt-Goring. "We are not discussing motives or intentions. I think. But she will tell you--if you care to ask her--that I advised her strongly against the course she elected to pursue."

"You would!" said Noel bitterly. "Well, get on! Let's hear this precious story. I've no doubt it's a damned lie from beginning to end, but if it's going the round I'd better know it."

"It may be a lie," said Hunt-Goring diplomatically. "But it was not concocted by me. I should conclude, however, from subsequent events that some portion of it bears at least some sort of resemblance to the truth." He stopped to light his cigarette while Noel looked on fuming. "The story is a very ordinary one, but might well prove somewhat damning to a doctor's career. It concerned a young lady with whom your brother was--somewhat intimate."

"Did you know her?" thrust in Noel.

Hunt-Goring looked at the end of his cigarette with a thoughtful smile. "Yes, I knew her rather well. I was not, however, prepared to lend my name to cloak a scandal--even to oblige your brother who had transferred his attentions to Miss Olga, so he had to take his own measures." He looked up with a glitter of malice in his eyes. "The girl died," he said, "rather suddenly. That's all the story."

It was received in a dead silence that lasted for the breathless passage of a dozen seconds. Then: "You--skunk!" said Noel.

He did not raise his voice to say it, but there was that in his tone that was more emphatic than violence. It warned Hunt-Goring of danger as surely as the growl of a tiger. His lazy complacence suddenly gave place to alertness. He straightened himself up. But even then he had not the sense to refrain from his abominable laugh.

"I've noticed," he said, "that present-day puppies are greater at snarling than fighting. I told you this story because you asked for it. Now I'll tell you one you didn't ask for. Max Wyndham transferred his attentions to Olga Ratcliffe, not because he cared for her, but because he wanted to put a spoke in my wheel. Little Olga and I were very thick at one time. You didn't know that, I daresay?"

"I don't believe it!" said Noel, breathing heavily.

Hunt-Goring inhaled a deep breath of smoke and blew it forth again in gentle puffs. "Ah! She never told you that? She was always a secretive young woman. Yes, we had some very jolly times together on the sly, till one day the doctor-fellow caught us kissing under the apple-trees. Then of course she was afraid he'd split, so it was all up." He smiled insolently into Noel's blazing eyes. "I flatter myself that she missed those stolen kisses," he said. "I must go round one of these days--when the dragon is out of ear-shot--and make up for it."

That loosed the devil in Noel at last. He took a swift step forward. His right hand gripped his riding-whip.

"If you ever go near her again," he said, "I'll break every bone in your body! You liar--you damned blackguard--you cur!"

Full into Hunt-Goring's face he hurled his furious words. He was more angry in that moment than he had ever been in his life. The force of his anger carried him along as a twig borne on a racing current. Till that instant he had forgotten that he carried his riding-whip. The sudden remembrance of it flashed like a streak of lightning through his brain.

Before he knew what he was doing, almost as if a will swifter than his own were at work, he had sprung upon Hunt-Goring and struck him a swinging blow across the shoulders.

Only that one blow, however! For Hunt-Goring was not an easy man to thrash. Ten years before, he had been the strongest man in his regiment, and he was powerful still. Before Noel could strike again, he was locked in an embrace that threatened to crush him to a pulp.

In awful silence they strained and fought together, and in a second or two it came to Noel through the silence that he had met his match. The Irish blood in him leaped exultant to the fray. He laughed a breathless laugh, and braced his muscles to a fierce resistance. He had been spoiling for a fight with this man for a long time.

But it was impossible to do anything scientific in that constrictor-like hold, and as they swayed and strove he began to realize that unless he could break it, it would very speedily break him. Hunt-Goring's face, purple and devilish, with lips drawn back and teeth clenched upon his cigarette, glared into his own. There was something unspeakably horrible about the eyes. They turned upwards, showing the whites all shot with blood.

"The man's a maniac!" was the thought that ran through Noel's brain.

His heart had begun to pump with painful hammering strokes. Not much of a fight this! Rather a grim struggle for life against a power he could not break. He braced himself again to burst that deadly grip. In his ears there arose a great surging. He felt his own eyes begin to start. By Heaven! Was he going to be squeezed to death ignominiously on the strength of that single blow? He gathered himself together for one mighty effort--the utmost of which he was capable--to force those iron arms asunder.

For about six seconds they stood the strain, holding him like a vice; then very suddenly they parted--so suddenly that Noel almost staggered as he drew his first great gasp of relief. Hunt-Goring reeled--almost fell--back against the wall of the bungalow. The sweat was streaming down his forehead. His face was livid. His eyes, sinister and awful, were turned up like the eyes of a dead man. He was chewing at his cigarette with a ceaseless working of the jaws indescribably horrible to watch.

Noel realized on the instant that the struggle was over, with small satisfaction to either side. He stood breathing deeply, all the mad blood in him racing at fever speed through his veins, burning to follow up the attack but conscious that he could not do so. For the man who leaned there facing him was old--a bitter fact which neither had realized until that moment--too old to fight, too old to thrash.

Noel swung round and turned his back upon him, utterly disgusted with the situation. He picked up his riding-whip with a savage gesture and stared at it with fierce regret. It was a serviceable weapon. He could have done good work with it-- on a younger man.

Hunt-Goring made a sudden movement, and he wheeled back. The livid look had gone from the man's face. He stood upright, and spat the cigarette from his lips. His eyes had drooped again, showing only a malicious glint between the lids. Yet there was something about him even then that made Noel aware that he was very near the end of his strength.

He was on the verge of speaking when there came the sudden rush of Peggy's eager feet, and she darted out upon the verandah, and raced to Noel with a squeal of delight.

Noel caught her in his arms. He had never been more pleased to see her. He did not look at Hunt-Goring again, and the words on Hunt-Goring's lips remained unspoken.

"Let's go! Let's go!" cried Peggy.

And Noel turned as if the atmosphere had suddenly become poisonous, and bore her swiftly away.

A few seconds later, Daisy, running out to see the start, came upon Hunt-Goring upright and motionless upon the verandah, and was somewhat surprised by the rigidity of his attitude. He relaxed almost at once, however, and sat down in his usual corner.

"I had no idea Noel was here," she said. "Has he been waiting long?"

"Not long," said Hunt-Goring. "I have been entertaining him."

"Isn't he a nice boy?" said Daisy impetuously. "Look at him in the saddle--so splendidly young and free!"

Hunt-Goring was silent a moment. Then, as he took out his cigarette-case, he remarked: "He is so altogether charming, Mrs. Musgrave, that I can't help thinking that he must be one of those fortunate people 'whom the gods love.'"

"But what a horrid thing to say!" protested Daisy. "I'm sure Noel won't die young. He is so full of vitality. He couldn't!"

Hunt-Goring smiled upon his cigarettes. "I wonder," he said slowly, and chose one with the words. "I--wonder!"

CHAPTER XX
THE POWER OF THE ENEMY

It so chanced that Noel did not find himself in any intimate conversation with Olga again until the great week arrived, and General Sir Reginald Bassett came upon the scene with much military pomp and ceremony.

Olga avoided all talk of a confidential nature with him with so obvious a reluctance that he could not force it upon her in the brief spaces of time which he had at his disposal when they met. They had become close friends, but the feeling that this friendship depended mainly upon his forbearance never left Noel, and he could not fail to see that she shrank from the bare mention of Max's name.

He bided his time, therefore, since there was no urgent need to broach the subject forthwith and he was still by no means sure of his ground. He would have discussed the matter with Nick, but Nick was never to be found. He came and went with astonishing rapidity, bewildering even Olga by the suddenness of his moves. Vaguely she heard of unrest in the city, but definite information she had none. Nick eluded all enquiries; but it seemed to her that the yellow face grew more wrinkled every day, and the shrewd eyes took on a vigilant, sleepless look that troubled her much in secret. The thought of him kept her from brooding overmuch upon her own trouble. She did not want to brood. If her own nights were sleepless, she took a book and resolutely read. She would not yield an inch to the ceaseless, weary ache of her heart, and very sternly she denied herself the relief of tears. Too much of her life had been wasted already, in the pursuit of what was not. She would not waste still more of it in bitter, fruitless mourning over that which was.

Perhaps it was the bravest stand she had ever made, and what it cost her not even Nick might guess. Certainly he had less time to bestow upon her than ever before. They met at meals, and very often that was all. But Olga, with her curious, new reserve, was not needing his companionship just then. Her attitude towards her beloved hero had subtly changed. Beloved he was still and would ever be, but he no longer dwelt apart from all other men on the special little pedestal on which her worship had placed him. He was no longer the demi-god of her childish adoration. Olga had grown up, and was shedding her illusions one by one. Nick was a man and she was a woman. Therefore it followed as a natural sequence that though she was fully capable of understanding him, she herself was--and must ever remain--a being beyond his comprehension. Not superior to him; Olga never aspired to be that. But with her woman's knowledge she realized that even Nick had his limitations. There were certain corners of her soul which he could never penetrate. He would have understood the wild crying of her heart, but her steady stifling of that crying would have been beyond him. Simply he stood on another plane, and he would not understand that her heart must break before she could listen to its passionate entreaty. Nor could she explain herself to him. She belonged to the inexplicable and unreasonable race called woman. Her motives and emotions were hidden, and she could never hope to make them understood even by the shrewdest of men.

So she veiled her sorrow from him, little guessing how the vigilant eyes took in that also when they did not apparently so much as glance her way.

On the morning of the day on which Sir Reginald was to arrive, he kept her waiting for breakfast, a most unusual occurrence. Olga was occupied with a letter from her father, one of his brief, kindly epistles that she valued for their very rarity; and it was not till this was finished that she realized the lateness of the hour.

Then in some surprise she went along the verandah in search of him.

His window stood open as usual. She paused outside it. "Nick, aren't you coming?"

There was no reply to her call, and she was about to repeat it when Kasur the khitmutgar came along the verandah behind her.

"Miss sahib, Ratcliffe sahib has not yet come back from the city," he said.

Olga turned in astonishment. "The city, Kasur! How long has he been there? When did he go?"

The man looked at her with the deferential vagueness which only the Oriental can express. "Miss sahib, how should I know? My lord goes in the night while his servant is asleep."

"In the night!" Again incredulously she repeated his words. "And to the city! Kasur, are you sure?"

Kasur became more vague. "Perhaps he goes to the cantonments, Miss sahib. How should I know whither he goes?"

It was an unsatisfactory conversation, obviously leading in every direction but the one desired. Olga turned from him, impatient and perplexed. She went slowly back round the corner of the bungalow to the breakfast-table, set in the shade of the cluster-roses that climbed over the verandah, and sat down before it with a sinking heart. What did this mean? Was it true that Nick went nightly and by stealth to the city? What did he do there? And how came he to be there at this hour? Moment by moment her uneasiness grew. The conviction that Nick was in danger came down upon her like a bird of evil omen, and inaction became intolerable. She turned in her chair with the intention of calling to Kasur to order her horse that she might go in search of him. But in that instant a voice spoke to her from the compound immediately below her, arresting the words on her lips,--a whining, ingratiating voice.

"Mem-sahib!""Mem-sahib!"

She looked down and saw an old, old man, more like a monkey than a human being, standing huddled in a ragged chuddah on the edge of the path. He seemed to be looking at her, obviously he must have seen her sitting there, and yet to Olga his eyes looked blind. They stared straight up at the sky while he spoke, and there was a dreadful paleness about them, a lifeless hue that contrasted very strangely with the deep copper of his bearded face.

"Do not be alarmed, most gracious!" he begged in a thin reedy voice. "I come with a message from the captain sahib. He has been detained in the city; but all is well with him. He bids me to say that he desires the mem to eat alone this morning, but to have no fear. He will be with her again ere the sun has reached its height."

Olga leaned upon the balustrade of the verandah and looked down at her strange visitor. She was not sorry that she was thus raised above him, for he was very dirty. The voluminous chuddah in which he was swathed looked as if it had wrapped him in those selfsame folds for many years.

"But what is the sahib doing?" she asked. "Why doesn't he come?"

The old man wagged a deferential beard. "Excellency, how should a poor old seller of moonstones know?"

"Oh!" Olga suddenly became interested in the messenger. "You are the moon-stone-seller, are you?" she said. "Have you ever been here before?"

He bent himself before her in a low salaam. "I am my lord's most humble servant," he told her meekly. "A very poor man, most gracious,--a very poor man. I come here at my lord's bidding--when he needs me."

Olga's brow puckered. "How queer!" she said. "I wonder I have never seen you before. Perhaps you only come at night."

"Only at night, most gracious," he said.

He made as if he would hobble away, but she called to him to wait, while she ran to her room to fetch a few annas for him. It took her but a second or two to find what she wanted, but when she emerged again upon the verandah her visitor had disappeared.

She stood and searched the compound with astonished eyes, but no sign of him was visible. He must have removed himself with considerable rapidity for so old a man, and remembering his extreme poverty, Olga was puzzled. She had never known a native run away from backsheesh before.

She sat down to her solitary breakfast, no longer actively anxious concerning Nick, but still by no means easy. She was firmly convinced that he was running risks in the city, and she longed to have him back.

The morning dragged away. She would not leave the bungalow lest he should return in her absence. She busied herself with the making of a fancy-dress which she and her ayah had concocted for the coming ball at the mess-house. It was to be quite an important affair, and every European within reach was to attend--according to Noel's decree. He had persuaded his colonel to have a purely European function for once, pleading that it would be so much more like Home; and Colonel Bradlaw, albeit with hesitation, had yielded the point. So to that one night's entertainment no native guests had been invited.

Noel was looking forward to the event with an enthusiasm that simply swept Olga along with it. She could not help being interested and in a measure excited. It was an absolute impossibility to be lukewarm about anything over which Noel was enthusiastic. He kindled enthusiasm wherever he went. Native fancy-dresses were tabooed by the regulations. Noel was supremely contemptuous of all things native. He meant to go as Dick Turpin himself, and she had promised to support him in a dress of the same period. It had taken considerable thought and skill to manufacture, but it was now well on the road to completion, and she sat and stitched at it throughout the morning, trying to stifle her uneasiness in the attention which it demanded.

It was not an easy matter. She found herself starting at every sound, and pausing to listen with nerves on edge. Still she persisted, determined not to give way to them; and she was in fact gradually schooling herself to a calmer frame of mind, when suddenly a thing happened that bereft her in a moment of all the composure she had striven so hard to attain. A man's hand shot--swiftly and stealthily--from behind her and covered her eyes in a flash, while a man's voice, soft and exultant, said mockingly above her head, "Guess!"

Olga uttered a cry that would have been a shriek had not the hand very swiftly shifted its position from her eyes to her mouth. She looked up into a face she knew--a face whose eyes of evil triumph made her heart stand still, and all her strength went suddenly from her. She turned as white as death and sank back into the chair from which she had half-risen. The total unexpectedness of the thing deprived her of all powers of resistance. She sat as one stunned.

He took his hand from her lips and brutally kissed them, laughing as she shrank away from him in sick horror. The gleaming mockery of his eyes was a thing she dared not meet.

"You will never guess what I have come for," he said, hanging over her, his hand gripping both of hers, his face still horribly near.

Her lips moved voicelessly in answer. She could not utter a word.

"You're awfully pleased to see me, aren't you?" he said. "That's nice of you. I wonder when you mean to pay that debt of yours--that old, sweet debt."

He spoke softly, smilingly, his eyes devouring her the while. She closed her own to avoid them. Her heart did not seem to be beating at all. She felt as if she were going to die of sheer horror there in his arms.

Softly again his voice came to her. "Come, you mustn't faint. That wouldn't be at all good for you. Open your eyes! Don't be afraid! Open them!"

They opened quiveringly, almost against her will. He was holding her closely, as if he anticipated some sudden resistance. But his eyes were on her still, burningly, possessively, menacingly. She met them shrinking, and felt as if thereby she gave herself to him body and soul.

He began to laugh again--that soft, silky laugh. "You're such a silly child," he said; "you always expect the worst. It's not wise of you. Aren't you old enough to know that yet?"

She found her voice at last, and with it came the consciousness of the slow, slow beating of her heart. "Let me go!" she said, in a breathless whisper.

"Presently; on one condition," he said.

"No, now!" The beating had begun to quicken a little, to harden into a distinct throbbing. But she felt deadly cold. Her hands, powerless in that unrelenting grasp, were as ice.

"Now don't be foolish!" said Hunt-Goring. "You're absolutely at my mercy, and it's very poor policy on your part not to recognize that fact. Just listen! You want me to let you go, you say. Well, I will let you go--for one small consideration on your part. You've never paid that debt of yours. You will pay it now--in full, freely, both arms round my neck. Come, I've a right to ask that much. It's just a whim that you can't refuse to gratify."

"I can refuse!" The words leaped from Olga. Her strength was returning, her heart quickening with every instant. "At least you can't make me do that!" she said.

"You would rather do it than marry me, I presume?" he said.

"I will never do either!" She stirred at last in his hold. She did not shrink from his eyes any longer; rather she challenged them as she stiffened herself to rise.

Hunt-Goring laughed in her face. "Oh, won't you?" he said. "I fancy you said that once before--and lived to regret it. It really is not wise of you to defy me. I warn you! I warn you!" His hold tightened upon her with sudden brutality, quelling her effort at freedom. "There are worse things than marriage," he said. "Are you utterly ignorant, I wonder, or deliberately foolhardy? Why do you always force upon me the role of villain? I tell you again, you are not wise!"

"I don't know what you mean," Olga said. She sat quite still in his hold now, for she knew that resistance was useless. Like Noel, she suddenly wondered if he were indeed sane. His eyes were unlike any she had ever seen in a human being. They glared upon her so devilishly, so murderously. She faced them with all her courage. "I don't know what you mean," she repeated. "I think you must be mad to persecute me in this way. I have always said that I would never marry you."

"But you will change your mind," he said.

She kept her eyes on his. "I shall never change my mind," she said very distinctly.

He laughed again, his lower lip between his teeth. "Even if I were mad," he said, "wouldn't you be wiser to humour me? Have you forgotten what happened when you flouted me before?"

"No, I have not forgotten." A quiver of anger went through Olga, and she suffered it, for it helped her courage. "I shall never forgive you for that," she said--"never, as long as I live!"

Hunt-Goring continued to laugh, and his laugh was an insult. "I shall get over that," he told her. "I don't want your forgiveness--especially as you had yourself alone to thank for that episode. But come now! About marrying me. You'd better give in at once; you'll have to in the end. And there are plenty of advantages to outweigh your present disinclination. For instance, my life is not considered a good one. As my widow, you would be quite a wealthy woman. Doesn't that appeal to you? And I'll give you plenty of rope even while I'm alive. I shan't interfere with your pleasures. Come, I shouldn't make such a bad husband. I'm quite respectable nowadays. I should want a little attention of course, but you wouldn't find me exacting. You'll get quite fond of me in time."

Olga barely repressed a shudder. "Never!" she said. "No, never!"

"Never?" said Hunt-Goring. He stooped a little lower over her, his arm about her shoulders despite her sick disgust. "Why never? You've sent that doctor chap about his business, haven't you?"

"He has gone, yes." She answered him briefly to hide the intolerable pain at her heart the words called up.

"But you're still hankering after him; is that it?" sneered Hunt-Goring. "Well, then, listen to me! I hold that man's future in my hands. I can ruin him utterly or--I can forbear. I'm not over-fond of him, as you know. I should rather like to see him ruined, though it would give me some little trouble to do it. What say you? I am the gladiator in the arena. I shall slay or spare--at your word alone."

Again his eyes overwhelmed her, so that she could not meet them. A great shiver went through her. She began to pant a little. "I--don't understand," she said.

"You know nothing--but gossip. You--you can prove nothing."

"Can I not?" said Hunt-Goring. "You haven't a very high opinion of my intelligence, have you? Colonel Campion--I believe you know him--is scarcely the man to sit still when such gossip as that reaches his ears. As for the proofs, I know how to find them. The worthy Mrs. Briggs was on the spot, you may remember. Her evidence would be valuable. And there are other well-known means which I needn't go into now. But I assure you the circumstances themselves, properly handled, are sufficiently suspicious. You would not care to see your friend Max on his trial for murder, I presume?"

She shivered again, shivered from head to foot. She did not utter a word.

"No, I thought not," said Hunt-Goring, after a moment. "It would be especially painful for you, as your evidence also would be required. You see the position quite clearly, don't you? Come, hadn't you better give in now--and save further trouble?"

She was silent still. Only her breath came fast--as the breath of one who nears exhaustion.

Hunt-Goring waited a little, watching her white face. "Come!" he said, "I don't want to play the villain any longer. Can't you give me something better to do? I always dance to your piping."

She spoke at last, forcing her trembling lips to utterance; after repeated effort. "Go--please!" she said.

"Go?" said Hunt-Goring.

"Yes! go!" She raised her eyes for an instant, piteously entreating, to his. "I--can't talk to you now,--can't--think even. I--will see you again--later."

"When?" he said.

Her breast was rising and falling. She could not for several seconds answer him. Then: "At the ball--on Thursday," she whispered.

"You will give me my answer then?" he said.

"Yes."

He smiled--a cruel smile. "After due consultation with Nick, I suppose? No, my dear. I think not. We'll keep this thing a secret for the present--and I'll have my answer now."

"I can't answer you now!" She flung the words wildly, and rose up between his hands with desperate strength. "I can't--I can't!" she cried. "You must give me--a little time. I shan't consult--Nick or anyone. I only want--to think--by myself."

"Really?" said Hunt-Goring.

"Yes, really." She set her hands against his breast, holding him from her, yet beseeching him. "Oh, you can't refuse me this!" she urged. "It's--too small a thing. I've got to find out if--if--if I can possibly do it."

"You won't run away?" he said.

"No--no! I've nowhere to go."

"And you mention the matter to no one--on your oath--till we meet again?" His eyes were cruel still, but they were not cold. They shone upon her with a fierce heat.

She could not avoid them, though they seemed to burn her through and through. "I promise," she said through white lips.

"Very well. Till Thursday then." He let her go; and then, as if repenting, caught her suddenly back to him, savagely, passionately. "I'll have that kiss anyway," he said, "whether you take me or not. It's the price of my good behaviour till Thursday. Come, a kiss never hurt anyone, so it isn't likely to kill you."

She did not resist him. She even gave him her lips; but she was shaking as one in an ague, and her whole weight was upon him as he crushed her in his arms. So deathly was her face that after a moment even he was slightly alarmed.

He put her down again in the chair with a laugh that was not wholly self-complacent. "That's all right, then. I'll leave you to get used to the idea. You will give me my answer on Thursday, then, and we will decide on the next step. I don't mean to be kept waiting, you know. I've had enough of that."

She did not answer him or move. She was staring straight before her, with hands fast gripped together in her lap.

He bent a little. "What's the matter? I haven't hurt you. Aren't you well?"

"Quite," she said, without stirring.

He laughed again--the soft laugh she so abhorred. "Jove! What a dance you've led me!" he said. "You'll have a good deal to make up for when the time comes. I shan't let you off that."

"Will you--please--go?" said Olga, in that still voice of hers, not looking at him yet, nor moving.

He laughed again caressingly. "Yes, I'll go. You want to have a good quiet think, I suppose. But there's only one way out, you know. You'll have to give in now. And the sooner the better."

"I shall see you on Thursday," she said.

"Yes, I shall be there. Keep the supper-dances for me! We'll find a quiet corner somewhere and enjoy ourselves. Till Thursday then! Good-bye!"

"Good-bye!" she said.

He was gone. Before her wide eyes he went away along the verandah, and passed from her sight, and there fell an intense silence.

Olga sat motionless as a statue, gazing straight before her. A squirrel skipped airily on to the further end of the verandah and sat there, washing its face. Below, on the path, a large lizard flicked out from behind a stone, looked hither and thither, spied the still figure, and darted away again. And then, somewhere away among the cypresses the silence was broken; a paroquet began to screech.

Olga stirred, and a great breath burst suddenly from her--the first she had drawn in many seconds. She stretched out her hands into emptiness.

"Oh, Max!" she said. "Max! Max!"

With that bitter cry, all her strength seemed to go from her. She bowed her head upon her knees and wept bitterly, despairingly....

It must have been a full quarter of an hour later that Nick came lightly along the verandah, paused an instant behind the bowed figure, then slipped round and knelt beside it.

"Kiddie! Kiddie! What's the matter?" he said.

His one arm gathered her to him, so that she lay against his shoulder in the old childish attitude, his cheek pressed against her forehead.

She was too exhausted, too spent by that bitter paroxysm of weeping, to be startled by his sudden coming. She only clung to him weakly, whispering, "Oh, Nick, have you come back at last?"

"But of course I have," he said. "Have you been worrying about me? I sent you a message."

"I know. But I--I couldn't help being anxious." She murmured the words into his neck, her arms tightening about him.

"What a silly little sweetheart!" he said. "Is that what you've been crying for?"

She was silent.

He passed rapidly on. "You mustn't cry any more, darling. Old Reggie will be here soon, you know. He'll think I've been bullying you. Have you been sitting here by yourself all the morning? Why didn't you go down to Daisy Musgrave?"

"I didn't want to, Nick. I--I don't in the least mind being by myself," she told him, mastering herself with difficulty. "Tell me what you've been doing--all this time!"

"I?" said Nick. "Watching and listening chiefly. Not much else. Is the post in? Come and help me read my letters!"

"They're here." Olga turned and began to feel about with one hand under her work.

"All right. I'll find 'em." He let her go, and fished out his correspondence himself. She was glad that he did not look at her very critically or press further for the cause of her woe.

He sat down on the mat at her feet, and proceeded to read his letters as she handed them to him.

After a little, she took up her work again. She had quite regained her composure, only she was utterly weary--too weary to feel anything but a numb aching. All violent emotion had passed.

Suddenly Nick dropped his correspondence, and turned. "Kiddie," he said. "I'm going to chuck this job."

She looked down at him with a surprise that would have been greater but for her great weariness. "Really, Nick?"

"Yes, really. I've done my poor best, but to make a success would be a life job. Moreover," Nick's eyes suddenly gleamed, "the Party want me--or say they do. There's going to be a big tug of war in the summer, and they want me to help pull. I'm rather good at pulling," here spoke Nick's innate modesty, "and so I've got to be there.'"

"We are going Home then?" Olga's voice was low. She spoke as one whom the decision scarcely touched.

Nick leaned back luxuriously against her knees. "Yes, sweetheart, Home--Home to Muriel and the kiddie--Home to good old Jim. You won't be sorry to see your old Dad again?"

"No," she said; then, as his brows went up, she stooped forward and kissed the top of his head. "But you've been very good to me, Nick," she said. "I--I've been happier with you, dear, than I could have been with anyone."

"Save one," said Nick, flashing a swift look upwards. "And you've struck him off the list, poor beggar."

She checked him quickly, her hand on his shoulder. "Please, Nick!" she whispered.

He nodded wisely. "Yes, that hurts, doesn't it? But you're not the only one to suffer. Ever think of that?"

She did not answer him. With a quiver in her voice she changed the subject. "When do you think we shall go Home then, Nick?"

"Soon," said Nick. "Very soon. They say I can't be spared much longer. Awfully sweet of 'em, isn't it? As for this immoral little State, it ought to be put under martial law for a spell. It won't be, of course; but old Reggie will understand. He'll take measures, and relieve me of my stewardship as soon as may be. I'm sorry in a way, but I only bargained for six months. And I want to get back to Muriel." He turned to her again, with his elastic smile. "But you've been a dear little pal. You've kept me from pining," he said. "Wish your affairs might have ended more cheerily; but we won't discuss that. Let's see; you don't know Sir Reginald Bassett, do you?"

"No, dear."

"Nor Lady Bassett his wife. Good for you. Pray that you never may, and the odds are in favour of the prayer being granted. She has decided not to come after all."

"Not to come, Nick! Why, I thought it was all settled!"

Nick grinned. "Her heart has failed her at the last moment. She doesn't like immoral States." He waved a letter jubilantly in the air. "No matter, my dear. We shall get on excellently without her. She isn't your sort at all." He broke into a laugh. "She's the only woman of my acquaintance I don't love, and the only one--literally--who doesn't love me."

"How horrid of her, Nick! I'm sure I should hate her."

"I'm sure you would, dear. So it's just as well--all things considered--that you are not going to meet. Well, I must go and get respectable." He rose with a quick, lithe movement, but paused, looking down at her quizzically to ask: "What did you think of my friend the moonstone-seller? Pretty, isn't he?"

She smiled for the first time. "I'm sure he's quite disreputable. He disappeared in the most mysterious fashion. I wonder if he's lurking about anywhere still, waiting to murder us in our beds."

"I wonder," said Nick.

But he did not trouble himself to look round for the mysterious one, nor did the possibility of being murdered seem to disturb him greatly. He went away to his room, humming a love-song below his breath. And Olga knew that his thoughts were far away in England, where Muriel was waiting to welcome him Home.

CHAPTER XXI
THE GATHERING STORM

Looking back in after days, the time that elapsed between the coming of Sir Reginald Bassett and the night of the Fancy-Dress Ball at the mess-house was to Olga as a whirling nightmare. She took part in all the gaieties that she and Noel had so busily planned, but she went through them as one in the grip of some ghastly dream, beholding through all the festivities the shadow of inexorable Fate drawing near. For she was caught in the net at last, hopelessly, irrevocably enmeshed. From the very outset she had realized that. There could no longer be any way of escape for her, for she could not accept deliverance at the price that must be paid for it. She did not so much as seek to escape, knowing her utter helplessness. Rebellion was a thing of the past. Her spirit was broken. Had she been still engaged to Max, the struggle, though hopeless, would have been more fierce. But since that was over, there was little left to fight for on her own account. Hate and loathe the man as she might, she was forced to own his mastery. To pass from the desert to an inferno was not so racking a contrast as if he had dragged her direct from her paradise.

Later, when the first paralysis of despair had passed, when her captor came to take full possession, she would rebel again wildly, madly. There would be a frightful struggle between them, the last fierce effort of her instinct to be free from a bondage that revolted her. Vaguely, from afar, she viewed that inevitable battle, and in her mind the conviction grew that she would not survive it. The thing was too monstrous. It would kill her.

But for the present her power of resistance was dead. Max must be protected, and this was the only way. She did not dare to think of him in those days, save as it were in the abstract. He filled a certain chamber in her heart which she never entered. He had gone out of her life more completely than if he had died, for she cherished no tender memory of him. She turned away from the bare thought of him, and in the naked horrors of the night, when she lay cold and staring while the hours crawled by, she deliberately banished him from her mind. She was going to do this thing for his sake--this thing that she firmly believed would kill her--but she barred him away from her agony. Not even in thought could she endure his presence at the sacrifice.

So, without struggle, those awful days passed, and she mingled with the gay crowd, instinctively hiding the plague-spot in her soul. Each day she encountered Hunt-Goring at one function or another, meeting the gleam in his dark eyes with no outward tremor but with a heart gone cold. He made no attempt to be alone with her; he was content to bide his time, knowing that the game was his. And each night the memory of his hateful kisses wound like a thread of evil through her brain, banishing all rest.

It was on the afternoon preceding the Ball that Nick called her out to the verandah where he and Sir Reginald were sitting. She liked Sir Reginald, he was genial and kindly and exceedingly easy to entertain.

He drew forward a chair beside him as she approached. "Come and join us, Miss Ratcliffe! Nick and I have been having a very lengthy confab. I am afraid you will accuse me of monopolizing him."

Olga came to the chair and sat beside him. "I hope you have been telling him to stop his visits to the native quarter at night," she said. "They are very bad for him. Look how thin he is getting!"

Nick laughed, but Sir Reginald shook his head. "If I may be allowed to say so, I don't think you are either of you looking very robust," he said. "India plays tricks with us, doesn't she? It doesn't do to let her get too strong a hold. I think Nick will be in a position to take you Home before the end of next month, Miss Ratcliffe. His work here is practically done, and a very brilliant service he has rendered the Government. It has been a very delicate task, and he has accomplished it with marked ability."

"Oh, is it finished?" said Olga.

"Not finished--no!" said Nick. "And never will be with Kobad Shikan in power. But I rather fancy the days of that old gentleman's supremacy are drawing to an end. I've been teaching friend Akbar a thing or two lately. He is beginning to see which way the cat jumps, and to realize that the only way to hold his own is to hold by his masters. I've been the antidote to a big dose of sedition administered by the hoary Kobad, and I fancy I've brought him round. Kobad's influence is undermined in all directions, and I fancy the old sinner is beginning to know it."

"I knew he was a horrid old man!" said Olga.

Nick laughed again. "He entertains a very lively hatred for all of us that nothing will ever eradicate. But he belongs to the old regime, so what could one expect? I have even heard it whispered that he served with the rebel sepoys in the Mutiny. However, his day is done. Akbar is no longer under his influence. He will strike out a line for himself now. I've won him round to the British raj, and if he isn't assassinated by Kobad's people, he'll do. It's a pity they can't have martial law for a bit," he added to Sir Reginald. "They would settle in half the time. Hang a few, shoot a few, and--"

"Nick!" said Olga, in astonishment.

He stretched out his one hand and laid it on her knee. "And flog a few," he finished, smiling at her. "There would be some chance for the State then. Yes, I'm a blood-thirsty creature. Didn't you know? One can't wear gloves for this game."

Olga held his hand in silence. She had learned more of Nick in the past five months than she had ever known before. Undoubtedly he had become more of the man to her and less of the hero. She did not love him any the less for it, but her attitude towards him was different.

She knew he had divined the change, and suspected him of being amused thereby--a suspicion which he strengthened by saying with a laugh, "You didn't know I could be such a brute, did you?"

She smiled back a little wistfully. "I begin to think you could be almost anything, Nick," she said.

He shot her a swift glance, and it seemed to her for a moment that he was looking for a double meaning to her words. But apparently he found none, for he smiled again with the comfortable remark, "Ah, well, it's a useful faculty if exercised with discretion. What are you going to wear to-night? Let's hear all about it!"

That was the new Nick all over, displaying the male denseness with which she had never been wont to credit him. She gave him details of her costume without much ardour, he listening with careless comments.

"You don't sound very keen," he said suddenly. "I believe you're getting blase."

"These things get a little monotonous, don't they?" said Sir Reginald.

His smile was sympathetic. She felt inexplicably that he understood her better than did Nick. He had fathomed the deadly weariness that Nick had overlooked.

"Go on!" commanded Nick. "Who are you going to dance with?"

She hesitated a little, and he turned his hand and pinched her fingers somewhat mercilessly. "Noel of course--he's too handsome to refuse, isn't he? And the rest of the boys will expect their share, doubtless. But remember--the supper-dances are mine."

She started a little. "Oh, Nick dear, I'm afraid I've promised those already."

"To whom?" said Nick swiftly.

"Major Hunt-Goring." Her voice was low; she did not look at him as she uttered the name.

Nick's eyebrows shot upwards with lightning rapidity; then drew into a frown. He was silent for a moment before he said very decidedly, "I'm not going to let you dance with Hunt-Goring, so you may as well pass his dances on to me. If he wants to know the reason, he can ask me--and I shall be delighted to tell him."

He spoke in a fighting tone; there was fight in the grip of his hand. Olga noted it, and foresaw trouble.

"I'm afraid it's too late now, Nick," she said rather wearily. "I must keep my engagements."

Nick turned and sent one of his keen glances over her. "You won't keep this one," he told her. "I am simply not going to allow it. Those supper-dances are mine, so make up your mind to that!"

He spoke with a finality that made protest seem futile. It seemed to Olga that the yellow face had never looked so grim. She made no further effort to withstand him, aware that to do so would entail a battle of wills which could only end in her defeat. Perhaps deep in the heart of her she was even thankful for this brief reprieve.

She said nothing therefore, and Sir Reginald considerately turned the subject by asking Nick what disguise he intended to assume.

"I?" said Nick. "I haven't absolutely decided, sir. I've got a fool's dress some-where that might serve."

He turned, releasing Olga's hand, to take a screw of paper from a salver with which Kasur at that moment approached him.

He glanced at Sir Reginald as he did so, muttered a word of excuse, and deftly opened it. The next instant he crumpled it again in his hand, and spoke over his shoulder to the waiting native.

"Say I will see the moonstone before it is sent away!"

The man departed, and Nick rose. "Afraid I shall have to go to the Palace, sir. Olga, you must take care of Sir Reginald in my absence."

"What! Now, Nick?" Olga looked up in swift surprise.

"Yes, now, my child. Good-bye!" He stooped and lightly kissed her. "I daresay I shan't be late back. If I am, you must go to the Ball without me, and get Sir Reginald to take care of you. I shall turn up some time, you may be sure."

"Important, is it?" asked Sir Reginald.

Nick nodded. "I ought to go, sir. Don't wait for me. I shall follow on if I'm late. In any case," he turned to Olga, "I shall be in time for those supper-dances."

His look flashed over her with a species of quizzical tenderness. "And you are not to give any dances to Hunt-Goring, mind, whatever the bounder says."

He was gone. Free, careless, upright, he strode humming along the verandah and swung round the corner out of sight.

A brief silence descended upon the two who were left. Olga glanced once or twice at Sir Reginald, whose brows were drawn in deep thought.

At length, with slight hesitation she spoke, voicing the anxiety that had been growing within her for many days. "Sir Reginald, do you think he is in any danger when he goes to the city?"

The old soldier came out of his reverie, and met her eyes. He smiled at her, albeit his own were grave. "He is extremely shrewd and capable," he said. "I do not think there is much likelihood of his being taken unawares."

"But it is dangerous?" Olga insisted.

"There is a certain amount of risk certainly." Gravely he admitted the fact. "But I think you need not be over-anxious," he added, with a kindly smile. "Nick is one of those clever people who always manage to win through somehow. They always used to say of him on the Frontier that he bore a charmed life. He has a positive genius for wriggling out of tight corners."

He wished to reassure her, she saw; but somehow she did not feel reassured. The conviction was growing upon her that Nick was exposing himself to a danger that would have appalled her had she realized it to its fullest extent.

She said no more to Sir Reginald, but her heart sank. The clouds were gathering thicker and ever thicker on her horizon. She did not dare to look forward any more.

CHAPTER XXII
THE REPRIEVE

I say, you're magnificent!" said Noel. His hand closed tightly upon Olga's with the words. He looked her up and down with a free admiration too boyish to be offensive. "You're an absolute darling in that get-up!" he told her with enthusiasm.

It was impossible to be indignant. Olga tried and failed. She had not been aware till that moment that she was making a particularly brave show in her eighteenth-century costume, with her pink satin finery and powdered hair. But there was no mistaking the adulation in the boy's eyes, and even in the midst of her misery she felt a little glow of gratification. He was looking alluringly disreputable in his high-wayman's dress, and the dark eyes shone upon her with fascinating audacity as he lifted her hand to his lips.

"So you haven't brought Nick with you?" he said, speaking with laughing haste to cut short her half-hearted rebuke.

"No, Nick was called away," she said. "He'll come later if he can."

"Called away, was he?" Noel paused, with her programme in his hand. "Is that what you are looking so worried about?"

She tried to laugh. "Yes, I am rather worried about him. I am afraid he is taking--big risks."

"Little idiot!" said Noel. "When he's got you to look after. But what do you mean by risks? Where has he gone?"

"I don't know," she said, with a shake of the head. "I don't know anything, Noel. He said something about going to see a moonstone, but I think that was only a blind. He can be rather subtle, you know, when he likes."

"Confound him!" said Noel. "Why doesn't he turn his attention to taking care of you? I've been wanting to have a talk to you for days, but I couldn't work it somehow."

Olga held out her hand for her programme; it shook ever so slightly. "I don't think we have anything very important to talk about," she said.

"But we have!" he said impetuously. "At least I have. Oh, damn!--a million apologies! I couldn't help it!--here's that brute Hunt-Goring. You're not going to dance with him? Say you're full up!"

Hunt-Goring, attired as a Turk, was crossing the room towards them. Olga cast a single glance over her shoulder, and turned to Noel with panic in her eyes.

"I've forgotten something," she said in a palpitating whisper. "I must run back to the cloak-room. Wait for me!"

She was gone with the words, fleeing like a hunted creature, till the gathering crowd hid her from sight.

Hunt-Goring smiled, and turned aside. He had no pressing desire for a public meeting. His turn was coming,--the very fact of her flight proclaimed it,--and he could very well afford to wait. He would make her pay full measure for that same waiting.

He passed Noel's scowl with a lazy sneer. The young man would pay also, and that reflection was nectar to his soul. Carelessly he betook himself to the verandah. The dancing did not attract him--so he had told Daisy Musgrave earlier in the day, a remark of which she had been swift to take advantage. For her weariness of her guest was very nearly apparent by that time, and it was a relief to be able to relax her duties as hostess for that evening at least.

The dancing began to the strains of the regimental band, and soon the motley throng were all gathered in the ball-room. It did not look like an all-British assembly, but the nationality of the laughing voices was quite unmistakable. All talked and laughed as they danced, and the hubbub was considerable.

Into it Olga came stealing back, and paused nervously in the doorway to look on. Daisy, dressed as a water-nymph, waved her a gay greeting over her husband's shoulder. Olga smiled and waved back, striving to smother away out of sight the sick fear at her heart.

Someone touched her shoulder, and she started round almost with a cry.

Noel bent to her. "Sorry I made you jump. Look here! There's no one in the ante-room. Come and sit out with me!"

He offered his arm, and she took it thankfully without a word. They went away together.

The ante-room was dimly lighted, and comparatively quiet, though the music and laughter and swish of dancing feet were fully audible there. Noel found her a comfortable chair, and seated himself upon the arm thereof.

He did not speak at once, but after a little, as Olga sat in silence, he turned and looked down at her.

She raised her eyes at once and smiled. "You must think me very foolish," she said.

"No, I don't," he rejoined bluntly. "That brute is enough to scare any woman. You hate him, don't you?"

There was insistence in his tone, insistence mingled with a touch of anxiety. But Olga did not answer him.

"Don't let us talk about him!" she said, with a shiver she could not repress.

Noel's mouth hardened a little. "I'm very sorry," he said. "But we must. He's been circulating a lot of lies about--Max." He paused an instant, looking straight down at her. "Max is a good chap, you know," he said. "It's up to me to defend him."

Olga's face quivered, but she kept her eyes lifted. "You can't," she said, her voice very low.

"Can't I, though?" Hotly he threw back the words. "You don't mean to say you believe it?"

"I know it is true," she said.

"My dear Olga,--" he began.

But she checked him, her hand upon his arm. "Noel," she said, "truly I can't talk about this. But that story is--true, in part at least. Max admitted it--himself--to me."

"Impossible!" ejaculated Noel.

Her fingers closed over his sleeve; her hold was beseeching. "I can't argue with you, Noel," she said. "But I know it is true. You see, I was there."

He stared at her in stupefaction. "Olga, I can't believe it!"

"It is true," she said again.

"But--" Noel began to waver in spite of himself--"if you were there, you must have known all along!"

Her brows drew into the old lines of perplexity. "You see, I was ill," she said. "I--I didn't remember. I don't remember all the details even now. I only know that--it happened. Max told me so--when I asked him."

"Good heavens above!" ejaculated Noel.

She went on drearily, as if he had not spoken. "That was the end of everything between us; and it's just as well now. For I shouldn't have been able to marry him even if it hadn't been."

"Why not?" said Noel.

She looked away from him, and was silent.

He leaned down towards her, and spoke quickly, urgently.

"Olga dear, forgive me for asking, but I must know. Don't you really love him?"

She made a little unconscious gesture of the hands as of pushing something from her. "No," she said.

"But you did?" he insisted.

She leaned her elbow on her knee, lodging her chin upon her hand. "I thought I did--once," she said slowly. "But--it was a mistake."

"It couldn't have been," he said.

She nodded slowly two or three times, not turning her head. "Yes," she said, with the air of one clinching an argument. "It was a mistake."

Noel was silent for a few moments. There was something in her set profile that hurt him. He longed to see her full face. But she did not move. She seemed almost to have forgotten that he was there.

He moved at last, bending nearer. "Olga!" he whispered.

"Yes?" Still she did not turn.

He slipped down to his knees beside her. "Olga!" he said again very pleadingly.

She stirred then, stirred and looked him full in the eyes. And all his life Noel remembered the awful despair that looked out at him from her soul "I--can't!" she said.

He clasped her two hands between his own. "Can't you even think of it?" he urged, under his breath. "You know--you said--you'd have married me if--if--poor old Max hadn't come first. I wouldn't cut him out for worlds; but that's happened already, hasn't it? Surely there's no one else?"

But Olga made no answer. Only the despair in her eyes deepened to a dumb agony.

"Darling," he whispered, gathering her hands up and holding them against his face, "I'd be awfully good to you. And I want you--I do want you. Won't you even consider it?"

A great shiver went through Olga.

"Won't you have my love?" he said.

But still for a little she was silent. It seemed that no words would come.

Then, as he pressed his lips to the hands he had taken, something seemed suddenly to break loose within her. With a great sob she leaned her head upon his shoulder. "Noel! Noel! I--can't!"

His arms clasped her in a moment; he held her close. "Dearest, what is it? Why can't you?"

She answered him with her face hidden and in a voice so low that he barely caught the words. "I am--not free!"

"Not free!" Sharply he repeated the phrase. Suspicion, keen-edged as a rapier, ran swiftly through him. His arms tightened. "Olga, tell me what you mean! Who is it? Not--not that devil Hunt-Goring!"

She did not answer him, save by her silence and the convulsive shudder that went through her at his words. But that in itself was answer enough, and over her head Noel swore a deep and terrible oath.

Only a few yards away the lilting waltz-music was quickening to a finish. In a few moments more their privacy would be invaded by the giddy dancers.

"Listen!" said Noel, and his voice fell short and stern. "He shan't have you! That I swear! It's monstrous--it's unthinkable! Why, he's old enough to be your father. And he's got the opium-habit. Max told me so. Olga, I say, haven't you the strength of mind to refuse him? If the brute pesters you, why don't you tell Nick?"

Slowly Olga raised herself, quitting his support. "I've promised not to tell any-one," she said dully. "You mustn't know either."

"But, my dear girl, something must be done," he objected. "You can't let him ride over you roughshod. You don't mean--you can't mean--to let him marry you?"

"I can't help it," she said.

"Can't help it!" He stared at her. "He really has some hold over you then? What is it?"

She was silent. The last crashing chords of the first waltz were being played. Noel got to his feet. His boyish face was set in grim lines.

"Do you want me to go and kill him?" he said.

"No!" She sprang up also, quickened to sudden fear by his words. "You're not to go near him," she said, "Noel, promise me you won't! Oh, if you only knew--how much harder--your interference makes things! Don't you see--I've given him my word to consult no one!" She was panting uncontrollably; her hands were fast closed upon his arm. "I refused him once before," she told him feverishly, "and he--he punished me--cruelly. I can't--I daren't--refuse him again!"

"You'd sooner marry him?" Noel stared at her incredulously.

She flung out her hands with a wide, despairing gesture. "Yes--yes--I would sooner marry him!"

The music had stopped. There came the sound of approaching voices. Their privacy was at an end.

Yet for full ten seconds Noel stood widely gazing at the girl before him with eyes in which surprise, hurt pride, and smouldering passion mingled; then very abruptly, as the first chattering couple reached the half-open door, he swung away from her.

"All right!" he said. "Good-bye!"

He went straight out without a glance behind, nearly running into the gay invaders.

Olga, with the instinct to escape notice, turned as swiftly to the window. She went out upon the verandah, blindly groping her way, scarcely aware of her sur-roundings. And a figure waiting there in the dimness laughed a cruel laugh and roughly caught her.

"'You'd sooner marry him,' eh?" gibed a voice close to her ear. "My dear, that's the wisest resolution you ever made in your life!"

She did not cry out or attempt to resist him. She had known that her fate was sealed. Only, as his lips sought hers, she shrank away with every fibre of her being in sick revolt, and for the first time in her life she begged for mercy.

"Please--please--give me to-night!" she pleaded. "Only to-night! Yes, I will marry you. But don't--don't ask--any more of me--to-night!"

He paused, still holding her in his arms, feeling the wild beat of her heart against his own, softened in spite of himself by that quivering, agonized appeal.

"And if I let you go to-night, what will you give me to-morrow?" he said.

"I shall be--your fiancee --to-morrow," she whispered, gasping.

"And you will marry me--when?"

"You shall decide," she murmured faintly.

He laughed rather brutally. "A somewhat empty favour, my dear, since I should have decided in any case. But if you give me your promise to come to me like a sensible girl, without any more nonsense of any kind--"

"I will!" she said. "I will!"

"Then--" he released her with the words--"I give you your freedom--till to-morrow. Go--and make the most of it!"

He had not kissed her. She slipped from his arms, thankful for his forbearance, and sped away down the veranda like a shadow.

As for Hunt-Goring, he cursed himself for a soft fool and took out his cigarettes to wile away what promised to be an evening of infernal dullness.

CHAPTER XXIII
THE GIFT OF THE RAJAH

Olga danced that night with the feeling that she danced upon her grave, reminding herself continually, as the hours slipped by, that it was her last night of freedom.

The failure of Nick to appear for the supper-dances diverted her thoughts from this but to send them with ever-growing anxiety into a new channel. Where was Nick? What was happening to him? What could be delaying him?

She had no partner to take her in to supper, refusing each one that offered with the repeated declaration that she must wait for Nick. But Nick came not, and momentarily her uneasiness increased.

Sir Reginald came to her at last, his kindly face full of sympathy. "There is probably no occasion for alarm, my dear," he said. "Come, give me the pleasure of your company at supper!"

She had to yield, for he would take no refusal; but she could eat nothing notwithstanding his utmost solicitude. She was in a state of mind to start at every sudden sound, and the food he put before her remained untasted on her plate.

Sir Reginald watched over her with fatherly concern, but he could do nothing to alleviate her anxiety. In his own private soul he shared it to a considerable degree.

As they left the supper-room together, she turned to him piteously. "Oh, do you think I might go back and see if he has returned? Really, I can't--I can't dance any more!"

"Wait a little longer!" he counselled. "You needn't dance of course. Stay quietly with me! He may walk in at any moment."

She longed to go, but could not refuse a suggestion so kindly proffered. She stayed with him therefore, glad of his protecting presence, refusing to dance any more on the plea of fatigue.

The whirling scene wearied her unspeakably. She found herself watching Noel, who was frankly flirting with every woman in the room. It was doubtless a safe pastime, but behind her gnawing anxiety a little spark of resentment kindled and burned. How hopelessly fickle he was!

Hunt-Goring had apparently removed himself from the gay company altogether, for she saw him not at all. His absence was the only palliating circumstance in that hour of sick suspense.

It was growing late and the remaining dances were few, when a native orderly entered the room and stepped up to Colonel Bradlaw, who was standing with Sir Reginald. He murmured a few low words to which the Colonel listened with a frown. It was his habit to frown always at the unexpected.

He turned after a moment to Sir Reginald. "There's a messenger arrived from the Palace with a box of sweets or something. What?" breaking off ferociously as the orderly's lips moved soundlessly.

"Moonstones, sahib," murmured the orderly with deference.

"Moonstones," repeated the Colonel, in a tone of vast contempt, "to be presented to the lady wearing the best make-up in the room. What on earth am I to do, sir?"

"Accept with thanks, I should say," said Sir Reginald, with a smile.

"Oh, I don't mean that," said the Colonel, frowning still more. "But who the dickens is going to decide as to the merits of the ladies' costumes? Not I--and not my wife! It's too big a responsibility--that."

Sir Reginald laughed. "That is a serious consideration, certainly. I should make them decide themselves. Vote by ballot. That ought to satisfy everyone."

The Colonel turned to the waiting orderly. "Very well. Tell the messenger to come in!" He made a sign to Noel, who had just ceased to dance, that brought the young man to his side.

"Look here, Wyndham! You organized this show, so you may as well take on this job. The Rajah has sent a prize for the lady wearing the best costume."

Noel frowned also at the news. "Confound him! What for, sir?"

"Oh, I suppose he wants to make himself popular," said the Colonel, still mightily contemptuous. "We can't refuse it anyway. Arrange for the ladies to vote by ballot, will you? They will probably all vote for themselves," he added to Sir Reginald. "But that's a detail. And I say, Noel, get a table from somewhere, will you? It's your show, not mine."

Noel smiled upon his commanding-officer, an impudent, affectionate smile. He and Badgers were close allies. "Very good, sir, I'll see to it," he said, and departed.

Under his directions a table was brought in and placed at the end of the room. The dancing was stopped temporarily, and the dancers lined up against the walls. Noel, armed with a sheaf of note-paper went the round, tearing off slips and distributing them as he went.

While this was in progress, the Rajah's messenger was admitted and conducted to the table behind which stood Sir Reginald with Olga and Colonel Bradlaw. He was a very magnificent person, turbaned and glittering; he bore himself like the servant of an emperor. In his hands he carried with extreme care an ivory casket, exquisitely carved, with a lock of wrought Indian gold. The key, also of gold, lay on the top of the casket.

The gift was plainly a costly one, and every eye in the room followed it.

The messenger reached the table and bowed low. "With the compliments of His Highness the Rajah of Sharapura!" he said, and deposited the casket upon the table.

The Colonel glanced at Sir Reginald who at once responded. "Convey our thanks to the Rajah," he said, "and say that the gracious gift will be much appreciated! I shall give myself the pleasure of calling upon him to assure him of this in person to-morrow."

The messenger salaamed again deeply, and withdrew.

"I wish he'd keep his precious moonstones!" grumbled the Colonel. "They are more bother than they're worth. Hurry up, there, Noel! It's getting late."

"Just finished, sir," came Noel's cheery answer. "I must just get a hat to hold the ballot-papers."

He did not offer a paper to Olga, who still kept her place by Sir Reginald, her young face white and tired under the pile of fair, powdered hair.

"I think I shall go when this is over," she whispered to Sir Reginald.

"So you shall," he said kindly. "I will escort you myself. I expect we shall find

Nick waiting for us," he added, with a smile. "Some business has delayed him, I have no doubt."

She tried to smile in answer, but her lips quivered in spite of her. She turned her face aside, ashamed of her weakness.

Noel came up with the ballot-papers, and emptied them out upon the table without a glance at her.

"I must get you to help," said Sir Reginald, drawing her gently forward.

"I can manage, sir," said Noel shortly.

But the Colonel broke in, "Nonsense, Wyndham! One scrutineer isn't enough."

And Noel pushed across a handful of papers to Olga without lifting his eyes.

With fingers that trembled slightly, she began to sort, assisted by Sir Reginald. Several of the papers bore her own name, a fact which at first she scarcely noticed, but which very soon became too conspicuous to be ignored.

"I believe it's yours," murmured Sir Reginald at her elbow.

"Oh, impossible!" she said, flushing.

But in a very few minutes the suspicion was verified. Noel looked up from his sorting with a brief, "You've won!"

Olga raised her eyes swiftly, but he instantly averted his, and turned to communicate the result to the Colonel.

The latter shook hands with her, and shouted the news in his loudest parade voice to the assembled company. There ensued applause and congratulations that Olga would gladly have foregone. Then, as her friends began to press round, Sir Reginald stepped forward.

"It is my proud privilege," he said, "to present to Miss Ratcliffe in the Rajah's name his very handsome gift."

He took the golden key from the top of the casket and handed it with a bow to Olga.

She took it with a murmur of thanks, and stood hesitating, possessed by a very curious feeling of dread.

"Open it!" said Noel impatiently.

"Open it for her!" said Sir Reginald, divining a certain amount of nervousness as the cause of her hesitation.

Noel held out a hand for the key, and she gave it to him. There was a sudden hush and a little thrill of expectation in the motley crowd gathered round as he turned to fit it into the lock.

The key did not fit in very easily; it seemed to meet with some obstruction. With a frown Noel pulled it out again. "What's the matter with the thing?" he said irritably.

"Try it the other way up!" suggested Sir Reginald.

"I believe it's a hoax," said a man in the crowd.

Noel turned the key upside down amid an interested silence, and began to insert it again in the lock.

As he did so, there came a sudden cry from the background, a man's voice shrill and warning.

"Leave the thing alone! It's a bomb! I tell you, it's a bomb!"

"What?" The crowd scattered backwards as though a thunderbolt had fallen in its midst, and a woman shrieked in panic.

A man--wild, unkempt, ragged--tore like a maniac over the polished floor, making for the group at the table, waving one skinny arm.

"Noel! You damn' fool! Leave the thing alone!"

Noel whizzed round with the key in his hand. "Hullo,--Nick!" he said.

"Leave it alone! Leave it alone!" The voice dropped to a hoarse croak. The man was close to the table now, and in amazement Olga recognized the face of the old moonstone-seller. But it was convulsed with a terror such as she had never seen on the face of any man.

The bony hand darted out towards the casket, and her heart stood still. She knew that hand--wiry, energetic, capable.

"Nick!" she whispered. "Nick!"

He brushed her aside, and, again in that dry, breathless croak, "There isn't--a moment--to lose!" he said.

In another instant he would have had the shining thing in his grasp, but in that instant Noel's wits leaped to full understanding. He wheeled, caught the newcomer by his tattered garment, and flung him violently away.

"All right, you old joker!" he said. "My job!"

Dazed with horror, though still scarcely realizing, Olga saw him turn and lift the ivory casket, holding it clasped firmly between his hands. Then, with a set face, stepping warily, he moved to the window close behind.

In the other part of the room women were crying and men deeply cursing; but there near the table no one uttered a sound, till the ragged creature on the floor sprang up crying hoarsely for a pail of water.

Noel's figure passed through the open window as he did so, smoothly, unfalteringly, and so out upon the dark verandah.

Deftly, warily, he made his way. The thing between his hands weighed heavily. It would have been no job for a one-armed man.

He passed down the verandah with every nerve strung to the moment's emergency. Unquestionably he was not afraid, but he could have wished that the place had been better illuminated. His progress would have been considerably quicker.

He neared the flight of six steps that led down to the compound, and suddenly became aware of a dark figure lounging in a wicker-chair ahead of him. He saw the glow of a cigarette.

He raised his voice. "Hi, you! Clear out! Git--if you value your life! There's going to be an explosion!"

He did not slacken his pace as he uttered his warning. He dared not pause. His whole heart was set on reaching the compound in time.

The figure in the chair turned towards him. He heard the creak of the bamboo. But it made no movement to rise.

"Confound you! Take your chance then!" said Noel between his teeth.

He came closer. He saw in a momentary glance the face behind the cigarette. Heavy, drugged eyes looked up to his. Then in the dimness he heard a sudden movement, a snarling, devilish laugh.

The next instant he kicked against an obstruction, staggered, fought madly to recover himself, tripped a second time, and with a yell of rage fell headlong.

There came a flash of blinding, intolerable brightness--a roar as of the roar of a cannon, stunning, deafening, devastating,--the smaller sound of wood splintering and falling,--and then a dumb and awful silence more fearful than Death.

*   *   *   *   *

The first to arrive on that scene of darkness and destruction was the old moon-stone-seller. He seemed to be gifted with eyes of extraordinary keenness, for he made his way unerringly, with the agility of a monkey among the splintered debris. One corner of the mess-house had completely gone, leaving a gaping hole into the ante-room. Dimly the lamps within shone upon the wreckage. The crowd from the ball-room, horror-stricken, fearful, were gathered about the doorway. The atmosphere was thick with dust and smoke.

Light as an acrobat the moonstone-seller stepped among the ruins, then paused to listen.

"Is there anyone here?" he asked aloud. "Noel, are you here?"

There was no answer. The awful, tragic silence closed in upon his words.

But it did not daunt him. Cautiously he crept a little further forward. And now there came a voice from the room behind him, Colonel Bradlaw's voice, harsh with suspense.

"Is the boy dead?"

"Don't know yet, sir," came back the answer. "Will you send a lantern? Ah! Hullo!"

Something had moved against his foot. Something writhed and groaned.

The searcher stooped. "Hullo!" he said again. "Noel, is it you, lad? I'm here. I'll help you."

A voice answered him--a smothered inarticulate voice. A groping hand came up, clutching for deliverance. There came the slip and crackle of broken wood beneath which some living object struggled and fought for freedom.

The one wiry arm of the moonstone-seller went down to the rescue. It did good service that night--such service as astonished even its owner when he had time to think.

The man under the debris was making titanic efforts, thrusting his way upwards with desperate, frantic strength. Once as he strove he uttered a sharp, agonized cry, and the man above him swore in fierce, instinctive sympathy.

"Where are you hurt, old chap? Keep your head, for Heaven's sake! Where is it worst?"

The gasping voice made answer with spasmodic effort: "My head--my face--my eyes! Oh, God,--my eyes!"

There followed a cough as if something choked all utterance, and then again that mute, gigantic struggle for freedom.

It was over at last. Out of the wreckage there staggered the dreadful likeness of a man. The lantern had been brought and shone full upon the ghastly sight. He was torn, battered, half-naked, and the whole of his face was blackened and streaming with blood.

"Noel! Is it Noel?" asked Colonel Bradlaw.

And the man himself made answer, spitting forth the blood that impeded his utterance.

"Yes, it's me! But I'm done, sir! I'm done! Bring a light someone! I can't see--where I'm going!"

The moonstone-seller's arm was round him, holding him up. "All right, lad! I've got you!" he said.

"But bring a light! Bring a light!" A note of panic ran through the reiterated words "Confound it! I must see--I will see--I--"

"My dear lad, you can't see for a minute." It was Nick's voice, quick and soothing. "This infernal blood has got into your eyes. Come and have them attended to! You'll be better directly."

"No! It's not the blood! It's not the blood!" The words tumbled over each other, well-nigh incoherent in their fevered utterance. And suddenly Noel flung up his arms above his head with a wild and anguished cry. "My God! I'm blind! I'm blind!"

With the cry his strength--that fiery strength born of emergency--collapsed quite suddenly. His knees doubled under him. He fell forward in utter, overwhelming impotence, and lay prone and senseless at the Colonel's feet....

CHAPTER XXIV
THE BIG, BIG GAME OF LIFE

It was many hours later that understanding returned to Noel. He came to himself abruptly, in utter darkness, with the horror of it still strong within his soul. His head was swathed in bandages. He turned it to and fro with restless jerks.

"And will ye please to lie quiet?" said the voice of the Irish regimental surgeon peremptorily by his side.

Noel, also Irish, collected his forces and made reply. "No. Why the devil should I? Where am I? What's going to happen to me? Am I--am I blind for life?"

The falter in the words spoke to the tenseness of his suspense. The doctor answered instantly, with more of kindliness than judgment. "Faith, no! It's not so bad as that. But ye'll have to pretend ye are for the present, or, egad, ye will be before ye've done. We brought ye to the Musgraves' shanty. Mrs. Musgrave wanted the care of ye. Damn' quare taste on her part, I'm thinking. And now ye're not to talk any more; but drink this stuff like a good boy and go to sleep."

Noel drank with disgust; the taste of blood was still in his mouth. He had never been ill in his life before, and he had not the smallest intention of obeying the doctor's orders.

"Let's hear what happened!" he said impatiently. "Oh, leave me alone, do! When can I have this beastly bandage off my eyes?"

"Not for a very long while, my son." The doctor's voice was jaunty, but the eyes that looked at the blind, swathed face were full of pity. "And don't ye go loosening it when my back's turned, or it isn't meself that'll be answerable for the consequences."

"Oh, damn the consequences!" said Noel. "I want to get up."

"And that ye can't!" was the doctor's prompt rejoinder. "Ye'll just lie quiet till further orders. Ye'll find yourself as weak as a rat moreover, when ye start to move about. It's only the fever in your veins that makes ye want to try."

Noel straightened himself in the bed. He was becoming aware of a fiery, throbbing torture beneath the bandages. With clenched teeth and hands hard gripped he set himself to endure.

But in a few minutes he turned his head again. "Are you still there, Maloney?"

"Still here, my son," said Maloney.

"Well, go and find someone--anyone who knows--to tell me exactly what happened last night."

"I can tell ye meself," began Maloney.

But Noel interrupted. "No; not you! You're such a liar. No offence meant! You can't help it. Find--find Nick, will you?"

"It isn't visitors ye ought to be having with your pulse in this state," objected Maloney.

"Do as I say!" commanded Noel stubbornly.

His will prevailed. The Irish doctor saw the futility of argument, and departed, having extracted a promise from his patient not to move during his absence.

And then came silence as well as darkness, an awful sense of being entombed, an isolation that appalled him added to the torture that racked. With an acuteness of consciousness more harrowing than delirium, he faced this thing that had come upon him, grabbing all his courage to endure the ordeal.

He felt as if his brain were on fire, each nerve-centre agonizing separately in the intolerable, all-enveloping flames. And through the dreadful stillness he heard the beat, beat, beat, of his heart, like the feet of a runaway along a desert road.

He turned his head again restlessly from side to side. The agony was beginning to master him. His powers of endurance were dwindling.

Suddenly he found himself speaking, scarcely knowing what he said, feeling that he must cry out or die.

"Lighten our darkness, we beseech Thee, O God!" Just the one sentence over and over to save him from raving insanity. "Lighten our darkness! Lighten our darkness! Lighten our darkness, we beseech Thee!"

He broke off abruptly. What was the good? Prayers were for white-souled children like Peggy. Was it likely that any cry of his would pierce the veil?

Yet the words came back to him, so urgent was his distress, so unbearable the silence of his desert. He said them again with a desperate earnestness, and almost instinctively began to listen for an answer. He felt almost a child again himself in his utter need, as he wrestled to drive the awful darkness from his soul. But no answer came to his cry and the brave heart of him slowly sank. He was deserted then, hurled down into hell to die a living death. In a single flashing second he had been torn from the world he loved--that bright, gay world in which he had revelled all his life--and flung into this inferno of endless darkness. The iron began to bite into his soul.

The glory of his youth was quenched. From thenceforth he would hear the music from afar, he would be barred out from the splendour of life, he would wander along the outside edge of things, forlorn and lonely. His popularity, his brilliance, his joy of living, had all been crushed to atoms with that single, sledge-hammer blow of Fate. Better--ten thousand times better--to have killed him outright! For this thing was infinitely worse than death.

The iron drove in a little deeper. His spirit, his pride, awoke and rebelled, raging impotently. He would not bear the burden. He would die somehow. He would find a means, do what they would to stop him. He would escape--somehow--from this particular hell. He would not be chained between life and death. He would burst the bonds. He would be free!

His pulses rose to fever pitch. He started up upon the bed. Now was the time--now--now! He might not have another chance. And there must be some means to his hand--some way out of this awful darkness!

The madness of fever urged him. In another moment he would have been on his feet, at grips with the fate that bound him; but even as he gathered himself together for the effort, something happened.

The door opened and a woman entered. He heard the swish of her draperies, and his heart gave a great throb and paused.

"Who is it?" he said, and his voice was harsh and dry even to his own hearing. "Who is it? Speak to me!"

She spoke, and his heart, released from the sudden check, leaped on at a pace that nearly suffocated him. "It's I, Noel,--Olga! They said I might come and see you.

You don't mind?"

"Mind!" he said, and suddenly a great sob burst from him. He felt out towards her with hands that wildly groped. "Let me feel you!" he entreated. "I--I'll let you go again!"

And then very suddenly her arms were all around him, closing him in, lifting him out of his hell. "Noel! My own Noel!" she whispered. "My own, splendid boy!"

He held her fast, his battered head pillowed against her while he fought for self-control. For many seconds he could not utter a word. And in the silence the world he knew opened its gates to him again and took him back. The darkness remained indeed, but it had been lightened. The horror of it no longer tore his soul. The iron had been withdrawn.

He moved at last, drawing her hand to his lips. "Olga, you don't know what you've saved me from. I was--in hell."

"Lie down, dear!" she murmured softly. "I'm going to take care of you now." She added, as she shook up the pillow, "It's my business, isn't it?"

He sank back with a sense of great comfort, holding her hand fast in his. It made the darkness less dark to hold her so.

"I want to know what happened," he said. "Sit down and tell me!"

"And you will try to keep quiet," she urged gently.

"Yes--yes! But don't keep anything back! Tell me everything!"

"I will, dear," she said, "though really there isn't much to tell. Is that quite comfy? You're not in bad pain?"

"I can bear it," he said. "Go on! Let's hear!"

So, sitting by his side, her hand in his, Olga told him.

The plot had been of Kobad Shikan's devising. Nick had been on the watch for it for some time, had penetrated the city nightly in the garb of a moonstone-seller, collecting evidence, and--most masterly stroke of all--he had drawn the Rajah into partnership with him. It was due to Nick's influence alone that the Rajah had not been caught in Kobad Shikan's toils. Thanks to Nick's steady call upon his loyalty, he had remained staunch. But Kobad Shikan had been too powerful a tactician to overthrow openly. They had been forced to work against him in secret.

"The Rajah calls Nick his brother," said Olga.

"Like his cheek!" said Noel. "Not that I can talk myself. I took the liberty of kicking him off his own premises once." He chuckled involuntarily at the recollection and commanded her to continue.

So Olga went on to tell of old Kobad's final coup and of how the Rajah, receiving news of some mischief afoot, had sent an urgent message of warning that had taken Nick straight to the Palace. Thence he had gone in disguise to the haunts of Kobad Shikan's conspirators, but here he had received a check. Kobad Shikan, fearing treachery among his followers, had taken elaborate precautions to conceal his proceedings, and for hours Nick had been kept searching vainly for a clue. Then at last he had succeeded in running the truth to earth, had discovered the whole ghastly plot barely half an hour before the time fixed for its consummation, and had raced to the mess-house with his warning.

"And that's all, is it?" said Noel.

"Yes, that's all; except that old Kobad has disappeared. Nick seems sorry, but everyone else is glad."

"And what about--Hunt-Goring?" said Noel at last.

Olga's fingers tightened in his hold. "Oh, did you know he was there?" she said.

Briefly he made answer. "Yes, he tripped me. I believe he was half-drunk with opium or something. What happened? Was he killed?"

Noel's voice was imperious. She answered him instantly, seeing he demanded it.

"Yes."

Noel drew a deep breath. "Thank God for that!" he said. "Then you are free'"

Olga was silent.

"You are free?" he repeated, with quick interrogation.

Yet an instant longer she hesitated. Then she leaned her head against his pillow with a little sob. "No,--I'm not free, Noel. I--have given myself--to you!"

"Because I'm blind!" he said.

"No, dear, no! Once free--I should have come to you--in any case."

"Would you?" he said. "Would you? You're quite sure? You're not saying it out of pity? I won't have you marry me out of pity, Olga. I couldn't stand it."

"Oh, you needn't be afraid of that!" she said. Then a moment later, "When I marry you," she murmured softly, "it will be--for love."

There was no mistaking the sincerity of the words, though even then as it were in spite of himself he knew that the passionate adoration he had poured out to her had awakened no answering rapture in her heart. The very fashion of her surrender told him this. He might come first with her indeed, but the full gift was no longer hers to offer.

"I wonder if you will be happy with me," he said, after a moment.

"It is my only chance of happiness," she made answer.

"How do you know?" There was curiosity in his voice: he made a movement of impatient impotence, putting a hand that trembled up to his bandaged head.

She took the hand, and drew it softly down. "I will tell you how I know," she said. "I know because when I thought you were killed I felt--I felt as if the world had stopped. And since then--since I knew that you would live--I have been able to think of only you--only you." Her voice broke upon a sound of tears. "That awful fear for you opened my eyes," she whispered. "I haven't been able to think of Major Hunt-Goring's death or anything else at all. I've even deserted Nick." Valiantly, through her tears, she smiled. "I never did such a thing as that before for anyone."

He clasped her hands tightly as he lay. "Don't cry, sweetheart!" he whispered. "You're not crying--for me?"

"I can't help it," she whispered back. "I can't bear to think of you suffering,--you, Noel, you!"

"Don't cry!" he said again, and this time there was a hint of grimness in his voice. "I shall win through--somehow--for your sweet sake. Maloney told me I wasn't blind just now. That, I know, was a lie. Or at least he didn't believe it himself. Personally I feel as if my eyes have been blown clean out of my head. But--blind or otherwise--I'll stick to it, I'll stick to it, Olga. I'll make you happy, so help me, God!"

"My dearest!" she murmured. "My dearest!"

"And you're not to cry over me," he said despotically. "You're not to fret--ever. If you do, I--I shall be furious." He uttered a quivering laugh. "We'll play the game, dear, shall we, the big, big game of life? It won't be easy, God knows; but He lightened my darkness--very first time of asking too. So perhaps He'll give us a tip now and then as to the moves."

He fell silent for a space, and she wondered if he were growing drowsy. Then as she sat motionless by his side, closely watching him, she saw the boyish lips part in their own sunny smile.

"Go and tell Mrs. Musgrave to hoist a flag!" he said. "Say it's the luckiest day of my life!"

The lips quivered a little over the words, but they continued bravely to smile.

And Olga understood. The boy had shouldered his burden with all his soldier's spirit, and nothing would daunt him now. He had begun to play the game.

She herself rose to the occasion with instant resolution, forcing back the tears he would not suffer, brave because he was brave.

"I shall tell her to hoist one for us both," she said, "and to keep it flying as long as we are under her roof."

CHAPTER XXV
MEMORIES THAT HURT

Well, Max! You're just off then?" Sir Kersley Whitton looked up with a smile to greet his partner as he entered.

"Just off," said Max.

He came to Sir Kersley, seated at his writing-table, and paused beside him. It was a day in April, showery, shot with fleeting gleams of sunshine that sent long golden shafts across the doctor's room.

"You will bring the boy here then?" said Sir Kersley.

"Yes, straight here. It's very good of you, Kersley." Max's hand lay for a moment on the great man's shoulder.

"Nonsense, my dear fellow! I'm as keen as you are." Sir Kersley leaned back in his chair. "I only hope we may be successful," he said. "Is he likely to be a good patient?"

"Quite the reverse, I should say." Max sounded grim. "But I expect I can manage him."

Sir Kersley smiled again. "Just as you managed me a couple of years ago, eh? Yes, I should say you will be fully competent in that respect. You have a way with you, eh, Max? What was it this Indian doctor said?"

"He believed a cure possible, but only under the most favourable conditions. The boy was in no state then to undergo an operation, and he funked the job." Max's tone was contemptuous.

"Ah, well! It's as well he didn't attempt it in that case," said Sir Kersley. "He will stand a better chance with us. And what about Captain Ratcliffe and Olga? Will they go straight home?"

"No," said, Max. He paused a moment, then said rather shortly, "I had a line from Dr. Jim. He says she won't leave Noel. He and Mrs. Ratcliffe are coming up to meet them, but he expects to go back alone."

"Captain and Mrs. Ratcliffe will stay in town with Olga, then?" asked Sir Kersley.

"I believe so."

Sir Kersley's grey eyes regarded him thoughtfully. "And she is still in the dark with regard to Miss Campion's death?" he asked, after a moment.

Max's eyes came swiftly downwards, meeting his look with something of the effect of a challenge. "Yes, absolutely," he said.

"It's an extraordinary case," observed Sir Kersley.

Max said nothing whatever. He took his pipe from his pocket, and began to fill it with a face of sardonic composure.

"I wonder if she ever asks herself how it came about," said Sir Kersley.

"Why should she?" said Max gruffly.

"My dear fellow, she must have wondered how it happened--why all details were kept from her--and so on."

"Why should she?" said Max again aggressively. "The subject is a painful one. She is willing enough to avoid it. Of course," he paused momentarily, "Noel doesn't know about that affair either. No one knows besides ourselves, but Dr. Jim and Nick."

"In my opinion Noel ought to know," said Sir Kersley, with quiet decision. "It would be a terrible thing for Olga if some day--after they were married--she remembered, and he were in ignorance of it."

Again Max's hand pressed his friend's shoulder, but this time the pressure was one of warning. "Kersley," he said, "I've been into all that. I've weighed every possible contingency that might arise. And I have decided against telling Noel. As you say, it would be a terrible thing if she ever remembered; but if Noel is left in ignorance, the chances are she never will remember. To tell him would be to put a shadow between them which he would never forget and she would in time come to be aware of. It would wreck their happiness sooner or later. No; in Heaven's name, leave them in peace!"

"I think you are wrong," Sir Kersley said. He was looking straight up into Max's face with eyes of shrewd kindliness. "I think it is extremely improbable that she never will remember. And I think, moreover, that it is hardly to be desired that she should not."

"I disagree with you!" said Max harshly.

"Yes, my dear fellow, I know you do. You are no impartial judge. You want--very naturally--to save her from any suffering. And I don't think you will succeed. If you could have persuaded her to marry you, you might have done it. Forewarned is forearmed; you would have known how to safeguard her. But utter ignorance is no safeguard at all. I don't think she would thank you for it--if she knew."

Max's mouth twisted in its most cynical smile. "I wonder," he said.

Sir Kersley said no more. Beyond the bare fact of his brief engagement and its rupture, Max had confided in him not at all. He had left him to infer that she had been caught by a nearer attraction in his absence--an inference which her present engagement to his brother had seemed to confirm. And Sir Kersley had been far too considerate to probe for further enlightenment. But he was not privately by any means satisfied with regard to the matter of Max's long and fruitless journey. He was not accustomed to seeing Max beaten, and the spectacle hurt him.

He urged his opinion no further, for it was evident that Max was firmly determined to withstand it; but when Max had gone he sat and contemplated the matter with a troubled frown. There seemed to be something he had not fathomed behind Max's silence.

As for Max he departed for the docks with that air of grimness that had somewhat grown on him of late. Though bound upon a welcoming errand, he knew that it was not going to be a particularly easy one.

He was somewhat late in arriving, and the great steamer had already come to her moorings. Among the waiting crowd he discerned Dr. Jim and Muriel, but he did not make his way to them. He knew they would meet later, and he was not feeling sociable that afternoon.

So he stood aloof and waited, searching the many faces that lined the deck-rails for the one face that alone he longed to see. He spied her at last, and was conscious of a momentary pang that he fiercely stifled. She was standing there at the rail above him, waving her handkerchief to Dr. Jim. Nick was on one side of her, also madly waving and yelling with futile energy. On the other side stood Noel. And at sight of him Max's grim face softened to tenderness.

"There's grit in the boy," he murmured.

For Noel, with a black shade covering his bandaged eyes, was obviously as merry as any there. He was holding Peggy Musgrave perched on his shoulder, and his thin, brown face was upturned and laughing. There seemed to be some joke going on between them, for Peggy was also chuckling vigorously, and as Max watched she slipped a caressing hand round Noel's chin and tenderly kissed him.

Daisy and Will Musgrave were standing next to them, but they were plainly not thinking of Peggy or her cavalier. They were very close together and hand in hand.

It was nearly an hour later that Max joined the party as they came ashore. Noel's pleasure at meeting him was very obvious. He gripped him by both hands.

"Old chap, you're a brick to come and meet me!" he said. "I was thinking of asking Trevor, but I'd ten times sooner have you."

"Trevor's away," Max said. "I've come to take possession of you altogether. I suppose you've no objection?"

"Objection!" laughed Noel. He pushed his hand through his brother's arm. "You'll have to pilot me," he said. "I'm getting used to things, but I can't find my way in a crowd yet."

And then came the meeting with Olga. It was very brief. For barely the fraction of a second her hand lay in Max's. Her greeting was quite inaudible.

Noel turned to her. "Olga, Max wants me to clear out at once with him. You're going to Marriot's with Nick of course. I shall come round and see you to-night."

"Perhaps Olga will come and see you instead," said Max. "Is Dr. Jim spending the night in town? Bring him to dine! I will speak to him, shall I?"

He passed on and made the arrangement with Dr. Jim, not waiting for her reply.

Then came a general rallying of the party, introductions and good-byes, fervent embraces from Peggy, good wishes and invitations on all sides, and at last the final departure of the two Wyndhams in Sir Kersley Whitton's motor.

Noel removed his hat and leaned back with a sigh. "It's been a ripping voyage," he said. "But I'm deuced glad it's over." He added with a laugh, as Max made no comment. "I shall miss Peggy though. She's been blind man's dog to me all through."

"Let us hope you won't need a dog to lead you about much longer!" said Max.

Whereat Noel's hand came out gropingly, with a certain diffidence. "Oh, man," he said, "I haven't dared to think of that!"

Max grasped the hand. "I'll do my best for you, old chap," he said. "But you'll need a thundering lot of patience."

"I've been cultivating that," said Noel. "The only thing I can't stand is not to know the truth."

"I shan't keep you in the dark," said Max. "It's not my way."

He was as good as his word. A few hours later he made his first examination of the injury, and curtly gave it as his opinion that it was not beyond remedy.

"I don't profess to be infallible," he said. "But there certainly seems to be just a chance that the sight has not been absolutely destroyed. I'm afraid you'll have a good deal to go through if it is to be restored, though. It will be a tough job for all concerned."

"Oh, I'm not afraid of that," said Noel sturdily. "I've the very best of reasons for sticking to it."

"Ah!" said Max, with his twisted smile. "I haven't congratulated you yet."

Noel turned with a quick movement. "I say, Max," he said, with a touch of embarrassment, "you weren't quite straight with me over that, were you?"

"I don't know what you mean," said Max in a voice that was utterly devoid of expression.

Noel's face was red, but he stuck to his point. "You didn't tell me why she broke with you," he said.

"Who did?" demanded Max.

"Hunt-Goring."

Max swallowed a remark which sounded more savage suppressed than if it had been fully audible.

"You had a row with him then?"

"Yes, I did. I couldn't help it. I told him it was a damned lie," said Noel.

Max grunted.

Noel proceeded with a hint of that doggedness that characterized them both. "After that, I saw Olga; it was before we got engaged. And I told her it was a lie too."

Max grunted again, stubbornly refraining from question or comment.

Noel, equally stubborn, continued. "She said it was the truth--said you had ad-mitted it to her. I didn't--quite--believe it even then. Thinking about it since, I am pretty sure you didn't do actually that. Or if you did, it was a lie."

Max maintained an uncompromising silence.

Noel waited a moment, then squarely tackled him. "Max, why did you lie to her?"

"And if I didn't?" said Max very deliberately.

Noel made instant and winning reply. "Oh, you needn't ask me to believe that tomfool tale, old chap! I know you too well for that."

"All right," said Max. "Then you know quite as much as is good for you. If you want to be ready in time to meet your fiancee, you had better let Kersley's man lend you a hand with your dressing. I will send him to you."

He was at the door with the words. Noel heard him open it and go out. He sat where Max had left him with a puzzled frown between his brows.

"I wish I knew the fellow's game," he murmured. "I wish--"

He broke off. What was the good of wishing? Moreover, to be quite honest, perhaps he was more or less satisfied with things as they were. Max had probably got over his disappointment to a certain extent by this time. It was quite obvious that he had no desire or intention to reopen the matter. No, on the whole perhaps it was indiscreet to probe too deeply. Every man had a right to his own secrets. And meantime, Olga was his--was his, and there remained this glorious possibility that his sight might be restored also.

He put up his hands suddenly, covering those useless, tortured eyes. A very cu-rious tremor went through him. His heart began to throb thick and hard. It seemed too good to be true. Since that first awful day he had not fought against Fate, refrain-ing himself even in his worst hours of darkness and suffering, and now it seemed that Fate was going to be kind after all. Like Job, he was to receive all--and more also--that he had lost.

He broke into a quivering laugh. "Good old Job!" he said. "We're not all such lucky beggars as that."

And then again that odd little tremor went through him. It was like a warning, almost a presentiment. His hands fell. He sat straight and still, as one waiting for a sign. No, such things didn't happen. Luck like Job's was apocryphal, abnormal, outside the bounds of human possibility. They might give him back his sight, but--He stopped here as if brought up by a sudden obstacle.

"I wonder if I'm a fool to have that operation," he said. "I wonder if--she--will like me as well if I get back my sight."

The doubt pressed cold at his heart. She had been so divinely kind to him ever since the catastrophe. She had literally given herself up to him, making his darkness light. And vaguely he knew that she had loved the doing of it, had loved to know that he needed her. How would it be, he asked himself, when he needed her thus no longer? Would she love him as well in strength as in weakness? Would she be as near to him when he no longer needed her to lead him by the hand?

He sprang to his feet with a gesture of fierce impatience. He flung the doubt away. Her love was not fashioned of so slender a fabric as this. What right had he to question it thus?

But yet, despite all self-reproach, the doubt remained, repudiate it as he might. It went with him even into her loved presence, refusing to be dislodged.

She came with her father to dine in accordance with Max's invitation. The evening passed with absolute smoothness. Sir Kersley and Dr. Jim were old friends, and had a good deal to say to one another. Max was present at the table, but withdrew early, alleging that he had a serious case to attend. Olga and Noel were left to themselves.

They retired to Sir Kersley's drawing-room and spent the rest of the evening there. Olga was evidently tired, and Noel provided most of the conversation. Noel was never silent for any length of time. He lay on the sofa talking with cheery inconsequence, scarcely pausing for any response, till presently he worked round to the subject of his blindness--a subject which by tacit consent they seldom discussed.

"Max has had a look at me," he said. "He thinks they may be able to switch the light on again. They will have to tighten up a few screws, or something of the kind. He didn't let me into the whole ghastly process, but gave me to understand it wouldn't be exactly a picnic. I don't know how long it's going to take; some time, I fancy. You'll pay me a visit now and then, won't you?"

It was then that Olga came very suddenly out of her silence, moved impulsively to him, and knelt by his side, her hands on his.

"Noel!" she said.

He turned to her swiftly, gathering her hands up to his lips. "What, darling?"

"Noel,--" she paused an instant, then with a rush came the words--"let us be married very soon! Let us be married--before the operation!"

"My darling girl!" said Noel in astonishment.

"Yes," she said rapidly. "I mean it! I wish it! Dad knows that I wish it. So does Nick. Nick is very good, you know. He--he is going to settle some money on me on my twenty-first birthday. So that needn't be a difficulty. We shall have enough to live upon."

"And you think I'm going to live on you?" said Noel, still with her hands pressed hard against his cheek.

"No," she said. "No. You've got something, I expect. That--with mine--would be enough."

"I've got what my good brother-in-law allows me--besides my pay," said Noel. "I daresay--if the worst happened--he would make a settlement too. But I can't count on that. Besides--the worst isn't going to happen. So cheer up, darling! I shall go back to Badgers yet. Poor old boy! It was decent of him to pay me the compliment of being so cut up, wasn't it? I mustn't forget to send him a cable when the deed is done."

He was switching the conversation into more normal channels with airy inconsequence, but Olga gently brought him back to the point.

"Won't you consider my suggestion?" she said.

He smiled then, his quick, boyish smile. "My darling, I have considered it. I'm afraid it isn't practicable. But thank you a million times over all the same!"

"Noel!" There was keen disappointment in her voice. "Why isn't it practicable?"

He let her hands go, and reached out, drawing her to him. "Don't tempt me, sweetheart!" he said softly. "I'm hound enough as it is to dream of letting you join your life to mine under present conditions. But this other is out of the question. I simply won't do it, dear, so don't ask me!"

"But why not?" she pleaded very earnestly. "I have told you I wish it."

He smiled--a smile that was very tender and yet whimsical also. "So like you, darling," he said. "But it can't be done. There are always chances to be taken in a serious operation; but I don't mean to take more than I can help. I'm not going to chance making you a widow almost before you are a wife."

"Oh, but, Noel--" she protested.

"Yes, really, darling. It's my final word on the subject. We will be married just as soon after the operation as can be decently managed. But not before it, sweetheart. Any fellow who let you do that would be a cur of the lowest degree."

He was holding her in his arms with the words. Her head was against his shoulder. A man had entered the conservatory behind them from an adjoining room, lounging in with his feet in carpet slippers that made no sound.

"And suppose--" it was Olga's voice very low and quivering--"suppose the operation doesn't succeed,--shall you--shall you refuse to marry me then?"

"Not much," said Noel cheerily. "If I'm alive and kicking, I shall want you all the more. No!" He caught himself up sharply. "I don't mean that! I couldn't want you more. Ill or well, I should want you just the same. I only meant--" his voice grew subtly softer, he spoke with great tenderness, his lips moving against her forehead--"I only meant that 'the desert were a paradise, if thou wert there, if thou wert there.'"

She raised her head quickly. There were tears in her eyes. "Noel, how strange that you should say that!"

"Say what, dear?"

"That old song," she said rather incoherently. "It--it has memories for me--memories that hurt."

"What memories?" he asked.

But she could not tell him, and he passed the matter by.

The man in the conservatory drew back with his hands deep in his pockets, and went back by the way he had come.

CHAPTER XXVI
A FOOL'S ERRAND

D r. Jim's expectations, so far as Olga was concerned, were fulfilled. When he went back to Weir, she remained in town with Nick and Muriel. But he did not go back alone. Will, Daisy, and Peggy went with him. Daisy's love for Dr. Jim was almost as great as her love for Nick, and Will had spent his boyhood under his care.

There was a cottage close to the doctor's house which Daisy had tenanted seven or eight years before when she had been obliged to come Home for her health and Will had been left behind in India. Dr. Jim had managed to secure this cottage a second time, and here they were soon installed with all the joy of exiles in an English spring.

"But we are not going to forego the honeymoon," Will said on their first evening, as he and Daisy stood together in the ivy-covered porch.

She laughed--that little laugh of hers half-gay, half-sad, that seemed like a reminiscence of more mirthful days. "Isn't this romantic enough for you?"

He slipped his arm about her waist. "I'm not altogether sure that I did right to let you come here," he said.

"Oh, nonsense!" She leaned her head against him with a very loving gesture. "I am not so morbid as that. I love to be here, and close to dear old Jim. He hasn't altered a bit. He is just as rugged--and as sweet--as ever."

Will laughed. "How you women, do love a masterful man!"

"Oh, not always," said Daisy. "There are certain forms of mastery in a man which to my mind are quite intolerable. Max Wyndham for instance!"

"What! You've still got your knife into him? I'm sorry for the man myself," said Will. "It must be--well, difficult, to say the least of it, to see his brother come home in possession of his girl and to keep smiling."

"He doesn't care!" said Daisy scathingly. "Geniuses haven't time to be human."

"I wonder," said Will.

He knew, and had never ceased to regret, his wife's share in the accomplishment of Max's discomfiture; and he fancied that secretly, her antipathy notwithstanding, she had begun to regret it also.

He changed the subject, and they went on to talk of Noel.

"Olga tells me that they think of operating next Sunday," Daisy said. "How anxious she will be, poor girl! I am thankful she has Nick and Muriel to take care of her. It has been a terrible time for her all through."

"Poor child!" said Will compassionately.

He shrewdly suspected that the time that lay ahead of Olga would be harder to face than any she had yet experienced.

Olga herself had already begun to realize that. Noel's refusal to consider her suggestion had surprised and disappointed her. She had not anticipated his refusal, though she fully understood it and respected him for it. But it made matters infinitely more difficult for her. She longed for the time when Max's part should be done and he should have passed finally out of her life. Not that he intruded upon her in any way. He scarcely so much as glanced in her direction; but his very presence was a perpetual trial to her. She had a feeling that the green eyes were watching continually for some sign of weakness, even though they never looked her way.

Nick was a great comfort to her in those days, but she felt that even he did not wholly grasp the difficulties of the situation. He supported her indeed, but he did not realize precisely where lay the strain. And it was the same with Dr. Jim. He had accepted her engagement without demur after a gruff enquiry as to whether she loved the fellow. But he had not asked for any details, and had made no reference to her former engagement. She supposed that he found out all he wanted to know on this subject from Nick; and she was grateful for his forbearance, albeit, after a woman's fashion, slightly hurt by it.

She had not, however, much time for reflection of any sort during those first days in town. Noel occupied all her thoughts.

On the day before that fixed for the operation, he went into a private nursing-home. He was extremely cheery over all the preparations, and made himself exceedingly popular with his nurses before he had been more than a few hours in the place.

Even Max was somewhat surprised by the boy's fund of high spirits, and Sir Kersley openly expressed his admiration.

"You Wyndhams are a very remarkable family," he said to Max that night.

Max smiled sardonically in recognition of the compliment. "But the boy has more backbone than I thought," he admitted. "I don't think he will give us much trouble after all, thanks to Olga."

"Ah!" Sir Kersley said. "You think this is due to her?"

"In a great measure," said Max.

Sir Kersley's face was grave. "I am afraid the strain is telling upon her," he said.

"You think she looks ill?" Max shot the question with none of his customary composure.

"No, not actually ill," Sir Kersley said, without looking at him. "But she is too thin in my opinion, and she looks to me very highly strung."

"She always was," said Max.

"Yes; well, she mustn't have a nervous break-down if we can prevent it," said Sir Kersley gently.

"No," Max agreed curtly. "She has got to keep up for Noel's sake."

That seemed to be his main idea just then--his brother's welfare. Very resolutely he kept his mind fixed, with all the strength of which it was capable, upon that one object, and he was impatient of every distraction outside his profession.

Late that night he went round for a last look at Noel, and was told by a smiling nurse that he had "gone to sleep as chirpy as a cricket." He went in to see him, and found him slumbering like an infant. The pulse under Max's fingers was absolutely normal, and an odd smile that had in it an element of respect touched Max's grim lips. Certainly the boy had grit.

The first sound he heard when he arrived at the home on the following day was Noel's heartiest laugh. He was enjoying a joke with one of the nurses who was Irish herself and extremely gay of heart. But the moment Max entered, he sobered and asked for Olga.

Olga was in the building with Nick, but they had thought it advisable to keep visitors away from him on the morning of the operation. Noel, however, was absolutely immovable on the point, refusing flatly to proceed until he had seen her. So for five short minutes Olga was admitted and left alone with him.

More than once during those minutes his cheery laugh made itself heard again. He had a hundred and one things to say, not one of which could Olga ever remember afterwards save the last, when, holding her close to him, he whispered, "And if I don't come out of it, sweetheart, you're to marry another fellow; see? No damn' sentimental rot on my account, mind! I never was good enough for you, God knows! There! Run along! Good-bye!"

His kiss was the briefest he had ever given her, but there was something in the manner of its bestowal that pierced her to the heart. Her own farewell was inarticulate. She was only just able to restrain her tears.

But she mastered her weakness almost immediately, for Max was waiting in the passage outside. He was talking to a nurse, and she would have slipped past him without recognition; but he broke off abruptly and joined her, walking back with her to the room where Nick was waiting.

"Look here!" he said, "I don't think you need be so anxious, I give you my word I believe the operation will be a success."

It was so contrary to his custom to express an opinion in this way that Olga raised her eyes almost involuntarily to gaze at him.

His eyes met and held them instantly. He looked at her with a species of stern kindness that seemed to thrust away all painful memories.

"Even if it isn't a success," he said, "I won't let him die, I promise you. Now, will you follow my advice for once?"

"Yes," she murmured, wondering at her own docility.

He smiled upon her with instant approval, and her heart gave a wild leap that almost made her gasp. "That's wise of you," he said in that voice of cool encouragement that she remembered so well--so well! "Then get Nick to take you for a walk that'll last for an hour and a half. Go and look at the frogs in the Serpentine! Awfully interesting things--frogs! And have a glass of milk before you start! Good-bye!"

Strong and steady, his hand closed upon hers, gave it a slight admonitory shake and set it free.

The next moment he had turned and was striding back along the corridor. Olga stood and watched him out of sight, but he did not turn his head.

*   *   *   *   *

The search for frogs in the Serpentine was scarcely as engrossing a pastime as Nick could have desired for the amusement of his charge on that sunny April morning, but he did his valiant best to keep her thoughts on the move. He compelled her to talk when she yearned to be silent, and again in a vague, disjointed fashion Olga wondered at his lack of penetration. Yet, since he was actually obtuse enough to misunderstand her preoccupation and to be even mildly hurt thereby, she exerted herself for his sake to respond intelligently to his remarks. So, with cheery indifference on his part and aching suspense on hers, they passed that dreadful interval of waiting.

On the return journey Olga's knees shook so much that they would scarcely support her; and then it was that Nick seemed suddenly to awake to the situation. He gave her a swift glance, and abruptly offered his arm.

"There, kiddie, there!" he said softly. "Keep a stiff upper lip! It's nearly over."

She accepted his help in silence, and in silence they pursued their way. Nick looked at her no more, nor spoke. His lips were twitching a little, but he showed no other sign of feeling.

So they came at last to the tall building behind its iron railings that hid so many troubles from the world.

The door opened to them, and they went within.

Silence and a curious, clinging perfume met them as they entered.

Olga stood still. She was white to the lips. "Nick," she said, in a voiceless whisper, "Nick, that is--the pain-killer!"

And then, very quietly from a room close by, Max came to them. He glanced at Nick and nodded. There was an odd, exultant look in the green eyes. He took Olga's hands very firmly into his own.

"It's all right," he said.

She stared at him, trying to make her white lips form a question.

"It's all right," he said again. "Well over. As satisfactory as it could possibly be. Now don't be silly!" Surely it was the Max of old times speaking! "Pull up while you can! Come in here and sit down for a minute! I am going to take you to see him directly."

That last remark did more towards restoring Olga's self-control than any of the preceding ones. She went with him submissively, making strenuous efforts to preserve her composure. She even took without a murmur the wineglass of sal volatile with which he presented her.

Max stood beside her, still holding one of her hands, his fingers grasping her wrist, and talked over her head to Nick.

"Absolutely normal in every way. Came round without the least trouble. He'll be on his legs again in a fortnight. Of course we shan't turn him loose for a month, and he will have to live in the dark. But he ought to be absolutely sound in six weeks from now."

"And--he will see?" whispered Olga.

Max bent and laid her hand down. He looked at her closely for a moment. "Yes," he said. "There is no reason why he shouldn't make a complete recovery. Are you all right now? I promised to let him have a word with you."

She stood up. "Yes, I am quite all right. Let us go!"

Her knees still felt weak, but she steadied them resolutely. They went out side by side.

In silence Max piloted her. When they reached the darkened room he took her hand again and led her forward. The cheerful Irish nurse was at the bedside, but she drew away at their approach. And Olga found herself standing above a swathed, motionless figure in hushed expectancy of she knew not what.

The hand that held hers made as if to withdraw itself, but she clung to it suddenly and convulsively, and it closed again.

"All right," said Max's leisurely tones. "He's a bit sleepy still. Noel!" He bent, still holding her hand. "I've brought Olga, old chap, as I promised. Say good-night to her, won't you?"

The voice was the voice of Max Wyndham, but its tenderness seemed to rend her heart. She could have wept for the pain of it, but she knew she must not weep.

The figure in the bed stirred, murmured an incoherent apology, seemed to awake.

"Oh, is Olga there?" said Noel drowsily. "Take care of her, Max, old boy! Make her as happy as you can! She's awfully--fond--of you--though I'm not--supposed--to know."

The voice trailed off, sank into unconsciousness. Max's hand had tightened to a hard grip. He straightened himself and spoke, coldly, grimly.

"He isn't quite himself yet. I'm afraid I've brought you on a fool's errand. You can kiss him if you like. He probably won't know."

But Olga could not. She turned from the bed with the gesture of one who could bear no more, and without further words he led her from the room.

CHAPTER XXVII
LOVE MAKES ALL THE DIFFERENCE

I've been prayin' for you, dear Noel," said Peggy importantly, with her arms round her hero's neck.

"Have you, though?" said Noel. "I say, little pal, how decent of you! How often?"

"Ever so many times," said Peggy. "Every mornin', every evenin', and after grace besides."

"By Jove!" said Noel. "What did you say?"

"I said," Peggy swelled with triumph, "'Lighten Noel's darkness, we beseech Thee, O Lord!'"

"Why, that's what I said!" ejaculated Noel.

"Did you?" cried Peggy excitedly. "Did you really? Oh, Noel, then that's how it was, isn't it?"

"Quite so," said Noel.

He sat on the sofa in Daisy's little drawing-room with his small playfellow on his knee. They had not seen each other for six weeks. And in those weeks Noel had been transformed from a blind man to a man who saw, albeit through thick blue spectacles that emphasized the pallor of illness to such an alarming degree that Daisy had almost wept over him at sight.

Peggy, more practical in her sympathy, had gathered him straightway to her small but ardent bosom, and refused to let him go.

So they sat in the drawing-room tightly locked and related to each other all the doings of their separation.

"I wonder you're not afraid of me in these hideous goggles," Noel said once.

To which Peggy replied with indignation. "I'm not a baby!"

"And Olga has gone to Brethaven, has she?" he asked presently.

"Yes," said Peggy wisely. "Dr. Jim said she must have some sea air to make her fat again. So Captain Nick came yesterday and took her away. And d'you know," said Peggy, "I'm goin' there too very soon?"

"What ho!" said Noel. "Are they going to let you stay there all by yourself?"

Peggy nodded. "Daddy and Mummy are goin' away all by theirselves, so I'm goin' away all by myself."

"And who's going to slap you and put you to bed when you're naughty?" Noel enquired rudely. "Nick?"

"No!" said Peggy, affronted, "Captain Nick's a gentleman!"

"Is he though? Nasty snub for Noel Wyndham Esquire!" observed Noel. "Sorry, Peggy! Then unless Mrs. Nick rises nobly to the occasion, I'm afraid you'll go un-slapped. Dear, dear! What a misfortune! I shall have to come down now and then and see what I can do."

Peggy embraced him again ecstatically at this suggestion. "Yes, dear Noel, yes! Come often, won't you?"

"Rather!" said Noel cheerily. "I believe I'm going to be married some time soon by the way," he added as an afterthought.

Peggy's face fell. "Oh, Noel, not really!"

"Why not really?" said Noel.

Peggy explained with a little quiver in her voice. "You did always say that when I was growed up you'd marry me."

"Oh, is that all?" said Noel. "That's easily done. I'll get permission to have two. Whom does one ask? The Pope, isn't it? I'll go and cultivate his acquaintance on my honeymoon."

"What's a honeymoon?" said Peggy.

Noel burst into his merriest laugh and sprang to his feet. "It's the nicest thing in the world. I'll tell you all about it when we're married, Peg-top! Meantime, will you take me to see the great Dr. Jim? I want to inveigle him into lending me his motor."

"Oh, are you goin' to Brethaven?" asked Peggy eagerly. "Take me! Do, dear Noel!"

"What for?" said Noel.

"Reggie lives there," said Peggy. "And Reggie's got some rabbits--big, white ones."

"But suppose they don't want you?" objected Noel.

"S'pose they don't want you?" countered Peggy, clinging ingratiatingly to his hand. "Then--you can come and play with me and the rabbits--and Reggie."

Noel stooped very suddenly and kissed her. "What an excellent idea, Peg-top!" he said. "There's nothing more useful when the road is blocked than to secure a good line of retreat."

Peggy looked up at him with puzzled eyes, but she did not ask him what he meant.

*   *   *   *   *

It was on that same afternoon that Olga found herself wandering along the tiny glen in the Redlands grounds that had been her favourite resort in childhood. It was only two days since she had left town, urged thereto by Dr. Jim who insisted that she had been there too long already. Nick, moreover, who had patiently chaperoned her for the past five weeks, was wanting to rejoin his wife who had returned to Redlands soon after Noel's operation. And Noel himself, though still undergoing treatment at his brother's hands, had so far recovered as to be able to leave the home and take up his abode temporarily with Sir Kersley Whitton and Max. He had cheerily promised to follow her in a day or two; and Olga, persuaded on all sides, had yielded without much resistance though not very willingly. She had a curious reluctance to return to her home. Something--that hovering phantom that she had almost forgotten--had arisen once more to menace her peace. And she was afraid; she knew not wherefore.

She was happier in Noel's society than in any other. To see him daily growing stronger was her one unalloyed pleasure, and, curiously, when with him she was never so acutely conscious of that chill shadow. Of Max she saw practically nothing. He was always busy, almost too busy to notice her presence, it seemed--a fact that hurt her vaguely even while it gave her relief.

There was another fact that imparted the same kind of miserable comfort, and that was that Noel, though impetuous and loving as ever, never made any but the most casual allusions to their marriage. She could only conclude that he was waiting to make a complete recovery, and she would not herself broach the subject a second time. She did not actually want him to speak, but it grieved her a little that he did not do so. She did not for a moment doubt his love, but she felt that she did not possess the whole of his confidence, and the feeling made her vaguely uneasy. She had been so ready to give all that he had desired. How was it he was slow to take?

These thoughts were running persistently in her mind as she moved along the edge of the stream. It was a day in the end of May, fragrant with many perfumes, crystallized with spring sunshine--such a day as she would have revelled in only last year. Only last year! How many things had happened since then! She was almost afraid to think.

There came the sound of feet on the drive above, and a cracked voice hailed her. "Hullo, Olga mia! How are you amusing yourself?"

She looked up with a smile. Last year she would have sprung to meet him; but she seemed to have outgrown all her impulsiveness lately. She moved to meet him indeed, but he was at her side before she had moved a couple of yards.

He caught her hand in his, and drew her to the water's edge. His eyes flickered over her and went beyond.

"Hullo! There goes the green dragon-fly!" he said.

She looked round startled. "Oh, Nick, where?"

"Gone away!" said Nick unconcernedly. "He'll come back again, I'll wager. What's the programme for this morning, kiddie? Anything special?"

"Nothing," said Olga.

Again rapidly his eyes comprehended her. "I'm going up to the Priory myself," he announced unexpectedly. "Care to come?"

She started again, coloured, then went very white. "I--don't know, Nick," she faltered.

"Might as well, dear," said Nick persuasively. "There's no one there. Did I tell you about the landslip? There was a bad one last February, and the old place is beginning to crack in all directions. It's been condemned as unsafe, and Campion is going to clear out bag and baggage. He hasn't lived there, you know, since last summer. They've taken to travelling. Wouldn't you like to come and see it once more before it is dismantled?"

Olga was standing very still. She did not seem to be breathing; only the hand Nick had taken vibrated in his hold.

"Don't come if you don't like!" he said. "But it's your last chance. They are going to start clearing it to-morrow. I've got to go myself to fetch poor old Cork. You remember Cork? Campion has handed him over to me."

Yes, Olga remembered Cork. She drew in a deep breath and spoke. "Dear old dog! I'm glad you are going to have him. Yes, Nick, I'll come. But is the place really doomed? What will happen to it?"

"It will probably fall in first," said Nick, "and the next big landslide it will go over the cliff."

"How--dreadful!" said Olga, and added half to herself, "Violet was wondering only that morning if she would--would--live to see it."

"Ah!" said Nick. He was leading her through the glen that led down to the shore. "It was bound to happen some time," he said, "but they didn't think it would be so soon."

Olga went with him as one moving in a dream, submitting though not of her own conscious volition.

Nick said no more. He had chosen the shortest route, and his main object was to accomplish the distance without disturbing her thoughts.

They came out at length upon the shore, where the stream from the glen gurgled and fell in bubbling cascades into its channel on the beach. The sun poured full over a sea of blue and purple, threaded with silvery pathways here and there.

Olga paused for a moment, as it were instinctively, because from her earliest childhood she had always paused in just that spot to drink in the beauty of the scene.

Nick waited beside her, alert but patient. When she turned along the beach, he turned also, walking close to her over the stones, saying no word.

They came to the hollow in the rocks where she and Violet had rested on that summer morning, and again Olga paused with her face to the sea. A curious little spasm passed across it as she looked. Far away a white sail floated over the blue, and the cries of circling gulls came to them over the water. There was no other sound but the long, long roar of the sea.

Again, in utter silence, Olga turned, pursuing her way. They reached the cliff-path that still remained intact, and began to climb.

The way was steep, but she did not seem aware of it. Nick, lithe and agile, followed her step for step. His yellow face was full of anxious wrinkles. He looked neither to right nor left, watching her only.

Olga never paused in the ascent. She went unswervingly, as though drawn by some magnetic force above. Reaching the summit of the cliff, she turned at once from the Redlands ground, and struck across towards the boundary of the Priory. Nick fell into pace beside her again, vigilant as an eagle guarding its young in the first terrifying flight, not offering help, but ready to give it at the first sign of weakness.

But Olga gave no such sign. Only as they came in sight of the old grey building, standing stark and gaunt above them, she uttered a sudden sigh that seemed to break from her in spite of rigid restraint. And a moment later she quickened her pace.

They passed at length around a buttressed corner and so on to the yew-lined drive that led to the front of the house. The Gothic archway gaped wide to the spring sunshine. Olga came swiftly to it, and there stood suddenly still.

"Nick!" she said. "Nick!"

Her voice was vibrant, her eyes widely staring into the gloom within.

He slipped his arm about her, that wiry arm of great strength that had served her so often. "I am here, darling," he said soothingly.

Olga turned to him in piteous appeal. "Nick," she whispered, "where is she? Where? Where?"

He answered her steadfastly, with the absolute conviction of one who knew. "She is there beyond the Door, dear. You'll find her some day, waiting for you where it is given to all of us to wait for those we love."

But Olga only trembled at his words. "What door, Nick?" she asked. "Do you--do you mean Death?"

"We call it Death," he said.

She scarcely heard his answer. She was shaking from head to foot. "Oh, Nick," she gasped, "I'm frightened--I'm frightened! I daren't go on!"

His arm encircled her more strongly still. He almost lifted her forward over the threshold into the cold and gloomy hall. "Don't be frightened, darling! I'm with you," he said.

She would have hung back, but her strength was gone. She tottered weakly whither he led. In a moment she was sitting on the old oak chest with her face to the sunshine, just as she had sat on that golden afternoon when she had come to summon Violet to her aid.

She covered her face and shivered. Surely the place was haunted--haunted! In a grim procession memories began to crowd upon her. With shrinking vision she beheld, and all the while Nick stood beside her, holding her hand, sustaining even while he compelled.

"Do you remember?" he said, and again, as she shrank and quivered, "Do you remember?"

There was something ruthless about him during those moments, something she had never encountered before, something against which she knew she would oppose herself in vain. For the first time she saw the man as he was, felt the colossal strength of him, quivered beneath his mastery. He was forcing her towards an obstacle from which every racked nerve winced in horror. He was driving her, and he meant to drive her, into conflict with a force that threatened to overwhelm her utterly.

"Oh, let me go, Nick! Let me go!" she cried in agonized entreaty. "It's more than I can bear."

He knelt beside her; he held her close. "Darling," he said, "face it--face it just this once! It's for your own peace of mind I'm doing it."

And then she knew that no cry of hers would move him. He was ready to help her--if he could; but he would not suffer her to flee before that dread procession that had begun to wind like a fiery serpent through her brain. So, in a quivering anguish of spirit such as she had never before known, she sat and faced it, faced the advancing phantom from the shadowy presence of which she had so often shrunk appalled. And the beat of her heart rose up in the silence above the sound of the sea till she thought the mad race of it would kill her.

Slowly the seconds throbbed away, the torture swept towards her. She was as one who, fascinated, watches a forest-fire while he waits to be engulfed.

Presently, from the shadows behind, the great dog Cork came like a ghost and gave them stately welcome. He licked Olga's quivering hands, standing beside her in earnest solicitude.

Nick rose to his feet and moved a little away. His hand was hard clenched against his side. He could not help, it seemed. He could only look on in impotence, while she suffered.

Slowly at last Olga raised her head and looked at him with tragic eyes. Her face was white and strained, but she had in a measure regained her self-control.

"I am going upstairs," she said, "just for a little while. Don't come with me, Nick! Wait for me! Wait for me!"

She rose with the words, swayed a little, then recovered herself, and, with her hand on Cork's head, moved slowly away down the great hall.

Dumbly Nick stood and watched the slim young figure with the wolf-hound pacing gravely beside it. At the end, immediately below the east window, she paused, and he saw her drawn face upraised to the dreadful picture above her; then, still slowly, she turned, and, with the dog, passed out of sight under the southern archway.

For a long, long space he waited in the utter stillness. He had faced a good many difficulties in his life and endured a good many adversities, but this thing stood by itself, unique in his experience, with a pain that was all its own. He would have given much to have gone with her, to have held her up while the storm raged round her, to have borne with her that which, it seemed, she could only bear alone. But, since this was denied him, he could only wait with set teeth while his little pal went through that fiery trial of hers, wait and picture her agonizing in solitude, wait till she should come back to him with all the gladness gone for ever from her eyes,--a woman who could never be young again.

Slowly the minutes dragged on till half an hour had passed. He fell to pacing up and down in a fever of anxiety. Would she never come back? She had begged him to wait for her, but he began to feel he could not wait any longer. The suspense was becoming intolerable.

Desperately he marked another quarter of an hour crawl by leaden-footed, moment by moment. And still she did not come. He went for the last time to the open door and looked forth restlessly. The warmth of the spring sunshine spread everywhere like a benediction. It was only within those walls of crumbling stone that it found no place. A sudden shiver went through him. He turned abruptly inwards. She should not stay alone in the vault-like solitude any longer. Surely anything--anything--must be better for her than that!

With quick strides he went down the old dim hall that once had been the chapel of the monks, turned sharply through the second archway, and approached the staircase beyond. And then very suddenly he stopped. For there above him at the open staircase-window that looked upon the sea stood Olga.

The afternoon sunshine streamed in upon her, and she seemed to be stretching out her hands to it, basking in the generous glow. Her face was upturned to the splendour. Her eyes were closed.

For a moment or two Nick stood narrowly watching her, then as suddenly as he had come he withdrew. For Olga's lips were moving, and it seemed to him that she was no longer alone....

He went back to the porch and stood in the sunshine waiting with renewed patience.

Ten minutes later a moist nose nozzled its way into his hand. He looked down into Cork's eyes of faithful friendliness. Then, hearing a light footfall, he turned. Olga had come back to him at last.

Straight to him she came, moving swiftly. Her face was still pale and very wan, but the strained look had utterly passed away. Her eyes sought his with fearless confidence, and Nick's heart gave a jerk of sheer relief. He had expected tragedy, and he beheld--peace.

She reached him. She laid her hands upon his shoulders. A tremulous smile hovered about her lips. "Nick--Nick darling," she said, "why--why--why didn't you tell me all this long ago?"

He stood before her dumb with astonishment. For once he was utterly and completely at a loss.

She slipped her hand through his arm, and drew him out. "Let us go into the sun!" she said. And then, as the glow fell around them, "Oh, Nick, I'm so thankful that I know the truth at last!"

"Are you, dear?" he said. "Well, I certainly think it is time you knew it now."

"I ought to have known it sooner," she said. "Why did you--you and Max--let me believe--a lie?"

He hesitated momentarily. "We thought it would be easier for you than the truth," he said then.

"You mean Max thought so," she said quickly. "You didn't, Nick!"

"Perhaps not," he admitted.

"I'm sure you didn't," she said. "You know me better than that." Again she stood still in the sunshine, lifting her face to the glory. "Love conquers so many things," she said.

"All things," put in Nick quickly.

She looked at him again. "I don't know about all things, Nick," she said.

"I have proved it," he said.

She shook her head slowly. "But I haven't." She passed from the subject as if it were one she could not bear to discuss openly. "What made you think the truth would hurt me so, I wonder? It was only the first great shock I couldn't bear. That nearly killed me. But now that it is over--and I can see clearly again--Nick, tell me,--as her friend--her only friend--could I have done anything else?"

Nick was silent. He had asked himself the same question many times, and had not found an answer.

"Nick," she said pleadingly, "none but a friend could have done it. It was--an act of love."

"I know it was," he said.

"And yet you blame me?" Her voice was low, full of the most earnest entreaty.

"You blamed Max," he pointed out.

"Oh, but Max didn't love her!" He heard a note of quick pain in her voice. "Oh, don't you see," she said, "how love makes all the difference? Surely that was what St. Paul meant when he said that love was the fulfilling of the law. Nick, you must agree with me in this. It was utterly hopeless. Think of it! Think of it! If she had been living now!" A sudden hard shiver went through her. "Nick, if I had been in her place--wouldn't you have done the same for me?"

"I don't know," he said.

But she clung to him more closely. "You do know, dear! You do know!"

And then Nick did a strange, impulsive thing. He suddenly flung down his reserve and bared to her his inmost soul.

"Yes, Olga mia, I do know," he said. "I would have done the same for you. I nearly did the same for Muriel when we were in a tight corner long ago at Wara. But whether it's right or whether it's wrong, God alone can judge. It may be we take too much upon us, or it may be He means us to do it. That is what I have never yet decided. But I solemnly believe with you that love makes all the difference. Love is the one extenuating circumstance which He will recognize and pass. It isn't the outward appearance that counts. It's just the heart of things."

He stopped. Olga was listening with earnest attention, her pale face rapt. For a moment, as he ceased to speak, their eyes met, and between them there ran the old electric current of sympathy, re-connected and entire.

"Oh, Nick," she said, "you never fail me! You always understand!"

But Nick shook his head in whimsical denial. "No, not always, believe me,--being but a man. But I've learnt to hide my ignorance by taking the difficult bits for granted. For instance, I didn't expect you to take this thing so sensibly. If I had, I should have acted very differently long ago."

"Do you call me sensible, Nick?" she said, with a wistful smile.

"Not in all respects, dear," said Nick. "But you have shown more sense than I expected on this occasion."

"Did you expect me to be very badly upset?" she asked. "Nick, shall I tell you something? You'll think me fanciful perhaps. Yet I don't know. Very likely you will understand. I've had a feeling for such a long, long time that she--that Violet--was calling to me, and I could never hear what she wanted to say. To-day--at last--I have been in touch with her, and I know that all is well." She turned her face up to the sun again, speaking with closed eyes. "I know that she is safe. I know that she is happy. And--Nick--Nick--" her voice thrilled on the words--"I know that she loves me still."

Nick bared his head with reverence. His face was strangely moved, but the restless eyes were steadfast as he made reply: "That, dear, is just the Omnipotence of Love. You can't explain it. It's too great a thing to grasp. You can only feel the pull of the everlasting Chain that binds us to those beyond."

"It is wonderful," she whispered, "wonderful!"

"It is Divine," said Nick.

CHAPTER XXVIII
A SOLDIER AND A GENTLEMAN

When Nick returned to Redlands, he was alone. Olga had gone down again to the shore. She wanted to be by herself a little longer, she said. He didn't mind? No, Nick minded nothing, so long as all went well with her; and, on her promise that all should be well, he left her with Cork for guardian.

He went back to Redlands over the cliffs, entering his own grounds by a low wire fence, and thence turning inwards towards the garden. The sounds of gay voices reached him as he approached, and he speedily found himself caught in a lively ambush that consisted of Peggy, Reggie, and Noel. He naturally fled for his life, but was overtaken by the latter and held down while the two accomplices rifled his pockets. By the rules of the game all coppers found therein were confiscated, and this regulation having been duly observed, the prisoner was allowed to sit up and converse with his principal captor while the rest of the gang divided the spoils.

"Have a cigarette?" said Noel.

"Thanks! Mighty generous of you!" Nick righted his tumbled attire and accepted the proffered weed. "If it isn't a rude question, what are you doing here?"

Noel's eyes laughed across at him gaily through the blue spectacles. "I should have thought you might have guessed that I'm spending a night or two with the Musgraves, but I am under a solemn oath to return to Max by noon on Friday in order to have another dose of some infernal stuff with which he is peppering my eyes. He didn't much want me to come away, as it meant postponing the torture for a few hours. But I managed to get on the soft side of him for once, though he is holding himself in preparation for an immediate summons in case my vision should take advantage of my absence from him to play any nasty tricks."

"I see," said Nick. "And how is the vision?"

"Oh, all right, so far as it goes. Gives me beans upon occasion, for which Max always swears at me as if it were my fault. I'm not allowed to see by artificial light at all, so after sunset I join the bats. Lucky for me the sun sits up late just now. By the way, I had a positively gushing epistle from old Badgers this morning. He seems almost hysterical at the thought of getting me back again; says that married or single, I've got to go." Noel stopped to take in a long breath of smoke; then, very abruptly, "Where's Olga?" he demanded.

Nick nodded in the direction whence he had come. "Down on the shore."

Noel was on his feet in a second. "All right. You can be nurse for a bit now. See you later!"

He would have swung away with the words, but Nick had also risen, and with a swift word he detained him. "I say, Noel!"

Noel stopped. "Hullo!"

"Look here!" said Nick rapidly. "She isn't wanting anyone just yet. We have just been to the Priory, she and I--in accordance with Sir Kersley's advice, of which I told you. She is having a quiet think. Don't disturb her!"

Noel stood still. He had stiffened somewhat at the words, but there was no dismay discernible about him. He faced that which had to be faced without flinching.

"You mean she knows?" he asked slowly.

"Yes," said Nick. "But I didn't tell her."

"Did she remember, then?"

"Yes. It all came back to her."

"What effect did it have? Was she--is she very badly upset?" The sharp falter in the words betrayed more than the speaker knew.

Nick turned away from him, grinding his heel into the turf. "No. She took it remarkably quietly on the whole--seemed relieved to know the truth."

"And Max--did she mention him?"

"Yes. She seemed glad to know that he was not responsible, but rather hurt that he had thought it necessary to concoct a lie for her benefit."

"Exactly what I should have felt myself," said Noel. He paused a moment; then: "It was decent of you to let me into that secret," he observed.

"Oh, that was Sir Kersley's doing." Nick still spoke with his back half-turned.

"He tackled me on the subject, said you ought to know, but that Max was averse to it. Then I told him why. It seems that he hadn't the vaguest notion till then as to why the engagement was broken off."

Noel nodded. "Just like Max! He's a bit too clever sometimes. Well, what did he say when he knew?"

"He said that if Max wouldn't take the responsibility of setting matters right, he would. And he advised me to tell you everything straight away; which I did," said Nick, "at peril of my life. I don't know how Max will take it, but it will doubtless be on my devoted head that his wrath will descend."

"You'll survive that," said Noel. "But look here! Tell me more about Olga! Wasn't she horribly shocked--just at first?"

"It was touch and go," said Nick. "I followed Sir Kersley's advice throughout. He didn't want me to tell her outright, and I didn't. The whole thing came to her gradually. Yes, it was a bit of a strain to begin with. But she has come through it all right. Give her time to settle, and I don't think she will be any the worse."

"I see," said Noel. He relaxed very suddenly, and passed a boyishly familiar arm around Nick's shoulders. "Well, that cooks my goose, quite effectually, doesn't it? Lucky it's come to me gradually too. I shouldn't have relished it all in a lump. The only person who is going to have a shock over this little business is Max. And you'll admit he deserves one."

"What are you going to do?" asked Nick.

"Do? Send him a wire of course."

"Who? Max?"

"Yes, Max. And I shall say, 'Come at once. Urgent. Noel.' That'll fetch him," said Noel with a twinkle. "He's making a speciality of me just now. He ought to be here before eight."

"And what about Olga?"

"Leave Olga to me!" said Noel.

Nick glanced up at him, and abruptly did so. "You're a sportsman, my son," he observed affectionately. "But to return to Max, doesn't it occur to you that it may not be precisely convenient for him to come posting down here at a moment's notice? He's an important man, remember."

But Noel here displayed a touch of his old imperious spirit. "Who the devil cares for Max?" he demanded. "He's just got to come; and if he doesn't like it, he can go hang. Surely a fellow may be permitted to settle who is to be asked to his own funeral!"

"Oh, if you put it like that--" said Nick.

"Well, it is like that; see?" There was a comic touch to Noel's tragedy notwithstanding, and Nick divined with a satisfaction that he was careful to conceal that the role he had taken upon himself was not altogether distasteful to him. The funeral arrangements obviously had their attractive side.

"Well, my boy, fix it up as you think best!" he said, giving him as ample a squeeze as his one arm could compass. "You're a soldier and a gentleman, and whatever you do will have my full approval."

"What ho!" said Noel, highly gratified.

They parted then, going their several ways. Noel to send his message, Nick in pursuit of the two children. And so the rest of the afternoon wore away.

Muriel had tea laid in the old oak-panelled dining-room, and thither Nick presently marshalled his charges, to find his wife serenely waiting for them in solitude.

"Hasn't Olga come in yet?" he asked.

"Yes, dear, some time ago. But she looked so tired, poor child!" said Muriel. "I persuaded her to go up to her room and lie down. She has had some tea."

"She will be all right?" asked Nick quickly.

"I think so. She looks quite worn out. She seems to need a sleep more than anything," said Muriel.

He gave her a quick look. "You saw Noel?"

"Yes. He came in and talked for a few minutes after he left you. He seems a very nice boy." A faint smile touched Muriel's lips.

Nick laughed, pulling her hand round his neck as she brought him his tea. "Lost your heart to him, eh? It's quite the usual thing to do. Where has he gone?"

"He came over in Jim's motor, and has gone away in it again. He didn't say where he was going."

"Gone away without me!" ejaculated Peggy in consternation.

"He'll come back again, my chicken. Don't you worry!" said Nick. "Here! Have a jam sandwich!"

"I want Noel," said Peggy. "Where is Noel?"

"He has gone out on business," said Nick. "Which reminds me," he added to Muriel. "His brother Max will probably be here this evening to spend the night."

"Max!"

"Yes. Don't mention it upstairs! Noel is pulling the wires, so be prepared for anything."

"What wires is Noel pullin'?" Peggy wanted to know.

"Telegraph wires," said Reggie brightly.

"Yes, telegraph wires," chuckled Nick. "I think I'll just go up for a second, Muriel. I shan't wake her up if she's asleep."

He was gone with the words, swift and noiseless as a bird on the wing, and five seconds later was scratching very softly at Olga's door.

Her voice bade him enter immediately, and he went in.

She was lying on her bed, but the blind was up and the windows wide. She held out her arms to him.

"Nick--darling!"

"Ever yours to command!" said Nick. He went to her, stooping while the arms wound round his neck.

She held him tightly. "Nick," she whispered, "is Noel still here?"

"No, darling. Do you want him?"

She drew a sharp breath. "I--I'm afraid I--dodged him a little while ago. I simply couldn't meet him just then. Has he been looking for me? Did he wonder where I was?"

"Don't think so," said Nick. "He was playing with the kids. He is spending a couple of nights with the Musgraves, and he brought Peggy over."

"And he has gone again?" Faint wonder sounded in her voice.

"Only temporarily. He wanted to send a message to someone from the post-office; but he is coming back--presumably--for Peggy."

"I see." She was silent for a few moments, and Nick sat down on the edge of the bed. "Nick," she said at length, speaking with obvious effort, "will he--will he be very hurt, do you think, if--if I don't see him to-day?"

"Shouldn't say so, darling," said Nick.

She slipped her hand into his. "I've got to do a lot of thinking, Nick," she said rather piteously.

"Can I help?" said Nick.

She shook her head with a quivering smile. "No, dear. It's a--it's a one-man job. But, if you don't mind, tell Noel I'm rather tired, but I'll come over to Weir in the morning. I'm going to tell him everything," she ended, squeezing his hand very tightly.

"Quite right, dear," said Nick.

"Yes, but--before I tell him--I want to--to write to Max." Olga's voice was very low. "I must put things right with him first. I must ask him to forgive me."

"Forgive you, sweetheart!"

"Yes, for--for being very unkind to him." Olga's lips quivered again, and suddenly her eyes were full of tears. "I feel as if--as if I've been running into things in the dark, and doing a lot of harm," she said. "Of course everything is quite over--quite over--between us. He will understand that. But I want--I want to be friends with him--if--he--will let me. Nick dear, that's all. Hadn't you better go and have your tea?"

"And leave you to weep?" said Nick, with his face screwed up. "No, I don't think so."

"I'm not going to," she assured him. "I'm going to be--awfully sensible. Really I am. Kiss me, Nick darling, and go!"

He bent over her. "You mustn't cry," he urged pathetically.

She clasped him close. "No, I won't! I won't! Nick--dearest, you're the very sweetest man in the world. I always have thought so, and I always shall. There!"

"Ah, well, it's a comparatively harmless illusion," said Nick, with his quizzical grimace. "I'll endeavour to live up to it. Sure you want me to go?"

"Yes. You must go, dear. I'm sure Muriel is wanting you. I've monopolized you long enough. You--you'll tell Noel, won't you? Is he all right?"

"At the very top of his form," said Nick.

She smiled. "I'm so very glad. Give him my love, Nick, my--my best love."

"I will," said Nick. He stood up. "He's a fine chap--Noel," he said. "He deserves the best, and I hope--some day--he'll get it."

With which enigmatical remark, he wheeled and left her.

CHAPTER XXIX
THE MAN'S POINT OF VIEW

That letter to Max was perhaps the hardest task that Olga had ever undertaken. She spent the greater part of three hours over it, oblivious of everything else; and then, close upon the dinner-hour, tore up all previous efforts in despair and scribbled a brief, informal note that was curiously reminiscent of one she had written once in a moment of impulsive penitence and pinned inside his hat.

"Dear Max," it ran, "I want to tell you that everything has come back to me, and I am very, very sorry. Will you forgive me and let us be friends for the future? Yours, Olga."

This letter she addressed and stamped and took downstairs with her, laying it upon the hall-table to be posted. Thence she passed on to the library to find a book she wanted.

The glow of sunset met her on the threshold, staying the hand she raised to the electric switch. She moved slowly through the dying light to the window and stood before it motionless, gazing forth into the glory. It poured around her in a rosy splendour, lighting her pale, tired face. For several minutes she stood drinking in the beauty of it, with a feeling at her heart as of unshed tears.

Then at last with a long sigh she slowly turned, and moved across to a row of bookshelves. Perhaps there was light enough for her purpose after all. She began to search along the backs of the books with her face close to them.

"Are you looking for Farrow's Treatise on Party Government by any chance?" asked a leisurely voice behind her.

She sprang round as if a gun had been discharged in the room. She stared widely, feeling back against the bookshelves for support.

He was lounging on the edge of the table immediately facing her--a square strong figure, with hands in his pockets, the red light of the sunset turning his hair to fire.

"Because if you are," he continued, a note of grim humour in his voice, "I'm afraid you won't find it--to-night. What's the matter with you, fair lady? You don't seem quite pleased to see me."

"I am pleased," she whispered. "I am pleased."

But her voice was utterly gone. Her throat worked spasmodically. She put up both hands to it as if she were choking.

He stood up abruptly and came to her. He took her hands and drew them gently away. "I shall begin to think I'm bad for you if you do that," he said. "What's the matter, child? Did I frighten you?"

"No!" she whispered back. "No! It was only--only--"

"Only--" he said. "Look here! You mustn't cry. It's one better than fainting, I admit; but I'm not going to let you do either if I can help it. Come over here to the window!"

He led her unresisting, one steady arm upholding her.

"Do you know," he said, "a curious thing happened just now? I'd only been in the house twenty minutes or so when, coming downstairs to look for you, I discovered a letter in the hall addressed to me. I took the liberty of opening and reading it, in spite of the fact that it was plainly intended for the post." He paused. "I thought that would make you angry," he observed, looking down at her critically.

She uttered a desperate little laugh and tried to disengage herself from his arm. "No, I'm glad you've got it," she said rather breathlessly.

"It was a very silly letter," remarked Max, calmly frustrating the attempt. "It didn't say half it might have said, and what it did say wasn't to the point."

"Yes, it was," she maintained quickly. "It--it--I meant to say just that."

"Then all I can say is that you have quite missed the crux of the situation," said Max. "Why are you very, very sorry? Why do you want me to forgive you? And why in the name of wonder do you suggest that we should become friends when you know that we are so constituted as to be incapable of being anything but the dearest of enemies?"

He looked down again suddenly into her quivering, averted face. "Still I shall value that letter," he said, "if only as a sample of the sweet unreasonableness of women. Are you still very sorry, Olga?"

She moved at the utterance of her name, moved and made a more decided effort to free herself.

"Not a bit of good," said Max. "Don't you know I'm waiting for the kiss of peace?"

"I can't!" she protested swiftly. "I can't!"

"Can't what?" said Max.

Her lips were trembling, but she shed no tears. He seemed in some magic fashion to keep her from that.

"I can't kiss you, Max, really--really!" she said.

"Why not?" said Max.

She was silent, but he persisted, still holding her pressed to him.

"Tell me why not! Is it because you don't want to Or you think you ought not to? Or because you are just--shy?"

She caught the smile in his voice and pictured the cocked-up corner of his mouth. "I think I ought not to," she murmured, with her head still turned from him.

"Conscientious objections?" suggested Max.

"Don't laugh!" she whispered.

"My dear child, I'm as serious as a judge. What are the objections?"

"There is--Noel," she said.

"You will have to chuck Noel," said Max coolly.

That vitalized her very effectually; she turned on him with burning cheeks. "Max, how dare you--how dare you suggest such a thing!"

His eyes met hers, green and dominant. She saw again that old mocking gleam of conscious mastery with which he had been wont to exasperate her. He answered her with a directness almost brutal.

"Because you don't love him."

"I do love him!" she declared fiercely. "I do love him!"

"Better than me?" said Max.

She shrank visibly from the question. "I love him too well to throw him over," she said.

His lips twisted cynically. "That is curious," he said.

She winced again from that which he left unsaid. "Oh, Max, don't hurt me!" she pleaded. "Try--try to understand!"

It was an appeal for mercy. But Max would not hear. He took her by the shoulders, compelling her to face him. "So you really mean to marry Noel," he said. "Do you think you will be happy with him?"

"I could never be happy if I didn't," she answered rather incoherently.

Max frowned. "Look here!" he said. "It's no good expecting me to understand if you won't even answer my questions."

She quivered in his hold. "You ask such--impossible things," she said.

"They are only impossible," Max said relentlessly, "because you are afraid to tell me the truth. You are afraid to tell me that you are sacrificing yourself. You are afraid to be honest--even with yourself."

"I am not!" she protested fierily. "Max, you have no right----"

"I have a right." He broke in upon her sternly. "I have the first and foremost right. Remember, you were mine before you were his. You gave yourself to me because you loved me. You only threw me over because of a fancied unworthiness. Now I am cleared of that, do you think you owe me nothing more than an apology?"

"Oh, but, Max," she pleaded, "think of Noel! Think of Noel!"

"Well?" said Max, "then think of him! Don't you think he can make a better bargain for himself than marriage with a woman who doesn't love him best? Why, nearly every woman he meets falls in love with him, and could offer him more than you do. You women who are so keen on sacrificing yourselves never look at the man's point of view, and so the only thing he really wants, you make it impossible for him to get."

"Max! Max!" she cried in distress.

"Well, isn't it so?" said Max. "Just admit that, and p'raps I won't bully you any more. You know he doesn't come first with you--and never would."

"But I could make him happy," she said.

"Oh, could you? And suppose his happiness depended upon yours? Suppose he were man enough to want you to be happy too? Could you do that for him?"

She hesitated.

He pressed on without mercy. "Could you drive me utterly out of your thoughts, your dreams? Could you stifle every regret, every secret longing? Could you empty your heart of me and put him in my place? Tell me! Could you?"

But she could not tell him. She only turned her face from him and wept.

He set her free then, just as he had set her free on that day long ago when her will had first bruised itself against the iron of his. He went away from her, went to the door as if he would leave her; then stood still, and after a space came back.

She trembled at his coming. She had a feeling that he had armed himself with another, stronger weapon to overcome her resistance.

He stopped in front of her. "Olga," he said, "have you thought about me at all?"

She made a sharp gesture--the involuntary wincing of the victim from the knife.

He went on, very quietly, as if he had not seen. "Do you think I'm going to be happy without you? I've got my career, haven't I, and all my brilliant successes? How much do you think they are worth to me? How far do you think they are going to satisfy me--make up for that which you have taken away?"

He paused, but she could not answer him, could not so much as lift her eyes to his.

He went on. "A little while ago you appealed to my love, and--I don't claim to be more than human--it stood the strain. I appealed to yours, and you sent me about my business. You had some excuse. I had deceived you. But this time--this time-- are you going to do the same this time, Olga?"

"I can't help it!" she whispered through her tears.

He came nearer to her, but he did not touch her. "Is that the truth?" he said. "Don't you love me well enough? Is that it? Is my love so little to you that you can afford to throw it away? You know I love you, don't you? You believe in my love?" His voice suddenly vibrated; his hands clenched. "It's stood a good deal," he said. "But, by Heaven! I don't think it will stand this!"

She lifted her face suddenly. "Max, stop! I can't bear it!"

"Neither can I!" He flung back fiercely. "It's too much to ask--too much to give! Olga, you shall come to me! You shall! You shall!"

He caught her to him with the words, holding her mercilessly in a grip that was savage. She felt the hard, passionate beat of his heart against her own. And she gasped and gasped again, as one suddenly immersed in deep waters.

She did not resist him, for she could not. He had her a helpless captive before she could even begin. Perhaps she might not have done so in any case. It was a point she never was able to decide. But from the moment his lips met hers the battle was over. With or without her will her lips clung to his; the flame of his passion kindled an answering flame in her; and the love which she had striven so desperately to re-strain leaped forth to him in wild, exultant freedom, so that she forgot all the world beside.

*   *   *   *   *

"So that's settled!" said Max a little later into the flushed face that lay against his shoulder. "It's taken a mighty long time to make you see reason."

"It isn't reason," said Olga faintly. "And oh, Max, what--what am I to say to Noel?"

Max's one-sided smile appeared. "I should just say, 'Thank you kindly, sir,' if it were me. There's nothing else left to say."

"Oh, but there is!" she protested.

"There isn't," said Max. "He is coming over to congratulate us to-morrow."

"Max!" She opened her eyes wide and lifted her head. "Max, you don't mean----"

"Yes, I do," said Max imperturbably. "Why do you suppose I came tearing down here to-night, leaving Kersley to kill all my patients as well as his own?"

"Not--surely--to see me?" said Olga, wonderingly.

He laughed grimly. "No. It was to see Noel. Odd how we both put him first, isn't it? The young cub sent me a message that brought me down post-haste, expecting to find him in a state of collapse. Instead of which I found him gaily awaiting me at the station to tell me he had run himself out--or some bosh of the kind--and it was now my innings, and I was to go in and win. On my soul, Olga, he was enjoying himself up to the hilt."

"But why didn't you tell me this before?" said Olga quickly.

Max's mouth went up a little higher. "Various reasons, fair lady."

"Don't be horrid!" she protested, giving him a shake. "And how did it happen? How did he come to know anything? I haven't seen him to-day. It must have been Nick!"

"Yes. I'm going to throttle Nick presently. I've often wanted to. After which I shall turn him into a mummy and send him to India to be worshipped as the little god of intrigue. I daresay he'll get on all right in that capacity. It ought to suit him down to the ground. He's a born meddler."

"How absurd you are!" Olga laughed in spite of herself. "Where is Nick? Don't you think we had better go and find him?"

It was at this point that the handle of the door was turned ostentatiously the wrong way, struggled with, sworn at, and finally put right.

"May I come in?" said Nick, briskly opening the door. "Muriel and I have finished dinner. We knew you wouldn't be wanting any."

"Nick!" Olga exclaimed. "I'm sure you haven't!"

"All right, we haven't," said Nick. "That is to say, we have saved you a little in case you were prosaic enough to want it. Max, my son, your presence here is an honour for which I have scarcely made fit preparation, but I am none the less proud to entertain you, and as your uncle-in-law elect I bid you welcome."

He held out his hand which Max took with a dry, "Thanks! One can't scrag a man under his own roof, I suppose, though it's a sore temptation."

"You will have ample opportunity in the future," Nick assured him genially, "though, as I think I told you long ago, I'm the most well-meaning little cuss that ever walked the earth. I threatened once to put a spoke in your wheel, didn't I? Well, I never did it. I've been pushing and straining to get it out of the bog ever since. And now I've done it, you want to scrag me. Olga, the man's a blood-thirsty scoundrel. If you have the smallest regard for my feelings, you will kick him out of the house at once."

But Olga was holding the two clasped hands in hers, and she would not let them part. "Nick, you're a darling--a darling! And Max knows it, don't you, Max? It was dear of you to make the wheels go round. They would never have done it without you, and we shall never, never forget it as long as we two shall live."

"Amen!" said Max.

"Bless your hearts!" said Nick benevolently. "Well, come and have something to eat!"

He turned towards the door, but Olga hung back. "Is--is Noel here?" she asked.

"Heavens, no!" said Nick. "He eloped with Peggy long ago."

"Oh!" A note of relief sounded in her voice. "I shall see him to-morrow," she said.

"Yes, he'll be over to-morrow." Nick shot her a swift look in the twilight. "Meantime, I have a message to give you from him," he said.

"So have I," cut in Max.

"I know what it is!" said Olga quickly.

"His love," said Max.

"His best love," said Nick.

There was an instant's silence in the room; then Olga bent her head and murmured softly, "God bless him!"

CHAPTER XXX
THE LINE OF RETREAT

No," said Daisy, with decision. "I shall never like Dr. Wyndham, though I am quite willing to admit that he may be admirable in many ways. He is not my ideal of a nice husband, but then of course--" she dimpled prettily--"I'm only just back from my honeymoon, and I've been thoroughly spoilt."

Will smiled upon her indulgently. "It's just as well we don't all like the same people. He looked happy enough anyhow."

"In his lordly, cynical fashion," objected Daisy. "He was quite the most self-possessed bridegroom I ever saw."

"Just as well perhaps," commented Will. "Olga was positively shaking with nervousness. Dr. Jim went grimly armed with a brandy-flask and smelling-salts."

"Will, did he really? How like him!"

"Yes. Sir Kersley told me. But he added that it is a well-known fact that brides never faint, so Jim's precautions were quite unnecessary. He also said--But perhaps it's hardly fair to tell you that!"

"What?" said Daisy eagerly. "Of course tell me! Tell me at once, Will!"

Will smiled again. "Well, if I must! He told me that Max himself was anything but as serene as he looked and had been dosing with bromide to steady his nerves."

Daisy broke into a laugh. "No, you certainly shouldn't have told me that! How mean of Sir Kersley! Still, it's nice to know that Max is a little human now and then. I shall like him better now. And so I don't mind telling you something in return. I've been making the most discreet enquiries, and I haven't unearthed the vaguest rumour of that tale Major Hunt-Goring told me. I believe it was all his own invention after all."

"Very likely," said Will. "Opium-smokers often get delusions."

Daisy caught and kissed her husband's hand. "How very charitable of you, Will! You're a perpetual antidote to my poison. Did you observe Nick during the ceremony? He was grinning like a Hindu idol--just as if he'd done it all."

"He has his finger in most pies," observed Will. "I daresay it wasn't altogether absent from this one. Muriel looked supremely proud of her C.S.I."

"And she has reason to be," declared Daisy warmly. "He is quite a king in his own line. I'm so glad he got the Star."

"It's time he got something of the sort certainly," said Will. "I suppose he'll be good now for another six years. Then he'll send the boy to school and inveigle her back to the East."

But Daisy shook her head. "No. I think she'll keep him now. This country is wanting men very badly--and there's plenty to be done."

"Oh, he's a bulwark of the Empire," smiled Will. "He'll do the work of ten. Where's the kiddie gone?"

"She's somewhere with Noel. Did you see those two come out of church together? It was the sweetest sight," said Daisy with enthusiasm.

"She ought to have been walking with Reggie," observed Will.

"Yes, I'm afraid she deserted him. But he ran after Dr. Jim. They are great pals. But Peggy and Noel--" Daisy suddenly laughed--"oh, Will, I do love that boy!" she said. "It is good to see him his gay, handsome self again. See, there they are together now, sitting on the grass! I wonder what they are talking about."

"Probably discussing to-day's event," said Will.

"And wishing it had been their turn," laughed Daisy. A guess which, as it chanced, was not altogether wide of the mark! Peggy, the while she leaned against her cavalier, was remarking at that very moment that she thought Midsummer Day the nicest day in all the year for a "weddin'."

"Why?" said Noel.

"All the fairies gets married then," said Peggy.

"Silly little duffers!" said Noel unsympathetically.

She looked at him round-eyed, then slipped a soft hand into his. "Dear Noel, don't you like weddin's?"

Noel cut short an involuntary sigh. "Not always, Peggy," he said.

"Not when you're best man and I'm chief bridesmaid?" persisted Peggy, with her cheek against his shoulder.

He laughed, without much gaiety. "Oh, well, of course that makes a difference," he said.

There was a pause during which Peggy rubbed her cheek up and down his coat in tender silence. At last coaxingly, "Why didn't you like this weddin', dear Noel?" she asked.

But at that he broke into a half-shamed laugh and springing up snatched her high into his arms. "I'll tell you when we're married, Peg-top," he promised her. "Till then--let's have some fun!"

"Yes, yes!" cried Peggy, laughing down at him alluringly. "Let's have some fun!"

And that ended the conversation.

The Codes Of Hammurabi And Moses
W. W. Davies

QTY

The discovery of the Hammurabi Code is one of the greatest achievements of archaeology, and is of paramount interest, not only to the student of the Bible, but also to all those interested in ancient history...

Religion   **ISBN:** *1-59462-338-4*

Pages:132
MSRP $12.95

The Theory of Moral Sentiments
Adam Smith

QTY

This work from 1749. contains original theories of conscience amd moral judgment and it is the foundation for systemof morals.

Philosophy   **ISBN:** *1-59462-777-0*

Pages:536
MSRP $19.95

Jessica's First Prayer
Hesba Stretton

QTY

In a screened and secluded corner of one of the many railway-bridges which span the streets of London there could be seen a few years ago, from five o'clock every morning until half past eight, a tidily set-out coffee-stall, consisting of a trestle and board, upon which stood two large tin cans, with a small fire of charcoal burning under each so as to keep the coffee boiling during the early hours of the morning when the work-people were thronging into the city on their way to their daily toil...

Pages:84

Childrens   **ISBN:** *1-59462-373-2*

MSRP $9.95

My Life and Work
Henry Ford

QTY

Henry Ford revolutionized the world with his implementation of mass production for the Model T automobile. Gain valuable business insight into his life and work with his own auto-biography... "We have only started on our development of our country we have not as yet, with all our talk of wonderful progress, done more than scratch the surface. The progress has been wonderful enough but..."

Pages:300

Biographies/   **ISBN:** *1-59462-198-5*

MSRP $21.95

The Art of Cross-Examination
Francis Wellman

QTY

I presume it is the experience of every author, after his first book is published upon an important subject, to be almost overwhelmed with a wealth of ideas and illustrations which could readily have been included in his book, and which to his own mind, at least, seem to make a second edition inevitable. Such certainly was the case with me; and when the first edition had reached its sixth impression in five months, I rejoiced to learn that it seemed to my publishers that the book had met with a sufficiently favorable reception to justify a second and considerably enlarged edition. ..

Reference   **ISBN:** *1-59462-647-2*

Pages:412

MSRP $19.95

On the Duty of Civil Disobedience
Henry David Thoreau

QTY

Thoreau wrote his famous essay, On the Duty of Civil Disobedience, as a protest against an unjust but popular war and the immoral but popular institution of slave-owning. He did more than write—he declined to pay his taxes, and was hauled off to gaol in consequence. Who can say how much this refusal of his hastened the end of the war and of slavery ?

Law   **ISBN:** *1-59462-747-9*

Pages:48

MSRP $7.45

Dream Psychology Psychoanalysis for Beginners
Sigmund Freud

QTY

Sigmund Freud, born Sigismund Schlomo Freud (May 6, 1856 - September 23, 1939), was a Jewish-Austrian neurologist and psychiatrist who co-founded the psychoanalytic school of psychology. Freud is best known for his theories of the unconscious mind, especially involving the mechanism of repression; his redefinition of sexual desire as mobile and directed towards a wide variety of objects; and his therapeutic techniques, especially his understanding of transference in the therapeutic relationship and the presumed value of dreams as sources of insight into unconscious desires.

Psychology   **ISBN:** *1-59462-905-6*

Pages:196

MSRP $15.45

The Miracle of Right Thought
Orison Swett Marden

QTY

Believe with all of your heart that you will do what you were made to do. When the mind has once formed the habit of holding cheerful, happy, prosperous pictures, it will not be easy to form the opposite habit. It does not matter how improbable or how far away this realization may see, or how dark the prospects may be, if we visualize them as best we can, as vividly as possible, hold tenaciously to them and vigorously struggle to attain them, they will gradually become actualized, realized in the life. But a desire, a longing without endeavor, a yearning abandoned or held indifferently will vanish without realization.

Pages:360

Self Help   **ISBN:** *1-59462-644-8*

MSRP $25.45

QTY

☐ **The Rosicrucian Cosmo-Conception Mystic Christianity** *by Max Heindel*　ISBN: *1-59462-188-8*　**$38.95**
The Rosicrucian Cosmo-conception is not dogmatic, neither does it appeal to any other authority than the reason of the student. It is: not controversial, but is: sent forth in the, hope that it may help to clear...　New Age/Religion Pages 646

☐ **Abandonment To Divine Providence** *by Jean-Pierre de Caussade*　ISBN: *1-59462-228-0*　**$25.95**
"The Rev. Jean Pierre de Caussade was one of the most remarkable spiritual writers of the Society of Jesus in France in the 18th Century. His death took place at Toulouse in 1751. His works have gone through many editions and have been republished...　Inspirational/Religion Pages 400

☐ **Mental Chemistry** *by Charles Haanel*　ISBN: *1-59462-192-6*　**$23.95**
Mental Chemistry allows the change of material conditions by combining and appropriately utilizing the power of the mind. Much like applied chemistry creates something new and unique out of careful combinations of chemicals the mastery of mental chemistry...　New Age Pages 354

☐ **The Letters of Robert Browning and Elizabeth Barret Barrett 1845-1846 vol II**　ISBN: *1-59462-193-4*　**$35.95**
by Robert Browning and Elizabeth Barrett　Biographies Pages 596

☐ **Gleanings In Genesis (volume I)** *by Arthur W. Pink*　ISBN: *1-59462-130-6*　**$27.45**
Appropriately has Genesis been termed "the seed plot of the Bible" for in it we have, in germ form, almost all of the great doctrines which are afterwards fully developed in the books of Scripture which follow...　Religion/Inspirational Pages 420

☐ **The Master Key** *by L. W. de Laurence*　ISBN: *1-59462-001-6*　**$30.95**
In no branch of human knowledge has there been a more lively increase of the spirit of research during the past few years than in the study of Psychology, Concentration and Mental Discipline. The requests for authentic lessons in Thought Control, Mental Discipline and...　New Age/Business Pages 422

☐ **The Lesser Key Of Solomon Goetia** *by L. W. de Laurence*　ISBN: *1-59462-092-X*　**$9.95**
This translation of the first book of the "Lernegton" which is now for the first time made accessible to students of Talismanic Magic was done, after careful collation and edition, from numerous Ancient Manuscripts in Hebrew, Latin, and French...　New Age/Occult Pages 92

☐ **Rubaiyat Of Omar Khayyam** *by Edward Fitzgerald*　ISBN:*1-59462-332-5*　**$13.95**
Edward Fitzgerald, whom the world has already learned, in spite of his own efforts to remain within the shadow of anonymity, to look upon as one of the rarest poets of the century, was born at Bredfield, in Suffolk, on the 31st of March, 1809. He was the third son of John Purcell...　Music Pages 172

☐ **Ancient Law** *by Henry Maine*　ISBN: *1-59462-128-4*　**$29.95**
The chief object of the following pages is to indicate some of the earliest ideas of mankind, as they are reflected in Ancient Law, and to point out the relation of those ideas to modern thought.　Religion/History Pages 452

☐ **Far-Away Stories** *by William J. Locke*　ISBN: *1-59462-129-2*　**$19.45**
"Good wine needs no bush,' but a collection of mixed vintages does. And this book is just such a collection. Some of the stories I do not want to remain buried for ever in the museum files of dead magazine-numbers an author's not unpardonable vanity..."　Fiction Pages 272

☐ **Life of David Crockett** *by David Crockett*　ISBN: *1-59462-250-7*　**$27.45**
"Colonel David Crockett was one of the most remarkable men of the times in which he lived. Born in humble life, but gifted with a strong will, an indomitable courage, and unremitting perseverance...　Biographies/New Age Pages 424

☐ **Lip-Reading** *by Edward Nitchie*　ISBN: *1-59462-206-X*　**$25.95**
Edward B. Nitchie, founder of the New York School for the Hard of Hearing, now the Nitchie School of Lip-Reading, Inc, wrote "LIP-READING Principles and Practice". The development and perfecting of this meritorious work on lip-reading was an undertaking...　How-to Pages 400

☐ **A Handbook of Suggestive Therapeutics, Applied Hypnotism, Psychic Science**　ISBN: *1-59462-214-0*　**$24.95**
by Henry Munro　Health/New Age/Health/Self-help Pages 376

☐ **A Doll's House: and Two Other Plays** *by Henrik Ibsen*　ISBN: *1-59462-112-8*　**$19.95**
Henrik Ibsen created this classic when in revolutionary 1848 Rome. Introducing some striking concepts in playwriting for the realist genre, this play has been studied the world over.　Fiction/Classics/Plays 308

☐ **The Light of Asia** *by sir Edwin Arnold*　ISBN: *1-59462-204-3*　**$13.95**
In this poetic masterpiece, Edwin Arnold describes the life and teachings of Buddha. The man who was to become known as Buddha to the world was born as Prince Gautama of India but he rejected the worldly riches and abandoned the reigns of power when...　Religion/History/Biographies Pages 170

☐ **The Complete Works of Guy de Maupassant** *by Guy de Maupassant*　ISBN: *1-59462-157-8*　**$16.95**
"For days and days, nights and nights, I had dreamed of that first kiss which was to consecrate our engagement, and I knew not on what spot I should put my lips..."　Fiction/Classics Pages 240

☐ **The Art of Cross-Examination** *by Francis L. Wellman*　ISBN: *1-59462-309-0*　**$26.95**
Written by a renowned trial lawyer, Wellman imparts his experience and uses case studies to explain how to use psychology to extract desired information through questioning.　How-to/Science/Reference Pages 408

☐ **Answered or Unanswered?** *by Louisa Vaughan*　ISBN: *1-59462-248-5*　**$10.95**
Miracles of Faith in China　Religion Pages 112

☐ **The Edinburgh Lectures on Mental Science (1909)** *by Thomas*　ISBN: *1-59462-008-3*　**$11.95**
This book contains the substance of a course of lectures recently given by the writer in the Queen Street Hall, Edinburgh. Its purpose is to indicate the Natural Principles governing the relation between Mental Action and Material Conditions...　New Age/Psychology Pages 148

☐ **Ayesha** *by H. Rider Haggard*　ISBN: *1-59462-301-5*　**$24.95**
Verily and indeed it is the unexpected that happens! Probably if there was one person upon the earth from whom the Editor of this, and of a certain previous history, did not expect to hear again...　Classics Pages 380

☐ **Ayala's Angel** *by Anthony Trollope*　ISBN: *1-59462-352-X*　**$29.95**
The two girls were both pretty, but Lucy who was twenty-one who supposed to be simple and comparatively unattractive, whereas Ayala was credited, as her Bombwhat romantic name might show, with poetic charm and a taste for romance. Ayala when her father died was nineteen...　Fiction Pages 484

☐ **The American Commonwealth** *by James Bryce*　ISBN: *1-59462-286-8*　**$34.45**
An interpretation of American democratic political theory. It examines political mechanics and society from the perspective of Scotsman James Bryce　Politics Pages 572

☐ **Stories of the Pilgrims** *by Margaret P. Pumphrey*　ISBN: *1-59462-116-0*　**$17.95**
This book explores pilgrims religious oppression in England as well as their escape to Holland and eventual crossing to America on the Mayflower, and their early days in New England...　History Pages 268

QTY

The Fasting Cure *by Sinclair Upton*　　　　ISBN: *1-59462-222-1*　**$13.95**
In the Cosmopolitan Magazine for May, 1910, and in the Contemporary Review (London) for April, 1910, I published an article dealing with my experiences in fasting. I have written a great many magazine articles, but never one which attracted so much attention... New Age/Self Help/Health Pages 164

Hebrew Astrology *by Sepharial*　　　　ISBN: *1-59462-308-2*　**$13.45**
In these days of advanced thinking it is a matter of common observation that we have left many of the old landmarks behind and that we are now pressing forward to greater heights and to a wider horizon than that which represented the mind-content of our progenitors... Astrology Pages 144

Thought Vibration or The Law of Attraction in the Thought World　　ISBN: *1-59462-127-6*　**$12.95**
by William Walker Atkinson　　　　Psychology/Religion Pages 144

Optimism *by Helen Keller*　　　　ISBN: *1-59462-108-X*　**$15.95**
Helen Keller was blind, deaf, and mute since 19 months old, yet famously learned how to overcome these handicaps, communicate with the world, and spread her lectures promoting optimism. An inspiring read for everyone... Biographies/Inspirational Pages 84

Sara Crewe *by Frances Burnett*　　　　ISBN: *1-59462-360-0*　**$9.45**
In the first place, Miss Minchin lived in London. Her home was a large, dull, tall one, in a large, dull square, where all the houses were alike, and all the sparrows were alike, and where all the door-knockers made the same heavy sound... Childrens/Classic Pages 88

The Autobiography of Benjamin Franklin *by Benjamin Franklin*　　ISBN: *1-59462-135-7*　**$24.95**
The Autobiography of Benjamin Franklin has probably been more extensively read than any other American historical work, and no other book of its kind has had such ups and downs of fortune. Franklin lived for many years in England, where he was agent... Biographies/History Pages 332

Name	
Email	
Telephone	
Address	
City, State ZIP	

☐ **Credit Card**　　　　☐ **Check / Money Order**

Credit Card Number	
Expiration Date	
Signature	

Please Mail to:　Book Jungle
　　　　　　　　PO Box 2226
　　　　　　　　Champaign, IL 61825
or Fax to:　　630-214-0564

ORDERING INFORMATION

web: *www.bookjungle.com*
email: *sales@bookjungle.com*
fax: *630-214-0564*
mail: *Book Jungle PO Box 2226 Champaign, IL 61825*
or PayPal *to sales@bookjungle.com*

Please contact us for bulk discounts

DIRECT-ORDER TERMS

**20% Discount if You Order
Two or More Books**
Free Domestic Shipping!
Accepted: Master Card, Visa,
Discover, American Express

www.ingramcontent.com/pod-product-compliance
Lightning Source LLC
Chambersburg PA
CBHW080722020726
47503CB00010B/2749

* 9 7 8 1 4 3 8 5 1 4 9 5 6 *